Wilde's fire

Darkness Falls: Book One

A Division of **Whampa, LLC**
P.O. Box 2540
Dulles, VA 20101
Tel/Fax: 800-998-2509
http://curiosityquills.com

© 2012 Krystal Wade
http://krystalwade.blogspot.com

All rights reserved, including the right to reproduce this book or portions thereof in any form whatsoever. For information about Subsidiary Rights, Bulk Purchases, Live Events, or any other questions - please contact Curiosity Quills Press at info@curiosityquills.com, or visit http://curiosityquills.com

Cover design by Harvey Bunda
http://soulspline.deviantart.com

ISBN: 978-1-62007-056-7 (ebook)
ISBN: 978-1-62007-057-4 (paperback)
ISBN: 978-1-62007-058-1 (hardcover)

Table of Contents

Prologue 7
Chapter One 8
Chapter Two 17
Chapter Three 25
Chapter Four 35
Chapter Five 41
Chapter Six 47
Chapter Seven 60
Chapter Eight 67
Chapter Nine 84
Chapter Ten 94
Chapter Eleven 112
Chapter Twelve 123
Chapter Thirteen 134
Chapter Fourteen 140
Chapter Fifteen 151
Chapter Sixteen 167
Chapter Seventeen 186
Chapter Eighteen 203
Chapter Nineteen 207
Chapter Twenty 215

Chapter Twenty-One 235
Chapter Twenty-Two 247
Chapter Twenty-Three 259
Chapter Twenty-Four 271
Chapter Twenty-Five 292
Chapter Twenty-Six 308
Sample Chapter from *Wilde's Army (Darkness Falls, Book Two)* 322
About the Author 332
More from Curiosity Quills Press 333

Not every author is offered an opportunity to handwrite a thank you to her fans, but I have an amazing publisher who goes above and beyond for their authors & readers!

So, to you, Dear Fans,

Thank you!

Not only have you purchased a book for your reading enjoyment, you've opened yourself up to a part of my world. I've spent many hours writing and revising Kate's story. Not all moments were pure brilliance, but hey, I tried!

And I hope you love the characters as much as I do!

Before you dedicate the next day or two to devouring Wilde's Fire, I want you to know how many wonderful people have helped bring you this novel. Aimee H. is probably the most influential. Without her, I may never have shared my words with anyone. Sarah B. and Dawna R., my amazing critique partners who always let me know when someone was out of line. Lisa G. & Eugene T. for giving my book freedom. Harvey B. for designing an amazing cover. Vicki K. for editing. Most importantly, my family. They put up with me when I seemed more involved with the computer or cell phone, when I stayed up late and woke up early, when I looked like hell because writing was more important than doing my hair. If I've missed you, it was not intentional, but my hand is cramping. Who writes anything by hand these days?

Love,

To my family.

Without you my words would have no meaning.

Prologue

I'm standing in the middle of a meadow, surrounded by tall wheat grasses. Dotted along the hillside are thousands of purple and yellow wildflowers. Bending down to pick one, I catch sight of him. Tall, strong, with looks piercing straight through me.

Stepping away from the dark shadows of the forest, he crosses into the meadow, then stops in front of me.

"Katriona." He utters my name as if there's no other name in the world he'd rather speak.

"Arland."

He reaches out to hug me, the way he has so many times before. His work-worn hands warm my skin with their touch. He leans in, closes his eyes—

The sun disappears. The sky turns black. Emerging from the forest, gray beasts with hollow eyes surround and watch us. Before Arland can turn and fight, a mangled creature rushes forward, then stabs him through the heart with a long, dagger-like claw.

My screams fill the darkness.

Chapter One

The light knock on my door doesn't awaken me—I have been staring at the ceiling for at least an hour, trying to push the memories of a troubling nightmare from my mind. Easing myself from bed, I tiptoe across the worn boards of our family's farmhouse. Before I reach the door, my younger sister pokes her head through. Her long, brown hair falls in waves in front of her face, giving her away before she walks into the room.

"You ready, Kate?" Brit asks, holding out a cup of coffee.

Glancing back at the bed, I watch my best friend, Brad, as he sleeps; the gray morning light glows on his skin.

"No. Let's get a later start." We're supposed to be loading up the truck to head out to Skyline Drive, but our Mom is sick—the occurrence should be marked in a book of world records—and for the first time in our family's history we're not all going together. Our Memorial Day tradition is ruined.

"Take it." Brit continues to hold out the hot promise of a good day for me. "You guys were up late, and you haven't slept . . . how bad was the nightmare?"

I grab the mug. "How'd you know?"

"I just had a feeling. You wanna talk about it?"

"No, I'm okay."

I sigh. One day I'll get used to my nightmares. Six years I've dreamed of Arland, an ancient, rugged warrior who looks like he came straight from the pages of a fairy-tale. My warrior and I spend a good portion of my nightmares wrapped in each other's arms, but always, at the happiest part, the dreams take a dark turn and end with him murdered in gruesome, unthinkable ways.

Years ago, I tried talking to my mom about Arland and how horrible the pain of his deaths feel, but I stopped confiding in her after hearing, "It's just a dream, dear," so many times. I even entrusted Brad with the details of my nightmares. He tried to be understanding, at least more than my mom was, but I could tell he thought the same way she did. I haven't spoken to him about the nightmares again.

Brit is the only person I can confide in.

"If you change your mind, I'll be downstairs." She glances behind me, then shakes her head. "I think you're blind."

"Why is that?"

Brit points to Brad. "He's gorgeous, and in love with you," she whispers. "I'm surprised Mom and Gary allow him to sleep in here when they know what he really wants."

Brad's dark-blonde hair, baby blue eyes, and body built for playing football—although he never has—makes most girls do a double-take when he walks by, but to me he is just my best friend. Some of my girlfriends used to ask permission before asking him out on a date. I don't know why they felt they needed it, but my answer was always yes. Unfortunately for my friends, Brad's was always no.

"I could put in a good word for you," I say.

"I'd probably be better for him, but he's no good for either of us."

"What's that supposed to mean?"

Brit looks behind me.

Following her gaze, I see Brad roll over in bed, his eyes half open.

"Nothing. I'll see you in a little while." She closes the door.

"You girls don't know the value of sleep, do you?" Brad asks, pressing the pillow over his head.

"This is late for us." I laugh. "I'm gonna go shower."

He waves his hand at me.

Grabbing the clothes I laid out yesterday, I head for the bathroom. My stepdad Gary passes me in the hall, worry lines on his forehead—Mom must not be feeling better.

"Good to see you up," he says, always the earlier riser to work the farm. "You in better spirits about the trip?"

"Still disappointed, but glad to be going."

"Don't worry, Kate. You kids will be fine. You know those trails like the back of your hand." He smiles. "Anyway, have a great time."

I nod and escape into the bathroom, then hurry through the shower.

Running a brush through my wet hair, I hear Brad and Brit chattering in the family room about how incredible the trip is going to be. Before leaving the bathroom, I make a mental decision to ensure they both have a good time.

Brit looks up as I walk down the stairs. "It's about time! You ready?"

"Yep, but we have to load the Jeep."

"Done. Brad took care of it while you were in the shower." Her smile stretches ear to ear.

"Okay, let me say goodbye to Mom—"

"You just missed them. Gary took Mom to the doctor's office."

"Well, let's go, then," I say, out of excuses.

The closest entry to Skyline Drive is about an hour from our home in Albemarle, Virginia. Brit and I have been singing at the top of our lungs the entire time. Brad, who usually sings along with us, sits without talking in the backseat, staring at the mountains forming on both sides of the road.

"What's wrong, Brad?" I ask.

Brit turns around and peeks over the seat at him. Her dark brown hair whips in the wind. "You aren't getting cold feet because of the time you got lost, are you?"

Keeping my eyes on the road, I manage to punch her arm. "*Brit.*"

Brad's baby-blue eyes meet mine in the rearview. "Actually, I was kind of thinking about that."

She crosses her arms over her chest and grunts, giving me a look of satisfaction.

I stick my tongue out at her. "Why on Earth would you want to think about that?"

"It's the first time I've been out here with you guys since I got lost. Without my mom to beg me not to go . . . ." It's been a year, but he still has trouble talking about his mom's death.

"You were ten, Brad. I can't believe it took this long for your dad to allow you to come with us again," Brit says.

"I didn't need his permission, just his—"

"Acceptance," I say.

Brad nods. "Do you remember how scared I was when the park rangers found me?"

"How could I forget?"

He was lost for only an hour, but for a few years, he couldn't even get near a tree without freaking out.

We fall silent as we take the exit and wind our way along Skyline Drive, watching deer graze on the side of the road, and gawking at the spectacular views of the valleys below us. The Jeep top is open. Warm sunshine beams down on our heads, and smells of honeysuckle waft through the air so strongly, I can almost taste the sweetness of the nectar.

Brit draws a deep breath, holding on to it as if she doesn't want to let it go.

We share a smile.

I feel safe here; some of my most special memories are here, and it's a place where I feel at home, even when I'm far from it.

Turning off the main road, I pull into the Turk Gap lot, then park in the shade.

On normal trips, we would have arrived much earlier so we could hike straight down the north fork of the Moormans River trail, but this is not a normal day. No parents, slow start . . . anything but normal in my book.

"It's late. We should camp at Goat Ridge," I say, standing by the Jeep after considering the time . . . and Brad's hiking abilities. Goat Ridge is two miles from the parking lot. If we stop there, we won't get stuck in the dark looking for our favorite campsite along the river, which is another five-hour hike farther along the trail.

Brit's green eyes widen. Her long, brown hair bounces with the rest of her. "I love Goat Ridge! The view of the valley in the morning is going to be so cool!"

"It's where we camped the first time we came out here with Mom and Gary," I tell Brad.

He slides his pack over his shoulders and shakes his head. "You guys are always so nostalgic."

"It must be a genetic thing," I say, looking at my sister, who is jittering in anticipation. My feelings equal hers, but I don't allow them to show. I've always found it ironic how we resemble each other so much in appearance, but not in personality.

I take the lead down the Appalachian Trail. The heavy foot traffic the path sees every year has deadened the grass. This path guides us along for almost an hour through a lush, green forest busy with the sounds of nature. Birds sing over our heads. Bees buzz by our faces. Every now and then, leaves scatter as squirrels chase each other through the trees. Brad and Brit stay behind me almost the entire time. We keep to ourselves, soaking in our surroundings.

The rocks protecting our sentimental campsite along Goat Ridge are not steep, but they are slippery. I watch each step I take to ensure I don't send any small stones sliding down into the others. Reaching the top, I turn to grasp Brit's hand, but everything in front of me fades to black.

Brad and Brit are gone.
The forest has dissolved around me.

I'm all alone in a dark, desolate space. My fingers, too cold to move, are stuck in fists across my chest. There are no lights, no sounds, no warmth in the air. Trembles start from my gut, working their way into every part of my body.

Ignoring the fear of what I might discover, I find my voice and call out for help. "Hello?" *The word echoes, betraying the panic inside me.*

Spinning in circles, heart pounding out of control, I look for any signs of life. There is a light, far away, but if I strain hard enough, I see it. My feet propel me forward, making no sounds as they meet the ground. The longer I travel, the farther away the light seems to get.

"Wait, I'm here!" *I call.*

The light responds to my plea and stops moving. I move faster, struggling to breathe when I reach it. The light is not coming from a flashlight; it's coming from a person. Her face is familiar, but I'm not sure why. Her skin is flawless, her cheekbones are high and colored with a light-pink hue, and her eyes are a brilliant shade of green.

She smiles at me.

"Who are you?" *I ask.*

"You have to wake up now," *she says, snapping her fingers.*

Everything flashes a warm yellow color before she, and everything around her, fades.

"Kate, you have to wake up. Please!"

I hear my sister sob as I come to. "Brit?"

"Oh thank God. Are you okay?" she cries.

"What happened?" Brad asks.

I blink my eyes clear and sit up. The rocks and sticks I'm lying on leave red, throbbing indents in my skin.

Brit's face has blood on it.

"I don't know, but why are you bleeding?" I ask, touching Brit's forehead with my thumb, revealing a small cut above her left eye.

"She fell when you fainted." Brad shares the same look of concern as my sister.

"I don't remember fainting. I thought I was asleep." Brushing off their protests with a wave of my hand, I stand. I always keep a first aid kit in my pack, and I am not about to allow my sister to bleed to death.

"Can you set up the tent while I clean her face?" I ask Brad.

Brit puts her hands on her hips and scowls. "I'll clean my own face. You need to sit down. He'll set up the tent."

I give her my best grimace.

"Don't look at me that way, or I'm going home."

I love how strong she becomes when she gets upset, but I give in to her demands and sip water while they take care of camp. In a matter of minutes, the tent is up and they both insist I take a nap. But there's only so much anyone can tell me to do before I get annoyed.

"I'm fine!" I yell, scaring all the birds from the trees.

After my outburst, Brad and Brit leave me alone.

We hang around the camp the remainder of the afternoon, collecting dry wood and sticks, then start a small fire and sit huddled on the ground around it. We pick at the sandwiches Brit and Mom prepared for dinner. Too bad she and Gary aren't here. They'd have us talking and laughing. Instead, silence looms over us for the rest of the evening.

The events of the day have been too strange.

I don't tell them about what I saw when I fainted, because it seems odd to talk about. And so far, I'm failing to keep my promise to myself to guarantee they both have a good time.

Brad encourages me to lay my head down in his lap; he runs his fingers through my tangled hair. At school, we spent many nights like this one, playing with each other's hair, talking . . . not talking . . . whatever we needed, to make ourselves feel better. Tonight, I need to think, and I appreciate his silence.

Brit watches us for a while, but then she suddenly jumps up and announces she's going to bed. She seems upset about something; however, I'm too tired to get up and talk to her about it.

"Kate?" Brad asks.

"Hmm?"

He rakes his fingers through my hair. "Are you sure you're okay?"

"Mmm-hmm," I say. My eyes are heavy; my body is losing the war against sleep.

"There is something—" He starts off, but even though I battle the overwhelming need to sleep, so I can hear him finish his thought—I'm out before I hear him say anything else.

"I love you," my imaginary lover says, voice full of longing.

"And I love you, Arland." I gaze into his emerald eyes, watching the firelight flicker in them.

He puts his arm around me, draws me near, the heat from his bare skin burning into mine. I feel his lips graze my neck, sending shivers down my spine.

"Do you miss him?" he whispers.

"Who?" I ask, barely able to concentrate past my desire for more of Arland.

"Brad."

Why would Arland ask me about Brad?

Arland disappears.

Brad lies in a barren field, surrounded by gray, mangled monsters, with a sword sticking out of his chest.

He is without a doubt dead.

Waking with a start, I realize Brad must have picked me up in his arms and carried me into the tent. The nightmare has upset me too much to go back to sleep. I've dreamed of Brad before, but none of those dreams were nightmares, and Brad never shared a spot in my brain with Arland.

Brad is still next to me, alive and well. I drink some water and remind myself, like my mother always did, that it *is* just a dream. But I need to get out of the tent. I need to breathe and think.

The zipper is so loud, I'm sure it will wake everyone in the forest, but my crew remains asleep behind me. A chill runs down my arms as I step into the morning. The stars still shine above us, although to the east, the night sky is losing the struggle with the sunrise; pale blues and grays tint the horizon.

It's 5:00 a.m. and I cannot sleep. This is nothing unusual for me, so I rekindle the fire, then prepare food for us to eat before our nine-mile hike.

The nightmare about Brad replays itself in my head; different from any I have experienced before, but somehow this one bothers me less than most of the dreams do. I wish Brit was awake so I could tell her about it. But after what happened last night, I don't want to trouble her.

I continue cooking the food.

The smell of sausages over the fire fills the air. Brit comes out and sits on the ground next to me, wrapped up in her sleeping bag.

"Mor-ning," I say, high-pitched.

She reaches for a sausage, takes a large bite, then speaks around a mouthful of food. "Morning."

"I'm sorry if I'm ruining our trip."

"Don't be sorry. I was just scared," she says, leaning into me. "Are *you* okay?"

"I really don't know what happened, but I'm okay. When you went to bed last night, I thought you might be mad at me."

Brit's facial expression changes from concern to serious in an instant. "No, but there's something I have to tell you."

The zipper on the tent jingles, signaling the end of our privacy. Figures.

Brad steps out and walks over to join us.

Brit stops talking as soon as she sees him.

He grabs a sausage and sits down beside me.

Whatever is bothering her is going to have to wait until later.

We enjoy our breakfast in peace.

Chapter Two

After breakfast, we throw dirt over the fire, break down the tent, and re-pack our bags. By 6:00 a.m., we're back on the trail and making our descent toward the river.

We don't pass any other hikers, but an abundance of wildlife crosses our path throughout the morning. We stop and watch a doe and her fawn while they chew flowers from a bush. So many beautiful birds sing their morning songs, replacing the chorus of crickets from last night. The canopy of trees over our heads is the only thing protecting us from the bright sun attempting to shine in our eyes.

"This way," Brit calls. She leads us off the trail to one of her favorite spots in the forest: a patch of ground where no trees grow.

A group of gray boulders rests in the middle of the opening. The sun beams down upon them, making the perfect spot for Brit to tan while listening to her iPod. I used to bring along some of my favorite books. Many times, we'd spend an entire day here.

"We found this place when we were searching for you ten years ago. Now, it's our favorite hideaway," I explain to Brad.

"Didn't your parents worry about you?"

"It's not like *we* were going to get lost," Brit says, her voice a little too harsh.

I shoot her a look.

She puts her hands in front of her. "Sorry."

After sharing some granola bars on the rocks, we walk back to the trail to continue our descent. As the day progresses, the air becomes hot. The heat lingers on my skin, making my thoughts dwell on the river and how refreshing crossing it will be.

The dry air flowing in and out of my mouth makes me long for a drink. I pause to take a sip of water.

A bright, yellow light darts between the trees.

I point into the woods. "Did you see that?"

"See what?" they ask in unison.

"Nothing. It must have been my imagination." I am speaking more to myself than to them, but as soon as I say the words, the light darts through the trees again. Having had enough weirdness for one trip, I keep walking and ignore whatever trick my mind is playing.

We proceed down the trail for a few more miles. The farther we travel, the louder the sounds of water flowing over rocks become.

Brit and I exchange glances.

"Keep up," I yell over my shoulder to Brad.

Our feet pound the earth as we run down the trail. Twigs and rocks crunch under our shoes. We reach the river; it's not anything spectacular this high up, but it's still exciting to have reached it. The water trickles over the stones. Little pools have formed, creating a home in which tiny mosquitofish swim.

Brit wanders off into the woods, while Brad and I take a break. We are alone, sitting on a huge river rock.

He dunks a stick in the small pool below his feet, attempting to drown an evasive water strider. "Are you glad we came yet?"

"No," I say, grinning from ear to ear. I am *of course* having fun, even though I'm concerned about the strange events.

Brad pulls me into his shoulder. "I am."

It's unusual for him to be touchy-feely. Something is definitely bothering him. I've suspected it since we were in the Jeep yesterday.

"Is everything okay?" I ask.

"I'm great." Brad's voice is nervous, shaky.

I lift my head from his shoulder and look him straight in the eyes, begging him to tell me the truth. His baby blues look like they are dying to share some deep, inner secret with me, but he laughs and pulls me back into him. My ear rests over his heart; the rapid beating indicates he's lying.

Brad's always been able to share things with me, but I decide not to push him. Whatever he's hiding, he will tell me in his own time. I'm uneasy that he and Brit each have things they want to tell me, but for some reason, not in front of each other.

"I found it!" Brit yells. She trips and falls over the dense undergrowth along the tree line, but remains smiling when she stands back up.

"What?" I ask, lifting my head from Brad's chest, waiting for Brit to come over to us.

He continues stabbing his stick at the bug.

"You remember that time we brought Uncle John and his girlfriend Cindy out here with us?" Brit asks.

I nod.

She pulls a dirt-encrusted bottle from behind her back. "Well, I stole this bottle of rum from them and buried it . . . with a little help from a stick." She's proud of herself—I haven't seen her look this giddy in months.

"You *didn't?*" They were such alcoholics. Gary was furious with how much they drank around us.

"It was Gary's idea for me to steal it and bury it. Well, *actually*, he told me to pour it out and hide the bottle, but I thought it might come in handy one day. And here we are . . . in need of something fun to do!" Her huge grin makes her look so young, too young to be holding up a bottle of rum. Of course, we *are* too young.

We've had our fair share of beers throughout our teenage years. At college, Brad and I are more exposed to alcohol, but I've never liked the way it makes me feel. I've seen people do way too many stupid things to ever become a drunk myself.

Appalled, I eye the nasty bottle. "You aren't honestly going to drink that, are you?"

"Not just me. You, me, and Brad!" Brit says, pointing to each of us.

I sigh. "Let's get to the next campsite before we do anything illegal."

Brad stands up. He leaps across the rocks to the other side of the riverbank, looking excited at the prospect of getting wasted. At parties, usually Brad convinced me to lighten up and have a beer or two. I'm not used to seeing him this enthusiastic about drinking, though.

Brit leads our trio of future alcoholics to our next stop, following the river the entire way. The trail is a constant up- and downhill battle. In the heat of the full afternoon sun, I'm sure we're *all* ready to get into the water.

She turns right, off the main trail. The last obstacle before our "reserved" campsite is right in front of us: Moormans River. The sun sparkles on the surface, begging us to get in the river, but the waters are deeper and rush much faster here than where we crossed upstream. We have to be careful, or we're liable to go for a crash ride into some rocks.

I'm in awe of the river's beauty. Watching the water, I try to gauge how hard a crossing we'll have. "I'll go first."

No one protests; they both know I'm the strongest swimmer.

Sliding my pack from my back, then holding it over my head, I walk in, taking each step with caution. The water is up to my calves, and so refreshing to my hot, sticky skin I want to jump in and soak the rest of my body, but I know better and move forward at a slow pace. At its deepest point, the water reaches my upper thighs. The rapids can still knock us down, but they aren't overpowering.

I wave my hand, indicating to the others they can follow me.

Brit enters first, then Brad.

While waiting for them on the other side, I see someone, who looks like he's in a ranger uniform, step off the trail. I motion for Brit and Brad to hurry across.

Brit looks behind her. When she sees the person, she grabs Brad's hand and urges him to wade faster.

They make their way out as quietly as possible; then, we duck behind some bushes along the bank. We can get in trouble if a ranger finds us out here, especially if he finds us with a bottle of liquor we're all still too young to buy. Someone other than a ranger walking along the trail wouldn't know we're doing anything wrong, but we don't want anyone to find our secret spot, either.

On the last half-mile stint before we reach our campsite, we laugh about being on the wrong side of the law. I lace my arms with Brit's and Brad's; my qualms from yesterday—about coming without Mom and Gary—all wash away.

"We're here," Brit says in a singsong voice.

Brad's eyes widen. "This isn't what I was expecting at all."

"What was it you were expecting?" she asks.

He spins around, arms out. "Nothing this amazing."

Brad must be thrilled he made it passed Goat Ridge without getting lost.

After all the years of listening to our stories, he can see for himself how magical our spot is. The lush, green grasses are so soft that we take our shoes off and walk around barefoot. Sprinkled all throughout the meadow are little white and purple wildflowers. Twelve wickedly shaped chestnut trees encircle the grassy area, creating an overhang so thick, the temperature must drop by five or ten degrees once we enter.

Brad picks two purple flowers and gives one to each of us.

"Thank you for escorting me out here, m'ladies," he says, with a formal bow.

Brit and I laugh and tuck the flowers behind our ears.

"You're quite welcome, sir," I say.

By the time we set up the tent and have a small fire built, the sun is saying its final farewell for the day, painting the clouds with magenta and lavender tones. We take the time to eat more of Mom's sandwiches before we set our sights on drinking the rum.

Brit pulls three sodas from her pack with a devilish smile. I shake my head. I love my sister. She planned to dig up this old bottle from the minute Mom and Gary said they weren't coming.

Brit hands us each a soda can that has bounced around in her pack all day. We crack open the sodas all at once; warm spray shoots in our faces. I pour a little out, then add a tiny bit of rum before passing it to Brad.

He leans over and adds more to mine, then doubles the amount in his own.

"You aren't getting off that easy," Brad says.

Brit laughs while pouring rum in her can, then takes a swig from the bottle before she replaces the cap.

My mouth hangs open in mock horror at what she's doing.

"That's it . . . I'm transferring closer to home. You need a baby-sitter. What on earth happened to you this year?" My sarcastic sister and our late night video chats about school and boys are what got me through my first year at Virginia Tech, but this side of her I don't recognize.

Brit rolls her eyes. "Don't be crazy. I'm just messing with you. Besides, I'll be with you next year."

"Thank God."

We sip our tainted sodas, the rum burning my throat on its way down to my stomach. I set the can aside after a few gulps and watch the sky as the stars begin to shine on the other side of the river. Brit babbles on about how excited she is to join us at Tech in the fall, while Brad and I nod and agree with her at the right times.

The rum makes me tired; not tipsy . . . just tired. I lie on my back, staring up at the trees, while Brad and Brit share drinking stories. The firelight dances off the leaves with colors so amazing, I must be hallucinating. Maybe the alcohol *is* affecting me.

The yellow light I saw earlier in the woods flashes again. It doesn't shock me, but I don't dare mention anything to the others. They'll surely laugh and tell me I'm drunk. Instead, I watch the peaceful light. It makes me feel happy, although there's no explanation as to why.

Brad plops down next to me on the sleeping bag.

The light darts off toward the river.

"Whatcha lookin' at?" he slurs. Obviously, Brad's finished his drink, and then some.

"Just the trees." I sit up.

Brit is missing.

The fire has died down; only a few embers remain.

"Where's Brit?"

"She went to the tent a while ago." His words come out in one long string.

I didn't even notice, weird. How long have I been lying here? "Are you ready to go to bed, too?"

Brad nods.

He gets up on his own, but I have to help him walk back to the tent. To support his drunken weight, Brad keeps his arm draped around my shoulders.

"I love you," he says, like an alley cat crying in the rain.

"Of course you do. You're drunk." I laugh at him, but he looks at me with confusion written all over his face. "You'll be okay once you sleep it off."

Brad slides from my shoulder, lands on his sleeping bag, and falls right to sleep.

I curl into a ball and stare at the top of the tent, pondering his words. There's no way he means he *loves* me, does he? The thought is so ridiculous. Sure, we've talked a thousand times about how we're happy to be each other's friend—without having to worry about relationship ups and down—but he's never shown an interest in me. In all honesty, I've always thought he might be a good match for Brit. The two of them can talk and laugh for hours about some of the most mundane things, but I cannot imagine he likes me romantically.

Determining his words are nothing more than the ramblings of a drunken guy, I fall asleep.

Chapter Three

My mind races through dreams, not pausing on any long enough for me to understand the scenes playing out, but none of them are nightmares. What wakes me now is the weight of two arms slung over my back. I feel smothered.

Struggling to turn over, I give up. My eyes pop open. I slide Brad and Brit's arms from me, then sneak out of the tent.

Outside, everything is dark and still. Other than the sound of the river flowing, there are no noticeable noises. Looking for a place to sit alone, I walk toward the water. A fallen pine tree resting along the bank makes a perfect seat.

There's a wet chill to the night. Wrapping my arms around my knees to keep myself warm, I close my eyes, take a deep breath of the fresh air, and clear my thoughts, allowing the tranquil mountains to refresh my soul. When I open them again, the yellow light dances over the water. I'm beginning to wonder if I'm going crazy. Passing out, seeing yellow lights, Brad telling me he loves me—none of these things are really happening. Maybe I hit my head yesterday and gave myself a concussion?

The longer I think about my level of sanity, the closer the light draws to me, until I'm surrounded. Pulsing more intensely, the brightness entices me to get to my feet. I'm ready to go back to the tent, but something deep inside says I should follow the yellow nuisance.

Ignoring the danger of walking away from camp, in the dark and by myself, I do exactly that.

The light remains ahead of me as I walk through a familiar part of the forest. Every now and then, I turn, prepared to give up and head back, thinking I have gone too far, but the curious part of me wills my feet to continue following the light.

After floating along the trail for quite some time, the light stops at my favorite swimming spot: Snake Hole. A few years ago, one of the harmless serpents bit Brit. The creepy thing must have slithered into her shorts on the bank while we swam. When she picked them up to get dressed, the snake bit her hand. Brit dropped her clothes and went screaming back to camp, bleeding like a stuck pig the entire way. I gathered her things and brought them back to her. The bite hasn't stopped my sister from returning. The water is too perfect and calm to stay away on hot summer days. But, now, she always pokes her clothes with a long stick before picking them up.

The light pulsates with energy, drawing me back from my memories of Brit.

"What is it you brought me out here for?" I ask, confirming I *have* gone crazy.

As if in direct response to my question, the light swirls around me faster and faster, then dives straight down into the water. Fish and turtles scatter away in frenzy, avoiding the light as it plunges to the bottom.

"Oh, no! I might be crazy for following a light into the darkness, but I am *not* jumping into the water at night and by myself!" I turn on my toes and march straight back to camp.

What was I thinking? I followed a yellow light through the forest at night with no flashlight. The path was bright before, but walking back, I cannot see anything.

My thoughts turn to Brad as a little boy, alone and scared, lost out here in the woods. At least *he'd* had enough sense to get lost in the middle of the day; but here I am, in the black night, knowing the exact place I stand, but even *I* feel cut off from civilization.

The river guides me; my knowledge of the trail steers my feet clear of anything that might make me fall. The return hike is painstaking in the dark. Turning off the path, I arrive back at camp almost an hour later. I half expect to see Brit waiting for me with her hands on her hips—furious I wandered off without her—but everything is as dark and still as before I left. I crawl into the tent, praying I'm undetected, and close my eyes, prepared to sleep away the nagging curiosity of what the yellow light is.

"Where were you?" Brit whispers.

So much for my future as a spy.

"I just went for a walk." The walk part is true; I leave out the minor detail about the strange light.

"I thought you saw something outside the tent, the way you were shining your flashlight around."

"I wasn't shining my flashlight near the tent." I'd smack my forehead, but that would draw more attention to my stupidity. How am I going to explain this to her?

Sitting up, Brit brings the sleeping bag around her head, like I told her there was a murderer standing just beyond the tent, waiting to kill us the second we realized he was here.

"Relax. There's some logical explanation for what you saw. It's either the rum, some random hikers walking by, or—" Or what? She must have seen the same light that's harassed me all afternoon. I know my next question will raise a lot more if the answer is not what I expect, but I am compelled to ask. "What color was the light?"

"Yellow," Brit says, still hiding under the sleeping bag.

"Yellow?" I hear the caution in my voice; I hope she can't.

"Yeah, just like the color of the light you took with you down the swimming hole trail."

A shiver runs through me, my heart pounds, and my hands turn clammy, but I try to maintain a calm façade for my sister. She saw the light!

Maybe I'm not crazy, after all, but what does all of this mean? Should I tell her about the light, and how it coerced me to follow the trail? Tell her how the light dove into the water? Will she go check out the swimming hole with me? All these thoughts speed through my mind in an instant.

Brit nudges my shoulder. "Kate?"

"Sorry," I say, giving myself a mental shake. "Come outside with me?"

I grab an actual flashlight, and we step outside the tent. Leading Brit over to the bank, I sit her down on the pine tree by the river, then take a seat next to her. "You can't tell Brad."

Brad would never believe us. If we tell him, he'll think we're playing a joke on him. He doesn't believe in the supernatural stuff—and before tonight, I might have sided with him. Unless he sees something himself, it didn't happen.

"Tell him *what*, exactly?"

I decide to tell her everything—from the familiar, glowing woman who told me to wake up when I passed out, to the light dancing off the trees and water, and then guiding me to Snake Hole.

Brit's face is full of disbelief, but she saw the yellow light with her own eyes, so she can't outright mock my story.

She stands up, ready to take off. "You want to go to the hole now?"

"No. I'm not going to leave Brad by himself."

"Are you girls planning on going somewhere without me?" Brad asks, sounding a little groggy as he walks toward us from the tent.

"Oh, we were thinking of taking a little walk down to the swimming hole." Brit's eyes are big and full of innocence.

Brad runs his hands up and down his arms. "It's a little cold for a swim, don't you think?"

"We weren't going to swim; just walk there and back. We do it every year when our parents fall asleep," Brit says.

First, I find my sister's been drinking, and now, I learn she's an excellent liar. Brit is surprising me. I have a sinking feeling I'm going to be doing a lot of baby-sitting at college next year.

"Well, what are we waiting for?" Brad takes me by the hand and helps me off the log, holding on to me a little longer than necessary. He gives my hand a light squeeze, then lets it go. The signals he's been sending me on this trip conflict with our friendship status.

The sun begins its daily battle with the night sky as we walk along the river to our favorite swimming spot; dim gray light breaks over the horizon when we arrive.

There is no yellow light in the river.

Brit looks at me; her eyes change from nervous anticipation to question-filled.

All I can do is shrug.

Brad walks over to the river, bends down, then dips in his fingers. "The water is really warm."

The warmth of the water takes me by surprise, when I kneel to touch it. It's late May, but the night air is chilly; the water shouldn't feel so tepid.

Brit doesn't wait for a written invitation. She slips out of her clothes, and then she walks right into the river.

I frown. I'm more reserved about taking my clothes off in front of people than she is.

"I'll turn my head," Brad says, like a gentleman.

I lift my shirt over my head, then slide my pants down my legs, tripping over my own feet as I pull the pants off. I cannot get over the feeling I'm being watched, and *not* by Brad.

"Okay," I say, *after* I'm in the water.

My muscles relax and my spirit re-energizes; the water's so warm, it feels like I'm soaking in a hot tub.

Brad steps into the river, moaning when the water reaches his waist.

My eyes fixate on him.

His sculpted chest muscles loosen as the warmth works its magic. Brad catches me staring at him; his eyes widen, and the corners of his mouth turn up a little.

Brit splashes me, bringing my attention to her. She gives me a look of disapproval. Brit's been grumpy with Brad and me on this trip, and now—more than ever—I wonder if what she wants to tell me has something to do with him.

Laughing, I splash her back. "What was that for?"

"Tell ya later," Brit says, her gaze resting on Brad.

Oh yeah, whatever it is has to do with him. I look between them, concerned about what they each want to talk to me about, but I have to let it go, because neither one plans to say anything right now.

Instead of worrying, I have fun. We splash around, dunk each other, float on our backs, and play Marco Polo. It's wonderful to feel like a kid again.

Brit pushes my head under the water.

I grab her arm and pull her down with me.

All of a sudden, the water explodes with yellow light.

Losing my breath, I struggle to get up for air.

Brad's arms close around my hips. He pulls me against his chest and swims to the surface.

I choke out water into his face, but he keeps his firm hold on me.

"She got you good." Brad laughs. "You okay?"

Still gasping for air, I nod and look over at Brit.

She's also coughing up water, but stares down into the brilliant, yellow river right along with me.

I return my gaze to Brad; the closeness of our almost-naked bodies causes my cheeks to heat up.

His arms release me as fast as they clasped around me under the water.

I'm positive he cannot see what Brit and I can. Instead of gazing deep into the river, the way we are, he watches me with a slight grin on his face.

Brit and I stare at the point where the light is brightest.

"Beat you to the bottom." I tease her.

Brad won't think this is out of the ordinary, considering how many games we've already played.

"Go!" Brit takes a deep breath, then dives under the water.

I follow right behind her, swimming toward the emanating light.

When we're about to reach the bottom, the light swirls and darts over to the far side of the swimming hole, revealing a chasm under the short falls. Part of it is above the water, but most of the crevasse is below. How have we never noticed this before?

Brit points up.

We're unable to hold our breath any longer.

"Took you guys long enough," Brad says, running his fingers along the surface of the water.

"We found a cave!" Brit says.

"Really? How can you see anything when it's so dark?"

"Well, we think it's a cave, but we'll have to come back later, when it's lighter. You want to check it out with us?" she asks.

"Absolutely."

The water loses its warmth; goose bumps pop up all over my skin. I step out of the river—my teeth chattering, body trembling—and put on my clothes as fast as possible. It doesn't take long for the others to follow.

I lead them back to camp, running the entire time, hoping to heat up. I throw some scrap wood into the fire pit while Brit works to get it lit again. Once I'm warm, my stomach growls.

We all shove a few granola bars in our mouths while sitting around the fire, shivering.

At least, Brit and Brad got some sleep. I've pretty much been running around all night. The tent is calling my name, and I give in to my exhaustion.

They follow.

We unzip our sleeping bags and huddle together to calm our trembling bodies.

Brit falls asleep and rolls away. Her absence makes my shaking worse.

Brad opens his arms, allowing me to burrow into his chest to get warmer. He kisses my forehead. Brad's never done that before, not that the kiss bothers me enough to move away from him. But the kiss—combined with his drunken love profession—is enough to make me unsure of his feelings, for the first time in our long friendship. I try not to think about the meaning behind his kiss, and instead, I wonder why he didn't see the light.

"Kate, wake up," Brit says, pushing my shoulder.

Judging by the heat in the tent, it must be late in the afternoon. I'm still wrapped in Brad's embrace, and there is nothing important enough to make me want to move. My best friend's arms make me feel safe and comfortable. I don't understand this new closeness between Brad and me. I want to talk to him about us, but not with Brit around.

My eyes stay closed tightly, and I try to ignore Brit's attempts to wake me.

"*Guys!*" Brit yells.

Brad and I jolt.

Opening his eyes, he tightens his hold on me and groans at Brit. "*What?*"

"It's almost five . . . you know, at night! Unless we want to waste the rest of the daylight, we should start exploring the cave soon." Brit looks deliberately at me.

"Cave time?" Brad asks.

"Yeah, come on, it'll be fun." I want to go, but I'm still unwilling to move from his arms.

"Would you two just get up already?" Brit is clearly peeved.

I give in, peel myself away from Brad—who looks unhappy about me getting up—then get dressed. He keeps his eyes averted while I change my dirty clothes, but I couldn't care less about who's in the tent—the crispy feel my shirt and pants have, from being wet and subsequently dried by a fire, means they have to come off.

After dressing, I grab another granola bar and gather some gear. "Let's see, a flashlight, some rope, and our waterproof camera. That should be enough. What do you think, Brit?"

"Great, let's go."

Brit and I have issues containing our excitement as we walk toward the swimming hole—she's practically running, and I keep tripping over things. Brad stays so close to me, I'm afraid my ability to hide my enthusiasm might fail, and we'll end up having to explain the whole odd story to him.

I don't understand why a light guided us to the cave, and, I find it odd Brit and I are both so willing to go exploring. But, I push these thoughts from my mind and rush on, hoping the cave is not totally under water, so we can stay in it longer without worrying about how we're going to breathe.

Shrill laughter rings out ahead of us. The closer we get, the more obvious it becomes that we're not going to be alone at the swimming hole.

Brit stops at the end of the trail.

"Crap." She stares at five children splashing around, while their parents watch from the other bank.

"Be nice. We can just wait for them to leave," I say to my impatient sister.

"What's the problem?" Brad asks.

"If they decide to follow us, do you want to be responsible for them getting hurt?" I come up with the one response that makes sense.

The children being here shouldn't bother us, but seeing as we found the cave using a mysterious light, I think we better wait. Not that Brad is aware of this, but he buys the excuse.

We sit on the bank, waiting. The parents watch us the entire time, not even attempting to make their stares inconspicuous. They must figure we're up to no good. Five or ten minutes pass before they collect their children from the river.

I tip my head in their direction. "Look, they're getting out."

At last, we're free to go explore our cave.

I place the gear on a rock and undress down to my underclothes while Brad turns his head, once again.

Brit eyes the gear. "Do you really think we need the rope and camera right now?"

"No," I say.

We each carry a flashlight; the rest of the gear we leave behind.

I can see at least a foot of the top of the cave above the water, but Brad cannot. "Are you sure you can't see it?"

"I swear," Brad says.

Brit and I exchange glances.

"Can you see it under the water?" she asks.

Brad dunks his head. "Yes."

With a quick wink, Brit and I decide we should enter from below.

I smile. "Ready?"

They both nod.

We all take a deep breath and immerse ourselves.

As soon as we swim through the mouth of the cave, the water evaporates, and our bodies slam into cold, hard ground. I stand, confused, and wipe off the dirt and stones covering my wet skin.

The air is at least twenty degrees cooler than the air on the other side, and smells of rotting wood and mildew.

Intuition tells me the situation is wrong.

We need to go back.

We are not in a cave.

"We should go—"

Something so horrible, so powerful, takes control over my body—I fall onto my hands and knees and scream.

Chapter Four

The cold ground makes my bones ache. My soul is in agony from the wicked atrocities playing through my mind. The vision of gruesome creatures slicing through the terrified, helpless people before me is too much to bear. Their misery becomes my own, like an overpowering poison simmering inside my skin. Fire ignites women and children; as they burn and are left to die, the flames scorch through me. Plumes of blackened smoke rise from cottages, bodies, and from the forest, making the air unbreathable.

"Please stop screaming, Kate. I promise we're gonna get out of here," Brad says, rocking me in his lap, forehead pressed against mine. His heart beats so hard, it thumps against my right shoulder.

Gasping for air, I wish I wasn't here. I wish we were back at home where this hallucination would be gone. But, for all my pleading, it doesn't go away; the painful vision of devastation only plays stronger in my head.

The beautiful blue sky turns black. Mothers cry out for their children, husbands for their wives. A shrill scream comes from a young girl standing alone. Men and women both run for her, but aren't fast enough. I watch as the child is torn limb from limb by fiends.

"Kate, shut up, please, just shut up," Brit says, her voice trembling.

I'm scaring her with my screams, but if she could understand I'm seeing and *feeling* the creatures of my nightmares from the past six years, she would never ask me to be quiet.

The tall, mangled beings murder hundreds, thousands of people. These beasts seem to become stronger with each life they steal, moving from one victim to the next, faster and faster until they look like blurs of gray. There is no hesitation, no remorse. They kill with excitement.

"K-Kate, s-s-stop screaming." I haven't heard Brad stutter since fifth grade, when he had to give a speech about Patrick Henry in front of our class.

The fear in Brad's and Brit's voices registers in my brain. It's not the breathless fumbling of my sister's words that bothers me so much, but that of Brad's. When his mom collapsed in front of us three years ago in his barn, he didn't even flinch. He grabbed his cell phone, dialed 9-1-1, and began CPR on her. Brad saved his mom's life then. Something tells me he's trying to save my life now.

I take slow breaths, in and out, force the visions to the back of my brain, and open my eyes onto this strange, dark place.

Brad helps me to my feet and holds onto my hand, steadying me.

There is no moon, there are no stars above our heads, no streetlights, nothing but darkness.

Brad and Brit grab our flashlights—providing the only light that can be seen—from the ground and point them on something approaching.

I freeze.

Sniffing the air while moving toward us, like a pack of dogs, are six creatures that could only be from Hell. What I see doesn't make any sense; the beings before us must be remnants of the visions I've experienced. But the panic on Brad's and Brit's faces tell me the beings are real.

These creatures have plagued my nightmares for years, but I've never seen them like this. Their bodies look somewhat human, but their bones are crooked and mangled beyond belief. They're naked, with pasty, gray skin and bony fingers. Long claws hang from the hands by their sides. Their eyes, hollow sockets of pitch-blackness, focus on us. Every smooth step they take seems unnatural for such deformed creatures.

Tears spill over the edges of Brit's deep green eyes, race down her cheeks, drop from her chin, and splatter on the dry earth under our feet. She must understand the finality of this situation.

We are all going to die.

Maybe this could have been avoided if I'd ignored the yellow light that led us into this disaster, or if my parents were with us, like they should have been.

I squeeze Brit's hand to get her attention.

She looks at me, eyes wide and tormented.

I know what I have to do to save her and Brad.

I love you, I mouth to her.

She mouths it back.

I turn around and shove Brit in the chest as hard as I can, knocking her through the entrance of the cave, and I pray she'll make it home to safety.

Shrieks of rage come from behind me; I hear the creatures begin to run.

Brad's eyes lock with mine.

I grab onto him. Tears rush down my face. I know he's going to shove me through the mouth of the cave, the same way I saved my sister.

"I'm not leaving you behind!"

"I'll be right behind you. You have to go now!"

Brad pushes me toward the hole and jumps after me, but we must be disoriented, because I don't find myself submerged in water. Instead, I land on my butt.

He plants himself on the ground in front of me, takes my hand, and helps me up. Grabbing me by the waist, Brad pulls me into him with all his strength. With one firm hand holding me at the small of my back against his body, and the other racing up to the back of my head, he leans his face down to mine and kisses me.

For a second, everything disappears. It's just Brad and me, as one. His lips are warm and soft, but his kiss is filled with so much built-up emotion it takes my breath away. I don't care that death is approaching at a rapid pace; I don't care that the first and last kiss of my life means something different to Brad than it does me—I'm going to enjoy this. Putting my arms around his neck, I return his kiss with as much intensity as he gives it.

Brad steps back with a smile, allowing me to look into his watering eyes long enough to see the pain in them. I don't think anyone understood the depth of his feelings for me.

I know I didn't.

We could've had a good relationship—we had the friendship part of it down—but even now, faced with death, I don't know if that's what I want from him.

"I'm so sorry I've never kissed you before now. I've dreamed of doing that since I met you in second grade. I've been trying to find a way to say this since we came out here, Kate. I love you. I've always loved you and will continue to until I die." Brad pushes me down, then spins around before the creatures reach us.

I land on my back, with the wind knocked out of me.

He runs away, trying to distract our attackers—and it's working.

They follow him. The first monster catches his arm and slices through his back with dagger-like claws.

"No!" I wheeze, gripping at my chest.

Struggling to fill my lungs with air and get to my feet, I fall onto my hands and knees. I look up to see if he's still fighting when, from all directions, burning arrows blaze through the dark sky. They hit the creatures by the hundreds, lighting them into brilliant, blue flames. But not before the disgusting things take Brad's life.

He lies motionless on the ground.

The air fills with the smells of burning flesh and hair, the aroma so foul, it causes me to gag. I put my hand over my nose and mouth in an attempt to block out the awful stench.

Fearing an arrow might find me as well, I crawl to him.

"Brad?" I choke out when I reach his feet.

He doesn't respond.

Tears fill my eyes. Throwing myself over his bleeding body, I allow his death to overwhelm me. I never told Brad I love him, too. I'm sure it's not the same way he loves me, but I do love him. Now he's dead, and will never know.

I will never know if I could've loved him the same way.

Someone—or something—touches my shoulder.

I scream.

A hand clamps over my mouth.

"Do not fear. We are here to help," a man says, picking me up under my arms.

Kicking and biting, I fight against him. No one can help me. I've killed my best friend and lost my sister. I shouldn't be alive, shouldn't be here—wherever *here* is.

"I will not hurt you, but there are plenty of things around that will. Please stop fighting."

Giving in, I allow him to help me onto a horse.

He drapes a blanket over my skin.

Unconcerned with where I'm being taken, I slump over the horse's back. The only thing I know is my heart is irreparably broken from the loss of my closest friend.

Riding in the dark for what feels like hours, I drift in and out of consciousness. My tears have dried. I have no tears left to cry.

We stop, and I'm eased from the horse by someone with gentle, warm hands. The man—whose wrinkled face I can now see—carries me like an infant.

I fall limp in his arms.

His face is hardened with concern, but he forces a smile when he catches me looking up at him. "You are going to be okay."

The man's words send me into another hysterical fit of crying. Can anything be okay? Not after what just happened; nothing can. Not for me. I might not ever be okay again.

He lays me in a bed, then pulls a blanket up to my chin.

Trembling under the weight of the woolen covers, I cannot hold back the misery any longer. Howls erupt from deep in my chest.

The man hangs his head.

Something jabs into my arm.

My muscles are unable to move.

My eyelids are heavy.

Chapter Five

I come into consciousness for the first time in what feels like months, or even years. Inside, the searing pain and guilt of losing Brad rips a hole through my chest. I have no idea what I'm going to see, where I am, or why I'm still alive. I open my eyes, then blink a few times before they clear. The little room is dark; a few candles burn on an old table next to the bed. Sounds of people shuffling about and dishes clanging in a sink come from a room somewhere else, but no one is here with me.

Surveying my surroundings—and judging by the clothes strewn about the floor—I assume I'm in a man's bedroom. Fear controls my muscles, forcing me to slink out of the rustic poster bed. Someone has slipped a clean, white nightgown over my underclothes. Drawn in below my breasts and flowing to the floor, the gown reminds me of clothing from another time. If I wasn't so afraid, I might be excited by how flattering the nightie is to my slight figure.

I rummage through the drawers, the pants on the floor, and the hole in the dirt wall someone uses as a closet, hoping to find a weapon. I spot a small knife leaning against the wall behind a wooden chair made out of intricate tree limbs twisted together. The metal blade is so shiny it almost hums when what little light the candles offer bounces off it. Putting the knife to my ear, I hear faint sounds of people singing.

I must still be experiencing the effects of the drugs they injected into my arm.

The handle has a carving of those deadly, vile creatures on it. Horrified, I drop it, then notice out of the corner of my left eye someone standing in the doorway, smiling.

He clears his throat, causing me to jump.

My knees weaken. My heart pounds.

"I see you are finally awake. You have been sleeping for the last two days," he says, taking a couple steps into the room.

Backing up against the wall, I almost fall over my own feet. I have to get to the knife lying on the floor, but he sees me looking at the weapon and rushes to pick it up before I can even take a breath.

"I am not going to hurt you. If I wanted you dead, I would not have bothered rescuing you. My name is Lann," he says, reaching out one hand to me while he pockets the blade with his other. Lann is tall, lean but strong, with dark hair and green eyes, similar to mine and Brit's. He appears to be in his mid-twenties. He has flawless skin, and a smile that would melt the hearts of any girl. The only imperfection I see is the puffiness surrounding his eyes, revealing how tired he is.

Eyebrow raised, Lann looks me up and down.

There's nothing stopping him from hurting me. Accepting that Lann must not intend to kill me, I reach for his hand.

"Katriona, but my friends call me Kate," I say, staying as firm in my grip as possible to mask the fear I'm still working to subdue in my voice.

For an instant, I see a flash of surprise in Lann's eyes, and then it disappears.

"Well, Kate. It is very nice to meet you. Would you like to go visit your friend?"

"B-Brad is a-alive?" My knees finally give out.

He catches me before I hit the floor.

"I am sure he has seen better days, but yes, your Brad is *alive*," Lann says, standing me back on my feet.

The way he hung on the last word makes me desperate; I feel like there might not be much time left for Brad at all.

"Please, yes, I have to see him," I whisper, barely audible—even to myself.

Lann leads me down the brown, earthen hallway at a pace that makes me want to punch him. Taking deep breaths, I focus straight ahead, and I imagine the horrors waiting for me in Brad's room. I expect he'll be hooked up to machines, monitored by doctors, and medicated beyond belief.

Lann pushes open the door, then stands aside.

Two doors down from me, Brad lies in bed—*alive*. His injured face is pale, but someone has taken great care in closing the gaping wounds with stitches. Blisters cover every exposed part of his body. I don't even want to imagine what his back looks like; the thought makes me shudder.

"If you will excuse me." Lann bows, then leaves Brad and me to be alone.

I speed across the room and sit next to him. Taking his hand in mine, I realize how bad he is. Fever wracks Brad's body.

He opens his bloodshot eyes. They're full of confusion, as if he's searching his memory to place who I am.

"Why didn't you go back?" Brad asks. His voice cracks, but even though he sounds like he could use a drink of water, I still hear how frustrated he is with me.

"When you pushed me, I fell to the ground, not back into the water. Don't you remember? We didn't make it; we must have been disoriented. I saw the arrows flying from the trees and those awful creatures die, and I came to you. I thought you were dead. Someone picked me up, and the next thing I know I'm here . . . and you're alive!" I say, through tears mixed with joy and sadness. I bury my head next to him, too ashamed to look him in the eyes.

Brad shouldn't be here.

Placing his fingers under my chin, he lifts my head. I look at the brokenness of my friend; his face contorts. He must be in so much pain.

"How bad does it hurt?" I ask.

Brad shakes his head. "Kate, have they talked to you about anything that's going on here?"

"No. I just woke up, for the first time since we were attacked." I look at my hands, too embarrassed to meet his eyes. Brad has endured a brutal attack, and I slept longer than he did.

"Hey there," he says, caressing my cheek with the back of his sweaty fingers.

Brad's touch leaves traces of fever burning across my face.

"Everything is going to be okay."

"What have they told you?" I stifle the sobs that are sure to betray me any moment.

"They say we're in a place called Encardia. One of the doctors, if you can call him that, thinks we might have accidentally travelled through a portal to this world. Then he went on to mutter some stuff about how that's impossible. I think he's crazy."

Brad pierces me with a hard stare, but his eyebrow raises just a little—he thinks this is some kind of sick joke. He's a literal person, but even without him knowing about the yellow light I followed, the portal makes sense. How else can he explain swimming into a cave in the middle of a river and landing flat on our faces inside this nightmare? From the moment our bodies slammed into the ground, I've suspected we left our own world. Now that I'm coherent, the only thing that makes sense is some sort of parallel universe.

"You don't believe him?" I'm curious as to why he cannot connect the dots or even *feel* the difference. Were the creatures not indication enough?

"Do *you*?"

"I've felt like we weren't at home from the second we left the water," I say. I should have known something was wrong much earlier on in our trip. The moment I had the first vision of the woman, while we climbed Goat Ridge, I should have led us all right back to the Jeep.

Brad holds me prisoner with his gaze. He's probably hoping I will change my mind and tell him I think the people he's been talking to are crazy, but I'm not budging. He must think *I'm* crazy for believing we've entered another world. I feel it, even if he cannot.

"Be careful, Kate. I've heard the two old doctors whispering about us all day. If I weren't stuck in this bed, I would have us home and never look back," Brad says, closing his eyes.

He's in pain and trying to hide it.

"What have they been whispering about?" I ask, breathless.

"I don't know; something about them makes me uncomfortable." Brad shifts in bed and lets out a muffled cry.

He's dying in front of me, and there's nothing I can do but watch. I'm useless to him here. What could they have been whispering about us, other than how lucky we are to be alive? Brad must be paranoid. He has bruises on his arm where someone has, more than likely, injected him with drugs. Those must be affecting him, too.

I have to figure out where we are and how to get home.

Swallowing hard, I stand and straighten the nightgown. "I don't think they mean to hurt us. I'll go talk to them and get some answers."

"Don't go yet. Stay with me for a while, please?" Brad whispers.

My surge of resolve melts away. "Okay."

I move a chair from the corner of the room, set it next to the bed, then I take a seat. I prop up my elbows, rest my head in my hands.

Brad drifts in and out of sleep for what feels like hours. Sitting and watching my lifelong friend die is painful. He's been here for me for almost as long as I can remember, held my hand when I was scared, made me smile when no one else could. I cannot imagine a life without him in it, without his witty remarks, his always knowing the right thing to say, and the warmth of his arms around me when I'm sad.

What's wrong with me? Why didn't I tell him about the light? At least, if I had, he could have decided whether he wanted to come with us. He might not be here, if I had said something. I want to cry, but I don't want Brad to see me upset. I don't want to make him any more worried than he is already.

Waking again, he watches me while I think over all the mistakes I made in the forest. He motions with his finger for me to come closer.

I lean over his body.

He smiles—or at least tries to—as he pulls my face down to his, finds my lips, and gives them a sweet kiss.

I cannot return his love. Other than how strange it feels, touching his swollen lips with mine while he burns with fever, I worry Brad wants more from me—more than I'm sure I want to give him. The only thing I'm positive of, in this moment, is that if he doesn't receive the proper treatment soon, this could be the last time I ever see or kiss him.

I stand. "I'm going to get answers."

"Come back soon."

"I promise."

A renewed strength builds, centering me. My mission is to save Brad, get home, and never dream of going near that swimming hole again. Reaching the door, I turn to look over my shoulder; Brad's eyes are closed. I pray this is not the last time I see him alive.

Chapter Six

The hall is empty. The clanging of dishes has stopped. To the left are two other doors; one at the end, and one diagonally across from Brad's room. I make the choice to go right.

Neither of the rooms I've been in have windows; small sconces with flickering candles line the wall and provide the only light.

Reliefs of people from a happier time decorate the length of the packed dirt walls. I run my fingers across the contours of the art-filled earth. The serenity displayed on the faces of the people in these scenes seems so unreal. With rings of flowers through their curly locks, children laugh and dance by a pond. Men play flutes, and women hug their babies. Everyone is smiling. The beauty of it is touching. Something nags at the back of my mind. The simple clothing, the wooden instruments, the love of the mothers for their children and the happy men—I know these people. I've seen them in so many of my dreams.

After getting lost in the beauty and familiarity of the walls, I walk to the end of the hall, just past the room I've been sleeping in. The corridor leads into a dining room. Five round tables, each with four wooden chairs, cluster throughout the little area. A buffet table made from a huge tree trunk, full of steaming, hot food sits against the far wall. My stomach growls furiously at me. When did I last eat?

Setting aside the fact I'm supposed to find answers, I look around, then make my way over to the table. Meat, potatoes, carrots—everything looks delicious. I grab a dish from one end and pile it full of enough food to feed Brad *and* me. But he's asleep; I'll take him something later.

Sitting at the closest table, I inhale the meal. Midway through a bite of chicken, guilt consumes me. So far, these people have been good to us. They've saved our lives, cleaned us up, and given us beds. In return, I'm stealing food from them, but now that I've done it, I might as well finish devouring what I put on my plate.

My mind wanders off and out of this gloomy little room, and I think about Brad's confession. I should have seen it coming. How could I not realize he loves me as much as he does? People tried to tell me, but he always denied it. Even if I had accepted the truth, he was my friend—my good friend—but I had deeper feelings for someone I've never met. A relationship with Brad wouldn't have been fair.

Tears stream down my face as I finish my meal. I wipe my cheeks with the back of my sleeve. Instead of sitting here, thinking about how stupid I am for the rest of my life, I should take food to Brad and wait for him to wake up so he can eat. If I'm going to steal, it should be for someone who is sick and more than likely going to die.

I put so much food on the plate, potatoes and chicken hang over the edge. Turning to take the treasures back to Brad's room, I bump into someone standing right behind me. My gaze works its way up a man's chest, neck, face, then finally comes to rest on eyes so familiar, my hands tremble, and all the blood in my body runs cold.

It's *him*.

The dish falls to the floor. Bits of food splatter all over the place.

"You must be Kate," he says, frowning at me.

"Y-yes. I came to find someone to talk to and saw all of the food and couldn't help myself. I'm sorry I've made such a mess." I kneel to gather pieces of plate, chicken, and potatoes from the floor and begin to whisper under my breath. "This is all just a dream, it's just a dream, and everything is going to be okay."

"A dream?" He laughs, joining me on the floor. "No, Kate, this is not a dream."

"Well, you have been in almost every one of my dreams since I was fourteen," I say, not meeting his eyes. Do concussions cause hallucinations? I rub the back of my head. The swelling from my meeting with the rocks on Goat Ridge has gone away.

He places his fingers under my elbow, then lifts me to my feet. Surges of excitement rush up my arm and into my chest; air catches in my lungs.

"That is not necessary. They will clean it up," he says, pointing to Lann and another man who looks like he could be Lann's twin.

The two men do not appear pleased about having to clean up my mess, but they move right in as they were instructed, while I'm brought to a table in the middle of the room.

Arland motions for me to sit down, facing away from them. "Have you eaten?"

"Y-yes, but I was taking something for my f-friend." Formulating fluid thoughts seems to be impossible. I'm flustered by his presence. His eyes, the beautiful emeralds I've stared into a hundred times, hold my gaze now. He's so intense, so handsome—so exactly how I dreamed.

"Flanna, will you please prepare a plate for our guest's friend?" he asks, without looking away from me.

I glance over my shoulder as Flanna rushes through the room, doing as she's been instructed. Her long, fiery-red hair bounces as she walks; her skin glows a pale white. I cannot get a good look at her face, but she must be as beautiful as the men I've seen here so far.

The intensity of Arland's eyes burns straight through me. I'm perplexed by his appearance—millions of questions buzz through my head, but nerves win out over my need for answers, rendering me mute. I allow him to speak first.

"So you say you have dreamed about me? Would you mind sharing?" He gives me a warm smile, but it transforms into a smirk. He's enjoying this.

I feel my whole face flush. A memory of a kiss flashes in my head, sending the heat rushing into my cheeks. "What do you want to know, Arland Maher?"

He laughs. "What did we do in these dreams?"

I stare at my hands, afraid to meet his eyes again—afraid he'll laugh me out of the room, but I might as well lay it all on the line. If this is a dream, it won't matter, but if it's real, well, he'll know what he's done to me. "We've fought side-by-side, worried for one another, lain in bed together for days, kissed passionately, and loved each other deeper than could ever be true in reality. I've also seen you die dozens of different ways and found myself alone and broken, each and every time. You are the only man I've ever loved with my whole heart."

Arland's smirk fades; his jaw tightens.

"Cadman, where did you report finding Kate and the boy?" he asks of a man entering from the kitchen.

I close my eyes. *Wake up. This is just a dream. It's not real. You're in your bed; you're at home. Brad is just fine. None of this is happening.*

Heat radiates into my shoulder blades. Looking up, I see the corner of Cadman's lip twist up—just a little. He is the same man who carried me into bed when I thought Brad had been killed.

"We found them in the clearing, sir. We heard the girl screaming from the edge of the forest and knew someone needed help."

"I believe I instructed you to inform me upon discovering *anyone* in the clearing!"

"I am sorry, sir. You were away upon the arrival of these two innocents. I should have informed you this morning, when you returned from Wickward, but failed to do so." Judging by the flecks of gray in his short, red hair, and the wrinkles around his mouth and deep-set eyes, I'd say Cadman is in his late fifties. He stands straight, waiting for someone much younger to mete out his punishment.

But it doesn't come.

Arland whispers into Cadman's ear. Without another word, he walks away, but before disappearing into the hallway, he steals one more glance at us.

"We have been expecting you for a very long time. How did you and your friend find the entrance to Encardia?" Arland asks, his attention back on me.

"Expecting me? What do you mean?"

"Are you Katriona Wilde? Daughter of Brian and Saraid Wilde?"

Arland knows my name, my parents' names, and he has been waiting for me. But how can this be? How can I dream of someone I've never met, never known, who's from another world?

And what does this mean for Brad?

What if my nightmares are visions of the future?

"Yes, but my dad died a long time ago," I say, making sure to keep my voice even.

"I am aware of your father's death." Arland shakes his head. "But surely your mother has informed you of this place?"

"No, she hasn't."

"Hmm." He rubs the chin I've seen him rub so many times in my dreams. "So how *did* you arrive here then?"

"We were swimming in the river. My sister and I saw something shimmering under the waterfall. We thought it was the entrance to a cave, so we decided to check it out, but when we swam through, we found ourselves here." I rub my hands, trying to calm my nerves.

"Your sister? It is only you and the boy who are here now."

"My sister was with us, but I was able to push her back the way we came, before we were attacked. You don't think she's here?" I ask, choking on the food rising in the back of my throat. The thought of Brit being here, alone and confused—or possibly dead—is too much.

"No one else was found in the clearing, otherwise my soldiers would have informed me," Arland says.

"Like they informed you where they found *me*?" Arland is confident, but I have to know for sure my sister is safe.

He places his hand over mine. "You have my word your sister is not here."

"I hope I can trust your word," I say, pulling my hand away so as not to be mortified by my sweaty palms. Arland's touch is not repulsive; in fact, it's the opposite. He's warm and exciting.

"So, you said you've been expecting me . . . . Why have you been expecting me? And what's wrong with Brad? He looks like he's d-dying. What were those things that attacked us?" I try as hard as I can to hold my composure.

"Take a walk with me?" Arland asks, standing up.

How can I say no to him? I've seen the love in his eyes, kissed his lips, and held his hands in my dreams for the past six years. Sure, they were *just* dreams, but they all felt so tangible. Nothing ever seemed the slightest bit imagined or made up. Now here he is, in front of me, and I don't know how to react. I'm too nervous to respond.

Arland reaches out his hand to me. "I promise I am not going to hurt you."

I take a tentative hold on it, *after* I dry my own on the gown.

I'm feeling underdressed, all of a sudden.

He leads me through a kitchen, to the left, upstairs, and then out two large, round-topped, wooden doors that open into a courtyard. It's still dark and cold outside. Too cold. Wherever I am, summer is not the season. The plants along the side of the building are all dead. By the way the barren chestnut tree in the center of the yard leans, I'm sure it will be dead soon, too.

He directs me to sit on a bench a few feet away from the tree. I follow a gray, flat stone path to the seat and take in the architecture of the building.

"It is beautiful, is it not?" Arland asks.

"Yes. I've never seen anything like it. Is everything made of earth, wood, and stone?" From what I can see, the outside walls of the building are made of packed dirt—like those inside the building—but out here, they also have one-foot wide wooden beams every five feet or so. In between the beams are reliefs, but I can't quite see the details from where I sit.

"It is. This is one of our many military bases. Most of this structure is underground. The only portion of the main building above ground is this courtyard where we sit. We come out here to remind ourselves why we fight."

"Why do you fight?"

"Survival." He pauses, then points at the wall. "If you look closely, you will see combat scenes carved into the walls. After harsh battles, some of us come out here and draw out the memories. It is a tool we use to heal our hearts."

Sadness fills Arland's words . . . a sadness I hope I never have to comprehend. I walk over to the walls—run my hands across them as I did inside and inspect some of the distressed art. One in particular stands out more than the others do. A stake impales a woman, driven through her chest and into the ground. A child with a sword in his hand sits, curled at her feet. A dead monster lies next to them. My hands shake. The person who experienced his mother's tragic death in such a dreadful way is the one who must have drawn this.

Arland stands next to me, leaning into the wall. He touches it with his own hand, closes his eyes, and mutters something inaudible—not to me, but to the wall.

"This was my mother," is all he says, before returning to the bench.

There's a part of me that wants to wrap my arms around him, caress his face, and tell him everything will be okay, but I'm sure that would be strange to him. To me, not so much, considering we've done that for each other so many times before, in my dreams. It's safer not to do or say anything, so I follow him back to the seat and fold my hands in my lap. "I'm sorry."

Arland's gaze returns to the courtyard. "There is a layer of magic protecting us from the enemy stumbling upon the base, but, unfortunately, there is not enough to protect our entire civilization."

"Magic?" I ask, careful not to reveal my disbelief.

"This might be difficult for you to accept, but please know I will *never* lie to you. You are Encardia's only hope of surviving this war."

Arland pauses and watches me, as if he's waiting for me to say something, but I remain silent. I don't know what else to do. As much as I'd like to tell him he's wrong, I cannot. I'm here, I've seen the monsters and the man from my dreams firsthand—running away is hardly an option.

"Many years ago, you and your family lived in this land. Six months before you were born, a Seer gave your mother and father a prophecy. It instructed them to protect you by using old magic to take you out of our world, immediately after your birth, for you would be the Light to end the Darkness seeking to destroy our kind."

"Me? Light?" War is not for me. Light and Darkness, prophecies and magic—none of this makes sense. I'm sitting on a bench next to a man I've dreamed of for years, he's touched me, he's telling me I'm some kind of savior—it's all too unreal.

"Yes," he says, watching my knees bounce up and down.

I cross my ankles, trying to control my nerves. "But, how?"

"Through old magic."

"What is old magic?"

"Something people of this world have long since forgotten how to use." He turns his head toward the sky.

"So a Seer said I'd save this world, but I couldn't live here—and my parents just did what they were told? No questions asked?"

"I am sure they had plenty of questions," he says, sitting like a statue—the total opposite of me.

"So why did they do it? Why did they leave?"

"When a Seer gives a prophecy as clear as yours, people listen. We lived in a time of great peace, but they had to protect you, even though it was hard for them to fathom, taking their child out of the only world they ever knew."

I look around the courtyard. Nothing I see has life. Everything reeks of death and misery. It's hard to imagine peace ever existed here.

"If my prophecy was clear, did it say where I'd learn this old magic?"

"Not that I am aware of."

"If no one knows it, how do I learn it?"

"I hoped you would already know, but it appears your mother never taught you."

I take a deep breath. "And my dad? If no one used the magic, how'd he get my family through the portal?"

"Your father was wise in the old magic—I believe his family continued to practice even though they were not supposed to—but even *he* struggled to find a way to open a portal. He worked tirelessly for weeks, before he informed my father of his plan, but no one else, as the Seer instructed. The two of them worked together at great length before they discovered how to open the portal to your world."

"Why did he die? If we were on Earth, what killed him?"

"Your father continued coming back to check on us and aid in the battles as often as he could. Conjuring magic powerful enough to allow him to go between two worlds fatigued him; after a few months of living two lives, he tried to return here and immediately stepped into a battle in the clearing. He was ill-prepared and, unfortunately, lost his life."

My dad is dead because of me. Mom could never talk about how he died. She would become distant and tell me he was lost in the war, but I assumed an American war—not one from another world. I wonder if that's why she was always closer with Brit, because somewhere, deep inside, Mom blamed me?

I'm not sure how, but I know Arland is telling the truth. I feel like I know him all too well. His presence is calming, comforting—the way it always has been. Except, this time, he's real.

"How long was it before all this"—I raise my hands and look around the courtyard—"happened?"

"Two days after your birth. Darkness appeared and slaughtered our people with such ferocity, its minions nearly wiped us out within a few months. We have never battled anything like this before. We drained most of the remaining old magic fueling life itself."

"Do you have any idea why it's here? What it wants?"

Arland shakes his head. "We do not know why Darkness is here, but as far as we can tell, it wants us to die. Can you not see it for yourself? There is no sunshine, the plants are decaying, the air smells of death, and people are worn and weary."

I nod. In the short time I've been here, I have noted all of these things: the darkness, the smell, the tired look on everyone's faces. How can I be from this world? Why hasn't Mom ever shared any of this with me? Why would she let me live a lie? My life, and everything I've ever wanted to be, have all been fake—and Mom knew it.

Arland looks down at me and wipes tears from my cheek with his thumb.

I didn't realize I was crying.

His touch is warm, gentle—familiar, even. I want to put my hand over his. His deep green eyes return my mixed feelings of longing and loss with what I interpret from him to be hope. His people—*my* people—are counting on me to save this world. This is too overwhelming to think about. What can a girl raised on a horse farm have to offer, in terms of war? My hands are sweating again; I ball them up in my lap.

"Are you afraid?" he asks.

"Only that I'll let everyone down," I admit. "What am I supposed to do?"

"Unfortunately, I do not know."

"So, I just get to embarrass myself in front of all these people until I discover whatever makes me Light?" I ask, wondering if I've ever done anything special or meaningful in my life . . . something that would help me now.

"You will not be embarrassed; not many people know of your prophecy. My father, myself, Flanna, and Lann are the only ones who have been informed officially, although some have discovered information unofficially," he says, clenching his jaw. "We will keep your identity a secret until the time is right."

"But someone is bound to find out. I mean, you're here because of me, aren't you?"

The muscles in his face relax, and somehow, I feel my own worries slip away when confronted by his resolve. "No one will find out. And yes, we set up Watcher's Hall to await your return."

"How long have you been here?"

"There was never an indication as to when you would return, so we have been here for many years. My father used to bring me on patrols with him when I was younger. He wanted me to know the surroundings, so I could maneuver through them with my eyes closed. Now that you are here, I am solely responsible for your well-being."

"Why are you solely responsible for me?" I ask, shocked and mildly elated.

"I was born five years before you. When my mother was carrying me, the Seer prophesied I would be Keeper of Light. At the time, my family did not understand what that meant. It was not until your father visited with *your* news that they were able to make sense of it. I am your Coimeádaí."

Arland pauses, then smiles. "You and I have met once before, a day after you were born. You were lying in a cradle your father crafted for you before the prophecy. I peeked in, and you smiled at me," he says, as if the memory is a good one.

"So that's why I've seen you die in so many of my dreams?" I ask, standing. My arms are at my sides, every muscle tight, fists balled. "You die trying to protect me? Like Brad lies in his room, dying, because of me."

"I do find your dreams quite interesting. I would like to learn more about them, but I do not believe you are a Seer—and I am not going to die." He raises his eyebrow, making me feel like a fool.

Taking a deep breath, I sit back down.

"We will have to research why you are having these dreams. Maybe it is a subconscious part of you. My father should know, since your parents informed him of your prophecy. I will communicate with him later, to fill him in on the full details of your arrival. Did your mother *never* speak with you about any of this?" Arland rambles on, avoiding my comment about Brad.

But Brad is all I can think about.

"He's going to die then, isn't he?" I say, scowling.

Arland's face softens.

"He should already be dead. Our Healers do not understand how the poison has not stopped his heart," he says, not meeting my eyes.

"What's happening to him?" I ask, my voice barely above a whimper.

"He was attacked by a daemon of Darkness. We call them coscarthas. They are the lowest ranking, but represent the largest population of daemons draining the life from our land."

"Are they why I need your protection?"

"Amongst other things . . . ." He stares at me, no hint of concern or fear in his features, like he's having a conversation with an old buddy on a park bench—only everything around us is dead.

"What other things?"

"Tairbs, hounds, shifters, serpents—those are much more powerful than coscarthas."

I'm not even sure I want to know what those things are. "So what do they do?"

"They kill without hesitation—like they have no conscience at all. When a coscartha cuts someone with its claws, a poison enters the victim's body, acting similar to a snakebite. Generally, the poison paralyzes and kills instantly. So why your friend lives, and as for what is happening to him . . . we do not know."

"A neurotoxin," I say, standing, ready to leave. "If I can get back home, I can probably get an antidote that will save him."

Arland catches my hand before I can go anywhere. "I cannot risk your life by taking you there right now. Your screams brought a lot of unwelcome daemons to the area. My soldiers have been trying to fight them off, but for now, the danger is too great. I will have Flanna and Lann continue to monitor the surrounding areas every morning. I am sorry about your friend, but the most you can do for him now is keep him comfortable while the poison takes over."

"I have to try. Please, take me back." I whisper urgently to him.

Arland shakes his head.

I'm not going to win this one. If his purpose is to protect me, he's going to do just that. Until he feels the circumstances are safe, I will not be able to see my family or save Brad.

"You won't mind if I stay with him, then?"

Tugging my hand free, I leave, without giving Arland a second glance. I'm sure he spoke the truth, but the pain of knowing Brad is going to die is too much for me to bear, and that's all I can think about now. I've already experienced the horrible, mind-numbing grief his death will cause me once; I don't think I can handle experiencing that again. For now, I want to spend as much time with my friend as possible.

Chapter Seven

Coughs echo through the base. *Brad.* I run from the kitchen to get to him.

The Healers work together to clean blood from his face and change his blankets. I catch only a glimpse of the crimson before they wipe it away, but I see enough to know his condition has worsened. All the strength I managed to gather throughout the course of today leaks from my soul, leaving me hollow. I stare at the alarming scene before me, afraid to step into the room.

"Would you like to be alone with him, miss?" an old man asks, his tired eyes full of pity.

My heart is heavy. "Yes, please."

I sigh and take a few steps toward the bed.

The Healers leave the room. The old man shakes his head as he closes the door behind him.

I turn to Brad. He's asleep. Curling up on the bed next to him, I attempt to sleep as well, but it's impossible. For the longest time, he doesn't move, making me think for sure, a few times, he might have died. But every so often, he draws in a ragged breath. When Brad breathes, I breathe.

All I can think about is how it's my fault we're here in the first place. If I'd told Brad about the light, or even put a little more thought into how weird it was that he couldn't see the entry to that stupid cave, we might not have come here. But the way Arland told it, I didn't have much choice. My eyes close, but the details of every error I made play across them.

Following the light into the cave was the biggest mistake of my life.

Brad's body is so hot that I have to get out of bed. He's soaked with sweat. I grab a chair from the corner of the room and place it next to the bed, then lay my head on the edge by his waist.

Time seems to stand still. An hour goes by—maybe two. Brad runs his fingers through my hair. I lift my head, groggy and confused by the overwhelming guilt, as well as the information Arland shared with me earlier. I shouldn't have walked away from him so soon; there are other things I want to ask, other things I *need* to understand.

Brad's expression asks the pressing question before he does.

"What's happening to me?" He plays with the loose hem on the bed sheets.

"They said it's a poison, similar to a neurotoxin. There's nothing here to treat it, and it's too dangerous right now to return home for medicines." I want to be strong for him, but weakness reveals itself in my strained voice.

"I was prepared to die for you, Kate; I still am."

I squeeze the edge of the bed for support. "I will try to get home after the daemons have either been killed off or left."

"*Daemons?* The things that attacked us? Don't!" Even though his face is swollen beyond recognition, his eyes are still my Brad's. I know the look he's giving me; he doesn't want me to risk my life for him.

"Why? I can't leave you here to die!" Tears mount an assault, but I hold them back—for now.

"I would rather die here, in bed, with you in my arms, than send you out there. The medicines probably won't work. Please, promise me you won't do anything reckless."

"I promise not to do anything reckless," I say, my voice flat.

He moans; the agonizing sound torments me.

"Shh, everything is going to be okay," I say, pushing Brad's tousled hair from his forehead and wiping his face with a cold cloth from the bedside table. The fabric becomes hot the instant it touches his skin. I remove the cloth, swirl it around the air, and then reapply. My attempts to cool him are futile, but I'd rather be busy. And if cooling him *does* help, then I'll continue until he's healed, if that's what it takes.

Brad's eyes close for a moment—as if he's going to sleep—then pop right back open. "Did you know I wanted to marry you? From the very first day I met you, I've known I wanted to be with you forever. Promise me you'll find someone who loves you the way you deserve; find someone who loves you like I do."

He grabs my hand, squeezes it. Dropping the cloth, I cannot respond, cannot keep up the façade of strength. Tears race down my cheeks, pain fills my heart, and air refuses to fill my lungs. Giving an automatic nod, I grab the cloth again, dab Brad's head, but remain quiet.

Two promises I cannot possibly keep, within five minutes of each other. This day keeps getting worse for us both.

Questions swim around the forefront of my mind. Would I have married him? Sure, I've thought about marriage, kids, and what kind of life I wanted to have, but I haven't had a boyfriend before, so I haven't considered who I might spend my future with. Would it have been Brad? I cannot see a life without him in it, in some fashion. I cannot fathom the depths of his love for me. Why did he never tell me? Why didn't he ask me if I'd date him? Was he afraid my answer would be no? *Would* my answer have been no? The rambling questions pop up as fast as corn kernels in the microwave, leaving me as battered as the bag they pop in.

Brad's eyes glaze over as he watches me think. I'm not sure what level of consciousness he's in. A few times, his eyes roll back in his head, causing me to go into a panic. Before I scream for help, his eyes always come back to their proper place, looking at me. After he falls asleep again, I lie beside him and fall asleep, too.

Flashes of violent images set on a loop plague my dreams: the coscarthas attack Brad and me, killing us both. Arland jumps into a lake to save me from being pulled under by a snake-like creature, only to drown. Everyone I've met here at base is set on fire, bodies flailing on the ground before me. I'm forced to watch as their skin melts. Something—some *creature*—stabs a woman through the heart with a stake; a child screams at her feet.

I awaken, trembling with fear. Sitting up, I realize it's not me trembling, it's Brad.

"Brad! Help! Someone, *please*!" I jump off the bed and continue to yell, trying to get someone's attention.

He convulses on the bed. Drool leaks from the corners of his mouth. The irises of his eyes roll into the back of his head, revealing only white.

Arland bursts through the door, along with the two elderly Healers. He backs me up to the wall, blocking my view of Brad. I cry out from the innermost recesses of my heart as I watch my best friend's body shut down.

The woman injects something into Brad's arm with a large copper syringe, stopping the convulsions.

"Kegan, bring the other," she says.

Kegan brings over another syringe, filled with something I hope will help Brad.

"This will place him in a deep sleep. He will not be in as much pain. We can take him out of it—if we find he is healing," the old woman says, looking at Arland.

He hangs his head. "Go ahead, Shay."

Arland returns his gaze to me and lets my arms go, when I stop fighting against him. I'm the definition of a mess. This is the beginning of the end. If they have to induce a coma, they're worried the neurotoxin is attacking Brad's brain. *If* he heals, they can bring him out of it, and it will be as though he were in a deep sleep, but *if* he does not heal, he will at least pass without pain.

Sinking to the floor, I rest my head against the wall. My heart already broke once, when I thought Brad died; now, my heart feels like it has been ripped from my chest.

Arland scoops me into his arms. He carries me into my room, where he lays me on the bed. Curling into a ball, I wrap my arms around my shins and bring my knees to my chest. There are no tears left, no emotions to express, no will left in me to live. I'm empty, and a terrible friend.

"How long have you two been mates?" Arland asks, stretching a wool blanket over me.

"He's not my *mate*." The word makes me feel like the friendship I've shared with Brad is cheap.

"Cadman informed me you two were in each other's arms, kissing, when they came upon you in the clearing. It is really none of my business. I am sorry to have asked. If you do not need anything, I will leave you." Arland is already by the door.

"No," I say, sitting up. I can't handle this. My emotions are out of control. I don't want Arland to leave. I don't want to be alone. I feel bad for being so nasty toward him. He has been kind to me; he deserves to have that kindness returned. "Please don't leave. I'm sorry I got upset."

"I should not have pried into your personal affairs," he says, still standing by the door.

"It's okay. I might have asked the same thing if I were you. Will you stay for a while?"

"Are you sure you do not wish to be alone?" His voice is full of apprehension.

"I'm sure. How did Cadman see us kissing in the dark?" I ask, desperate to start a conversation before he walks out.

Arland grabs the rickety old chair from beside the dresser, then sets it down by the foot of the bed. "Our eyes have become accustomed to seeing great distances in the dark. It is not a trait we are proud of, but one we could not survive without."

I cross my legs over each other to get more comfortable. "So you don't need light to see? You've evolved?"

"Light helps, but no, we do not need it."

"If it had not been for our flashlights, the three of us might not have known the daemons were coming," I say, shuddering at the memory.

"Your eyes will adjust," he says, as if it will happen overnight. "If you do not mind, what is your relationship with the boy?"

"Brad has been my best friend since we were eight. Until we wound up here, I never realized how much he loved me. People have brought it to my attention over the years, but when I asked him how he felt, he always denied it. Maybe because he knew I didn't feel the same, and if he admitted it, he might lose me. I don't know. I can't figure it out. Before the coscarthas attacked, he kissed me. I imagine he figured it would be the last chance he would ever have to share his feelings," I say, rambling on way too long.

"You do not share the same feelings for him?"

"I don't know what I feel. I do love him, but it's not the same kind of love he has for me." Now, I'll never have the opportunity to explore a relationship with Brad. Lying back down, I pull the blanket up to my chin and close my burning eyes. All the happy memories of Brad flash across them. "My mom always told me to be honest with him about how I felt, so I wouldn't end up hurting us both in the future. If I'd listened to her, he might not be here with me right now. He could be safe at home, with someone who deserves him. Not stuck in a coma here, because of me."

"You cannot blame yourself. I do not believe the boy would ever have given up on you, even if you had said you hated him. If he has waited this long for an opportunity to be with you, he would not have easily left your side. That kind of love does not burn out." Arland pats my hand, then heads for the door.

The simple touch leaves me even more confused about my love life than before I met Arland. My dreams of him have always been filled with intimate passions I've never experienced with anyone. His light touch is not enough to quench the intense desires I feel, because of what we've shared over the years.

He stops before the door closes all the way. "If you are willing, I would like to begin training you how to use weapons in the morning. I will not take you away from the safety of this base without you having knowledge of some basic self-defense techniques."

I nod.

Arland disappears behind the heavy, wooden door.

What am I supposed to do here? This world may be where I came from, but it doesn't feel like my own. Somehow, I'm supposed to fight Darkness for these people, and I've never so much as punched a person. I miss Brit. If she were here, I'm sure she would love the opportunity to save the world. Scratch that; I'm glad she isn't here. I hope she's at home, safe in her own bed.

Picturing home for a moment, I wonder what Brit told our parents. Sure, Mom probably wasn't shocked, but what are Gary and Mr. Tanner doing right now? The thought of Mr. Tanner brings me back to Brad's comment about marrying me. I could have been Mrs. Kate Tanner. The thought causes me to choke. The way I felt so comfortable in his arms that evening in the tent: was it because of how familiar we are with each other, or because there is something more?

I no longer want to think about anything—not about Brad, not about Brit, and not about Arland. The flickering candle next to the bed illuminates roots poking through the ceiling. I count them until my thoughts slow and my breathing becomes heavy. After fifty-two, I begin drifting to sleep.

Chapter Eight

The smell of eggs drifts into my dreams. Hunger gnaws at my stomach. Opening my eyes, I stretch my arms, muscles sore and stiff. There's no way I could have been sleeping more than an hour.

Someone has left a tray of food and some clean clothes next to the bed. I grab the tray, pick at the eggs and potatoes, but wait to get dressed. My skin is dirty. There would be no point in putting on clean clothes. I climb from the bed, grab the burning candle from the table, and then walk from the room to check out the other two doors in the hall. No one else I've seen is as dirty as I am; there must be a shower or something somewhere.

The door at the end of the hall is locked, but the one across from Brad's opens into the most peculiar of bathrooms. The floor on the right side of the room has a stone enclosure built over a natural spring. Water flows in and out of the basin, probably making it the cleanest bath anyone could ever sit in.

The sound of the spring flowing is consistent, tranquil. The candle in my hand flickers in the holder. I set it down, and then slip off my borrowed nightgown, allowing it to fall to the floor around my ankles. I walk up the stone stairs to the opening of the enclosure, and then step into it with caution.

The water temperature is perfect. Submerging myself, I allow the warmth to refresh my tired skin. My eyes close, and I float on top of the spring. I don't think about Brad, or home, or anything else for as long as it takes for my fingers and toes to prune.

Next to the enclosure, sitting on a large rock, is a bar of soap. I grab it, rub the soap all over my skin, and through my hair. The smell of summer lilacs drifts through the bathroom, along with the steam.

The bath is so comforting, I have to force myself to climb out. Reaching the bottom step, I find someone has replaced my nightgown with the clean clothes I forgot to bring from the bedroom—and a towel. The fresh linens are folded and laying on an old oak counter next to the door. My senses must be relaxed; I never observed anyone come into the room.

For fear someone else might come in while I'm not decent, I rush to dress. The pants are tight and brown. The leather boots lace up to my knees and are a perfect fit. I slip a long-sleeved, white linen tunic over my head—the shirt hangs down to my thighs—and cinch a wide, brown belt around my waist. My hair is still dripping wet. I towel it dry, run my fingers through to comb the tangles, pulling out a ton of russet strands.

When my hair dries, I leave the bathroom and peek into Brad's room. Shay shakes her head. I look from her to Brad; there hasn't been any change in his condition.

"I will find you if I notice any improvement," she says, getting up from her chair.

"I-I—" I want to run to him, sit next to him, hold his hand and tell him everything's going to be okay, but he's not there.

"Go." She crosses the room, puts her hands on my shoulders, then guides me through the door. "There is nothing you can do."

The old Healer is right. There's no sense in going in; it wouldn't help me find a way to get him home, and it would only make me feel worse, watching him as he lies motionless on the bed.

Shay eases the heavy door closed behind me.

Dirty dishes litter the tables in the dining room, chairs are not in their proper places, and the buffet table is empty. I go into the kitchen, hoping to find someone soon because I'm beginning to feel alone, but there's no one in here either. It appears everyone has already eaten and gone about their business for the day.

Cleaning is the best idea I have for busying myself. I collect the plates from the dining room, take them to the sink—already full of water—and begin washing.

Back home, in periods of stress, I'd clean. After mailing out college applications, I'd work on the house until it gleamed. Every day, I came home from school and vacuumed, did the dishes, dusted—anything to get my mind off the waiting game. The afternoon my first acceptance letter came, the cleaning sessions became more intense. The acceptance wasn't from the school I wanted to attend; they were merely the first to write back. Twelve more acceptance letters graced our mailbox, but the one for Virginia Tech came last. During those few months, Mom never had to lift a finger. I inherited my habits from her, anyway. Mom did the same thing I did. When Gary had a heart attack and had to stay in the hospital for a week, Mom could barely find time to visit him with all the straightening up she was doing.

After a few trips back and forth between the kitchen and dining room, I've managed to wash all the dishes. The tables also get a good wipe down, and I push the old chairs, similar to the wooden one in my room, back into their places. I look around the rooms, smiling, proud of my work.

"Well," someone behind me says in a high-pitched voice.

Sucking in a sharp breath, I turn around. The redheaded woman who prepared food for Brad yesterday enters the dining room from the hallway.

"It appears as though you have finished up *my* job. Now what am I going to do with myself?" she says, her tone layered with irony. Laughing, she moves beside me. "We have not formally met; my name is Flanna."

"It's nice to meet you, Flanna." I'm able to see her face in full detail now. Flanna appears to be a year or two older than I am. She has crystal blue eyes, a short nose, and a pointed chin. She's smiling and absolutely stunning.

"Arland said you were beautiful, but with all that muck covering you, it was hard to tell for sure. I am glad you discovered the washroom this morning," she says, winking.

It's a little embarrassing to hear that Arland spoke about me *and* that everyone noticed how disgusting I was, but Flanna doesn't seem to understand this.

"Did I frighten you when I brought in your towel and clothes? I did not want to see you running down the hall wearing nothing but your skin."

"No, you didn't scare me. I never even knew you were there, but thank you. I appreciate your kindness." I like Flanna. Her gentle humor reminds me a great deal of Brit's sarcasm.

Flanna wraps her arm around me. She drags me up the stairs and into the kitchen.

"You washed all the dishes, too?" she asks, appraising the sink.

"Yep."

She kisses me on the cheek. "You and I are going to be very good friends!"

"I see you have met Flanna. Do not listen to anything my cousin says about me; she would only tell lies," Arland says.

I don't notice him enter the room, but when I hear him speak in his unmistakable, sultry voice, a jolt of excitement surges through me.

"I was telling Kate how you believe she is the most beautiful woman in the world." Flanna walks over to where Arland stands in the entryway and punches his shoulder.

"Ah, then you spoke the truth." He smiles wryly and comes closer to me.

My cheeks warm, and I pretend to look at something on the floor.

"I am sorry we left you alone for so long this morning," Arland says.

I'm beginning to worry he'll hear my heart pounding, he's standing so close. "It's okay."

I hope Arland's apology means I won't be left alone that long again: I need to be busy or else I'm going to go insane.

"I had my entire crew scouring the perimeter for daemons. We cannot risk any being around, if we plan to take you to our training facility. Are you still willing?"

"Yes!" Flanna answers for me.

Arland scowls at her.

"Oh, sorry."

"Yes, as long as Flanna can join us," I say, winking at her.

Flanna's face radiates excitement. Yes, she and I *are* going to be good friends. She makes me miss Brit, but I'm glad someone like my sister is here to keep me company.

"Since it appears Flanna has finished her duties already, I do not see that as a problem."

"I finished a few minutes ago, Arland. Can we go now?" Flanna asks, giving me a conspiratorial look.

"Follow me."

Arland leads us through a narrow corridor at the far side of the kitchen. There's a door on either side of the corridor, just before we reach a set of steps. Curiosity begs me to ask what's on the other side of these doors, but I'll have to save my questions for later, because we're moving up the steps too fast.

Split logs sunk into the dirt make up each tread. They don't creak as we walk up, like the steps do in our farmhouse back home. We stop.

Arland reaches into the dark space above him, unlatching a lock, and then swings a heavy metal bar from its braces. He pushes up the ceiling, then walks out slowly, looking from side to side. He motions for Flanna and me to wait below.

No light pours in from outside. There is no warmth, no songs of birds, no smells of summer; the outdoors are as dark, cold, and quiet as the indoors.

"How long has Darkness kept the sunshine from you?" I whisper.

"As soon as Darkness entered our world, it began stealing our light. But for the last seven months, it has been completely black. Is it not disturbing?" Flanna asks.

"Depressing, disturbing . . . . I can think of a lot of ways to describe it."

Creepy, cold, eerie . . . .

"The nights grew longer as more people died."

"Does that mean there aren't many people left to die?"

She shrugs. "In all our bases around the world, we have a few thousand left—"

"Out of how many?"

"Millions."

I suck in a sharp breath.

"But you are here now," she says.

Flanna points up to Arland; he waves, indicating we should meet him outside the stairwell. I climb the remaining distance while Flanna pushes me to move faster, but I feel like there are lead weights in my boots.

When I reach the top step, Arland takes my hand. He leads me through the forest, his touch gentle—as if he holds the hand of a small child—but it reminds me of a dream I once had of him.

We walked together through a meadow full of wildflowers. Two young children followed behind us, picking flowers, and laughing. The little girl ran to me—her curly, brown locks bounced in her excitement—and put a ring of white and purple flowers she'd fashioned on my head. I twirled around for her, displaying how beautiful her creation made me feel. She smiled and hugged my leg. The four of us were happy together, playing in the meadow. The sun beamed down on us as we set out a picnic blanket and ate our lunch. I curled into Arland's arms, watching the small boy and girl chase each other through the tall grasses. Arland ran his fingers through my hair until I fell asleep. Warm from the happiness of my life, I slept the afternoon away. When I awoke, the sun was gone; no stars or moon were in the sky. Arland and the children lay next to me—their skin cold, their breathing stopped. Panic consumed me, not knowing what killed them, or why whatever killed them left me alive.

I shudder.

"Are you cold?" Arland asks.

"Yes." The temperature isn't the reason I shuddered, but I'm definitely freezing.

When I left Virginia, summer was beginning to make its presence known, but the chilly air here feels like the middle of winter. It could be any month; without the sunlight and not being able to see the leaves on the trees, it's impossible for me to tell.

"I apologize, we did not think of how cold you would be. Our people are accustomed to life without the warmth of the sun. Flanna will ensure you have something more appropriate to put on tomorrow," Arland says, giving Flanna a pointed look.

"Warmer. Got it," she says.

We walk in complete silence the remaining twenty feet or so between the trees.

Lann appears in front of us. Kneeling, he opens a door in the ground similar to the one we came out of at the base.

Arland steps down first, showing me where I need to walk, then he turns, takes me by the hand again, and leads me in.

Once I'm in the stairwell, he releases me, leaving me cold. I feel my way along the wall until we reach the bottom of the steps. The screeching sounds of the locks and bar swinging closed come from behind me.

The room opens up into an expansive training space. This is, by far, the most well lit area in any part of the base I've seen. Candles burn in metal chandeliers overhead, in sconces lining almost the entire length of the middle of every wall, they sit in glass jars on tables, along the floor—pretty much everywhere possible, a candle is burning, providing beautiful, warm light.

At the far left of the room are three long aisles, ending in targets painted on the wall. Each aisle has a person armed with a bow and arrow, accurately releasing shafts into the center of their targets.

There are so many soldiers here—young and old—and they all stop training and focus their attention on me. I know they don't realize *who* I am, but there's no doubt they identify me as a stranger. Fighting off an overwhelming desire to run and hide somewhere, I rake my fingers through my hair and eye my clothes to make sure everything is in the right place.

Flanna takes off to the other end of the room, while Arland introduces me as a new recruit from an area called "The Meadows." I almost fall over. Is it possible The Meadows is a place like the meadow in my dream of him? Could life be that beautiful there, where endless fields of tall, green grasses and wild flowers in purples, yellows, and whites all grow together? The last part of my dream—the unhappy part where I woke up and found everyone dead—tells me that, no, life couldn't be that beautiful here . . . at least, it hasn't been for a long time.

Some soldiers introduce themselves. There are so many, sorting out any of their names becomes difficult. Once the last of the soldiers who come up for introductions shakes my hand and welcomes me, Arland instructs everyone to return to their assignments.

In the middle of the room, men are teaching young children how to wield swords. They stop as we pass. A couple children, who didn't come up for introductions, wave at me. They wear huge smiles on their faces. I cannot imagine these young boys and girls going into a war against the types of monsters that attacked Brad and me. How would they even be able to fight against something so strong? When I was a child, if I ever thought something was scary, I would run and hide under the covers, or behind the couch, or wherever I felt safe, but these kids train to run headfirst into a battle. They have to be brave.

We stop at the far end of the room, where Flanna had run. Multiple types of weapons lay arranged on a series of tables. Knives, bows, axes, spears; things I've never dreamed of having a reason to use. Of course, I did dream about fighting with swords, but I don't think I've ever seen one in real life until now.

"Have you had any formal training with weapons?" Arland asks.

"I've never used anything like these, but my stepdad and I shot clay pigeons with one of his rifles on our farm once," I say, running my fingers across the different weapons.

"You will not find any guns here," Arland whispers. "Fire seems to be the only weapon that takes life from the daemons. Our swords still have some old magic in them, aiding greatly in taking daemons down, but in the end, it is fire we use to deliver the final blow. We light the arrows before releasing them. So what would you like to begin with: swords or bows?"

Old magic in the swords? Maybe I did hear the knife humming yesterday? I wonder if I should ask Arland about it, but it doesn't seem all that important. If there's magic in them, then that's probably what I heard.

"Umm, swords." Does it matter? No chance I'll know what I'm doing with either one.

"Choose one of the claymores from the table. Flanna will fit you with a shield. When you are ready, meet me in the middle of the room and I will give you your first lesson," Arland says, walking toward the men and children in the center of the room.

Great, I get to embarrass myself in front of everyone.

My palms are sweating so profusely I'm positive anything I pick up will slide out of my hands. I try to calm myself, wiping my palms on my pants. The first sword is long, and too heavy to use in a fight. I put it down, then pick up another. This sword also weighs too much for me. While half as long as I am tall, the third sword seems manageable. The claymore's blade is polished silver, the hilt an antiqued brass.

I hold onto the sword and look to Flanna.

She raises her eyebrow.

I shrug.

Flanna gives me an angelic smile.

I am in for it. Could Arland not have found a better way to train me? Why does it have to be in front of a bunch of people I've just met?

"Calm down, Kate. Arland is an excellent instructor; he will have you ready to fight daemons in no time," Flanna says, loud enough for only my ears to hear.

I'm doing this for Brad. I exhale and draw in a deep, composing breath. "Right, calm."

"This is your shield. Put your arm through here, hold firm to the handhold, here." She positions the shield on my arm, then scoots me forward, toward Arland . . . toward utter humiliation.

I make my way to the center of the room with trepidation. The children were all training here moments ago. They've spread out toward the edges, giving Arland and me more room to work. Everyone watches me fumbling my sword and shield in my hands.

"Are you ready?" he asks.

"As ready as I'll ever be . . . I guess."

The way Arland looks at me, as if I'm some sort of zoo animal he's never seen before, drives me crazy. He expects me to save the world. Like, magically, I will somehow know what I'm doing, but I don't have a clue. I've never held a sword before. This thing is half my size, and heavy. I can't fight—and I certainly can't kill anything. Only one thing will happen here today: everyone will find out what an ass I can make out of myself. At least, when we finish, Arland won't expect much of me anymore.

"First, you need to focus on protecting yourself. Hold your shield in front of your torso to block an attack aimed at your heart." Arland holds the shield in front of him. "During most fights, your opponents will battle without a sword, but unfortunately, there are a few you will encounter who are masterfully skilled with them."

"So some of the daemons are human-like?" I ask, glad to be able to stall for a minute.

Arland's eyes scan through the room before he continues with his instructions. "Well, only as human as the rest of us are. Darkness has tainted some of our own, taken control of their minds, and turned them against their brothers and sisters."

Did I interpret Arland correctly? Is he implying we're not human? I'm pretty sure I have hands and feet and a brain, two eyes, a heart, a skeleton . . . all the DNA of a regular human. I've had my blood drawn at the doctor's office, donated it to needy patients in the hospitals. No one has ever come back and said anything about my blood having something wrong with it. Judging by Arland's nervous expression when I asked that, now is not the time to ask him about it, but I know this will drive me crazy until I find out what he means.

"I'm sorry." I don't know what else to say about our own people being turned against us; my mind is still trying to figure out the news about my genetic make-up.

"I pray once Darkness is defeated, the hold it has over our own will be released," Arland says, staring beyond me.

I wait for my next instruction . . . without talking.

Shaking his head, Arland snaps out of his trance and steps behind me. He presses his firm chest against my back, takes my right wrist in his hand, then goes through the motions of fighting with a sword.

Paying attention becomes difficult as I battle a sensation of déjà vu; I'm trying to focus on his instructions. Arland demonstrates a move, and I mirror it. The longer I hold the sword, the stronger the déjà vu becomes, but I force it from my thoughts. Parts of my body that have never been used before ache, as I lunge and jab the claymore through the air at my imaginary opponent.

"You are doing great. Now do a vertical slash."

I drag the sword through the air from high above my head, and it stops near the floor.

"Perfect. Are you sure you have never used a sword before?" Arland asks.

"I'm sure," I say, proud of myself. The claymore feels good in my hands now. It doesn't feel heavy or awkward to hold, like it did before. I haven't embarrassed myself, yet.

Arland shows me another technique, kneeling and stabbing at the same time, and it becomes clear where the déjà vu has been coming from—my first dream of him.

He didn't die that night. He taught me how to fight with a sword, how to protect myself with a shield, and showed me how much he was in love with me. He was a high-ranking military official whose purpose was to train and protect me . . . no more than that.

I'd been sad when I learned of this; my desire was to be more to Arland than someone he was ordered to be around. We had spent months working together, spent countless hours talking to each other about nothing and everything.

After a long day of training, he shared his feelings with me. They equaled mine. Arland wanted us to escape the confines of the military base where we lived and go out on our own, if I would have him. But I was scared, and procrastinated about leaving.

One night, he snuck us out. We walked down to a river in the night, stars shining above our heads. We made love for hours on a blanket, under an old weeping willow tree by the water. Arland built a small fire for us to sit by and asked me, again, if I'd be willing to leave with him. I waited too long to respond. Two officials caught us and demanded we return to the base.

Arland was allowed to remain by my side as my protector only, but we were never left alone again. When we discovered what it was that made me so special, the military forced me to go out into the world—to fight alone.

What was it that made me special? That part of the dream seems locked away in a section of my mind I cannot access.

"We are going to try something a little more difficult," Arland says, bringing me out of my thoughts. "Try to stay on your feet. If your enemy knocks you down, you will surely be killed."

He attempts to knock me off my feet with a swipe from his leg. I can almost feel his attack before he moves in, and, without hesitation, I swipe his legs out from under him, knocking *him* down first.

"Oh! I'm sorry." I run to help him up.

How did I do that?

"Do not be sorry. That was an excellent reaction." Arland straightens his shirt. "Lann, Tristan, please join us for a moment."

"Yes, sir." Tristan rushes up to Arland before Lann even takes a step.

"Tristan, I want you to partner with Kate. Lann and I will attack. You two need to work as a team to defeat us."

Okay, so I was feeling a little bit of confidence building, but now that's turning back into fear. If Arland could use some of that magic to read my mind, he would know I'm *not* okay with this. I fidget with the sword again.

"I am new at this, too," Tristan says, trying to make me feel better while we walk away from Arland and Lann.

"How old are you?"

"Sixteen. I arrived here last month, after my parents were killed. Some soldiers were passing through the area when my family was attacked, but they arrived too late to save anyone other than me." Tristan hangs his head low; his words are flat.

"I am so sorry."

I need to get over my fears of embarrassment and learn to fight; even the children here have had harder lives than I have. I also need to learn to be strong for myself, but more than anything, I need to learn to be strong for them.

"When Arland attacks, he prefers to be direct. If they corner us, put your back to mine. They will be forced to fight each of us individually," Tristan says, sounding eager for an opportunity to show off his fighting skills.

"Okay, and if they don't corner us?"

"Corner them." He smiles.

Tristan is intelligent; he's going to be a strong fighter as he ages. I hope the war ends before he ever needs to use these skills.

"Are you two ready?" Arland asks.

"Yes," we say in unison, but Tristan adds, "Sir."

Lann attacks first, directing his assault at me, slashing his sword, and hitting my shield. His blows come one right after the other. I spin on my toes to get away. The short distance between us gives me the opportunity to get a firmer grip on my sword. I stab it into him, hitting his shield. We push each other back and forth. He swings his sword from under him, meeting mine with what feels like his entire strength put into it. I force back the urge to let my sword fly from my hand and, instead, push harder.

Lann and Arland share a look and twist around each other.

Now, I'm fighting Arland, and Tristan is fighting Lann. It's obvious who the stronger swordsman is here—Arland.

They are trying to make me tired.

"Switch with me," Tristan whispers.

I run around Tristan, taking my place in front of Lann again. They don't corner us, as Tristan had expected, but I can tell they are both tiring. It's odd, but I'm not tired. I swap strikes with Lann until his sword flies out of his hand, leaving only Arland to contend with. Tristan lunges, swipes, ducks, and strikes Arland's shield, trying with all his might to win. It's clear Arland has much more experience; he allows Tristan to wear himself out, then knocks him to the floor with an easy swipe of the leg.

"Get him from the side, Kate," Tristan says.

Running up to Arland, I try to knock his sword free before he sees me coming, but he jumps and braces for my blow. He slashes, stabs, pushes, hits my shield with his, then backs me up against the wall, his sword locked onto mine. I have nowhere to go, no leverage to use. Or do I? Using my right foot, I push myself away from the wall and knock him back a few steps. Arland swings his sword; I duck and try to trip him.

Everyone in the room has stopped what they were doing; they watch the two of us. Arland is in front of me, stabbing, slashing, blocking, and I return each of his strikes with one of my own. Our swords meet again, mine under his. Using every muscle in my body, I push up and knock his sword out of his hand. The metal clangs on the floor, echoing through the facility. Everyone is quiet except for one small shriek of excitement, coming from a little girl in a corner.

"I believe we have confirmed you are skilled with swords," Arland says with a laugh, walking back to the center of the room.

Flanna gasps. "You can say that again."

Excited murmurs rise out of the gathered crowd.

"Sorry I couldn't protect you." I offer my hand to Tristan.

"It was my fault. I know Arland is weaker from the side, but I was surprised by how well you were doing and did not pay enough attention to him."

"Well, thank you for practicing with me," I say, then rejoin Arland.

"I think that will be enough for today. Would you like to head back to the base for lunch?"

"Are you scared to fight me again?" I taunt, pointing at his sword. I don't know what makes me do it; the thrill of the fight is so addictive. "Let's go one more time?"

Flanna laughs in the background; our audience cheers for us to go on. Arland cannot resist. He picks up his sword, winks at Lann, and takes his position in front of me. It's as if I can read Arland's mind; for every move his feet make, mine move away in defense, and then my arm commands the sword into his, crashing against the shiny metal of the claymore, over and over again. The battle takes no exertion on my part.

After a few minutes, he looks frustrated. Fighting the instinct to stab at him, I allow Arland to get his sword under mine, then knock it from my hand.

"Got ya. Good work," he says, wiping sweat from his brow, then turns to address the rest of the room. "Now, if you all will excuse us."

My deflated strength seems to be returning. Maybe if I can fight, I'll have a chance to save Brad, to see my family again, and maybe even save my people.

The others give a short bow to Arland. He points at Flanna and Lann; they run up the stairs in front of us.

"Oh, I forgot to put this back." I return to the weapons table, intending to replace the sword and shield.

Arland comes up behind me and clasps his hand around mine where I still hold the sword's hilt. "Keep this. I believe you should remain armed from now on. You can certainly handle yourself, if the need to use it should arise. There is a leather strap on your belt right here—"

He tugs at my belt, helping me slide the claymore through the loop. His fingers graze my stomach, sending a shiver through me.

Clanging of iron, feet scuffling, thuds when quivers hit their targets, bring the room to life. A little boy and girl, who had been practicing with knives, wave goodbye to me as Arland and I leave the room.

The locks open and the hinges creak.

"All clear," Lann says.

We step out into the dark forest, Arland takes me by the hand, and we proceed along the path between the two buildings.

"You are full of surprises."

"That was the most amazing experience. I really don't know where I learned to move like that." I smile, adrenaline still pumping through my veins.

"I am beginning to think that is the first of many surprises to come from you."

The way Arland speaks makes me nervous—not about what kind of surprises will come from me, but in a *nervous about being around a guy* kind of way. For the first time in my life, I'm concerned with what my hair looks like, how I smell, if I'm sweating, but I'm not about to do anything that would make him aware of how I feel. I shake away the thoughts.

He leads me through the door to the base and abruptly drops my hand. The absence of his touch leaves me empty. I know it's wrong to think like this, with Brad stuck in a coma, but I can't ignore six years' worth of romantic dreams.

Arland turns to face me. "I must attend a meeting."

"I'll help Flanna in the kitchen while you're gone. Will you be back soon?"

The memory of that first dream has me utterly confused. I want to spend more time with Arland, have him hold my hand longer, but then where does that leave me and Brad? Arland said he doesn't understand my dreams, but there's no way he can deny I had them. I know his name, his position in the military, and his mission to protect me. Maybe portions of the dreams are wrong, but my familiarity with him, and ability to predict his moves, make me wonder if I might be a Seer, like the one who prophesied about me before my birth. If I'm not, I must have some other strong connection to Arland.

"I am afraid I will be gone the remainder of the afternoon. I will come by your room tonight, after I finish my meetings. Oh, and Kate, try not to be too nice to Flanna, or she will want to keep you for herself. No one has ever offered to help her in the kitchen like you did this morning."

He reaches for my hand again, then brings it to his lips and kisses it. My heart skips a beat—or three—as he heads back into the corridor, then goes through the door on the right.

When Arland is out of the room, Flanna—who had been staring at us without shame—smiles, hands me a knife, and points to a basket of potatoes.

Chapter Nine

Flanna and I busy ourselves with preparations for the two upcoming lunch rounds. Since there's not enough room for everyone to sit in the dining area at one time, the children eat first, followed by the adults.

Twenty-five or so young boys and girls eat their stew and bread in less than five minutes. Two of them stop to talk to me in the kitchen before leaving for their afternoon chores; they have to wash clothes and bed linens. Marcus and Anna, who Flanna tells me are brother and sister, ask in high-pitched voices if I'll give them lessons in sword fighting. I have to stifle the laughter rising inside me, because in all honesty, they probably know a lot more than I do.

"I will talk to Arland to see if he will allow it," I tell them, after a moment's pause. Since he appears to be in charge here, I figure this is my best bet at getting out of teaching anyone anything.

"Thank you!" Marcus trills.

The two of them, who I'm guessing are about ten and twelve, run to the corridor and through the door on the left.

A distant memory of Brad and me running through the barn, a delighted Gary promising to teach us how to break the young horses, surfaces and sends a fresh, stabbing pain through my chest. I wonder what Brad would think of all this—if he'd try to sneak us out while everyone was asleep, or if he'd support the notion I'm some sort of hero. Forcing my thoughts onto other things, I serve lunch to the adult crowd.

The older soldiers stare at me while they eat. None of them asks questions or tries to talk to me. They just watch. I can't help feeling like I'm on display, carrying food from the kitchen to the buffet table, walking between the tables, and collecting empty plates when people finish their meals.

After everyone finishes eating, I help Flanna clean the kitchen, and allow my curiosity to get the best of me.

"So what's behind the two doors in the corridor?" I ask.

"The door on the left leads to the soldiers' sleeping quarters. There are forty-two soldiers and children currently sharing that room."

"Forty-two! That means there are more children here than adults! What happened to their parents?" I'm not sure I want to hear the answer. I swallow hard, remembering the coldhearted slaughtering I witnessed in my vision when we entered Encardia.

"We are at war, Kate; people die." Flanna shrugs as if it's no big deal people die, but there are only thousands of people left alive.

I'd say that's a big deal, but I don't respond. I understand it's a war, and a war the children here will soon have to fight in, a war in which I lost my own father. It scares me to think that, all too soon, any one of the boys and girls who ate lunch in here today could be killed.

Flanna washes dishes. I wipe down the tables and push the chairs back into their places. After we finish, she sits down with me and gives me some stew, since we didn't eat when everyone else did.

She watches me with her captivating eyes, as if I'm some sort of freak show at the fair—as if she's expecting horns to suddenly pop out the top of my head. "This world is not an easy one to live in, Kate. I know it is difficult for you to understand, but none of these children fears what lies before them. They are eager for their opportunity to fight and help our people regain control of our home."

Starving, I spoon a big bite of the stew into my mouth, chew, and swallow, before I speak. The warmth of the potatoes and sweetness of the carrots remind me of my farm and set my nerves at ease.

"Where I'm from, it would be unheard of for anyone under the age of eighteen to fight. Even fighting at that age was sad, but the world I live in is difficult, too. Earth is riddled with problems, but nothing as powerful as what's happening here. Children there are expected to go to school to learn, and then to college to learn more, before going off into the world on their own. Although some do join the military early. But most have an easy life there."

She hasn't touched the food sitting in front of her. "Hopefully, it stays that way there, but here, most children are considered adults by the age of fifteen. Many of us choose to get married and have children before we reach our twentieth year. Otherwise, our race would die out all too soon."

"Are you, Arland, or Lann married? Do any of you have children?" I ask before I can stop myself. The thought of Arland being married to someone makes me uncomfortable. Considering what we've shared in my dreams, I think my presence would make his wife uneasy . . . if she knew.

"No, but we are different." Flanna's eyes light up, and she pats my hand.

"Why?"

"Timing." That's all she says about their love lives, but Flanna doesn't appear sad—not at all. In fact, she's all smiles. "Would you like me to tell you more?"

Propping my elbows on the table, I rest my chin in my hands. "Please do."

"Good. Well, Lann, Arland, and I *were* the only three with private quarters. In case you have not figured it out, we are the highest ranked soldiers. Arland has been in charge since his father left, ten years ago."

"So, since he was fifteen, he's been in charge?"

"Yes, and he is the youngest we have assigned to lead a base, and the best at containing the daemons."

When he took over, Arland was a year younger than the eager soldier, Tristan. I picture Arland as a fifteen-year-old boy, giving orders to men and women, many of whom were much older than he was—which is still the case. It must have been hard for Arland and the soldiers under him. The fact he has run this base for so long, with so many reporting to him, means they have a great deal of respect for him. I've seen, firsthand, how they treat him when he enters and exits a room. They give formal bows, step out of his way while he walks, and rush around following his instructions. He's not a stern leader. When giving orders, he doesn't talk down to them like they are beneath him—he shows kindness and smiles. At least, that's what I've noticed, so far.

"Wasn't he ever afraid?"

"You have seen him. Does he appear fearful of anything?"

I laugh. "No, I guess not. How did he learn to fight the daemons?"

"He had no choice. We were just children when the early battles took place, but Arland seemed to have a natural instinct for killing them."

"Is that why he was put in charge here? Because he was so good at killing and containing them?"

"Part of the reason is due to his strength and talent, but it is in his blood to lead—and he was anxious to take on the role from his prophecy . . . waiting for you. His father trained him for it before you were born, before they even knew what they were training for," she says with a pointed look. "You know, I have never seen him sleep anywhere other than the room you are in, but since your arrival, he now sleeps in the soldier's quarters with the others."

I set the spoon down and push away my bowl. "I didn't realize."

"Of course not, how were you to know? At least Arland is not sharing my room, along with Lann. He snores!" Flanna teases.

"Did Lann have to move because of Brad?"

She nods.

"I can sleep somewhere else, so you don't have to share with him." So many people have had their lives turned upside down because of me—it doesn't seem fair.

"No, no, no. Please do not go runnin' off to sleep with the soldiers. Arland would never let me hear the end of it—and I do not mind."

"It really doesn't make a difference to me where I sleep." I feel horrible. Why should anyone have to move because of me? I don't care who I am or might be or whatever it is they think . . . a regular bed is more than okay. Their lives are tragic, compared to mine. "I can sleep on the floor."

Flanna narrows her eyes, and I decide to let it go.

"Back to your original question. The door on the right conceals a hallway. There is a communications room on the left, where Arland went earlier, and a storage room on the right, next to a flight of stairs leading up to the stables." Flanna has given me a glimmer of hope.

Animals, they have animals!

"So you're telling me that in the middle of a forest there are stables, containing a bunch of noisy animals where there are no other buildings? How odd does that look . . . and sound?"

"The layer of magic which protects us also protects the stables. We have used some of our strongest magical spells on it. I promise you, the stables are not visible to an untrained eye."

"I would love to see the animals." I imagine the smells of the farm back home.

"I do not believe Arland would appreciate me taking you aboveground," she says, looking as though she already regrets telling me about the stables in the first place.

"I thought you said it's heavily protected by magic?"

"The magic is strong, but not perfect."

I cringe; maybe I don't want to go up. "So, it's possible for something to get in?"

She sighs. "Nothing ever has."

"Well, then what are you worried about? Please?"

"I cannot *take* you—I do not enjoy getting in trouble—but if you were to accidentally stumble upon the stairs to the stables, I would be more than happy to pretend I had no idea where you were." Flanna winks.

"Thanks!" I hand her my dish and bolt from the table.

"Please do not try to leave the stables, or Arland will have my head on a platter," she yells as I run off.

Pushing through the door on the right, I enter an unlit hallway. Running my hand along the wall for a guide, I find the stairs leading up to the stables and begin climbing up them—two at a time. After a good fifty steps, I reach the top. I slide my hands over the door in search of the locks. Three bolts have to be pushed aside. Lifting the bar, I push the door open on its squeaky hinges, willing the old metal to be quiet so no one catches me coming up here.

The well-lit stables, while not large compared to our barn back home, are big enough to maintain a few different animals. There are chickens housed in a coop on the left across from the door leading downstairs, clucking away. Next to the chickens are four cows, and another stall with a bunch of goats. They stand on their hind legs, leaning against the wooden railing, chewing straw and watching me as I pass. I inhale the earthy scent of the stables and feel like I'm back at home, working in the barn with Gary.

At the end of the first section, there's a bay where feed, straw, and tools are stored. I turn to my right and discover horses. Standing in the first stall before me is the most magnificent brown and white Paint I've ever seen. He stands tall, neck straight, eyes watching me. He's knows he's beautiful. So as not to startle him, I approach slowly, with my hand up, and offer some oats from a burlap bag next to his gate. He watches me, his ears pricked back, then somewhere he seems to find resolve and eats from my palm. When he finishes, I rub his forehead.

"I'll be right back, Big Guy!"

He snorts.

"I'm only checking out your friends."

There are six other stalls occupied by a mare and her foal, two fillies, and two stallions. Most of them ignore me, so I walk back to the Big Guy.

He sighs, long and heavy, when I return.

"You sure are friendly." I want to get closer. Between his stall and the mare and foal's, I find a brush hanging on the wall. I grab the brush and some oats, open his gate, and walk right up to him.

His coat is well groomed, but I run the brush from his head to his haunches anyway.

"I just got a new horse at home," I say to him. The day before our trip, Gary and I had finished cleaning the horses' stalls, then he took me into the arena behind the barn and showed her to me. A beautiful brown and white Paint—just like this Big Guy—trotted over our rolling, green pastures toward us. Her eyes were wide, and her tail was curled up over her back. She was such a happy girl. "She was supposed to be my summer project. I never even gave her a name, Big Guy. Can you believe that? My poor girl doesn't have a name."

I talk to him about my life on the farm for about an hour or so. He sighs every now and then. He's so sweet. He nudges me with his head, and he sighs again. Leaning into Big Guy, I wrap my arm over his back, listening to him as he breathes.

During the summers on the farm, my stepdad took me out to work full days with him. As with most kids, I'd become bored, and after a few hours of following alongside him in the fields—or wherever it was I was supposed to be working—I would sneak away into the barn and find the horses. I don't think Gary cared when I wandered off. At the end of the day, my stepdad would come to get me, worn and weary, but always repeating his favorite line, "All you need is five minutes, and you can make any horse love you."

On the farm is where Gary and I are the closest. I wonder if I'll ever return. If I see my mom again, I'll have so many things to talk to her about. First, why she never trusted me with my truth, and second—well, there are a lot of second questions. I'm upset with her.

My mom and I have been able to talk to one another about most things, but now I think all she did was keep a lot of information from me.

"I miss my family. Do you think I'll ever see them again?" I ask, feeding the horse more oats. He neighs, pricks his ears forward, and shakes his head at me. "Well, I hope I do soon, Big Guy. I need someone I know to talk to."

Someone clears their throat.

I'm no longer alone.

Butterflies float in my stomach as I turn around. Arland and Flanna stare at me, disbelief on their faces.

"I see you have met Bowen," Arland says, not looking as angry as I thought he might.

"Is that your name, Big Guy? Bowen?" I ask, rubbing his soft nose.

Flanna snickers and puts her hands on her hips. "Arland, why is Bowen allowing Kate to touch him? He will not allow any of us to get near his stall."

"Flanna, why is Kate up here without anyone protecting her?" he asks, without looking away from me.

"Please don't be upset with Flanna. She told me about the stables being off-limits, but I couldn't help myself. I had to come up here." I hope she doesn't get in trouble for telling me about this place.

Arland's expression lightens, but I can tell he's still unhappy with her. "Flanna, you may return downstairs, now that Kate has been found."

"Yes, sir." Flanna hangs her head and kicks up dirt as she walks away.

Arland joins me on the other side of Bowen, receiving the same affection from the horse as I did. Arland rewards Bowen by feeding him some oats from his hand.

The hinges of the door creak.

"Kate, I will do everything in my power to make sure you see your family again," he says, making my face heat up.

I didn't realize he and Flanna stood behind me long enough to hear my conversation with Bowen. "I want to get Brad home to his family, too. Brad's family deserves to see him, healthy or sick, again."

"Does that mean you are willing to help us?" Arland asks, coming around Bowen to stand in front of me.

"I don't know what it is you think I can do." I shake my head. "But I'll stay as long as I know it will help Brad. We have to get him home; he won't live if he doesn't get better care."

Arland nods, then takes my hand in his and kneels on the ground before me. "Kate, as your Coimeádaí, I promise to protect and serve you until I draw my last breath, or you release me. Do you willingly accept?"

His actions are totally unexpected. He'd mentioned he was my Coimeádaí before, but I didn't realize it came with a formal proposal and acceptance. I've never been good at reacting when someone puts me on the spot; I'm standing here with my mouth gaping, not sure how to respond.

"A simple yes or no will be fine. It is not like he asked to be bound to you," Flanna chides, peeking her head above the stall door, grinning ear-to-ear.

"*Bound?*"

She exhales sharply. "Just answer him."

So the moment is not further lost, and he does not have to repeat this again in the future, I nod. "Yes. I accept."

Arland stands and kisses my hand, leaving me a little weak in the knees. They're expecting me to be their hero, and now he's sworn his life to protect mine. I don't even know how to process any of this. Brad is dying. My family is a world away. People here need me to save them. My life is not my own. The only thing I'm pleased with is Arland's hand wrapped around mine.

"I thought I ordered you back downstairs." Arland shoots a scowl speaking more than any words ever could at Flanna.

"You did, but I forgot this, umm, bucket. Yes, I need the bucket to gather hot water from the spring for dinner," Flanna says.

I laugh at her halfhearted lie; even Arland cracks a smile. Flanna watches him as if she's waiting for him to scold her, but he doesn't move or speak.

She runs from the stables, leaving the bucket behind.

"You seem to have warmed Bowen's heart. He is not usually so accepting of anyone other than me." Arland pats his beautiful horse's white shoulder.

"I've always had the ability to calm even the most capricious of horses. Bowen isn't that bad, though. He's a little proud, but nothing a little extra attention won't cure." I yawn.

"You are tired. We should go back inside," Arland says, offering me his arm. "Shall we?"

I hook my arm around his, then lean toward Bowen. "I'll see you later, Big Guy."

Arland leads me through the stables. "Please do not come up here by yourself again. The magic is strong, but I would feel safer if someone were with you."

"I promise I won't, but I would like to come up more often and visit all of the animals."

"We can work out a schedule for you," he says, which is definitely more than what I was expecting.

Chapter Ten

*I*gnoring Lann and Flanna in the kitchen—and the eyes of the young crowd gathered in the dining area waiting for dinner—Arland and I head into the hall and stand outside my room.

"Do you mind if I come in?" he asks.

I'm standing in the doorway, but I step aside. "It is *your* room."

"It *was* my room. The bed and everything in here now belongs to you while we remain at base," he says, pulling me inside by the hand and closing the door.

I take a seat on the edge of the bed, holding on to one of the wooden posts. "How long is that going to be?"

Arland sits next to me. "Considering how well you did in training today, it would be possible for us to leave any time. But I feel, if we can get to your mother, we might be able to obtain the medicines you mentioned that can help with healing your friend."

"*Brad!*"

I haven't checked on him since early this morning. I spring to my feet, burst through the door, and run through the hall, with Arland on my heels. I open Brad's door, revealing Kegan reading a leather-bound book by candlelight. He's sitting in the same chair Shay occupied earlier.

"I am sorry, miss; there has not been any change in his condition," Kegan says, not lifting his eyes from the pages of his book.

I guess he knew I was coming in to check on Brad; it's not like anyone else here would care. I'm not sure if many people even know he's here. Walking to the bed, I touch his cold, still hand. A tear runs down my cheek and hangs from my chin.

"Heal him. Please, God." I whisper the prayer.

"We cannot leave here while he is still in this bed. You would never be able to focus on the journey before us, and it could result in you and a lot of my soldiers getting hurt," Arland says.

I move my hand from Brad's, gently place the back of my fingers on his face, then walk away.

Arland closes the door behind us; the finality of the latch clicking startles me. I take a deep, shaky breath. "W-why do you think my mom can help him?"

"Your mother was one of our greatest Healers. I believe with the knowledge she has gained from your world, combined with their medicines, Brad's chance of survival will greatly improve," Arland says, holding my door open for me. "I would like to make a trip to the clearing to see if we can reopen the portal."

My mom's constant good health makes a lot more sense now. I wonder if she was really sick, or if she pretended, as a way to get me to go on the trip without her? I shake the thought. Of course, she wasn't feeling well; I held her hair while she threw up. "When do we leave?"

"We will begin at 4:00 a.m. the day after tomorrow. Most daemons sleep as we do. The hounds could pose a potential issue, but there has not been much activity since the night you arrived. I am not all that concerned about them."

"The hounds are worse than the others?" I don't think I want to know. As long as they aren't like hellhounds from the movies . . . .

"Yes, they have smaller numbers, but are a bigger threat."

"How so?"

"They are faster, larger, and smarter than the coscarthas. You will understand when you see one," he says, still standing in the doorway.

The fact that Arland is willing to risk both our lives to save Brad is touching. I'm sure if Arland's father knew of this plan, he would not approve of taking Encardia's only hope out of this world again. The thought of being *Encardia's only hope* makes me laugh to myself.

"We'll share the room," I say.

"That will not be necessary. The soldiers' quarters are more than adequate for my needs."

"Yes, it is necessary."

"Kate, I—"

"I don't want to be alone, and I can't bear the thought of you, Flanna, and Lann all being forced out of your rooms."

Part of me offers to share the room with him as repayment for his willingness to help, but the biggest part of me does this for selfish reasons. Being here without my mom, sister, Brad, or even Gary to talk to, is driving me crazy. Plus, I'm still trying to sort out all these mixed-up emotions I have for Arland; his presence draws me in, makes me forget about all the bad going on around us. I consider him to be a friend, even though we've known each other for only a short time. How many people will pledge to protect you with their life after just meeting?

"I will sleep . . . in the chair," Arland says, coming in and closing the door.

"No, I'm not forcing you to sleep in a chair. You can share the bed with me." I lean the claymore I've been carrying in my holster all day against the wall. Brad and I shared a bed together many times, and so have Brit and I. Sleeping with Arland won't be that much different.

That's not true, I feel differently toward him. But, now more than ever, I need someone to stay next to me.

Removing the belt and boots, I look around for something else to wear.

Arland grabs my folded cotton nightgown from the dresser and hands it to me. "Here."

"Oh!" When did I become so unobservant? After Arland turns to face the wall, I slip out of my clothes and into the gown. "I'm finished."

He turns around; his eyes widen as they roam up and down my body. "You look beautiful."

The way he looks at me now—not like a zoo animal, the way he did earlier, but as a woman—makes me feel beautiful, too. "Thank you."

"I am going to sleep in the chair." Arland pulls the seat away from the wall.

"Ar—"

"I will move the chair next to the bed. I know you do not want to be alone, but it would make me feel as though I were taking advantage of you, if I join you in that bed," he says, his tone firm.

It's nice to know he wants to sleep next to me, but it's frustrating that he won't. There's no point in arguing the matter. Arland is a gentleman. I'm sure he didn't grow up sharing a bed with friends, and definitely not members of the opposite sex, like I did. I'm lucky he even agreed to come in the room with me in the first place.

I lie down, pull the blanket up to my chin, and turn on my side to face him. In the dark room, with only a candle burning on the bedside table, we talk for hours. He asks questions about my life back home; where we live, what it is like, and what kind of work we do. I tell him I was in college, and he asks about school, what my stepdad is like, my friends, and about my mom. Our conversation becomes more serious when Arland brings up the subject of my past.

"As I told you yesterday, when your family left, it was only the three of you. Your father never told us about your sister, but since you were only a few months old when he died, he might not have known about her."

"She and I were born one year apart, so no, he probably didn't know about her." It breaks my heart Dad didn't know he had another daughter—and that we never knew him.

Arland laughs. "So you are twins?"

"Well, Irish twins, as we called it back home."

"Who does your sister resemble?"

"We look exactly alike, but we're complete opposites as far as our personalities. She's more outgoing than I am."

"You both resemble your father, then. I remember him well. During those three months before he was killed, he visited my father often."

"I don't know anything about him." The lengths my dad went through to protect my life are unimaginable. To be told to run away from the only home he ever knew so his child could grow up to save the world—was he proud, or was he afraid?

"From what my father has shared with me, your father was a good man. He loved your mother greatly, and she, him. He had a difficult time leaving the family behind during the early battles. But, the amount he learned about the daemons in that period is what gave us our chance to survive. He discovered fire kills them."

"You said I look like him, but how? Can you describe him to me?" I hope to build an image of my father, to replace the silhouette of him in my mind.

"Like you, he had dark wavy hair, but not nearly as long. You share his same big green eyes and fair skin. Your father was tall, so you must get your height from your mother."

"She *is* short," I say, laughing at the thought of my vertically challenged mom. All three of us have to stand on stools to reach the top shelf in the kitchen. Being five-foot-four can be a hassle at times, but one I've overcome.

"Your beauty certainly comes from your mother, too." Arland's compliment is smooth, and he says it without a hint of amusement.

A flash of heat rises in my cheeks; I'm glad the room is lit by only one candle.

"You have more family here."

"I-I do?"

"Your mother's younger sister Cairine and I used to keep in contact, but I have not heard from her recently. She lives in The Meadows, where you and I are both from."

"What does The Meadows look like?" I hope an area exists that's as perfect as my dream of the meadows.

"There are endless fields, with tall grasses and hundreds of wildflowers. In town, we had small homes, built into the hillsides. Some of us chose to live completely underground, but many of us enjoyed life above, with the light."

"Why would anyone want to live underground? It's so gloomy."

"I cannot begin to understand why someone would choose to live that way without the threat we face now, but they did."

"What was life like for you? What did your parents do for work?"

"Compared to some, my life was simple. I was in a private school to learn our history, how to use magic, and how to fight. My parents were always summoned away to meetings with your mother and father, as well as our highest leader. When I was not in school, I spent a lot of time listening to them and wishing to be like other children. That is how I met your aunt; she kept me company when no one else had time."

"Is that why you stayed in contact with her?"

"We remained in contact for personal reasons—she was like a second mother to me—but she would also give me reports on daemon activity in the surrounding areas. Daemons have mostly left The Meadows alone since they wiped out almost everyone when the war began, but our remaining people there have grown weary and are ready to join in the fight to end this war."

"Why did they not fight before?"

"Fear. The people who survived the initial attacks went into hiding. My father brought me and Flanna here because we had prophecies to fulfill."

"Do I have other family there?"

He nods. "You have relatives from your father's side, though I have never met any of them."

"And my mother's?"

"The rest of your mother's family was killed in the early days."

The more I learn, the more I realize I truly don't know anything about my life.

Arland switches the subject and asks me lots of other little quirky questions, like if I enjoy singing or dancing, or other ordinary things. I tell him about our family's annual trip to the mountains, and how I've felt most at peace in the forest—with nature. I tell him how—starting from the time I was about four years old—I could always be found in the barn, talking to the horses and interacting as if they were my friends.

He falls silent.

"Why were you so eager to be in charge?" I ask.

"I see you have been talking to Flanna." He smiles.

"She told me you took over here when you were fifteen and your dad left."

"She told you the truth. I was eager because of my prophecy, Kate. I knew my being in charge was part of the end of the war. I want, more than anything, for it to be over—for my mother, that her death not be in vain, for my people, and for myself. This world will not survive much longer if the war continues." He shakes his head.

"What else did your prophecy tell you about yourself?"

"Enough, but we can save that for another time," Arland says.

I've made him uncomfortable. It worries me to know speaking of his prophecy makes him edgy. I wonder if he *is* going to die, and maybe he's already aware of that? Pushing past my concerns, I continue to ask questions. Most of them are the same off-the-wall ones he asked me.

"What would life be like here if there wasn't a war going on?" I have to know the answer to this.

He opens and closes his mouth a few times, pausing on what I expected to be an easy answer. "It has been so long since life was normal, I am no longer sure. When this is all over, I will have to show you." Arland's eyes smile at me, but his mouth doesn't—like he's hiding something.

I'm not going to have an answer for a long time . . . if ever.

Marcus and Anna were born into this world full of turmoil, and haven't been able to enjoy a normal life, and I'm sorry for that. They've never experienced the full effects of sunshine, or even happiness, like what's displayed on the walls outside my room. I'm sure they haven't been able to explore the forest or caves, or go fishing in a river, or swim in a lake. It must be a sad life. Even if they are willing to go headfirst into battle to try to end the war, there must still be some fear in their hearts, some hesitation, some strong will to live that makes them want to run and hide to save themselves.

We've carried on our conversation for so long it feels as though I'm talking in my sleep. I cover my mouth and yawn.

Arland traces the outline of my face with his fingers; his touch so comforting it forces me to give in to the looming slumber.

Arland and I are swimming in a river, cleaning ourselves by the waterfall. The day is long, and we're both ready to rest for our next journey. He kisses me before lifting me up out of the water. I keep my legs wrapped around his body as he carries me into our hidden cave behind the falls. He sets me down near the back so I can dress, and lights a fire with some timber we collected earlier in the day. I join him and we eat the rabbit we snared. Food is hard to come by in the wild, but Arland is a skilled hunter and we rarely go without. After our bellies are full, we move to the back of the cave and lie on our bed of animal furs, holding on to each other as though we never want to let go.

Arland stares into my eyes. "If I die, Kate, do not stop fighting."

"You are not going to die," I tell him.

"I pray you are correct, but if not, you must go on," he says, more commanding.

I close my eyes. "I can't think about it."

He takes my face in his hand, pulling me into him. Our mouths meet and we make love behind the cover of the falls, but it feels more like a goodbye than anything else.

Tears stream across our faces while we rest in each other's arms. This is the end, and somehow we both know it. Our time with one another has been too short. We want to give each other years, decades even, but the sound of rocks tumbling against the side of the cave tells us we are not going to be afforded that time.

"They have found us." He grabs his sword and sits up, ready to protect my life. "You have to run."

"I will not. I am going to fight," I say, with more fervor.

He looks at me, and we share what for sure is our last goodbye kiss. We approach the opening of the cave, holding our swords. The falls block our view of what approaches, but we don't need to see them to know the army of mangled creatures has found us.

"Please run, Kate," Arland begs.

"Do not make me tell you again."

The first line of daemons approaches along the side of the falls.

"Stad," he mutters, waving his hand in front of us.

The waters stop flowing, and we find ourselves looking out onto thousands of daemons. It is as if Darkness sent the entire army after us. A rock falls from above and hits me on my head. Looking up, I realize we are both going to die. Daemons are everywhere. There is no time for either of us to run, hide, or even fight. They jump onto Arland from the rocks overhead. I scream for him, stab and slash my sword at the beasts, but there are too many.

I cannot see him.

"I love you, Katriona," he chokes out. They are the last words he says before letting out bloodcurdling screams of pain.

I've never heard someone cry with so much anguish before. I call for Arland, but he doesn't say anything.

He's gone. My love is gone.

"Why don't you just kill me?" I clench my fists and scream. "Why leave me here? Just do it!"

Trembling, I collapse beside Arland and wait for my own terrifying death, but it doesn't come.

The daemons slink away, leaving me at the mouth of the cave next to Arland's destroyed body.

"Now you no longer have protection, little girl. You could have prevented this, but now you are weak, and I will find and kill you myself." An unfamiliar voice laughs as I mourn.

I cry myself awake; I always do, from this dream. It's always been one of the worst I've had of Arland. Most start out more pleasant, but in this one, we know we have no future, no life to live, and no hope throughout the entire dream. I sit up, alone—seems to be the usual here.

The door opens. Candlelight illuminates Arland's face as he walks in the room.

"Are you crying?" He sits down in the chair and sets the candle next to the bed.

"Yes." The sheets make the perfect tissue to wipe the tears from my face.

"We will find a way to help your friend. I promise," Arland says, misinterpreting my sadness.

"I'm not crying over Brad. I had a dream about your death."

"Oh, I am sorry." His voice and face soften a little.

I'm ridiculous. The dreams aren't real. Arland is here, he's alive, and yet I'm crying.

"I've seen these dreams replay so many different times, I guess I should be used to them, but each time the pain of your death seems to hurt me even more," I say, telling him too much—once again.

He remains quiet for a moment, as though looking for the right words. "And some of these dreams make you cry over me?"

I cover my face with the sheet. "Yes."

I'm embarrassed for saying anything at all. I keep sharing my deepest feelings with Arland, as if I *am* in one of my dreams.

"Get dressed." Arland tugs the sheet away and offers me his hand.

"W-what are we going to do?" I take hold of him and he pulls me out of bed.

"I have something to show you." He heads for the door. "Meet me in the dining room—and bring your sword."

"My sword? Where is this *something* you want to show me?" I'm frozen in the middle of the room.

"Out."

I break free of my cold panic and march toward him. "*Outside* out?"

"Yes." He laughs.

"You have got to be kidding me!" I hug myself; trembles threaten to bring me to my knees.

"No, I want you to see the daemons the way I do. We are going to make rounds along the perimeter of Watchers Hall." He smiles as he leaves the room.

Going outside this base to look for daemons seems foolish. I've seen the monsters up close and personal. I'm positive I don't want to see them ever again. I also don't want to be alone.

I grab my clothes from the dresser, lift the nightgown over my head, and pull on the tunic, pants, and boots. Before opening the door, I see my sword resting against the wall. I jog back over to pick it up.

I slide the weapon through my holster, and find Arland waiting by a table in the dining area. The way he holds himself, straight, calm—like he doesn't have a care in the world—is comforting, but I'm still shaking.

My teeth chatter.

"Relax, Kate."

I look up at Arland and fight against an urge, deep inside, to wrap my arms around him and beg to be taken back to my room. "You want me to relax when I've seen exactly what those things are capable of? And you've told me Brad is lucky—everyone else dies instantly. So why, exactly, should I relax?"

He puts his hand in the middle of my back—warmth spreads along my skin, rushing through me like fire—and pushes me toward the kitchen. "Because you will not come in direct contact with any daemons. I have plenty of my men in the forest, and most daemons should be asleep by now."

"How can you know that for sure? If you have perimeter patrols, then some daemons try to get through, right?"

"If one makes its way through, I have plenty of guards to take care of it." Arland pushes open the door leading to the stables and communications room. "Wait right here. I am going to inform Keith of our departure."

I nod.

Rubbing the cold hilt of my sword, I look all around. No sounds of happy children or soldiers eating fill the dining room—everything is empty and quiet.

The door squeaks as it opens behind me. Turning around, I see Arland emerge from the dark hallway with a smile on his face and a lantern in his grip. "Keith will have the other guards on high alert."

"So you told him you were taking this world's supposed hero out?"

Reaching for my hand, Arland laughs and starts up the stairs. "Not exactly."

"What did you tell him?" I ask, trying to keep up.

"Here, hold this," Arland says, handing me the lantern, then lighting the wick.

"What's this for?"

"I thought you might be more comfortable if you could see." He unlocks the door and pushes it open.

I gasp for breath; the hairs on my arm stand straight. "W-Won't the daemons be able to see this?"

"No, our perimeter and everything inside it are invisible to them."

"What?"

"We have multiple layers of magic over the base, stables and perimeter. Daemons cannot see us. They can stand next to us, but will not know we are here—and Keith is under the impression I am taking a soldier out for training. It is not a lie. Are you coming?" He tugs at my hand, but my feet feel glued in place.

"Training?"

"Yes, training. Again, I want you to see the daemons as I do. I am not asking you to fight them, only observe how easily they can be killed."

"We're going to walk right up to one and kill it?"

"No, if it were that easy, we would have already won the war. You will be safe . . . ."

"Okay." I follow him up the remaining steps and away from the safety of base.

I see my breath comes out in white clouds of steam. My heart races, but somehow not as fast as I think it should. Arland wraps his hand around mine, and I stay within inches of him. The lantern does little to illuminate the forest. I cannot see past the small radius of light floating on the ground next to me, and beyond it, everything appears even darker than before.

"How long did it take for everyone's eyes to adjust?" I ask, ready to abandon the failing light.

"Mine took a month, but I refused to use artificial light after the sun was taken from us. Other people's eyes took longer. The sooner you accept it, the easier it is to overcome," he says, glancing at the lantern.

I lift the lantern to my face, open the small glass window in the wooden frame, then blow out the candle.

"Are you sure you want to do that? Your eyes will not adjust that fast."

"The sooner I accept it, the easier it is to overcome, right?"

He nods.

"I'm accepting it, then . . . so where are we going?"

Arland points to his left and leads us off the worn footpath between the base and the training facility.

We enter an area overrun with thick underbrush, snapping and echoing around us. I check over my shoulder, but cannot see more than a couple feet around me.

He puts his finger over his lips and has me walk behind him. If Arland wants us to be quiet, there's something out here that can hear us. My stomach twists and knots around; my mouth waters. I'm sure the stew I had for dinner is going to come back up.

"We are here," he says.

"Where?"

"We have been monitoring a growing population of daemons in the area, waiting for the right moment to attack." Arland stops and sits on the ground, pulling a bow and arrows from a quiver strapped to his back.

"Now is not the right moment, is it?" I ask, ready to retreat.

"No. We are here to kill daemons that break off from the rest of the group or get anywhere near us."

"You brought me out here to watch you kill stragglers?" I plop onto the soggy ground next to him.

"More or less," he says, shrugging. "And to show you the differences between the daemons—assuming you can see."

"I can't see much of anything."

"I believe I have something that will help with your vision." He closes his fingers into a fist and reopens them, revealing a tiny blue flame in the palm of his hand.

"Arland . . . ." I grab his hand and watch the flame dance. I reach out to touch it—like a child swiping her finger over a candle—laughing as the soft heat caresses me. "How did you do this?"

He gently pulls free, then transplants the fire to the tip of an arrow. "Squeeze your hand into a fist and whisper, *Solas*."

"Like it's that easy," I say, with as much sarcasm as I can.

Arland creates another flame. "When you have been practicing as long as I have, it *is* that easy. Try thinking of what you want to happen."

I want Brad to be healed. I want to see my family.

Crossing my legs over each other, I hold up my left palm. "Is this old magic?"

"No, old magic is more powerful than this."

"What does it do?"

"Stories have been passed down through generations of how everyone could command fire, and fire would listen. But we know little. It has been so long since it has been practiced."

Arland notches his arrow and pulls back. "Go ahead, try it while I take care of this stray daemon."

My muscles tense. I desert the plan to create fire and grip Arland's thigh. He looks down at my misplaced hand and grins.

"I am sorry," I say, moving it.

"Do not be sorry," Arland says, deep and seductive.

Pulling the arrow, he squints his eye, then lets go. The burning wood shoots through the air, creating a trail of blue in its path. Spinning and whistling, the weapon suddenly stops and ignites something into flames. Faint grunting sounds make their way back to us. Whatever he hit appears to be a hundred feet below. We're sitting on a ledge high above the daemons, and it's so dark, I didn't even realize.

"Why didn't you tell me we were so far away from them?"

"Did you believe I would put you in harm's way?" he asks, imprisoning me with his smile.

"I-I . . . I guess I did—you did tell me to bring my sword." Afraid to meet his eyes, I trace lines in my palm with my fingertip. "So what was that you hit?"

"A tairb. They are fast, smart daemons."

"Won't the others realize one has been killed and look for—?"

Arland creates another flame, then lets an arrow fly through the air. "From the information we have gathered, they do only what they are told."

"And the coscarthas?"

"They *all* do what they are told."

"And whoever leads the daemons doesn't care that you kill them?"

He looks down at me, all playfulness wiped from his face. "I am sure whoever leads them does not *care* about anything."

"Why don't you kill all of them right now?"

"My men have watched and followed these daemons for weeks, trying to discover where their orders come from. If we kill them all, our chances of obtaining information will diminish. We kill only the ones who get too close to our perimeter."

He repeats his assault on the creatures, one right after the other. Every now and then, blue streaks the sky from other areas, aiding the effort to kill the daemons below. Watching how easy it is for Arland to end their lives, and how the beasts don't retaliate, makes me feel somewhat safer.

"I am going to miss the next one on purpose. Pay close attention."

Arland released three consecutive arrows, then points to the ground, where a small deer grazes.

"I think you *really* missed." I laugh.

"No, that is a Shifter," he says, his tone serious.

"A what?"

"Shifters were the worst kind of daemons, until we discovered them. They would turn into cattle or chickens, wait until we brought them into our stables, then shift into their real forms and kill everyone." He grits his teeth. "But we are aware of them now. Any stray animal causes a great deal of concern."

"Do they ever turn into anything other than animals?"

He shakes his head.

"Are there other types down there?"

"There are other daemons, but none visible tonight. Would you like to try that spell now?"

No, but I promised I would try to discover what makes me Light, and I'm doing this for my friend. Closing my eyes, I focus on Brad, home, and magic, then make a fist. "Solas," I whisper.

Nothing happens.

"Try again," Arland says, his voice low, deflated.

"I'm sorry, but I don't know magic. I don't know spells, and I certainly don't know how to kill anything." My hands tremble. My face burns. The Seers got the prophecy wrong. I am not the Light.

I'm not even sure I'm from this world. Looking around, I try to remember how we got here, so I can run back.

Arland's smile fades. Standing, he looks me over, then glances toward the daemons below.

"We should return inside. There is nothing remaining out here for you to see. If my men find any hounds or serpents, they will inform me, and we can make another trip." He offers me his hand.

"I'm a disappointment, aren't I?" I wipe my sweaty palms on my pants and allow him to help me up.

Keeping his hold on me, Arland tugs me back the way we came. "You are not a disappointment. I can imagine many people in your position running far away from this, but here you are. You are doing incredibly well. Have faith in yourself; discovering magic may take time."

"Time Brad doesn't have—time this *world* doesn't have."

"There will be time," he says, leading me away from the ledge. "There must be time."

On our way back to base, Arland remains quiet. We travel through the underbrush, twigs breaking under our feet. He turns his head turns toward every sound and movement in the forest, but Arland never tenses up the way I do.

Reaching the door in the ground, he bends to open it. I enter first, walking halfway down the stairwell. Sliding the bar and locks, he follows me, then heads down the corridor toward communications.

"I will meet you in your room."

I nod. Making my way through the kitchen and dining area, my spirit feels empty. How am I supposed to learn old magic, when no one knows how to use it? How can I help this world, when I cannot create a simple spark in my hand? How will I save Brad? See Mom? Brit?

Pushing through the door, I remove the useless sword from my holster, then lean it back against the wall. I change into my nightgown, then crawl into bed.

Arland enters the room, breathing heavily. Picking up the chair, he returns it to its spot along the wall, then stands beside me.

"If I am next to you, maybe the dreams will not appear as real," Arland says, undressing. He lifts the covers on the bed, then lies on the spot next to me.

"Are you sure you're okay with this?" I ask, my heart racing, chest tight.

He drapes his arm over me, providing extra comfort.

"I would not offer if I were not okay with this." Arland was hesitant earlier, but somewhere between seeing my reaction to the dream and taking me out to kill the daemons, he must have found resolve.

The thought crosses my mind about how this would look to Brad, if he woke up and found me in here with another man, but it's not like we're dating. Unfortunately, I think Arland is joining me only because he feels bad about the dreams I've had of him dying. But already, with my sworn protector next to me, the isolation is going away.

We face each other, bodies pressed together. I close my eyes and force myself to drift back to sleep—before he changes his mind.

Chapter Eleven

The morning comes. I'm refreshed for the first time in years. Arland's arms are wrapped around me. I snuggle into him closer, breathing in the warmth of his body. I enjoy his touch; it's familiar and welcome.

"You are awake," he says, voice smooth and confident. Arland doesn't speak with even a hint of the nervousness I'm experiencing.

"Barely," I tease.

"No more dreams?"

"None at all. Did you speak to your dad about my dreams?" Sudden curiosity about what they mean hits me like a ton of bricks. I cannot believe the question didn't occur to me when we were talking last night.

Dreams have been such a major part of my life for so long I cannot think of the last time I slept without having a single glimpse of one. Well, other than the two days I was drugged, but those don't count. Last night started out rough, but I wonder if having Arland next to me worked like he believed it would, or if the dreams decided to stop for the night. Whatever the case, I'm glad to have gotten some decent rest.

"He does not have an answer. He said your mother should know. All the more reason for us to get to her." Arland brings my hope of knowledge crashing right back down. His arms unclasp the hold he has on me, leaving me in the bed by myself, so he can dress. He slides his long muscular legs into his pants—every bit of him is perfection.

"You should get dressed, too. We have a full day of training and stable duty," he says, without looking at me.

I scramble out of bed, tripping over my boots and almost falling on my face.

"Are you okay?" Arland asks, sliding his hand around my arm and helping me up.

Nodding, I grab my clothes, then jump on one leg while trying to shove the other in pants. "Stable duty? How come you didn't tell me last night?"

Arland gives a hearty laugh. "I came up with the idea this morning. You know, you might be the only person here who finds the stables exciting. You are not afraid of hard work, are you?" A tinge of doubt peppers his question.

"I don't consider taking care of animals a chore. I'm happy to take over that duty from now on, if that's okay?"

"Flanna is going to love you even more than she already does."

Arland turns his head; I take off the gown, then slip on my shirt. After we're dressed, we walk from the room and into our busy day together. I'm feeling the happiest I've been since Brad and I arrived, but Arland appears emotionless.

On our way to the kitchen, Arland gathers soldiers from the dining tables and tells them to meet him in the communications room.

"I will return shortly," Arland says.

I shrug. "I'll be here."

Leaving me with Flanna, he continues down the corridor.

Flanna prepares breakfast for the two morning rushes, darting between the fire, the sink, and a bag of potatoes.

I walk over to stand next to her, watching as she chops with precision, then tosses the food into a skillet. "Can I help you with anything?"

"I thought you would never ask," Flanna says, handing me her knife and pointing to the bag on the floor. She must hate potatoes; this is the second time she's given me the vegetables to work on.

She scrambles eggs over the fire burning in the stone hearth and teaches me how to roast the potatoes I wash and finish cubing. The smells of breakfast float through the air. Yawning children stumble into the kitchen on their way to the dining room; Flanna and I rush plates of warm food to them, rather than making them serve themselves from the buffet table.

"So how was your night with Arland?" she asks with a wink when we re-enter the kitchen.

"It was nice. We talked all night long." I fight back a yawn of my own.

Her eyebrow raises. "Uh-huh."

"Trust me." I gather more filled plates and run them out to the next group of children streaming in.

"You know you can tell me anything," she says, after I return to collect more food.

I ignore Flanna, and by the time we finish preparing the second round of breakfast, she stops asking. She's either given up and believes me, or she figures I'll never tell her—either is fine by me.

Arland comes back from the communications room with the small group of soldiers. "Sit with me," he tells me, as if I'm one of his men.

"Yes, sir," I say, deepening my voice.

He cocks his head to the side, then turns away, setting off wild flutters in my stomach. Maybe teasing him in front of the others isn't such a good idea?

I bite my lip and follow him to a table in the center of the dining room; Flanna and Cadman join us, and we eat our meal.

"I cannot wait to see you take Arland down today, Kate," Flanna says.

There's shuffling under the table, followed by a loud thump.

"Ow! What was that for?" Flanna scowls at Arland.

He ignores her, but they share a serious look.

"Your fighting skills are quite advanced. I was not aware people in The Meadows had been so well trained," Cadman says.

"I—"

"Her family had been growing frustrated from the lack of light. They were prepared to join in the fight even before they were attacked." Arland breaks his staring contest with Flanna, answering for me.

Cadman returns to eating his breakfast without looking at me again.

Arland seems to be going to great lengths to protect my identity, but I wonder why he does it. My presence could bring the people hope; as much as I'm glad not everyone knows my prophecy, it's unfair to withhold hope from them.

Banging echoes through the dining area. Lann bursts from the kitchen and rushes up to our table. He gives Arland a wild-eyed look that forces him out of his chair in an instant.

"Excuse me." Arland's tone is calm, but he runs to the kitchen with Lann on his heels.

I've never seen Arland react so fast. What could upset him like this? Have the spells failed? Have daemons found us? My heart races; I'm paralyzed and I don't even know why.

"What was that?" I ask Flanna.

"Do I look like a mind reader?" she says, staring after Arland.

We sit in silence for a few minutes, then Lann returns and seats himself next to me.

"Arland instructed me to continue with your training this morning. He will meet you over there as soon as he can. Flanna and Cadman will inspect the trail before we head over," Lann says.

"Okay. Is everything alright?" I ask not sure how to respond to him. Lann was so at ease the first time we met, and now he regards me with formality.

"We had a small security breach at the perimeter; nothing too far out of the ordinary." He steals a glance at Flanna.

My instincts tell me whatever Arland is up to is not ordinary. His agonizing screams when the daemons attacked him in my dream inundate my thoughts.

"So are we ready to go now?" I stand, hoping to busy myself with training so I can try to stop worrying about Arland.

"Do you still want something warmer to wear?" Flanna asks.

"I'll be fine, thanks." I might as well begin acclimating to the cold now.

Lann nods, sending Flanna and Cadman up through the door in the earth to make sure the path is secure. We follow close behind, pausing at the top. A double rap comes on the old wood above our heads; Lann pushes it open, so we can step into the dark forest for our short walk to the training facility.

I didn't look around the woods much yesterday—with Arland by my side, I didn't feel the need to. Without his supporting hand around mine, I constantly look over my shoulder, sure that a daemon will attack any moment. Focusing on the trees, I find we're in a dense forest of mixed pines, oaks, maples, and chestnuts. Most of those I see only as we pass a couple feet from them.

Grasses tall enough to reach my waist still grow along either side of us, but even those are dry and ready to die. The majority of the trees, with their wilted—and some dead—leaves, look as though they will fall over any day. I try to imagine a world without a forest like the one I've hiked in my entire life. All I can think of is the vision I had on Goat's Ridge. Nothing but Darkness, and one light, very far away. Is that what would happen if all of life was smothered out?

Arriving at the entry of the training facility, I sense my paranoia at being exposed subside. My shoulders lower and I take a deep breath. We descend the stairs into the candlelit room, then Lann and I take our spots in the middle. A small crowd gathers around us while we go through the motions of sword fighting.

My heart is not into the lesson today; all I can think about is Arland out there, fighting off some horrible monsters in my name, dying some death I've already seen him die in my dreams a thousand times over.

Everyone is watching, eyes boring through me. No one should expect anything out of me, but I'm sure the soldiers know something is different, since I'm sharing a room with their leader.

Lann knocks my sword out of my hand a dozen or so times. "Do you plan on allowing daemons to kill you so easily?"

"I'm sorry. I can't seem to focus."

"You will not be given a second opportunity out there," he says, pointing his sword at the ceiling.

It's true. If Lann were a daemon, I'd be dead. I know if I don't step up soon, he's going to throw in the towel and practice with someone else. I'm worthless today.

We keep practicing, for now, but my attempts to fight go on without enthusiasm, until the crowd gathered around us breaks up. With me moping about, they have nothing to watch.

A few small groups form around the room, training with different weapons. All of the soldiers seem tired, many show signs of old injuries, and some have new ones. I wonder how many battles they've seen, if their families are still alive, if they have a home to go to, once this is over.

"I realize I haven't met too many of the other soldiers. Can we trade partners?" I ask Lann.

"Saidear, would you like to train with Kate?" He sounds hopeful.

Saidear, who looks to be about the same age as my stepfather, gives a quick shake of his head, indicating he would not like that at all.

"Tristan?" Lann asks.

Even the eager Tristan refuses to train with me, when we did so well together yesterday. Why is it they refuse to work with me? Sure, I'm pathetic today, but is there something about me they don't like?

Lann calls out to a couple others, but young and old alike, no one is willing to step up.

Now I feel like a jerk.

"I will train with her," says a soldier, stepping from the back of the room.

I haven't met, or even seen, him around the base. He has blond hair, pale green eyes that could almost pass for white, and skin fairer than most—which is saying something, since none of these people has seen the full sun in twenty years. Most of the men have strong, well-built bodies, but this one appears only an inch or so taller than me. He's not muscular, and he seems even smaller in stature than the child, Marcus. No way can this man be a soldier.

"No, Perth, that will not be necessary. Go back to training with your assigned partner." Lann's voice is cold.

"You called for anyone willing to work with her. Well, *I* am willing." One corner of Perth's mouth twists up into a wicked grin.

Reading this situation is easy enough: Lann doesn't like Perth, but I wish to know why. My lips stay closed as the two of them exchange harsh spoken words in a strange language I cannot understand.

"Fine." Lann steps aside, allowing Perth to take a defensive stance in front of me.

I look to Lann for approval.

He nods, but his narrowed eyes suggest he's unhappy.

"Are you ready?" Perth asks.

"Yes." I hold my shield in front of my heart.

He attacks.

Our swords clang off each other, I step back, forward, back, to the side. I'm still not as agile as when Arland is around, but I'm certainly more involved than when fighting with Lann.

I'm positive it's Lann's formality which bothers me. I need someone to fight with who doesn't expect me to be a hero. We go on like this for what feels like twenty minutes or so, before I become tired of fighting and am ready to stop. Yesterday was different. Not once after we started did I feel like my sword was heavy, and not once did I feel as though I couldn't breathe.

"You must be special." Perth swings his sword over my head, missing me.

"Why do you say that?" I ask, trying to take his feet out from under him.

"The Great Arland Maher has taken you into his bed," he says, loud enough to bring the eyes of the crowd upon him.

"It's not what you think." I have to defend Arland. His people respect him, and it needs to remain that way. I should never have asked him to stay with me last night, but even as I think that, I still wish for him to be near me again tonight.

I lower my sword, intending to take a break. Being partnered with someone who is obviously trying to cause some sort of trouble is not a good idea.

Perth strikes my shield, slicing straight through the wood and leather. His blade stops an inch from my neck. His hold does not loosen. I look from the tip of his sword up to his ice-cold gaze. The way he regards me is disturbing; there's something in him not quite right. Maybe this is why Lann didn't want him to train with me in the first place.

Lann rushes forward, but before he reaches us, instincts take over and I hit Perth's head with the flat side of my sword.

"Ow!" He yelps. "Why did you do that?" The cold look in his eyes is replaced with something normal and playful.

"Next time, remember I'm not your *real* enemy." My voice comes out like a growl.

"You will never learn if you are not scared." Perth walks away, rubbing his head.

His words strike me; I wonder if he knows something about the prophecy. Maybe the people here are not as in the dark as Arland believes they are.

Flanna approaches, replacing Perth as my partner. "He deserved that. If you had not defused that minor situation, Lann probably would have killed Perth for coming that close to hurting you," she whispers, then spins around me, striking my broken shield without enthusiasm.

We're not really fighting. It's more like gossiping.

"What's his problem?" I ask with a hushed voice.

"You should talk to Arland about that," Flanna says.

Oh, My, God, I have a lot to talk to Arland about. It's beyond me how I could have forgotten to ask him what he meant by *Only as human as the rest of us are,* and now I have to ask about Perth, too.

Flanna and I take a break and sit in the back corner of the facility for a while. Anna and Marcus join us. The two of them ramble on about what they want to be when they grow up.

"What are you?" Anna asks me.

"A soldier."

Anna crosses her eyes and laughs. "What will you do *after* you are done being a soldier?"

The small army assembled here is supposed to believe I'm a new recruit from their world. I'm sure it will get out eventually I'm not from here—or rather, I am, and I have a prophecy, but for now I must act *normal.*

"I'd like to be an animal Healer," I say, which is the truth, but I'm not sure in what world that future lies.

"That is what I wish to become!"

"What's your favorite animal?" I ask.

"The horse."

"You know, Anna, horses are my favorite animal, too."

She claps her hands together; her eyes are wide and excited. "Do you think we might work together one day, and live in the same area, and be friends?"

"Of course." Ten-year-olds are so cute when they think of the future, hoping for happy endings and forever-afters. I pray a day comes when all of her dreams might come true, because at this moment, they are the only things she has to hold on to.

After our break, Lann decides it's safer for him, rather than anyone else, to work with me. Considering what happened with Perth, I couldn't agree more. Lann doesn't smile; that's something about him that has changed. When I first met him, he did. Am I causing that much stress? Does he have to work extra because of me? I'm beginning to think, instead of being Encardia's hope, I might be Encardia's nuisance.

I'm distracted by my thoughts, and—as usual—Lann knocks the sword out of my grip, then throws his hands up with frustration. I think he's about to walk away from me for good, but Arland graces the room—alive and uninjured. His high cheekbones are red from the chilly air, and his hair looks windblown.

Has he been riding?

Relief flows through me and wipes out the desperation I've been feeling all morning. I pick up my sword. "One more round?"

Lann looks at Arland.

"Okay," Lann agrees.

The mood of the soldiers in the room is different, now that Arland has returned. Some of them stared with curiosity earlier, but now, they return to their tasks and smile when I catch sight of them.

If I could hide under a rock, I would.

"Ready?" Lann asks.

"Yes."

We move in harmony with each other. Lann jabs; I immediately block, and slash back. He rushes forward. Spinning around him, I strike his shield as he ducks by me. I catch him off guard, and he stumbles over his feet and falls to the ground. I point my sword at his chest.

"Now that is what you need to do *every* time," Lann says.

His reflexes are much slower than my strikes, and I fake kill him at least three more times.

"My turn!" Flanna sings.

I nod in agreement. She must have expected me to be an easy target after all that goofing off she and I did earlier. Flanna cannot keep her sword in her hand for longer than a few seconds. I knock it from her grip on my first attempt, every time. The crowd regroups and cheers me on.

"May I try?" Anna asks.

"Sure," I say.

She's adorable, and so determined. I let her knock my sword from my hand.

"I did it!" she squeals.

"You did!"

Marcus and a few other children all take turns with me. I fight a little harder with the boys, but I still allow them all to win.

After my last battle, I holster my claymore and stand beside Arland. He's been leaning against the wall—legs crossed casually at the ankles—through the remainder of my training session, watching what must have been an entertaining show.

"Did you have fun?" Arland asks.

"Toward the end, I did. Where were you all morning?"

He leans his head toward mine.

"I will tell you soon." His lips move against my ear.

My stomach stirs with butterflies from the closeness of our faces. The heat from his cheeks radiates into mine. I notice his nose is a tiny bit crooked, but I find that makes him even more attractive.

Lann assured me Arland's absence was due to a routine security breach, but now that I've been given a cryptic reply, my already high doubts are even higher.

"Are we still going to work in the stables?" I ask, hopeful our plans will not change due to this *routine* breach.

"If you are ready to scoop manure, I guess I am, too," Arland says, shaking his head.

Chapter Twelve

Arland doesn't send any scouts out ahead of us to look for daemons, but I'm not concerned. He holds my hand on our trip to the stables. It's amazing how safe I feel in his presence. We've known each other for only a few days, but my mind tells me it's been a lot longer. Truthfully, we have known each other our entire lives. He met me when I was an infant, and was aware he would have to protect me; I was introduced to him through dreams.

Arland holds me the way Brad always did when leading me through a crowded concert; like a friend would, although, *Arland's* touch leaves me longing for more. I'm sure that's the way Brad always felt. I've never held another guy's hand before; Brad barely left my side long enough for anyone to dare get close.

I wonder how many would have, if he hadn't been there.

"I would love to know what you are thinking right now," Arland says, staring straight ahead.

"I'm sure you would, but it's not going to happen."

"You are blending in with the others quite well, Kate," he says, now looking at me.

"I'm not so sure."

Arland stops walking and turns to me. "What makes you say that?"

"Before you returned to the training room, no one wanted to work with me or look at me, except for Perth."

Arland flinches at the mere mention of Perth's name. "We need to keep moving," he says, glancing around. "The others will eventually warm up to you. Since you are from The Meadows, they all look at you differently."

"What does being from The Meadows have to do with anything?"

"In time, you will understand." His curious response leaves me feeling even more in the dark.

"O-kay." I draw out the word. "Well, why do they treat me differently when you're not around?"

"There are a few reasons I can think of. None that you should concern yourself with, but once they get to know you, they will become more comfortable with your presence." Arland stops in the middle of the forest. "We are here."

"Where?" He must be joking. We haven't even gone through the base, and there's nothing in front of us but trees and Darkness.

"Nochtann," Arland whispers, waving his hand in front of him.

Two large, wooden doors appear before us, adorned by intricate carvings of ivy with jasmine flowers blooming all over. Live ivy grows along the walls, covering every part of the visible structure.

Leave it to the vines to grow with no sunlight.

"Amazing." I feel like a child in wonder.

"Not nearly as amazing as you when you swing that sword around." Arland's comment makes my cheeks burn.

"What happens if a daemon bumps into the building?" I ask, pressing my cool hands to my face.

"It would pass through as though the stables were not here."

I stop trying to hide my embarrassment and stare up at him. "So, why is everything else underground?"

"We feel safer that way. Hiding large buildings takes time, and if a spell fails, we would prefer to already be somewhere we cannot be seen."

"So spells can fail?" I glance over my shoulder as we walk in next to the feed bay.

"Yes, but you should not concern yourself with that. The spell over these stables has never failed."

"What about the perimeter breach this morning?"

"I am sorry for causing you concern. The spell was not broken."

"So . . . ?"

Arland holds his arm in front of him. "I will tell you when we have finished cleaning stalls."

The doors close, and then disappear behind us, without any more words from Arland. I wonder if the reason he didn't want me up here by myself was not due to something coming in and attacking me, but rather me leaving. That's a funny thought.

Arland hands me a shovel. "First, the chickens, cows, then goats, and we will end with the horses."

"Got it." I lean the shovel against the wall and tie my hair back.

With my shovel, I make my way to the top of the L-shaped stables then enter the chicken coop. Arland pushes in a wooden wheelbarrow, and I set to work, scooping the droppings while he carries in fresh bales of straw, then scatters it around. After I finish cleaning, I collect the eggs from the hen's small nests and place them in a basket.

Working out here reminds me so much of my childhood. Mom used to say I needed to know how to run every part of a farm, even if it meant taking care of the smallest of animals. It makes sense now that she wanted me to learn those ways, since life here doesn't seem to be as convenient as life back home.

If I want to stay here after the war and survive, I'll have to be able to cultivate the land and grow my own food. A long time ago, it used to be that way at home, too, but the old ways of life have been replaced by modern conveniences—like electricity, for instance. It would be a lot easier to spot daemons, if Encardia had streetlights.

Arland and I make a fast working team. In a short time, we finish the chickens and cows, then move on to the goat pen. We don't talk much while working—just like on the farm with Gary. Unlike when I help my stepfather, Arland and I steal glances at each other every now and then. A few times, I'm sure I catch him standing and staring at me. I smile, and he goes right back to work.

Flanna walks in, carrying a small tray with two cups of water. "Would you like a drink?"

"Thank you." I take the cup, guzzle the water, then immediately return to work.

Arland drinks his, and also goes back to scooping and refreshing.

The usually nosey Flanna takes off toward the stairs, humming something.

I'm surprised she went away without being yelled at.

The goats take longer for me and Arland to care for, due to their curiosity about the taste of my clothing. Two of them are so interested in my shirt, they trot right up to take a bite out of it.

"Hey," I yell. "This is not food, and it's the only shirt I have!"

"We have more clothes for you. These brainless goats will eat just about anything."

It's true; goats *will* eat anything. Even senior term papers. I've never looked at the little monsters the same way since.

"I have a surprise for you. Close your eyes," Arland says, after we finish the pen.

What could he possibly have for me? I close my eyes, as Arland instructs. He stands behind me, then cups his hands over my face, so I can't peek.

"Walk forward," he says in my ear—causing my pulse to race—pushing me forward in the direction of the horses. "Okay, open them."

He removes his hands. I take a minute to process what I see. A snow-white mare stands tall and proud before me, in her new stall. She stares so hard, I feel like I'm being studied.

"She's stunning." I'm awe-struck; she's so white, her coat appears to be glowing.

"She is yours," Arland says, eyes lit with excitement.

I turn to face him. "What?"

He strides over to stand in front of the horse's stall. "This fine mare was our *security breach* from this morning. We found her standing on our perimeter. It was as though she was waiting for something, or someone. Lann and his brother Keith could not get her to move. I was informed of the issue and rode Bowen out to check on her; she followed him right back to the stables."

"She followed Bowen?"

"Yes."

Grabbing Arland by the arm, I back away from the horse. "W-what i-if she's a shifter?"

He peels my fingers from his forearm, then takes me by the hand. "She is not a shifter."

"But how do you know? You said—"

"I know what I said, and we also know how to tell if our animals have been infected. Their eyes turn solid black. Look at this horse's eyes." He points at the creature. "They are perfectly blue."

I take a deep breath and release my death grip on Arland's hand. "And she's mine?"

"I figured you are going to need one, and she seems the perfect fit for you . . . temperamental like Bowen," Arland says, leaning on his elbow against one of the wooden rails of her stall gate . . . smiling at me. "I have named her Mirain. It means beautiful."

"Mirain. You *are* a beautiful girl." I step on the bottom rail of the gate and offer her some oats.

She neighs and stomps her feet a couple times, then she eats from my palm. I reach up and rub between her eyes, the same spot that wins all the horses over. Mirain presses her forehead into my hand, and all control of my body disappears.

I fall and land on the floor.

The stables fade away.

Arland and I battle a group of daemons led by a man covered in dirt and blood. His eyes are black, and he glares at me. The closer he gets the more I recognize him.

"Brad?"

He laughs as the daemons surround me and Arland.

Mirain and Bowen both lay, slain, on the bloodstained earth next to us. We know our own time is up. Arland stops fighting and lowers his sword.

He picks me up at the waist. "I love you."

We kiss goodbye, but in this goodbye, there is no doubt I'm in love with him.

Anger flashes in Brad's eyes. He lunges forward, holding a black, iron sword, and strikes Arland through the heart. Brad laughs as my protector falls to the ground.

"No," I scream, throwing myself over Arland. "How could you? You were my friend. I trusted you!"

I don't attempt to fight off the attacking daemons; I sit and wait for them to kill me, so I can join Arland. There is no pain in this death, only peace, knowing I am going to die with the one I love the most.

A coscartha rushes forward, then thrusts its claw through my chest.

From over their heads, my spirit watches the daemons and Brad dance around my lifeless body, but it fights back. As they begin ripping me limb from limb, a bright yellow light escapes from my insides, blasting the daemons and Brad into nothing, and lighting the world.

"No," I scream, startling all the horses, except Mirain.

She reaches her head through the gate to rub her cold nose on my neck.

Arland takes my hand and helps me to my feet, concern written all over his face. "What happened?"

"A v-vision of us b-both dying." Tears fill my eyes; the muscles in my throat constrict. "T-this time it was B-Brad who killed you, and daemons killed me. When I died, l-light filled the world."

He kneels until we're eye level, holding me with his gaze. "Have you had waking dreams before?"

"Y-yes. The first time was a couple days before we arrived here."

He wraps his powerful arms around me, trying to make me feel better, but the tears continue to flow. "We are not going to die."

Returning his embrace, I rest my head against his chest. For a few minutes, we stay encased in each other's arms, and he calms me with "shh's." The warmth of Arland, his kind whispered words, his familiar hold—they almost make me feel as though we *are* safe.

I cannot handle these erratic visions anymore. Before, they were just realistic nightmares about someone I didn't know, but now that Arland is alive, warm, and standing here with me, they've turned unbearable. The addition of Brad makes them even more painful.

I have to get him home.

"Would you like to go back inside, while I finish up the stalls?" Arland asks, taking a step back, rubbing the side of my arms.

I wipe the tears with my shirtsleeve. "No, I'll be okay. I'd like to spend some time getting to know Mirain."

"Let me know if you change your mind," he says, and he leaves me alone.

The sounds of Arland's shovel hitting the earth echo through the stables. I grab the brush and hold it out to Mirain. She doesn't move away from me, or show any fear, so I open the gate and walk right in. Although she's already a model of perfection, I run the brush through her coat, mane, then tail.

"Will you let me sit on you, Mirain?" I ask when I'm finished, keeping my voice tender and bracing myself on a wallboard of her stall.

Mirain moves closer to me—as though understanding my intentions—and allows me to climb onto her back. I take the ends of her mane in my hands, and explain when I ride her, that I'll hold her here. Her head bobs.

I laugh.

My legs drape down Mirain's sides. We're a perfect fit. I praise her, rubbing from her neck down to her haunches, then I practice walking her. She has not shown uncertainty with anything I've requested her to do.

"You are such a good girl."

Arland stands outside her stall, his eyes wide. "It is as though she was made for you alone. Horses really seem to trust you. I have a feeling if I tried that, she would have had me flat on my back by now."

I grab one of her ears and rub it. "You wouldn't hurt anyone, would you, girl?"

Mirain takes two steps forward then nudges Arland in the shoulder with her nose. Now I know she comprehends my words. I slide from her back, then Arland and I both curry her.

I figure while we're standing here alone, it's now or never for my questions. I don't know how I've been able to hold back on them for as long as I have. "Can I ask you something?"

"Anything," Arland says, looking from Mirain's face to mine.

"If we are not *completely* human . . . what are we?"

"I was waiting for you to ask that question last night." He laughs. "We are human. As you can see, we do not look any different from the people of the world you were raised in. However, we are capable of using much more of our brain's abilities than the people you know."

My mouth hangs open.

"Allow me to finish." Arland puts up his hand. "Long ago, our worlds were open to each other. Our kind would frequently pass through the portal to your mad world. We learned a great deal from those humans, although we could not teach them anything in return. Our magical powers were invisible to them; their minds would interpret our actions as something daemonic. They accused us of great misdeeds, usually caused by their own kind. Mobs of men and woman began searching us out, and also killing anyone who might have associated with us. They burned innocent people at stakes, hanged them from nooses; or if we were not caught, we were forced into hiding. After watching people killed, merely because of our presence, our Leaders decided to close the portals forever."

"So . . . we are witches?" I ask with caution.

"No. Not witches, although the witches of that world may be descendants of our kind. Long ago, Kate, the human world called us by another name, but one we did not give ourselves: Álfar." Arland says the word as if it's offensive.

"What does that mean?" I hope not to sound ignorant, but I don't remember learning about anything called *Álfar* in history.

Arland grits his teeth. "Elf."

Imagining Santa and The North Pole, I laugh. "No way. Elves have pointed ears and are short people who make presents at Christmas time," I tease, but I can tell by Arland's scowl, he does *not* find this funny.

"Many people died because of narrow-minded humans. They could not see the magic and confused the willingness of our people to help them with a daemonic plaguing."

I think about the Salem Witch trials and realize just how cruel people can be when they're scared.

"So I'm an elf?" It's really hard to keep myself from laughing right now.

He shakes his head. "No. You are a Draíochta. You will find no one here calls themselves an Álfar; it refers to a tragic time in our history, and it is not a name we had given to ourselves."

The term *Elf* must be extremely offensive, if Arland is not even willing to say it in English.

"If the Leaders closed the portals forever, does that mean my dad broke the law?"

Arland's face softens, and he returns to rubbing Mirain, watching me from the corner of his eyes. "Multiple laws. They also banned those who were familiar with the old magic—the force used to operate the portals—from conjuring it to go to *any* other world."

"What would have happened if he'd been caught?" I ask, picturing my mom and dad sneaking off into the night, an infant bundled under their arms.

"Laws of that magnitude have rarely been broken in Encardia. I am positive an example would have been made out of your father, because of his status."

"What was his status?"

"He was a Leader of Encardia. A powerful one. Many people loved your father; a few hated him. Those who envied him would have seen him severely punished for breaking *any* law."

"And my mom? Would an example have been made of her?"

He nods. "She was also a Leader."

"If we get to her, should she stay away from here?"

"No, not now. I cannot see her being punished for protecting hope. If your parents had not done what they were told, we would be doomed."

An image of my mother in shackles, bound to some dirt wall in the ground, fills my head. I shake the thought. "If I'm magical, then why don't I know any magic?"

Arland smiles. "The magic is in you somewhere. We just need to help you figure out how to use it."

"So far I've been unable to replicate regular magic. How am I supposed to save everyone with the forbidden magic no one knows how to use?"

"I do not know," he says, with an air of exasperation.

"And Darkness? Where did it come from?" I'm disappointed he doesn't know more about me.

"For many years after the portals were closed, everything appeared peaceful. As time wore on, and those who knew the old magic died, it began to sleep, too. Old magic upheld barriers of protection that kept us safe from the evil of other worlds—only those with pure hearts could pass through portals. When magic slept, the barriers came down, allowing Darkness to enter."

Mirain snorts.

I pat her shoulder. "How many other worlds are there?"

"There were nine, including The Heavens."

"*Were?*"

"One disappeared long ago. A few Draíochtans passed through the portal to Elysia, but found themselves floating in a black abyss. Everything was gone. They were lucky to return."

"Do you think Darkness attacked there?"

"We are unsure of what happened."

"Who commands Darkness?"

"We do not know that, either. No one has come forth as a leader. We only fight off the daemons when they attack, or when a scout has found a hiding place," he says, sounding as frustrated as I am.

"Or when stragglers get too close?"

Arland nods.

"So you don't even know what it is I'm supposed to save everyone from?" My voice is filled with irritation.

"No." He narrows his eyes; Arland's probably worried I'm so frustrated I'll storm off.

"Who is Perth?" I ask, trying to get off the subject of me.

Arland's eyelids constrict into slits; his jaw hardens. "Tomorrow, I will tell you about Perth. We should head back downstairs. If we are going to the clearing in the morning, we need rest."

His sudden mood change has me wishing I never asked. "Okay."

Taking deep breaths, I calm myself. I don't want to press Arland with questions now, not on the eve of riding out to potentially traveling home for help. Arland and Lann have both shared the same reaction to Perth. I'm afraid the tension runs so deep, if I keep asking about him, I will upset Arland.

He holds out his arm for me; I happily hook mine through his.

"I have to go now, Mirain, I'll be back soon."

She whinnies when we're out of her sight.

"The poor girl is in love with you already," Arland says, lightening the mood.

"She's very sweet." I try to smile, but the tense muscles in my face probably make it look more like a grimace.

Chapter Thirteen

Arland and I leave the stables and join the dinner crowd. Having both missed lunch today, we don't let food remain on our plates long. When we're ready for second helpings, Marcus and Anna rush over to our table, then ask to sit.

"Of course." I'm glad the children don't look at me the way some of the adults do.

Arland takes our plates to be refilled, while the children gush over the details of today's training session. They explain how some of their friends, who missed it, were jealous each of them was able to fight with me.

"You shouldn't try to make your friends jealous."

Anna glares at Marcus. "We did not mean to."

"Tell you what—if you each bring someone with you to training tomorrow, I will reward the four of you with a private session, but only if Arland will excuse you from your other duties," I say, meeting Arland's eyes as he returns to the table.

He nods.

Marcus and Anna dart from us to a group of children. They talk amongst themselves, and, every now and then, look in our direction. After some quiet debating, a couple of children smile widely at me. From their elated expressions, I know which two I'll be training first.

"You have a way with children, as well as the horses." Arland looks at me with what I think may be admiration.

Something tells me he has a harder time relating to them than the adults. He had to grow up fast; children may not make sense to him. "I love them. On our farm, I worked with kids in the summertime. I would give riding lessons. It was really win-win for me. Not only did I get to spend time with the children and the horses, but I got paid for it, too," I say, smiling to myself. All those wonderful summer days, riding through the pastures with little kids who were almost too excited to pay attention, make up some of my fondest memories.

"I bet you would have done it even if you were not getting paid." Arland shakes his head.

Somehow, he knows that about me; I absolutely would work with children without getting paid, but Gary would never allow that. "This is a business. We are not giving out any freebies," he used to say with a stern voice when I'd ask to take on a couple kids whose families couldn't afford what he charged.

I've been yawning all throughout dinner. I'm more than done for the day.

"Tired?" Arland asks, standing to hold my chair out for me.

"Extremely." I yawn again.

We make our way into *our* room after the dinner rush. Luckily, the dining area is empty, so no one watches us go in together.

"Turn around," I say, then tear off my dirty shirt and pants. I look down at myself and realize I, too, am filthy. "I can't go to bed like this; I'm disgusting."

Arland turns back to face me, but quickly returns his gaze to the wall. "I am sorry."

"It's okay. Can you hand me my towel from the chair? I'm going to take a bath."

Without looking in my direction, Arland picks up the towel, then hands it to me. Our fingers brush; his skin warms mine.

"Would you like to join me?"

"That would definitely not be appropriate," Arland says, as though he's not entirely sure he means no.

"We can keep our underclothes on. Please?"

I dress, then stand next to him. He clasps his hands behind his back and looks at me with one eyebrow raised. I can tell part of Arland wants to come with me, but the decision is tearing him up inside.

What's gotten into me?

His reaction makes me regret confusing him. "I'm sorry. I shouldn't have asked. Will you please wait outside the door for me?"

"Kate, did you not mention earlier how you feel the others look at you differently?" Arland asks. His eyes burn into me, making my heart pick up its pace.

"Yes, but—"

"Do you understand, if we go into the washroom together, the others will not only look at you differently, but also think more about us than what is truth? Quite a few of them already suspect more than what has happened."

"People will believe whatever they want, no matter what the truth is; why should we let that bother us? You and I know what's happened, or not happened, between us, and we're all that matter," I say, hoping to make him feel better—even though I know in my heart it won't.

What is it that's happening between us? We've shared a bed, trained to fight, cleaned a few stalls, but all of a sudden, I feel it might mean something more. It's as though the relationship we had in those dreams is coming into fruition, but how can that be? A few days ago, I hadn't kissed anyone, never had a boyfriend. Now I've kissed one guy, and am hopefully becoming closer than I've ever been to a relationship with another man.

The difference between Brad and Arland is, with Brad, I never thought this way about him, didn't accept he had feelings for me. My heart hasn't rushed for Brad the way it does in this moment, while I stand next to Arland and await an answer that might say he feels the same. Before crossing into this world, I thought something was changing between Brad and me. But growing close to him didn't have the same excitement as growing close to Arland does. Brad was familiar, friendly, and comforting, but if what we had was anything more, I don't recognize the feeling.

"Flanna is going to give me hell." Arland grabs a towel out of the top drawer of the old oak dresser.

"You don't have to come," I say, desperately hoping he still does.

"You are attempting to make me feel less guilty, but if you wish for me to join you, I will." He shakes his head.

I check on Brad before going to the washroom. Kegan looks excited when the door swings open, but then he sees me and frowns. His eyelids are heavy, and he stretches his arms above his head; I hope Shay will replace him soon.

"There has not been any change," he says.

"Thank you." I close the door.

The washroom is empty. Arland slides the lock across the door, so no one—Flanna—can *accidentally* come in. Arland turns his head while I slip out of my clothes again, then he takes off his. We leave on only our undergarments.

Climbing in first, he holds his hand out for me while I step in. The water is still the same perfect temperature it was when I bathed yesterday. We submerge ourselves to wash off the dirt.

Our bath together doesn't feel wrong or rushed. I find it comparable to sitting in a hot tub with someone; I'm enjoying myself. I cannot help but stare at Arland's flawless figure sitting across from me. He leans against the edge of the enclosure, keeping his distance.

Arland is well built for battle. He's much taller than I am—about six-foot-two—has broad shoulders, well-defined muscles on his arms and abdomen. His slightly wavy, dark brown hair hangs straight past his ears, and is dripping wet. Even in the dimly lit room, I can tell he's blushing. I must be staring at him with too much intensity.

"Has anyone ever told you how beautiful *you* are?" I ask.

"Only my mother, when I was a child," Arland says, looking down at the water.

Moving to his side of the enclosure, I sit next to him. "Well, now I have, too."

Arland puts his arm around my shoulders, eases my head onto his chest, then caresses my back with the tips of his fingers. His heart thuds rapidly.

I'm making *him* nervous. The thought makes me smile.

We do nothing but lie here in silence, until our skin prunes from staying in the water too long. I take the bar of soap from next to the enclosure and run it all over my body. Passing the bar to Arland, I fumble it in my hands.

He laughs.

The closeness we share is simple and pure. I don't want Arland to feel as though he's taking advantage of my vulnerability, like he said yesterday; although, I might be taking advantage of him. If Arland only knew the details of the intimacies we share in my dreams, how close we have been, or how close I want us to be . . . .

After we finish washing, Arland steps from the bath, then holds my hand while I walk down the stairs behind him. We face away from each other, take off our wet undergarments, then replace them with our nightclothes. We sneak through the empty hall to our room.

Arland lies in bed first and holds the blankets up for me. He doesn't even glance at the chair he tried to sleep in yesterday. I climb in next to him, and he wraps the covers over us.

"I will not leave you tonight," Arland says, his voice soft.

"Where did you go last night?" He never did explain to me where he had been, not that he had to.

"I checked in on the Watchers."

"The Watchers are the night soldiers? The ones who guard the perimeter and shoot at stray daemons?"

He wears a crooked smile. "Yes, and I have put Keith on duty again for tonight. They will come for me only if there is a problem, and I will awaken you if anything requires me to leave." Arland pushes a strand of hair from my face, sending heat rushing to where our skin meets.

I suck in a sharp breath. "Keeping you from your work is not my intention. You should do whatever it is you need and not worry about me." I don't mean what I say. I need him here with me, and I don't know why. There is no explanation.

"You are not keeping me from anything someone else cannot handle. You, Kate, are my main concern, now that you are here." Putting his arm over me, he pulls me closer.

Our legs touch. My heart races. His dewy scent fills my nose. I close my eyes, take a deep breath of Arland. Enjoy his soothing presence.

"But the others don't know that." I keep my hands clasped together in front of me, for fear a touch would chase him out of the room.

"They do not require knowledge of my affairs to follow my orders," he says with authority. "My father is anxious to meet you."

I'm thankful for the change of subject. "Is he?"

"Yes. He was excited to learn of your return. As we speak, he is mobilizing his army to prepare for our arrival."

My muscles tense; desire runs away. "*His* army?"

"He became the High Leader of Encardia a year after the war began."

I feel faint.

"Relax. Why are you tense?" His voice is soothing, but doesn't help calm me.

"The thought of being introduced to someone who knew my dad so well, and helped save my life, makes me a little nervous."

"Not the fact he is our world's Highest Leader?" he asks, his words layered with doubt.

"That doesn't seem as frightening as having to impress one of my dad's friends."

Arland laughs. "You are very interesting."

We don't talk about anything else; we lie here, staring at each other. I think about my dad and what life would have been like, if he lived, about Arland's father, and about all the sacrifices people have had to make for me. After what feels like hours of gazing into Arland's eyes, sleep consumes me.

Chapter Fourteen

"Wake up," Arland whispers.

I feel him pushing hair from my face before his words truly stir me.

"Hmm?"

"We are leaving in an hour for the clearing; I thought you might like to eat first."

"I'm awake," I say, eyes closed, body unwilling to move.

"Kate? Brad needs you. Do you want to see your sister and mother again?" His words are like daggers, even though he speaks kindly.

I open my eyes to the dark room. Arland's face is an inch from mine; he watches me. His chest rests on mine, but he holds himself up by his arms. A flood of emotions pumps through my veins. If emotions were colorful, I'm sure they could be seen covering every portion of my body right now, especially over my heart. Building up the courage to kiss him, I close my eyes . . . .

He sits back. "You are not easy to wake up."

My stomach twists with nervous anticipation. "It's been so long since I've slept without dreams; my body must be making up for lost time."

Arland smiles. "Then you should be well rested for when we see your mother and sister today."

"I can't wait," I say, jumping from bed.

The thought of seeing Brit and my mom is overwhelming. I rush to get dressed, then run from the room for breakfast.

Flanna raises her eyebrows when I come barreling toward the kitchen. Whatever she's thinking, I'm sure it's not the truth. That's all I know. Even if I wanted to do something with Arland last night, I don't think it would have happened.

"Kate, are you forgetting something?" Flanna asks.

Following her gaze, I look at my feet. "Oh, my boots!"

I turn back for the bedroom, but Arland carries my boots to me. I sit at the closest table and slide them on, fumbling with the laces.

"I am going to check in with the Watchers. Try not to run off without me," Arland says, then disappears into the corridor.

"Why is he going down there, if the Watchers are outside?" I ask, cinching my bootlace.

"He does not need to go outside to communicate with them."

"So how—?"

"Arland can tell you later." Flanna waves. "I am dying to know, did you have a nice night?" She adds a hint of amusement to her question.

After lacing my other boot, I get up to walk past her into the kitchen. "Yes."

Trailing behind me, she grabs my shoulder and spins me around. "Would you like to tell me about it?"

"No, it's not what you think." For Arland's sake, I don't want people to read more into us than they need to.

"You are no fun." Flanna abandons me to stir some sort of slop over the fire.

"We just talked."

She flashes a grin over her shoulder. "Call it what you will, but I saw you go into the washroom together."

"There wasn't anyone out here when we went in. How could you have seen us?"

"I have my ways." Flanna continues stirring her slop. "So, are you going to tell me, or do I have to get it from Arland?"

"We *just* talked."

"Arland it is." She smiles wickedly. "My cousin tells me everything."

"Sure he does," I say, giving her the same wicked smile. "I'm going to go in the other room and wait for him."

Pulling out a chair at the closest table, I sit and put my face in my hands. My legs bounce; my palms sweat. I'm messing up Arland's relationship with his people. They cannot lose respect for him. I need to focus on what's important. Getting help for Brad. Figuring out who I am.

I picture Brit's smiling face, her sarcasm, and her enthusiasm for life . . . think of the way she makes me feel needed and loved. And I picture Mom's open arms, and how wonderful a hug from her would be right now. No matter how many questions I have, I need her.

The door creaks open; Arland returns to the kitchen, scoops some of Flanna's slop into two bowls. He carries them out and hands one to me.

"Eat this," he says.

"What is it?" I ask, stabbing my spoon at the mushy, brown substance.

"I know it looks terrible, but it tastes wonderful. Flanna prepares this using magic, when she does not like what there is to choose from in our food supplies." Arland takes a heaping bite.

I spoon some of the slop into my mouth. The taste surprises me; it's good. The texture becomes chunky, like I'm biting into potatoes and chewing on meat. "Mmm. It *is* delicious."

"She calls it Flanna's Surprise."

I take another bite. "It's definitely a surprise." Lowering my voice so Flanna doesn't overhear, I say, "Oh, and I don't think she's going to give you hell about the bath."

"Oh?"

"She already gave it to me."

"I knew my cousin would not let us off easy." Arland laughs then takes another huge bite of Flanna's Surprise.

On cue, she walks into the dining area, hands up in surrender, eyes big and demure.

"Flanna, go wake Cadman and bring him to the stables," Arland says.

She nods, then bounces off to get the older soldier.

"We are bringing the two of them with us for extra security."

The door to the soldier's quarters squeaks on its hinges, echoing into the dining room.

"Do you intend to tell Cadman the truth about me?"

"No." Arland answers too fast to have thought about the question.

"Won't he find it a little odd for us to be riding out to the clearing, possibly disappearing into a chasm in the earth, or even potentially standing around until we give up and head back?"

Arland stops eating and turns his head toward me. "Cadman is a good soldier. He will not question it."

"I think you should tell him. If he's going to risk his life protecting us, he should at least know what he's willing to die for." If I were Cadman, I would appreciate the truth.

"It does not make you nervous to have another learn of your prophecy?" Arland whispers.

"Anyone who is willing to risk their life to protect me should be informed." It does make me nervous to have more people find out, but they will discover the truth anyway. I don't want people dying for me without knowing why.

"That is very honorable of you, but there are many here who should not know who you are," he says, still keeping his voice low.

I'd bet Perth is one of those people.

I take my last bite, and Arland swipes my bowl to carry it into the kitchen. "Are you ready?" he calls.

"Y-yes."

The stables are quiet. Almost all of the animals rest in their stalls. Mirain and Bowen are the only creatures awake, and they appear to have been waiting for us, nearly confirming my suspicions of the horses being magical.

I offer Mirain a treat before entering her stall. Arland follows behind me. He clasps his hands together, creating a footrest for me to mount, then he goes inside the other stall and mounts Bowen.

We ride the horses toward the exit by the storage bay and wait for the others. Arland quietly watches me—I'm going to need a new heart if all this racing doesn't stop.

The door opens; Cadman and Flanna climb the last of the stairs, then join us in the stables. "Where are we riding to, sir?" Cadman asks, riding out one of the stallions and halting next to us.

"We are going to the clearing. Upon our arrival, you and Flanna will stand guard over the horses and watch for daemons," Arland says, sitting tall on Bowen's back.

Cadman nods.

I flash Arland a pointed look.

"Kate has also asked me to inform you of our mission. If you have not already discovered, she is no normal recruit."

"I see she is gifted with swords, as well as having your favor, sir." Cadman glances at me.

"She is my choimeád, Cadman. It is my duty to keep her safe, so she may fulfill her prophecy. It has been foretold she will end this wretched war." Arland is devoid of any emotion, on his face or in his voice.

So that's all I am to him? I'm just someone he has to protect?

I should have expected this. It's not like Arland has dreamed of *me* for six years. The bond I thought we shared must be how any Coimeádaí treats the one he's protecting. Chagrin fills me; I cannot meet anyone's eyes.

I'd like to find a rock and hide under it now.

Flanna leads her mare over and stands by my side. "This is Luatha."

"What does it mean?" I stare at my fingers laced through Mirain's mane.

"It was just a name I picked. What has you down all of a sudden?" Arland turns from speaking to Cadman to look at me.

"I'm okay . . . nerves I guess." I lie, but it makes Arland return to his conversation with Cadman, and that's better than having him see me.

"How gullible do you think I am?" she whispers, pursing her lips.

"Flanna. I. Am. Fine."

She keeps watching me, but I ignore her and train my eyes on my hands.

"You and Flanna are to ride ten paces ahead of us. Do not exceed a trot." Arland barks out orders in a firm, authoritative tone. There hasn't been any reason for him to speak this way since I've been here. He appears at ease in his leadership role, sitting straight on Bowen, with shoulders squared and no emotion on his face. "Once we pass the perimeter, we will need to cover the remaining distance as fast as possible."

Everyone nods in agreement to the plan.

"Oscailte." Arland mutters the word.

The doors swing open; Cadman and Flanna take the lead. We wait for them to get far enough ahead of us, then follow. Mirain and Bowen's nostrils huff out steam in big, white clouds. A shiver runs through me, but my hands and legs are kept warm by Mirain's body heat.

I cannot look at Arland. I'm still too embarrassed by the way he cast me down in front of the others. Maybe he knows it, too, because he doesn't say anything, either. The silence between us makes the ride to the clearing painfully slow.

We travel through the thick forest, cold bearing down on us, Darkness everywhere. How long has it been since *I* have seen the sun? The world appears so much smaller when the stars don't shine. I try hard to think of positive things, but instead of being excited at the prospect of seeing my home, Brit, and Mom, all I can think about is what Arland said about me.

Mirain gives an irritated sigh, startling Bowen; he bumps into her. "What is it, girl?"

She shakes her head and continues walking.

Great, now she's as moody as I am.

"I believe she is sensing your spirit. Is something other than nerves bothering you?" Arland asks, bringing me out of my solitary thoughts.

"There is *nothing* wrong with my mood," I say, only proving there is something seriously wrong with my mood.

"You do not have to talk about it." Arland again falls silent.

By the time we reach the edge of the perimeter, I'm ready to turn around and head back to base. I should be excited about the opportunity before us, but I'm not.

There are two guards standing watch at the end of the trail. I recognize them from the training facility.

"Gavin." Arland tips his head at the nearer soldier, who looks to be in his mid-thirties. "Has there been any activity recently?"

Gavin locks eyes with me, but responds to Arland.

"No, sir. How far is your group traveling?" His face is strong, but his voice reveals submissiveness to the authority before him.

"Two more miles. We are going to the clearing. When your replacements come, you and Dunn need to hold your posts. If we do not return by the end of Sayer's and Ogilvie's shifts, you and Dunn need to come to the clearing, heavily armed. Once you reach us—if we have not already been killed—try your best to help us fight. Do you understand?"

"Yes, sir," Gavin says, perking up. He looks excited at the chance to run a rescue mission. Keeping guard over the perimeter must become boring after months, or maybe even years, of doing it.

Finished giving instructions to Gavin, Arland leads us to the edge of the forest, then we wait. He holds up his hand, closing his eyes and turning his head to the side.

"Go!" Arland shouts.

Cadman and Flanna race their horses ahead of us; Mirain and Bowen follow without any instruction. Riding a horse bareback, with only her mane to hold on to, is exhilarating. But now that we're in the open, it's hard to stay focused. There are so many reasons to look over my shoulder.

Mirain and her graceful strides make me feel like we're flying. Cold air fills my lungs, causing my chest to burn, and tears to stream down my face. I hold my breath to suppress the coughing fits attempting to take control, but I find that almost impossible at this speed. When we arrive, I take a deep breath, regretting not getting warmer clothes from Flanna.

Mirain stops next to Bowen. I jump off her back.

Arland takes my hand into his. "Show me where the portal was located?"

The spot where Arland and I stand is where, just a few days ago, my life changed forever. My palms sweat at the memory of Brad being attacked. I'm frozen in place. Arland squeezes my hand, but his touch hurts my feelings even more.

I am so stupid for thinking he feels the same way I do. I know I have to pull myself together, but I've never experienced anything as strong as this. The only one who's ever rejected me was Mark Evans, in the ninth grade. I had a big crush on Mark, my biology lab partner. Each day we worked together, our friendship grew stronger. The winter social was coming up; he asked me to go with him. Of course, I said yes. My sister and I spent multiple weekends trying to pick out the perfect dress, but a week before the dance, Mark told me he was taking Allison Moore instead. He switched lab partners that day, and never talked to me again. I was crushed, but it was nothing compared to how I feel right now.

I look from my memories to where the portal was.

"It's closed," I say, stating the obvious. "So, now what?"

"Try asking the portal to open." Arland rubs his thumb over my knuckles.

"Oh, sweet hole between two worlds, won't you please open?" I add a little too much sarcasm, and receive three equally impatient scowls. "Sorry. I don't know what you expect me to say."

"What were you doing when you discovered the portal?" Arland asks.

"We were swimming. Brit dunked me in the water, and I dragged her under with me. That's when we saw a bright, yellow light dive into the water, revealing the portal."

The three of them stare at me, their mouths gaping open. You would think I told them I'm Jesus Christ Himself. I haven't mentioned the light to Arland before now. I didn't know him well enough to entrust him with this information, nor did I know anything about being a Draíochta. The truth is, I didn't want him to think I am crazy—especially after everything else I told him.

"I knew she was special, Arland, but for the magic to lead her here is something else entirely," Flanna says.

"Had you ever seen the light prior to swimming?" Arland asks.

"Yes. I saw it a few times while we were in the forest. It's the reason we were at the swimming hole in the first place. The night before we arrived here, I was sitting by myself next to the river, and followed the light to the hole. I wasn't going swimming alone, in the middle of the night, so I went back to bed, but Brad and my sister woke up, so we all went. I didn't mention the light to Brad, but he couldn't see it after it slammed into the water. Just Brit and I could still see the light," I admit.

After listening to Arland's little history lesson, about the difference between our two kinds, Brad's inability to see the light all makes sense now.

"Do you think the gods used the magic to summons her here, sir?" Cadman asks.

"It does appear that way."

"Do you believe they will allow her to leave so easily, if they went to the trouble of sending magic into the human world to bring her home?"

Apparently, Arland shared quite a bit of my history when I was lamenting in the stables.

"Gods rarely involve themselves in our affairs, but if they did, I do not believe they wish for Kate to lose her friend, or never see her family again. Although, it is clear the portal is not going to open until Kate has satisfied them in some way."

"Gods?" I ask.

"Yes, gods." Arland stares at the sky. "If they are involved, I am sure it is Griandor. He is the god of sunlight, and his desire would be for you to fulfill your prophecy . . . for obvious reasons. There is nothing more we can do here."

Arland seems more upset than I am. Out of concern for his people, he didn't want to leave to meet his father until Brad was safe. Now that the portal is closed indefinitely, I'm sure Arland is even more worried about his people . . . because of me.

He drops my hand and turns away. "We should return."

Giving up on getting through the portal, we mount our horses and ride back toward base. Our return pace is much slower than it was on our way to the clearing. I'm glad to have more time to think to myself.

First, I was their hope, but now, I have to make the gods happy, too? I want to get Brad home to safety, see my sister, my mom, and not fight in a war, or please the gods. I don't even know what makes me special enough to bring light back into this world.

So many things keep disappointing me today. The connection I felt with Arland is not real, Brad is more than likely going to die, and my sister and mom are stuck on the other side of the portal, when I want—need—them here with me.

Entering the forest, we pass Gavin and Dunn. They both frown, seeming a tad too disappointed at our safe arrival. My suspicions of their boredom are confirmed. Maybe Arland should send them out to shoot stray daemons for a while.

Inside the cover of the trees, Cadman and Flanna stop riding ten paces in front of me and Arland, and hold up until we reach them.

"Why have you stopped?" he asks.

Flanna holds my gaze. "May I speak with Kate for a moment?"

Everyone looks at me, but I'm not focused on them or their conversation. I stare out into the black space in front of us.

"No," Arland says, his voice firm. "We will wait here until you get ahead of us again."

The silence between Arland and me is upsetting. Talking seemed so natural between us, but now I'm afraid to say anything to him. Arriving at the stables, we return the horses to their stalls, but still haven't spoken a word to one another. The animals are the only ones who seem happy. At least, the ride did them good.

"Will you require anything else this morning, sir?" Cadman asks.

"No, Cadman, thank you for your service."

Cadman and Flanna take off toward the stairs, leaving Arland and me alone.

He turns to me, but I cannot meet his eyes. "I am sorry we could not get through the portal today. There has to be some way around it. My father might understand the reasoning of the gods, but I would not wish to speak to him about such things unless we were in his presence."

"So, we leave Brad here to die *and* risk all of your soldier's lives?" I ask, upset that I haven't been able to come through for my friend, and that Arland is worried about me unintentionally hurting his people.

"Kate—"

"Don't. I need to be left alone for a while." I storm off to spend some time with Brad. How selfish of me for thinking about my own personal love life, when he is ill, and so many others are being murdered every day. I have to make a point not to be so much like a drama queen.

Chapter Fifteen

I don't pass anyone on my way to Brad's room. It's a good thing too, because I hate when people see me cry. Wiping tears from my face with my shirtsleeve, I push through the door to Brad's room.

Shay's head snaps up when the door squeaks. "I am sorry, Kate. Your friend has not shown any signs of improvement."

"May I spend some time alone with him?"

"Have Flanna come for me when you are finished," she says, patting my shoulder on her way out.

When Shay closes the door, I move the chair closer to Brad's bed, then take his hand in mine. "I'm sorry. We couldn't get through the portal, Brad. I know you made me promise not to go, but I still had to try. We didn't run into any daemons, but it didn't matter. The stupid thing was closed tight. They think *gods* brought me here. I should've told you why Brit and I wanted to go to the swimming hole that night. I just . . . I didn't think you would believe us. You deserve someone better than me. I'm not even human in the same way as you." I ramble on, watching his chest as it rises and falls—the only thing he does that makes him seem alive.

Brad has to come out of this. If he hears me, maybe he will. I laugh. Talking to him is no use, considering they forced him into this coma. Blisters and swelling cover his skin. His body is so lifeless; it's impossible to be near him—the pain of watching him die hurts too much. I need my friend to be here with me, to tell me everything is going to be okay. More than anything, I need to get him home, so he can be safe from this place.

Tears fall in a steady stream. Coming to spend time with Brad was not the best idea. I miss being able to talk to him, tell him what's on my mind, have him tell *me* everything is going to be great. We haven't spent this much time apart since we met. I never realized how much his friendship means. Finding his hand, I give a gentle squeeze. I stand, then leave the room.

Walking down the hall is unnerving. I don't want anyone to see me, but I have to find Flanna. The dining area is empty. Chopping sounds come from the kitchen, so I follow them.

Flanna's red hair bounces as she cuts through potatoes.

"Can you please tell Shay I'm finished visiting with Brad?" I ask the back of her head.

She turns and gives a nervous smile. "Yes, wait right here."

Flanna heads toward the soldier's quarters, but I don't wait for her. Once she disappears, I go back to my room and shut the door. I sit on the edge of the bed in the dark room, refusing to light a candle, close my eyes, and try to think of nothing.

A few minutes pass, and I hear Flanna talking loudly about how wonderful Shay is, clearly wanting me to be aware of their presence. I will not come out of this room until I know for sure Flanna is gone; I don't want to be around someone so happy.

I wait here in the dark, isolating myself from the rest of the world, for what feels like half an hour. It could be longer, could be less. I don't know how anyone tells time around here. There are no clocks on the walls. No one wears watches. The sun doesn't rise and set, so I can't use nature to judge time.

To make sure no one is outside, I put my ear to the door. Cracking it open inch by inch, I look both ways.

The hall is empty.

Sneaking out, I tiptoe to Brad's room then nudge open the door a bit.

Shay clambers from her chair.

"No, don't get up. I wanted to make sure you were with him."

"I will keep you updated, if his condition changes," she says, easing herself back down.

"Thank you." I close the door, then return to my room.

Throwing myself onto the bed, I grab the pillow and bury my head under it. There's never been a time in my life where I've felt I don't fit in. I know what I want, and have been working toward that future. College is the stepping-stone to my veterinary career. I hoped to one day take over our farm, but I guess that life isn't ever going to be mine.

Now that I'm here, almost everyone looks at me like I have two heads, with the exception of Flanna and the children. I was beginning to feel like Arland was accepting me, maybe even liking me, but now I know that's not the truth.

I miss my sister. Brit would know what to do now; she would tell me I could still have the world if I wanted it, she would tell me I deserve better than Arland, she would make me feel loved.

Now, I am alone.

My worst dream—the one of Arland and me inside the cave behind the falls—kindly replays for me. Of course, when he's not here, the dreams invade, when I don't know whether he's alive or dead, and I refuse to walk out of this room to go check.

I sit up. How long have I been asleep? There isn't even the faintest bit of light creeping under the door. It could be late, or early, who knows? Getting out of bed, I move quietly across the floor. Putting my ear up to the wooden slab between me and the rest of the world, I check to see if anyone is in the dining area or hall.

"Kate?" Arland whispers.

I ignore him. He knocks a few times, but I don't answer. Instead, I return to bed and close my eyes again.

Another knock.

"Kate? Open the door, please? If you do not, I will open it myself," Flanna threatens.

"Please, go away."

"Fine." Flanna's voice resonates with irritation.

I stare into the dark space above me for what feels like another hour, or two. Standing, I hug myself as I leave the room. The hallway is quiet, just as before. I sneak to the bathroom, slip out of my clothes, then step into the enclosure, letting the water wash away my tension—the way it did the other day.

The last few days I haven't wanted to be alone, but now solitude is the only thing I crave. I don't want to be away from Brit or Brad, Mom or Gary, just from the pressures of this place, the people who stare at me, Arland . . . especially Arland.

The door groans.

Arland walks in, holding a rusty old lantern in front of him. He doesn't notice me, so I splash around. Startling, he freezes in place.

We lock eyes.

"I am sorry. I was not aware anyone was in here." He takes a few steps backward, toward the door, then stops—as though waiting for me to say something.

"I should have locked the door." My voice is flat, emotionless, revealing probably more than I'd like.

"I . . . I will leave," he says, placing one foot into the hall, then he turns back to me. "Kate?"

I glare at him. "Yeah?"

"Never mind. I should go." He steps out of the bathroom then closes the door.

Is there something he wants to say? Whatever his indecision concerns, I don't care. I know he's alive. But being around him is still too painful and embarrassing.

Arland's disturbance was enough to ruin the ambiance of my dark and solitary bath. I climb out, dry off, then get dressed.

Leaving the bathroom, I discover the hall is not as quiet as before. Flanna and Arland are in the middle of some sort of argument. He has a firm hold on her elbow; she's scowling, with her fists balled at her sides. I swear it looks like she wants to hit him.

Let them argue. Whatever they're fighting over, I don't want to know.

"What time is it?" I ask.

Arland forces a smile. "Midnight."

Midnight? Other than Flanna's slop, I haven't eaten anything today, but I'm not hungry. In five more hours, she'll be up preparing breakfast for the soldiers. I should come out of my room then. Keeping myself isolated is not fair to her, or to the others.

Dreams wouldn't leave me alone last night. I awoke so many times, crying for Arland, Brad, my family, for the loss of a normal life. Sitting up, I clutch the wool blanket to my chest and watch the candle's flickering blue flame. I have to get out of this room and on with my life, but the thought of talking to people makes me dizzy.

No, I won't wallow like this. I sit on the edge of the bed and lean over to put on my boots. I stand and walk toward the door, trembling harder with each step.

Looking down, I make sure I'm somewhat together. The claymore is the only thing missing, but I don't plan on training or going outside today. The sword will stay next to the dresser.

Candles light the hallway, revealing happiness on every inch of the wall. I won't look; the smiles and love are torture to my heart. Staring straight ahead, I enter the dining room, then pull a chair to the loneliest corner, thinking only of myself.

Flanna walks out of her way to brush my arm, but doesn't speak, as she enters the kitchen. Children stream in for their breakfast. Marcus and Anna approach, but Flanna sends them the other direction.

Keeping my eyes down, I don't look at anyone, don't do anything other than play with my fingers, while they eat.

The children filter out as the adults make their way into the dining area. No one attempts to talk to me. The one time I do lift my eyes, my stare meets Perth's. He stares back, but I look away and investigate the back of my hands—the ones Gary says I know the woods like. Does anyone ever really know the back of their hands? Would I recognize mine in a pile of pictures? Probably not.

The adults finish their breakfasts and leave to go about their duties for the day. I don't care that I should be helping with kitchen or stable duties, or that I have not seen Arland since last night, and I don't care that everyone stares at me while I mope about in a funk.

My life is not my own. Even if I want to go back through the portal and leave this world to its own war, I cannot. Not unless I please the gods. Since this *is* my world, being stuck here shouldn't upset me so much, but I wasn't raised in Encardia. I've always thought I was born free and, therefore, able to make my own choices in life. That privilege is not my own.

Spending so much time by myself, I've come to the realization it's not only Arland's lack of feelings that upset me so much; I'm hurt from everything combined. With him protecting me from my dreams of his death, my thoughts of home and Brad, and showing an interest in me, Arland was the bandage I so badly needed. There was still pain, but I was healing.

Flanna interrupts my self-centered thoughts sometime after the second lunch or dinner rush. I really don't know what time of day it is. She put a plate of food in front of me hours ago; I only picked at the chicken, but the thought was appreciated.

"Would you mind helping me clean up? I was thinking of going to the stables afterward," Flanna says, her tone gentle.

I look around the dining room. Flanna has to handle this huge mess by herself. Nodding, I get up, gather plates, push in chairs, and do whatever does not require talk. She doesn't talk to me, either, which I appreciate. The silence must be difficult for her.

Instead, Flanna sings.

Let go of all your fears

May Griandor's light shine upon you
Let go, our world will heal
And one day our moon you will sleep to

Flanna sings the rest of her slow, warming song in a foreign tongue. Her voice is beyond any I have ever heard. I get lost in her melody, even though most of the words, I cannot understand. I hum the tune while she sings, and my heart lifts in my chest.

"Your song is beautiful."

She smiles, but her blue eyes look to be a million miles away. "My mother sang it to me as a child, when I was afraid. But, now, I sing for you."

"Is your mom—?"

"No," Flanna says, before I can finish asking my question about whether her mom is alive or not. "She was killed within the first year. I was three, but I remember it well."

My face warms. "I-I'm s-sorry."

"I would not be alive, if it were not for my cousin. Arland was only a child himself, but somehow he was able to kill the daemon that attacked my mother, and get me inside our home to safety. Neither of us has been there, since that day. My father and uncle took us into hiding. We lived in caves, hunted for our food, moved around every day, but eventually we made it into these underground buildings." She stares into the stone hearth.

"Who built these places?"

"They were built by the Ground Dwellers, years before the war started."

"The Ground Dwellers?"

Shaking her head, Flanna returns to washing dishes. "Arland has not spoken to you about them?"

I gather more plates and cups, then run them into the kitchen. "No."

"They are similar beings to us, but they prefer life underground. If we were not already at war with Darkness, we would most likely be at war with them." She rushes through the explanation as though she'd like to change the subject.

"Why would we be at war with them?" Stopping what I'm doing, I wait for a response.

"They are dark beings. Their magic is used against nature, but at times, we find we need their craftsmanship. Like building these bases."

"Who asked them to build these bases?"

"Our former High Leader."

"He knew the war was coming?"

"I am not aware of what he knew, just that he wanted these bases built. His request might have been an instruction from his prophecy." She picks up a wooden bucket to pour fresh water into the sink. "The Ground Dwellers also create our weapons."

"It sounds like they've done nothing but help. Why would we be at war?"

"Unfortunately, their services always come with a price."

"What kind of price?" I ask, drying a bowl.

"We can talk about it later." Flanna stops to survey the room.

The dishes are washed, tables are clean, and chairs are pushed in. Standing proud, we head through the corridor, up the stairs, and into the stables.

I'm sure Flanna understands, better than anyone else does, why I'm upset. Yesterday, in the stables, she recognized something was wrong with me from the moment my mood changed. I think her song was for Brad, my family, and my life, but her motivation was for my heart. Flanna has become a true friend.

We gather eggs, then sprinkle grain about the floor for the chickens.

Flanna turns on her heel, glowering at me.

"He did not mean it," she says, her voice low and rumbling.

Nearly dropping some eggs, I look at Flanna, dumbfounded. She was just singing to me, talking to me about her mom and life, and now she's angry with me?

"Arland. He. Did. Not. Mean. It."

"If I'm not just someone he has to protect, why would he say it?"

"He was speaking from a leadership position, not from his heart. Most of the soldiers already feel he shows you too much favor, but once Cadman spreads the news of his service to you, their attitudes will change. More importantly, if anyone knew his true feelings, they could use you against him, if they turn from our side," she says impatiently, as though I should have figured this out on my own.

"Did Arland tell you this?"

"No. I know my cousin, and I have never seen him look at anyone the way he looks at you." A crooked smile grows on her face—she's returning to the Flanna I'm used to seeing.

"Thank you."

"You are welcome," she says, closing the feedbag. "Next time I ask you what is bothering you, I expect you to be honest with me."

Flanna's words put the bandage back over my wounded heart, but they have not fixed how upset I am about being trapped here. The gods and goddesses should know I'd be happier to serve out my prophecy, if my family was with me and my friend was safe, but I dare not question a higher power.

"Flanna?"

"Yes?"

"What were you and Arland arguing about in the hall last night?"

"I wanted to speak to you alone. He would not allow it. He felt you were sad about not being able to get through the portal, and that you needed alone time. Men can be obtuse at times."

Arland might be obtuse and not realize his words hurt me, but he was correct in telling her I needed to be alone. I will have to thank him for keeping her away.

We return to our work in the stables. Flanna sings her soothing song while she milks the cows, and I the goats. A few of the little monsters try to eat my hair. I flee their stall, screaming.

Flanna runs out to meet me, hands on her hips. She reminds me so much of Brit. "Why are you going on in hysterics?"

I hold my hair in one hand and point at the animals with the other. "They won't stop eating my hair."

"You might have a way with horses, but these goats have you under their control." She laughs. "Shall we switch?"

"My hero!"

Flanna finishes caring for the goats with no issues. I'm guessing she's had years of experience shooing them away, because none of them tries to eat *her* hair.

Hurrying with the horses, we leave Mirain snorting and stomping her feet as we head back to the kitchen.

Flanna shows me how to make goat cheese, and skims the fat from the cows' milk to make butter. I'm surprised by how little of the soldiers' food supplies are wasted. No more is taken from the animals than what's needed on a daily basis. There's no electricity, so storing would not be an option, but there doesn't seem to be a need for storage, since nothing much is left over. Such a huge difference between our two worlds.

My bones ache from working in the stables and churning butter. Cramps run up my arms and legs, like I've been hard at work forever. "What time is it?"

"I believe it is close to 9:00 p.m."

"Was I really sitting in the corner by myself for that long?"

She lifts her gaze from the vegetables she's chopping. "You were like a rock."

"I'm sorry," I say. And I am; being such a horrible person for nearly two full days was wrong and unfair.

"Do not apologize to me. Arland is the one who had to explain to everyone how you thought your family must have died."

I stop turning the crank on the butter barrel and stare at her, mouth wide open. "What?"

"How else was he to excuse you from duties for two days? You are lucky we kept everyone away from you. You would have felt pretty bad when the others tried to share their stories of pain and suffering with you, in an attempt to make you feel better," she says, full of sarcasm.

"Make me feel *better*?" I ask, not sure how stories of painful loss can help anyone.

"Commiserate, make you feel good; however you wish to look at it."

Flanna is right; if everyone shared their stories of loss with me, I probably would've locked myself in my room for a month. Brad might be sick, but I have not lost him, and I still have a chance to see my sister and mom again. These people have gone through hell. Nothing in my life can compare to anything they've experienced.

"How can you tell what time it is?" This has been bothering me since I arrived.

"We can feel what time it is. You may not see the sun in the sky, but it is there, hidden by Darkness. I can sense it when it rises and sets. Has the sun not always been something you have focused on?"

"I always notice the sun, but here, I cannot feel it." I remember stepping onto the porch the day before our trip, watching the sunrise, and feeling the warmth of its rays on my skin.

Chills crawl across my arms.

"Clear your mind. Close your eyes, and think about the sun."

I do as she instructs, and think only of the bright, orange fireball in the sky, but I don't feel anything. "Nothing."

She closes her eyes and smiles. "Try every day. If you try hard enough, you will feel it."

"Do you do this every night?"

"What?"

"Cook, clean, work in the stables, prepare for the next day."

"Before you arrived here, I had kitchen *and* stable duties. Your help in both has allowed me a lot more free time. I would have finished with everything much earlier, but I allowed you to wallow all day, so we could be alone for a while after dinner."

"It hardly seems fair you have both duties."

"A lot of things are unfair, but we live in difficult times. If you have not noticed, there are not a lot of women around here. When Darkness attacked, most of the women and children were killed first. We were the easiest ones to attack, and the pain of losing us made the men easier targets. It also nearly made breeding impossible, so our chances of survival went down further. Only the strongest of us survived. I am good in the kitchen, and more patient with the animals than most of the men. I was willing to accept these duties."

"You will not have to do them alone again."

"I know, that is why I love you so much. Now, get back to work. I am sure Arland will be here looking for you soon, and we have not peeled the potatoes yet."

"You love me?" I say, playing along.

"How can I not? You have shown me more kindness than most. And you make my cousin smile."

"Where has Arland been for the last two days?" I ask, worrying about his safety for the first time since I stormed away in the stables yesterday.

"He is more than likely trying to figure out how to get you through that portal."

"Oh." I've treated Arland unjustly these last couple days. I don't know if he assumed I was upset with him or not, but he did not deserve the temper tantrum I threw—or the silent treatment.

Flanna hands me a knife, and we peel the potatoes without talking, cubing them and setting them aside for breakfast in the morning. She tells me to go to bed, after I yawn for what feels like the thousandth time, but I'm not skipping out on her. If she has to be awake, I will stay up with her.

We take only a few more minutes to finish preparing the kitchen for tomorrow. Turning to head off to bed, I stop when I see Arland leaning against the wall, with his arms crossed over his chest. He looks nervous, and doesn't greet me with the smile I'm used to seeing.

"Hi!" I say in a high-pitched tone, taking a few steps toward him.

He offers a nervous smile, as he stands straight. "Do you still wish to have alone time?"

I look over my shoulder at Flanna and mouth a silent *thank you*. If it weren't for our talk earlier, I might have told him I *did* want more alone time, and that I'd never bother him again. "No. I'm sorry I was so rude to you earlier."

"You have nothing to apologize for." Arland holds out his arm for me.

I accept, and we go to our room.

Pushing open the door and moving aside, Arland allows me to enter first. I walk toward the bed, but he grabs some towels and my hand, then pulls me toward the bathroom without offering time to protest.

"That bad, huh?" I ask, bringing him into a full fit of laughter.

"You only smell a little like goats," he teases.

"Well you smell like—" I put my nose to his chest and sniff his shirt. "Good. No, I mean, bad." Truthfully, he does smell good; like a man, but also like the forest on a dew-filled morning.

Arland snuffs out the candles burning in the hall while we walk. The only light left burning in the base—at least on this side—comes from the candles we hold in our hands. He opens the bathroom door. Steam from the spring greets us as we enter; the candles flicker out of control. He sets his on the floor next to the enclosure, and I do the same on the other side.

We take off our clothes. I climb into the water first. The bath is refreshing in more than one way—my skin gets clean, Arland and I are talking again, and my heart is less broken. I tell him all about my day with Flanna—leaving out the part about my misunderstanding of his feelings—and how I'm going to help her from now on. He doesn't disagree; she shouldn't be the only woman responsible for feeding an entire army, but he's going to take on stable duty with me. The task will be ours to share. Flanna will no longer be responsible, unless we're not around. Everything seems equal, so I agree; plus, it gives me guaranteed alone time with him.

"Has she professed her love for you yet?" Arland asks, pulling my head to his chest.

I place my hand on the surface of the water and wiggle my fingers, watching the ripples. "She has."

"My cousin does not normally make friends with others."

"She seems nice enough. Why would anyone not want to be her friend?" I lift my head to see his face.

"She is born of Leader blood. People treat her differently."

"Like they do you?"

"As they soon will you."

"If I live." I place my cheek against his chest; warm water plays at the corner of my lips.

"You will live."

"Are people appointed to leadership by blood lines? No elections, no choice?"

"There is only choice for High Leader, but even that is not for the public to decide."

"Who decides?"

"All the Leaders come together to choose."

"How was your father chosen, if he took the position a year after the war began?"

"The decision was made years before. Fifteen men and women are chosen as High Leaders, well in advance of their terms. If something happens, and the duty cannot be fulfilled, another person is ready to take their place. Some on the list never serve."

"Then you know who will take your father's place after he quits—or however that works? How long does someone remain in that position?"

"I will tell you more about being a Leader, but later."

Does he not want to talk about politics? Is there something he has to hide? I listen to his heartbeat speeding up, then slowing down, speeding up, then slowing down. I don't ask, but I am dying to know what he's keeping from me. He opens his mouth, as if to say something, then lets out a deep breath and sits in silence.

I'm so comfortable in his arms, in this endless supply of perfectly warm water, that I drift in and out of sleep.

"Kate?" my sister says.

"Brit?"

"I'm sorry I never told you the truth about who you are. Brit and I are waiting for you to come get us." These are Mom's words, but my sister's voice.

"We can't get through; we've already tried. Arland says Griandor has closed the portal until I fulfill my prophecy."

"Griandor would not do such a thing, but his sister would. Explore your heart, Kate."

"What does that mean?"

"Figure out who . . . ."

"Mom?"

"Kate?" Arland's gentle voice interrupts.

"Mom?" I ask, hoping to hold onto the strangest dream I've ever had.

"I asked if you were ready to sleep, but I already know your answer."

Arland scoops me out of the bath, then sets me down on the floor. He wraps a towel around my body, one around himself, then carries me to our room. Arland returns me to my feet and turns his head.

I strip out of the soggy things, then slip my nightgown over my clean skin. Once dressed, we crawl into our bed, and I curl into him. I've become addicted to the feel of his arms around me, the warmth of his touch on my skin.

"You never allowed me to apologize for not getting through the portal to your family," he says.

Portal? The dream. My mom talking with Brit's voice . . . .

"I believe we should meet my father, soon. Two weeks should be long enough to get everyone ready."

I rest my head on his chest. "Everyone?"

"We will leave a few behind, to care for Brad."

The thought of leaving Brad behind steals air from my lungs. I don't know what to say, so I shake my head. "Does Griandor have a sister?"

"He does. Her name is Gramhara. What makes you ask?"

Yawning, I close my eyes. "A dream I had about my mom."

The rapid beating of his heart fills my ears. "You have very interesting dreams."

"What is Gramhara the goddess of?"

"Love," he says, breathless.

Pulling my head from his chest, I look into his eyes; he stares at the ceiling. Whatever he's thinking about, his thoughts are far away from here. I duck my head back into him and fall asleep.

Chapter Sixteen

Waking up in Arland's arms, after a dreamless night, makes me happier than I imagined a man could make me feel. I'm safe, calm, warm, and happy when I'm with him.

He's still sleeping. Sitting up in our bed, I practice *feeling* the sun. Flanna said I should clear my mind, reach out for it. What better time than now, while I have no one distracting me?

Crossing my legs, I rest my hands on my knees, as if to meditate. Really, I have no idea what I'm doing, but I guess starting this way is as good as any.

Where are you, sun? What time is it?

I don't honestly expect an answer. And of course, I don't get one.

I picture blue ridges on mountains, green leaves on trees, the bright orange horizon, and the rolling pastures of our farm back in Virginia. I think of the swimming hole, the clearing, Darkness, the dying trees, what Encardia would look like if the sun were shining right now. "Where are you, sun?" I ask again, this time a little too loudly.

Arland sits up in bed, concern written all over his face. "Are you having dreams again?"

"No. I'm trying to tell what time it is."

He smiles. "I could tell you."

"No. Flanna told me you can feel it."

"We can . . . *you* can. You have to think about the sky, and where the sun is."

As if I haven't been doing that.

"I'm trying, shh."

He lies back down on the pillow, staring at me, distracting me terribly. "I will be quiet."

Closing my eyes, I think of the pale grays and blues in the morning sky at 5:00 a.m., and the pinks and purples of the clouds when the sun sets. I miss the sun, I need the sun, I *want* the sun. "Where are you?"

My skin warms. I receive a flash of the moon in the western sky, the bright, orange sun peeking over the eastern horizon—like it does around 7:00 a.m. I'm not sure if I'm imagining what I want to see, or if I'm actually *feeling* the sun, like Flanna and Arland tell me I can.

"Is it 7:00 in the morning?"

He sits up. "Yes! You did it. What did the time feel like?"

"Warm. I saw the sun peeking over the horizon."

"You *saw* it?"

My thoughts turn frantic. "Yes, I *saw* it. Why are we still in bed? I promised Flanna I would help her in the kitchen from now on, and we have to go to training and—"

"Calm down, Kate. Flanna was made aware of my plans for us for the day," Arland says, placing his hand over mine. "I have never been able to *see* the sun, and I do not believe anyone else has, either."

I ignore Arland's comment about what he can see. They've already told me I'm different from them; this doesn't shock me as much as it seems to shock him. "What plans?"

He shakes his head; the corner of his mouth twists up. "I would like to take you on a tour."

"I'd like that, but it's so late. Why we are still in bed?"

"I felt you could use the extra rest."

"Arland, I really don't need any special treatment."

He looks deep into my eyes, touching my soul with his gaze. "Kate, you *are* special."

There is something within his eyes, something that tells me he wants more, something that makes my heart race. Every piece of me begs to lean forward and kiss him, but after what happened in the stables, in front of Cadman, I'm not sure I could handle the rejection if Arland denied me.

I laugh nervously and push desire aside. "I hope so; otherwise there's a Seer out there who has wasted a lot of people's time."

Arland crawls from bed then holds out his hand. "Are you ready to get started, then?"

I take hold of him. "Yes."

He pulls me up, and his chest presses against mine. My heart pounds harder. "W-what will we do first?"

He tugs me behind him toward the dresser. "We should eat."

Opening a drawer on the right side, Arland hands me a shirt and pants, then opens the drawer on the left and pulls out clothes for himself. "The children wash and put the clothes away, every day."

"Marcus and Anna told me they had to wash clothes and bed linens."

Arland faces away from me while we dress. "Yes, Marcus and Anna wash. Glenna and Keely gather the dirty clothes and linens and make the beds. Art and Farrell put everything away—and there are so many more that have jobs to do."

I slide the last item into my holster . . . my claymore. "I'm ready."

"After you," he says, holding the door open for me.

The candles burn in the sconces along the walls, flames flickering wildly. "Who lights all the candles?"

He presses his hand against the small of my back, guiding me toward the dining room. "Food first, then questions."

Flanna sings to herself while she wipes the tables clean and pushes in the chairs. When she notices us, she winks at me, then continues with her happy, little song.

I smile at my friend. "Good morning, Flanna."

"Good morning, Kate. Going for a tour today?" she asks, returning my smile.

"Yes."

She clasps her hands together and gets down on one knee. "Promise me that you will not offer to help everyone else with their jobs, too."

"I don't intend to break the promise I already made to help *you*, Flanna."

She dances across the room. Standing in front of Arland and me, Flanna kisses me on the cheek, like she did the first morning I helped around the kitchen. "Arland, you better not let anything ever happen to her."

He places his hand on my shoulder and pushes me forward, into the kitchen. "She will be safe with me, Flanna. You do not have to worry about her."

"What would you like to eat? Eggs, or Flanna's Surprise? It appears as though we have both to choose from," Arland asks, eyeing the food on the counter.

"Flanna's Surprise will be faster."

"I had a feeling you might say that." He spoons some of her slop into two bowls. "Here."

I take the bowls to the nearest table in the dining area, sit down, then inhale my breakfast—which magically tastes like bacon and eggs—before Arland has a chance to set down two cups of water. "You ready?"

He laughs. "May I at least eat half?"

Pushing out my chair, I stand. "Sorry. I'll help Flanna while you finish."

"Not today." Arland catches my hand. "Sit with me."

"O-kay," I say, taking a seat next to him again.

"You do not have to help anyone today."

Almost on cue, Flanna comes by the table, grabs my bowl, then twirls along as she takes them back into the kitchen.

"For the last part of your tour, I would like to take you for a ride."

My breath catches. "Will we be passing the perimeter?"

"No. I have something special I want to show you."

"You're sure nothing can get past the magic?"

"You will be safe." Arland raises his eyebrow. "Are you going to make me beg? Or are you going to trust me?"

I blow my hair from my face. "O-okay," I stutter.

Finishing the last bite of his slop, Arland stands, then pulls out my chair. I expected him to present his arm for me to hold, but instead, he points in front of him, indicating he wants me to walk first.

"We will begin in the soldier's quarters," Arland says, at the same time a group of children stomp down the stairs.

"Hi, Kate," Anna calls, her eyes big.

The other children push past us, and they all run in different directions.

"Hi, Anna. How are you doing today?" I ask my favorite child here.

She hugs onto my waist. "Good. I have missed you."

Her love for me brings on a new wave of guilt from acting like such a baby the last couple days. I hug her back. "I've missed you, too."

"Anna, I am giving Kate a tour of the base today. Would you like to show her where you and your brother wash the clothes and linens?" Arland asks.

She grabs my hand and bounces through the cavernous room where the soldiers sleep. Their thin mattresses, no wider than a twin bed, lay in rows, and appear to be made from down. Gray feathers tumble across the floor like balls of dust. Everyone has a sheet, a lumpy pillow, and a gray wool blanket—not nearly as nice as what Arland and I have. In the right corner of the room, more mattresses are rolled up and tied with rope.

I stop. "Who are those for?" I ask, pointing at them.

Anna smiles. "For new people."

"Where do they come from?"

"Some find us, others we find. Tristan came to us that way," Arland says.

"He told me his family was attacked, but your soldiers saved him before he was killed."

Arland nods. "Yes."

"So these mattresses are waiting for more people like Tristan to come along and occupy them?"

"That is our hope; unfortunately, the soldiers have not found many people to rescue, not like they used to."

"But you found me and my brother, and we have not been here long." Anna bats her lashes at him. "My mother told me you would become the greatest High Leader Encardia has ever seen. She said if anyone could end the war, it would be you."

Arland was chosen to be a High Leader? Why didn't he tell me this? I look at his eyes to check for shock, anger, or some emotion indicating he's upset with her, but he just stands still.

I kneel beside Anna. "Are you from The Meadows, too?"

"No, my brother and I are from the Gorm Mountains."

"Oh." I shouldn't have asked; I have no idea where or what the Gorm Mountains are. "How did your mother know about Arland?"

"Everyone knows, but he has to be bound first—"

"*Anna*," Arland snaps.

She sucks in a sharp breath and stares at her hands. "Sorry."

I don't know how to react. Whatever Anna was about to say, Arland didn't want me to hear. But he's shared so much with me, why would he hide this?

He lifts her chin with his finger and smiles. "We are on a tour . . . ."

Anna nods, then walks to the far left corner of the sleeping quarters. Opening a door, she pulls me into their version of a laundry-bath combo. The room smells of sweet lilacs. Five washboards and tubs are built over the spring. Candles placed in wrought iron chandeliers burn brightly overhead.

Marcus scrubs bed linens over his washboard. Anna runs to her place and adds linens to her tub, alongside her brother.

Arland leans next to my ear. "I am sorry," he whispers.

"Why didn't you tell me?" I keep my voice low, so the children don't overhear.

"I had planned to tell you when I took you on our ride."

Crossing my arms over my chest, I turn and face him. "You couldn't give me a hint? And what does *bound* mean?"

He straightens. "I promise to share everything with you, but not inside."

So many people have kept things from me; I don't want Arland on that list. "Okay, but if you hold any—"

"I will not keep anything from you."

Two little girls walk into the room, carrying more soiled things for Marcus and Anna to wash. I've seen these children before; they're the ones Marcus and Anna are supposed to bring to the next training session.

Arland kneels to speak with the girls. "Glenna, Keely, this is Kate. I know you have seen her around, but I would like you to introduce yourselves."

They dump their loads next to the washtubs, then offer their hands to me.

"I am Glenna, this is Keely." Glenna is the older of the two. She's about a foot taller than Keely, and a foot shorter than I am.

"Nice to meet you. What do you two have to do now that you have brought the dirty things in here to be washed?"

"Make beds," Keely says. She might be all of five years old; brown ringlets hang down to her waist.

My mom carries a picture of my sister and me in her purse. The photograph was taken when we were around Keely's age; she looks like she could be one of us.

"All of them?"

"Yes." Glenna sounds agitated, probably from me slowing them down.

Arland and I follow them out and watch as they make the beds. Experience has made them quite the experts; I've never seen anyone wrap sheets and blankets around a bed that fast.

The door opens behind us while we're watching the children. A woman, whom I've not met, steps in.

"Good morning, Enid," Arland says.

His words bring Enid to a standstill. Her eyes widen, and she wobbles like she wants to take a step back out of the room, but composes herself.

"Morning." Avoiding our eyes, she rushes by and enters the laundry room.

I give Arland what I hope to be a questioning look.

"Ask Flanna," he says. "Thank you, girls, for showing us how well you make beds. We are going to the gardens now."

"Okay." Glenna gives Arland the same smile as Anna did earlier.

"It seems you are good with children, too," I whisper. He's definitely better with them than I thought he was.

"I have a soft spot for them," he whispers.

I wave goodbye to the girls as we head out of the room.

Arland leads me through the dining area, down the hall, and pushes open the door that had been locked when I tried to get through, the other day.

"Why do you keep this door locked?"

"In the past, when our own turned against us, they always attacked the food supplies first. Kill the source of life; kill the people surviving off it."

We come into a huge underground garden. I've never seen anything quite like it. Vegetables cannot grow without natural light, but, somehow, here they do. Everywhere I look, green, lush plants sprout from the ground. All the other children are in here, digging, watering, wheeling dirt around, and collecting food in bins.

"How do the plants grow?" I ask.

Arland clears his throat.

The children look up.

"Most of you know Kate by name, or have seen her around, but I would like you to show her how our garden grows. Will you all, please, give her a demonstration?"

Stopping what they're doing, the boys and girls sit on the ground, hold hands, and chant something. The air warms. The room feels so bright, it becomes difficult to look around, even though there's no more light than before. I have the urge to avert my eyes, but there isn't anything from which to avert them.

The plants grow before my eyes, shooting up about an inch or two. "This is amazing!"

"That is enough. Thank you." Arland turns from the children to me. "The plants respond to our magic. We never farmed food like this, before Darkness came. It is another way we learned to adapt," he says.

"When our own attacked the food, why didn't you just regrow the plants with magic?"

"We need seeds to start a garden; those who turned against us left nothing." Arland shakes his head. "I pray one day I understand their motivation."

"Why don't you use magic against Darkness' army?"

"We do as much as we can, but our magic works with nature, not against it. Even if we could use it to kill, it would not be enough to fight against this kind of evil." Arland whispers as the children work.

"But you can fight with fire, that's magic?"

"Correct. Some magic can be manipulated into fighting. We can use magic to hide things, or open and close doors, make food grow, but—aside from fire—we cannot use our magic to kill."

"Will you help me learn to use magic?" I squeeze my fist and whisper *Solas*, but nothing happens.

He chuckles. "Of course. Have you seen enough, or would you like to see more?"

"We can keep going; I have definitely not seen enough."

Leading me from the garden, Arland explains how Flanna lights the candles throughout both buildings in the morning, and he snuffs them out at night.

The next stop is the communications room. It's the first time I've been able to peek in here. My expectations have not been met. Back home, if someone had said a military communications room would be full of nothing more than a few chairs, I would have laughed. But that's pretty much all there is here—three chairs, and one long table with a small wooden box sitting on the corner, buzzing with static. The contraption appears to be an old radio, but there's no electricity in Encardia.

"What is that on the table?"

"That is a chatter box. When someone wishes to send a message, an announcement is made through the box. We connect to it mentally, but when the message is delivered, an apparition appears in the room."

"An apparition? Like a ghost?"

"No, the person fully materializes, but cannot stay for long. Staying in the device takes a lot of energy and concentration. Aside from the box to communicate with other bases, we can also connect with people, which is why we have this quiet room back here."

"You don't need the box for that?"

"No."

I nod. It's the best I can come up with. A telepathic army is like something from science-fiction movies, not from reality—certainly not my own.

Arland closes the door and leads me up to the stables. "Mirain has missed you."

"I was acting very selfishly," I say, guilt creeping into my thoughts once again.

"You have handled yourself quite well. If it had been me leaving a happy world full of sunshine, I might have tried to escape this place to get back there, several times by now."

So he did think I'd try to escape. I knew he wasn't worried about anything getting into the stables. "No, you wouldn't."

Arland looks down at me and smiles. I know he would never leave his people, and neither will I. It wouldn't be right, even if I have only recently discovered Draíochtans; they are my own and need help.

Mirain sighs a few times when I walk into her stall.

I rub her between her eyes. "Hey there, girl."

I use the wall to help me mount, but Arland stands in the stall with me. "Are you going to get on Bowen?"

"I would like for you to ride with me."

I slide from Mirain. "Next time, girl."

She whinnies when I leave.

Arland climbs onto Bowen, offers me his hand, then pulls me up. Wrapping my arms around Arland's waist, I lean into his back.

"Where are we going?"

"To the river."

Once clear of the stables, Bowen gallops at full speed, following the familiar path toward the perimeter. I'm not used to sitting on the rear of a horse, but I could get used to holding on to Arland this way. I lock my hands around him. His torso blocks the cold air from hitting me, and his muscles flex more strongly, the harder he rides. I enjoy the closeness of our bodies, how right I feel when we touch.

Arland turns Bowen left off the path. Our pace is much slower through the trees. I try blocking the thoughts of daemons jumping onto me from the branches, but I can't. Fear pricks up my arms. My hold on Arland tightens, and I look all around.

He glances over his shoulder. "Kate, there is nothing to be afraid of. I had my men run a thorough check of the spell around the perimeter, before bringing you out here."

"But daemons can get through, though, right?"

"They can pass through, but would not know you are here."

"Flanna told me the spells can fail."

Arland clasps one of his hands over mine. "Everything is going to be okay."

His touch calms me; I decide to trust him—not that I ever haven't. I rest my head on his back again and allow him to ride Bowen without further distractions.

The sounds of rushing water become louder, the farther along we ride. I cannot see anything, but we must be very close to the river. The trees here are greener than those closer to the main path; the grasses growing up around us still have life in them. Bowen's hooves clop as he steps on small rocks lining the ground. Arland rides us forward for another five minutes, then stops at the edge of a cliff. The sound of the water is deafening.

"We are here."

"Where?"

"As close to home as we can get."

"The Meadows?"

"Yes." He climbs down Bowen, then offers me a hand.

I take hold of Arland and slide from the horse. "Do you miss your home?"

"I miss my mother, mostly." His voice is quiet and full of sadness.

"I'm sorry. I wasn't old enough to understand the loss of my dad, but I wish I knew him," I say, trying to empathize with Arland.

He points across the dark space in front of us. "The Meadows is about thirty miles on the other side of this river."

I feel the emptiness around us, and hear the river flowing below, but I cannot see more than ten feet.

Arland turns to me. "From time to time, I come out here by myself, so I can think. I feel close to my mother here, to the past, to hope for a better future. All the leaders from around the world lived there; it is where we will live when this is over."

Part of me wants to blurt the question *together*, but I don't. He's brought me to his special place, where he feels close to his mother, and where he comes to think when times are tough—I'm not going to take anything away from what this section of the forest means to him.

"You asked who Perth is," Arland says, his tone flat.

Fear builds and rises in me. "Y-yes."

"Perth is a Ground Dweller. His people built the underground structures we now call home."

"Flanna told me. She also said there was a price that had to be paid." My palms sweat. Something tells me this conversation is not going to end well. "Arland, what price had to be paid for their help?"

Arland grips my hands in his. "*You* were the price."

Thankfully he's holding me up, because I could fall over any second. "Excuse me?" I say, shivering.

His words stole warmth from the air.

"Perth's father, Leader Dufaigh, was jealous of your father and the reverence so many people had for him. The Ground Dwellers knew from their own Seer, a war was coming, and they were aware you were going to be an important part of that war, but they did not know, fully, to what extent."

"What did my involvement in the war have to do with my father?"

"Dufaigh, and our High Leader at the time, were threatened. Your father was already powerful; having a daughter who would play an important part in ending a war made him practically unconquerable."

"Unconquerable? What could conquer him?"

"A quest for power. The Ground Dwellers wanted it—and still do—and the High Leader did not want to lose it. Your father had plans to restructure the way we govern our world. He wanted Leaders to be chosen, not appointed by blood."

"He wanted a democracy? Elections?"

"Yes. He did not think it was fair to have High Leaders chosen years in advance, before knowing what their true personalities were like."

"But that's fair. Why would they not want that?"

"Your father would have won the initial elections without any problems. Dufaigh and the High Leader were selfish, and afraid of losing everything, so they made a deal for you to be bound to Perth by marriage."

I ball my fists, clench my teeth. "So bound means marriage?"

"Yes."

"Then that's it? My life is not my own. I already belong to Perth?"

"No, not yet. Before a proper marriage takes place, your mother must cast a Binding spell over you and Perth. Even if she were here, I doubt she would willingly do so. However, if you are discovered, I am positive the Ground Dwellers would seek a way around your mother."

I draw in a deep breath. "And why would any of this hurt my father?"

"They were sure your father would lose the election if he was connected to the Ground Dwellers."

"Were they right?"

"The changes never took place. Shortly after the deal was made, your family disappeared."

"Because I was born, and my parents had to get me away?"

"Yes, and Dufaigh could not have been more pleased by the disappearance."

"With my father out of the picture, why am I still promised to Perth?"

"When the war began, news of your prophecy made it around to some of the other Leaders. Dufaigh thirsted for power, so he decided not to rescind the marriage agreement. For fear of what the Ground Dwellers might try to do to me, my father kept quiet about my part in your future. But I imagine when they learn we have been sharing a bed, they will try to kill me," Arland says, taking my hands and squeezing.

My head feels like it will explode. I cannot believe someone would think it's okay for my marriage rights to be *taken* away. As if I'm something that can be traded for favors.

I want to yell at the world, tell off whoever it was who made this deal. "Arland, I am not the type to be told what I can and cannot do. *I* will decide who and when I will marry."

Arland doesn't respond.

There's so much he's been holding back, about me, about him, about *everything*. "What did your prophecy say about you?" I demand.

"That I would be Keeper of Light," Arland says, leaving out loads of detail, I'm sure.

"What else?" I demand again.

Arland kicks a pebble into a tree.

"What else?" I ask, my voice a little weaker this time.

He leads me to a boulder a few feet away, and we sit down. "Are you sure you want to know?"

"Yes, I'm sick of not knowing as much as everyone else."

"Prophecies are not always definite—people and visions can change. Sometimes they do not make any sense to us, and sometimes they are clear."

"I get it."

"My prophecy said I would be Keeper of Light, forever, even after Darkness fades. It stated, as long as I held Light in my arms, she would be safe, powerful, and the world would be guarded from evil. Light's happiness means Encardia's Light. There is a lot of other information that does not make much, if any, sense."

He's already given me enough to make my heart stop.

We have to be together for Encardia to be safe, but how can Arland and I have a future when there are those who seek power, and know he stands in their way? "So, if Perth's father was aware of this, he would kill you for it?"

Arland stares at our fingers laced together. "If Perth, or any Ground Dweller, knew who you were, they would kill me. Never in our history has a Coimeádaí *not* fallen in love with the one he was protecting."

Is he trying to tell me something? The dreams I've had for years—of Arland holding me, us making love—they were all true. Maybe not entirely, but I was so happy in his arms, so at ease. The world was almost always bright and cheerful when we were together. It wasn't until he died that the dreams became dark, except for the one of us in the cave behind the falls. "Can't your father reverse the promise made to Leader Dufaigh?"

"While it is possible for my father to do that, he will not. Our people do not need a reason to war with each other while Darkness is here."

"But—"

"He has to maintain peace, Kate. There is nothing he can do—no matter what he knows."

"So, he'll let the Ground Dwellers make decisions for him and allow the world to die?"

"He is not controlled by the Ground Dwellers, and the world will not die. But another war would give Darkness the opportunity to finish us off."

"Did your prophecy mention anything about *you* dying?"

"No. And Perth does not know, and cannot find out, who you are."

"But you told him I'm from The Meadows. Won't he be able to put it together?" I ask, suddenly concerned about everything I've said and done and every step taken since I've been here. Would it be enough for Perth to realize who I am? He stared at me for the longest time while I sat in the dining room yesterday; does he already know?

"He would not be expecting you to say you are from The Meadows. Your family has been missing for over twenty years. But I am sure his father has told him of your prophecy. If we discover your magic, we will have to keep it from him. I will not allow him to be Bound to you, even if I have to fight everyone to protect you."

"Why would you do that for me?"

"Tell me something. Do you feel different when you are around me?"

"Y-yes," I stammer. I'm afraid I might have a heart attack if this rapid pace keeps up.

"You fight better around me, you can *see* the sun when you are near me—"

"Do you think you have something to do with my magic?"

Arland smiles nervously. "My prophecy said you would be safe *and* powerful in my arms. I believe I might have something to do with it."

If I had to describe every feeling coursing through me right now, my explanation would come out all confused—which is probably the best way to sum them up. I get the sinking suspicion I'm not the only one with emotions here, but he still resists getting any nearer to me.

I'm shaking; anticipation, frustration, fear, excitement, anger . . . I'm not even sure why.

Arland puts his arm around my shoulder and pulls my head onto his chest; his heart pounds.

"I am sorry," he says.

"What are you sorry for?"

"That I had to bring you out here to tell you this. I did not feel comfortable talking about it where someone might overhear."

"It was for the best; if you told me back there, I might have hurt someone." I try to make light of the situation.

"And I am sorry for what Anna said."

"She's a child; they know nothing about secrets."

He laughs.

"So, in order for you to become High Leader, you have to be Bound to someone?"

"Yes."

I bite my tongue, afraid to ask if he's been promised to someone else, the way I have. His response has the potential to break my heart.

"Perth watches you."

"I've noticed."

Sitting alone in the dark on a huge rock by the rushing river, we both fall silent.

Arland caresses my arm, fingers trailing lightly over my skin. Even in times like these, he makes me feel different, happy, *strong*. The thought of him being killed for spending time with me—for helping me figure out how to save this world—angers me. He has been so kind, honorable, and honest.

Bowen trots over, stands next to us, then grazes on the grass. The jingles of his gear make me think about church bells, weddings, white dresses, cakes, Perth.

The sound makes me want to vomit.

"If the High Leader had not promised me to Perth, would I have had the choice of who I wanted to marry?"

Arland shifts on the rock. "No."

"If not Perth, then who?"

"Me. But I would not have allowed the Binding if you did not wish to marry me," Arland rushes the words out on one long breath.

"Interesting." I would not have enjoyed being *forced* to marry anyone, but the thought of being Bound to Arland is not a bad one. I already know what sleeping with him would be like. We've spent happy and sad moments together—my dreams as well as my time here have shown me these things. He will make a good leader; his people here love him. By the way he acts around the children, I can tell he would make a good father.

"The plans for restructuring were never adopted, leaving you and me third in line to rule. Encardia has never had two High Leaders at one time; we were to be the first. While my father favored the idea of elections, he also favored the idea of his son being a major part of history. He was furious at the deal made between Leader Dufaigh and Maoilriain, the High Leader," Arland says, interrupting my daydream of a marriage between us.

"And if I'm with Perth, we can't be High Leaders together?"

"You would be considered a Ground Dweller. All of their kind is dark; peace is not a word they understand or appreciate. Many years ago, a council of Draíochtans decided Ground Dwellers would never be appointed as High Leaders. I am sure Leader Dufaigh has a plan to change that, as well. One more reason they cannot discover who you are."

"Why don't you send Perth to another base, somewhere far away?"

"I wish I could do that, but I cannot," he says, his tone flat, defeated.

"But you're a Leader, and this is your base. Why can't you?"

"When the war began, Perth's father felt it would be a good idea to put him here, as a reminder to me—to any future Leader—the Ground Dwellers are powerful. If we outright refused Perth being placed here, suspicions would be raised."

"Dufaigh put Perth here to hurt you, because he stole your future from you?"

"Yes, I believe that was the point." In bed this morning, I noticed something within Arland's eyes, but thought it was desire for more of me. He's in pain—his life and future have been stolen from him.

There has to be a way to sway Arland's father, or even Dufaigh. "Maybe we can change all of their minds."

"What are you planning?"

"I'll think of something." Really, I have nothing, but I will not stop searching until I find a way.

"I hope whatever you come up with is crafty enough to convince them."

"I hope so, too." I want to live in a world where I'm free to choose—I also want others to be free to choose—and right now I want nothing more than to stay in Arland's arms forever.

We ride Bowen back to base. I clasp my arms around Arland even tighter than before. He rests one palm over my hand. We don't speak, but I know he feels something as strong for me as I do for him. If something happens to Arland, and a future comes where I have to marry Perth, I'm going to jump into the first portal I find and go somewhere else, assuming I figure out how to open one.

Chapter Seventeen

"Are you sure I should come in? It's a meeting with people other than Lann and Flanna. Won't someone be suspicious?" I ask Arland, arms crossed over my chest.

He sighs, placing his hand on the communications room door. "You do not have to worry about anyone inside here. Even if one of them discovers your identity, they would not share with Perth."

I swallow hard. Two weeks have gone by since I learned of my future with Perth. The knowledge has not negatively impacted my relationship with Arland. If anything, it's made us closer, but concern for his life guides my every decision. "I'm ready."

Arland pushes open the door then stands aside, allowing me to enter the room first.

Flanna turns away from a conversation with Saidear and grins. "Took you long enough. I was beginning to think the goats finally ate *you*, Kate."

I smooth my new shirt, free of goat holes. "Not today, but they tried."

Laughter fills the room.

Lann, Kegan, Cadman, Keith, and Dunn sit around the table with Flanna and Saidear; yellowed maps lay before them.

The night Arland and I returned from our ride to the river, Flanna was waiting. She looked from our connected hands to him and said, "We have to find a way."

Flanna didn't have to say anything else; I knew what she meant. My mind has been in constant motion, trying to find a way around the Ground Dwellers without creating another war, but so far, I've come up empty. Now, instead of focusing on Perth, we're planning a move for the soldiers. Arland and I are going to Wickward to meet his father, but the others will relocate to Willow Falls, another base about fifty miles from here.

Cadman stands and pulls out a chair at the head of the table.

"Kate," he says, pointing at the seat.

"Thank you." I join the soldiers and glance over the aged maps. They appear to have been balled up, smoothed out, and straightened so many times, I'm afraid to touch them.

"We are here," Cadman says, pointing at a group of trees labeled *Measctha Forest*, in the middle of a map.

Keeping my hands to myself, I study the landscape; the Gorm Mountains are located to the west and form an arc leading northeast of us. The Iníon na Réaltaí River is to our east. Beyond the river are The Meadows and Attaigh Ocean. The clearing is to our south. "Where is Willow Falls?"

Arland moves a chair from the opposite end of the table, then places it next to me, but remains standing. "I forget how few families owned maps. Willow Falls is located to the north . . . here, along the same river we are near, and Wickward is just northeast of that."

I keep my eyes down, afraid to look up. Anyone from this world should know its geography. I may have just revealed too much. Put Arland even more at risk. Put *this world* even more at risk.

"As most of you are aware, Kate and I need to move to Wickward," Arland interrupts my state of panic, and everyone directs their attention to him. "The population of daemons in the area has increased rapidly. I have never seen such a large gathering. I cannot, in good conscience, leave everyone here . . . ."

Saidear clears his throat and stands.

"Do you have something to say?" Arland asks.

The soldier places his hand over the bronze hilt of his sword, gripping so hard, his knuckles turn white. "This has become our home. We should fight."

"Saidear, I understand your connection to this place. We have been here together many years, but it is time to go."

Saidear tips his head in my direction. "Time, because of your connection with Kate? She is the reason we need to leave?"

Cadman did exactly as Flanna said he would, and now everyone knows Arland is my Coimeádaí.

Arland paces in front of the table, meeting eyes with each soldier he passes. "We have been in hiding too long. We will fight, just as you wish for us to do, but not here. Our numbers will be stronger once we are with the others at Willow Falls—"

"But you and Kate are continuing to Wickward. What is her place in all this?" Saidear asks, staring at me, eyebrow arched.

I knew they'd be suspicious. I shouldn't be in this meeting. It could cost everyone's life. Scooting out of my chair, I stand.

"Sit down," Arland says, his voice heavy.

Defiance makes me want to stick out my tongue and run from the room, but I do as he instructs.

Arland stops pacing and rubs his chin between his thumb and forefinger. "My father is High Leader; I do not expect him to inform me of every decision he has made. He wants Kate and me at Wickward, and he wants us to come alone. As your Leader, I am telling you that you cannot stay here. There is something brewing with those daemons, and our numbers will be stronger at Willow Falls. My father wants to fight, he wants to end this war, but we must pick our battles wisely."

Saidear releases the grip on his sword and returns to his seat, but scrutinizes me.

He knows. I don't know what, but he knows something about me. I pray Arland is right; none of these soldiers will tell Perth I am someone different.

"Keith, are you still willing to stay behind with Kegan to watch over Brad?"

"I will remain behind, but I wonder why we will not bring the boy with us."

Arland turns his head toward me, holding my gaze, while he answers Keith. "His condition has not improved. Traveling with someone as ill as he is would slow us down and increase our chances of encountering daemons. It will be safer to move him when the Collectors come by boat for the animals."

This morning, when Arland informed me we'd make the trip to Wickward Mountain in three days, the reality of leaving my friend behind hit me hard. How could Arland want Brad to be carted off with the animals, like an afterthought? I cried . . . a lot, but the more Arland explained how it was safer for Brad *and* everyone else, the more it made sense.

I nod.

Keith leans back in his seat and smiles. "I can handle a week without responsibility."

Arland jerks his head in Keith's direction. "You will have plenty to be responsible for. Kegan is not a trained soldier; he is a Healer. And Brad has no defense. You will be responsible for both their lives."

The smile fades from his face.

"Cadman, you need to move weapons from the training facility and take an inventory. Everyone should have at least three methods of protecting themselves."

"Yes, sir. When would you like me to begin?"

"Tomorrow." Arland sets to pacing again. "Flanna, Willow Falls is at least a two-day trip; make sure we take enough food with us for two meals a day."

Flanna crosses her arms over her chest. "Of course."

He stops in front of Lann. "I want you to keep watch over the daemons. If you find their numbers increase dramatically, or if they get any closer to our perimeter, we will leave sooner. Saidear and Dunn," Arland says, moving toward the other soldiers, "choose four of our best. You two will be in charge of maintaining security while we are moving."

The two men tip their heads at Arland.

"Again, we will leave in three days. Kate and I will part ways with you when we arrive at Willow Falls. Now, if you will excuse us, she and I need to go to the training facility while the others tend to their duties."

He's scheduled a private training session to work with bows. Since they are the weapon of choice for most of the soldiers, Arland's under the impression I will find them valuable, as well. I don't mind, since the training will afford me alone time with him. *And* I won't have an audience to be embarrassed in front of, if I'm horrible.

Flanna gets up first, then stands next to me. "Thanks for getting the milk. Lunch would not have been the same without it—and since I no longer have *time* . . . ." She glares at Arland, but it's all in good humor.

Last week, he cleared me from lunch preparations. I was a little overwhelmed with my rigorous schedule of kitchen duty, training, private lessons with the children, cleaning the stables, working with the horses, and spending time with Brad.

But Flanna hasn't let her cousin hear the end of it.

I don't know how she handles everything around here with such ease; I have to give her credit. She's always in such a pleasant mood, too—singing, laughing, and playing jokes on the children and soldiers. The sun may not shine, but Flanna adds as much, if not more, warmth as the sun.

"It was your idea," Arland says, eyebrow arched.

She sighs. "Just because I said she was falling asleep during lunch did not mean I wanted her to be taken away from me. I miss her. Who else can I nag to cut potatoes?"

He laughs. "In a few days, we will be at Willow Falls, and you will no longer be responsible for cooking." Arland pulls out my chair, then takes me by the hand, helping me up. "We must go."

We leave the room and walk up the stairs leading outside.

I don't expect to be skilled with bows, just like I'm not good with magic. Of all the spells he's shown me, I've not been able to do more than create a quick spark in my hand—like a lighter without fluid—or slam a few doors in my own face.

Arland has been kind not to laugh at me. I've never had a boyfriend before, but I'd like Arland to be my first. The gentle, caring nature he shows me, and his people, is so alluring, it makes him even more desirable. Any doubts I had about his feelings for me have disappeared. Instead of holding my hand, he now laces his fingers with mine when we walk through the woods or up to the stables. When he has to leave me, even for a short time, his absence is preceded by a kiss to my hand, or my forehead when we're somewhere private.

We enter the training facility alone.

"Choose a bow from the table, and meet me back at the first long hall," Arland says.

I pick up the first bow on the table, then hurry back to him.

He steps behind me, puts his right arm over mine, guides my hands and fingers to the proper places on the weapon, then takes the bow in his left hand. "Relax your muscles, Kate."

Arland shows me how to notch the arrow. "Keep your bow facing the ground until you are ready to aim and shoot. Aim slightly above your target to make up for the drop the arrow will have over the distance. When you release, do not think about it; just let it fly." He takes a step back.

"Like this?" I look at the target and aim slightly above the bull's-eye, lift the bow, pull back, then let the arrow go, as he said.

It falls to the ground, about ten feet in front of the target.

"Oops." I laugh.

Arland steps up with his own bow and demonstrates how it should be done. He hits the target dead in the center.

"Show-off!" I exclaim.

Arland gives me an encouraging smile. "Try again."

On my second try, the arrow skids across the floor about fifteen feet in front of the target. Twelve more times I attempt, each time missing terribly. The arrow hurts my fingers. The bow feels awkward in my hand. Thankfully, this is a private lesson; otherwise, I would have been humiliated in front of the others.

Arland releases another arrow into the center of the target. "I believe we have found a weapon you are not skilled with. It is a good thing, too. I was beginning to feel like you might not need me."

"Of course I need you," I say, putting a double meaning on my words.

Arland smiles wryly. "Would you like to try again?"

I glare at him.

"It was just an offer." He puts up his hands in surrender. "We do not have to continue. You will be much better off with a sword. But I will never leave your side, so the likelihood you will even need to use it is slim."

Arland points me toward the weapons table.

"Thanks for the vote of confidence," I tease.

We leave my bow behind, and I re-arm myself with the claymore. Arland holds my hand as we exit the center; his thumb caresses mine. Every time he shows these simple little affections, my heart hurts for more of him—for us finally to take that step. But, then I worry about Perth, and I try to push the longing away.

Halfway between the training center and the base, Arland stops.

"What is it?" I ask, as quietly as possible, afraid something might be following us.

Arland faces me. His jaw is set, his eyes serious. "I need to share something with you."

My heart skips a few beats. "Is something out here?"

Arland puts his hands on my shoulders and gives them a slight squeeze, dissolving my tension. He pulls me against him and wraps his arms around me. "Everything is okay."

With us this close, I think he's right—everything *will* be okay.

"Kate, I pray to the gods this does not come across the wrong way." Arland looks up to the black sky, then returns his burning green gaze to me.

I tip my head back to see him; our faces are so close.

"The last few weeks, since you arrived, I have changed. I never in my life expected to feel so connected, so in-tune, so close to someone. I have not been this happy since before my mother was killed."

Arland doesn't have to say anything else; my feelings equal his.

I smile up at him. "Me, too."

His confession was much nicer than mine was; I'm afraid if I try to speak, my words will all come out in a jumble. But I think what I said was enough for Arland to understand my feelings.

Our bodies press against each other, sending excitement over every inch of my skin. He uses one hand on my back to pull me closer to him, as if I'm fragile, while his other hand cups my cheek. I'm surrounded by Arland's warmth. He gazes into my eyes—into my soul—and my pulse races. I wrap my arms around his neck.

Arland takes his time, giving *me* time to memorize this moment, as he leans his head down, closes his eyes, and presses his mouth to mine. He parts my lips, slowly and sweetly. I ignore the fact we're in a dark forest in a world full of turmoil, ignore everything while we kiss. Arland digs his fingertips into my back, pulling me even closer, stealing my breath away, and making me want this to last forever.

My body is on fire; everything I've felt for Arland, since meeting him in real life and from years of dreaming of him, all flows freely out of me and into this greeting of our lips.

Arland's kiss deepens, becoming more intimate. He moves his hand from my face to caress my shoulder. Tracing his fingertips down my arms, Arland sends chills along them. He takes my hands into his own and moves his head back.

"Mmm," he manages to say through my favorite wide smile.

"Arland—" I begin, but he cuts me off with another sweet kiss, making me gasp for air.

His lips are so warm, so soft, so gentle; I'm totally lost in this moment. I have no idea what I was going to say to him.

He pulls back with another smile.

"You wanted to say something." His voice is low, throaty, flooded with seduction.

"I-I—" I'm unable to formulate a coherent thought. There is so much I want to say. I want to tell him we should stay this way forever, that we should run away together, that I've fallen head over heels for him, but my brain melts into mush, leaving me flustered by his kisses.

He squeezes me in his arms. "You do not have to say anything."

This moment is so much different from what I experienced with Brad. There is no confusion for me or Arland; we both wanted this kiss. *I've* wanted to share this exchange since the first night we bathed together. The buildup of anticipation wasn't ever there with Brad. When he heals—if he heals—this is going to break his heart, but I push these thoughts from my mind and enjoy myself.

Locked in an embrace, Arland and I stare into each other's eyes. There are so many unspoken words and new concerns, but I try not to worry. I stand on my toes to kiss Arland again.

The bushes rustle.

He tightens his hold on me. "Move away slowly. Remember, the daemons cannot see us, but you will be able to see them."

We turn and walk toward the base, but I look over my shoulder.

A coscartha emerges from the Darkness.

I close my eyes. "I-it's behind us . . . ."

"Open your eyes, Kate. It has turned off the path," Arland says, rubbing my hand.

Trembling, I glance around and take a deep breath. "I-I'm sorry. I don't have any idea how I'm supposed to save everyone when *one* daemon scares me so much."

"We will—"

Shrieks come from our right.

Arland stops and stands still.

"What? W-What is it?" I look everywhere, at everything. Arland is listening. Is he afraid? Has the spell broken?

A twig snaps, echoing through the forest.

He jerks his head toward the sound.

"Run," Arland says, pushing my shoulder.

The blood in my hands runs cold; my knees wobble. I can't run. I look up at him. "Ar—"

A lone coscartha jumps at Arland from behind a tree, claws poised to kill.

I push him to the side, and in one concise motion, remove my sword from my holster and stab the daemon through the chest.

All around us, the forest lights up with millions of brilliant colors; reds, golds, whites, blues, and so many others. I look down at my sword; it blazes with bright, blue flames, similar to the one Arland created in his hand, but a million times more powerful.

The daemon writhes on the ground, twisting and screaming as the fire steals its life.

The yellow light I followed in the forest, which led me to Encardia, swirls around me, more intense than the other colors.

Arland stares, probably in shock, at the bright forest around us. He shakes his head, snapping out of his trance. "We have to get you inside. Now!"

Turning me by my shoulders, Arland pushes me to run as fast as I can.

More creatures approach behind us. I hear each of their feet hit the earth as they run, trying to catch us.

I count footsteps, making notes about our opponents.

"If we run to the base, they'll know where we are. Everyone will be at risk." I gasp for air.

"Let's turn and fight. There are only three of them." I have absolutely no idea where this bravery comes from.

Arland pushes me forward. "I do not want you to get hurt."

"Then help me fight."

I stop running.

Arland crashes into me, but I move around him and face the daemons.

I'm so mad at these creatures for ruining our first kiss. An angry rage burns inside me, boiling in my blood. I let it flow through me, but instead of being blinded by rage, I feel powerful, capable . . . willing.

Three of the gray, mangled coscarthas move forward, encircling us as a predator might hunt down its prey.

Holding my sword ready to strike, I close my eyes.

Please help us, God.

Opening my eyes again, I find the world has taken on a different appearance. Everything is filled with bright light. The Darkness above our heads has split open; the sun shines through the trees, illuminating the brown forest. It's been so long since I've seen the sunshine, I have to shield myself from the blinding rays.

The plants around us don't waste time—they stretch up their limp leaves and limbs toward the sky, reaching for the same thing from which I'm shielding myself.

Slinking back into the surrounding Darkness, the daemons squint their black eyes and stare up at the sky. They look at each other, then us. Without a fight, they run away.

Arland turns me around again. "Go!"

Reaching the base, I pull up the door in the ground and jump inside with him right behind me. He slides the bar over the door, locking it.

The dark stairwell pulsates with blue light.

I am glowing.

Arland pins me against the wall by the stairs. "You never cease to amaze me. You *are* Light!" he says, moving in to kiss me again, this time much more intensely. Near-death experiences seem to make people's emotions run wild.

Pulling away, he breathes heavily. "It would have been much easier if this did not happen."

"If what didn't happen?" I ask, just as breathless.

Captivating me with his eyes, he cups my cheek in his palm and rubs his thumb across my skin. "If I did not fall in love with you."

I smile, but have no words to offer. I *am* deeply in love with Arland. I've never imagined how easy it could be, but here I am, a few weeks into knowing someone, and I've fallen for him. No longer am I confused by my feelings for Brad. While I know I love him, it's nothing like what I feel now. And no longer do I believe these are remnant emotions from my dreams. For the first time in my life, I know what I want, and I have him.

Arland releases me from the wall. The distance between us drains me. "I have to speak with Lann and figure out how we had a perimeter breach. Then we should ride out to the clearing."

"Why are we going to go there again?" I ask, not wanting to move from this spot.

"The yellow light, your dream about Griandor having a sister, the portal being closed—everything is connected. It *was* Griandor's sister who brought you here; I am almost positive. Gramhara is the goddess of love. It is love that brings magic out of you."

All this time, the answer has been right in front of me. The key to getting Brad home, the key to seeing my sister, my mom, the farm—it all springs from my love for Arland. My dreams—all of the passionate moments, all the *I love you*s, and the pain of losing him—must have been clues to my magic, my power.

Arland gives me a slight shake. "Kate, breathe!"

I let out the breath I didn't realize I was holding. "I'm breathing. I'm just in shock. We're really going back to the clearing? Do you think it will work?" I think of my sister's witty comments, and my mom, and how much I need to talk to her . . . and how much I miss them both. We might even have a chance to get Brad home before we have to leave for Wickward. I want to kiss Arland again, but it's too dangerous. We've already risked enough.

"Yes, of course I believe it will work. We will take Flanna and Cadman with us again. Let me go speak to Lann. Wait inside the corridor, so no one sees you." Arland pushes open the door, pulls me through, then runs to the communications room.

I've daydreamed about our first kiss since I arrived here; this was not what I thought we'd be doing after our moment. I definitely didn't expect to be riding off to the clearing afterward, but I'm excited at the prospect of us getting through this time.

Arland entered the communications room alone, but he comes out with Cadman following on his heels.

"Flanna," Arland yells.

"I hear we are going to the clearing again," Flanna says, poking her head inside the doorway.

I smile broadly at my little spy friend.

"Whoa, you are radiant." She grabs my shoulders and looks me up and down.

"Since you have been eavesdropping, I do not need to repeat the mission to *you*. Go ready the horses," Arland barks at her.

Flanna practically skips from the room.

"Cadman, we are riding to the clearing again. I believe we may have found a way to get through."

Glancing at my glowing body, Cadman nods, then heads up the stairwell.

Arland grabs my hand and pulls me toward the communications room.

Lann meets us outside the door, offering a short bow to Arland, but doesn't look at me. How could he not find my appearance strange?

I stare at my hands for a moment, smiling as the blue fire dances on my skin and up my arms. *I* find my appearance strange.

"Gather any soldiers remaining outside, and bring them in. Leave only the best fighters to hunt down the rogue daemons, then reset the spell. If we do not return, you are not to come looking for us. If you do not hear from us by tomorrow, send word to my father, then leave for Willow Falls." Arland's instructions are clear, as usual.

Lann nods. "I am sorry for failing you, sir. I am glad you two are okay."

"We were lucky, but I am worried we need to move sooner. We will discuss this upon our return."

Arland laces his fingers with mine again, and we head down the hall. Instead of him leading me up the stairs into the stables, I lead him. We run up, still full of energy from the kiss, fight, and power—at least, that's how I feel.

Mirain's wild neighs fill the stables. Rushing toward her, we round the corner and discover she's only being miserable for Cadman.

"Mirain! Calm down, girl," I say, keeping my voice firm.

She looks me over, snorting and shaking her head.

"I'll take her from here, Cadman. Thank you."

We all mount our horses and wait for the doors to open.

"Kate, follow close on my right," Arland shouts. "Cadman, Flanna, I want you two to flank us. Ride fast!"

"Uh, Arland, why are we riding in a tactical formation?" Flanna asks.

"We were attacked in the woods by daemons. I am concerned they will communicate our location to the others. Now, we need to move."

"Why are we riding to the clearing, if the base may be attacked while we're gone? What about Brad? The children? If we leave them while the perimeter is down, will they be able to fight off the daemons?" I ask before I can stop myself. More than anything, I want to go; I'm desperate to get to my family, but I don't want anyone here to get hurt.

"There are plenty of soldiers here to protect everyone. My men are scouring the forest as we speak. They will reset the spell, and everyone will be safe."

"What if—?"

"I do not know how it broke. Spells can fail, but they can also be reset." He leans over and presses his hand to my thigh. "And we are going because I promised you would see your family again. If your mother has any shred of this world left in her, she has been waiting for you on the other side of the portal since your sister returned home."

"The dream I had a couple weeks ago—Mom was the one who told me about Griandor's sister. She also said she and Brit were waiting for me. Even if that was real, do you think they'll still be there?"

He nods. "Yes, I believe they will still be waiting for you."

Anna's smile, and her big brown eyes, flash in my mind. I cannot risk everyone's lives for another possible failed mission. They've already lost so much. "Do you honestly think this is going to work?"

"Kate, until tonight I did not know how we were going to re-open the portal. The way old magic swirled around you was incredible. It did your will without instruction from you. The daemons were scared. Right now, they are probably telling the others about the incident in the woods, which means we have very little time to test my theory on the portal," Arland rushes out his words.

Blinking away Anna's image, I push my reservations aside. "Then, let's go!"

"Oscailte!" he says.

The doors swing open. We walk the horses out, take our positions, then immediately urge them to a gallop. There are no daemons, no sounds other than our horses' hooves hitting the earth and heavy breathing through their nostrils.

We speed down the trail, the wind blowing past my ears.

In what seems like no time at all, we arrive at the perimeter checkpoint. Any normal horse wouldn't be able to run at a pace like this, but as with most things in this world, they *have* to be magical. We don't waste a moment's pause to explain to the soldiers what we're doing.

My body is not glowing as brightly as it was earlier, but my skin still radiates blue light. I wonder what it looks like to the soldiers, or if they notice anything at all. I'll have to make sure Arland speaks to them about keeping quiet.

At the edge of the forest, he draws Bowen to a stop. The rest of us follow his lead. He looks from me to Flanna to Cadman.

"Ready?" Arland whispers.

We nod in unison.

"Ride as fast as you can."

We break through the last of the trees into the clearing, stressing the horses to run harder than before.

At the spot where the portal is located, I jump from Mirain's back.

"Be a good girl for Cadman." I pat her shoulder.

Arland hands Bowen's reins to Flanna. "Keep guard over a twenty-foot perimeter. If anything attacks, leave Bowen and Mirain and head back to base to warn the others."

"We will see you soon."

Arland takes my hand and leads me to the portal. We fall to our knees next to it. I see the glistening edges better than the last time we traveled out here, but it's still not open. He pokes his finger at the center, but nothing happens.

This was all for nothing.

Arland smiles. "I want you to concentrate on what you need the magic to do for you. Imagine the portal opening, and seeing your family."

I close my eyes. *I need the portal to open, so I can get home, so I can see my sister and mom again.*

Nothing happens.

Please, open the portal, so I can see Brit and my mom again.

Nothing, still.

"I am sorry it took me so long to figure this out," Arland says.

I open my eyes, looking back into the dark reality of our situation.

The magic may have responded to me earlier, but it certainly isn't now.

I give up. "Arland, you have nothing to be sorry for. You have done everything you could to help me see my family again. I could never be upset with you over this, but it's just not going to work. We need to get back before something happens to the others."

A grin plays across Arland's face. "It is going to work. Now kiss me."

I laugh. "Yes, sir."

He leans forward, and our mouths meet with so much depth and love, I have to pull away. Arland takes me by the waist and draws me into him.

I give in and kiss him, longer and harder, until I feel our bodies meld into one. I'm not worried about Flanna and Cadman watching us; they won't share what's happening between Arland and me with anyone else.

"Well, look at that. You are both radiating fire now," Flanna says, staring at us. Golden yellow light reflects in her eyes and gleams on her skin.

The blue is gone, and we both burn in the same brilliant, golden-yellow fire that swirled around me in the woods before.

Smiling, Arland looks down at himself. His eyes widen.

"Close your eyes, and ask the magic to open the portal, Kate," he says, his voice smooth, calm, knowing.

God, I need you, please open this portal. I need to see my sister and mom.

"Incredible." Arland's word hangs in the air.

The glow is so bright it appears in my vision, even before I open my eyes. When I do, my jaw falls slack. The beautiful light from our bodies shimmers through the portal, illuminating the water on the other side. I can't move. My legs are useless. I'm stuck where I kneel, clutching tightly onto Arland's hands.

Sensing my nerves, he lifts me to my feet and chuckles.

I squeeze his fingers between mine. "Step through at the same time as me, please. I don't want the door to close and lose you, too."

Arland holds me steady and meets my eyes. "I promised I would never leave your side . . . unless you want me to."

I shake my head. "Hold your breath."

We each place one foot through the portal. Warm water soaks through my boot. Thrusting the rest of my body into the rippling wave between two worlds, I hold tightly to Arland's hand.

Chapter Eighteen

The water is warm and inviting. We could stay here forever, be happy, be free, be at peace. It would be so easy to run away from everything. But we can't. Everything depends on us.

We swim the short distance to the surface. It's midday. The sunshine sends delightful tingles over my skin; the earthy smells of living trees and plants fill my nose, easing my nerves.

Arland squints at the sky and smiles. The sun has a captivating beauty I could get lost in; I think Arland is already lost in it. He looks back at me, his skin glowing. The worn look in his eyes has been replaced with a healthy, youthful one. Arland is beautiful. He catches me watching him; I shake my head at the déjà vu feeling.

Was I not staring at Brad in this swimming hole a few weeks ago?

"The sun makes me want to leave it all behind and stay here with you, forever," Arland says, looking at me with hungry eyes.

"We would never get over the guilt that would cause us both." I lead him from the water to one of the rocks along the edge of the river.

"I have not seen the sun in such a long time. I was only five years old when Darkness began stealing our light, Kate. Although, since I met you, Darkness has not seemed as lonely." Arland takes my hand and spins me around, as though he'd like to kiss me again, but there will be time for that later.

"We're going to fix it all. Then, we can live wherever we want," I say, trying to pull Arland out of his obvious desire to sit in the sunlight the rest of the day.

"Come on, let's move. If Brit and my mom have been waiting for us, I know exactly where they'll be."

My feet are so familiar with this trail, I run at a full sprint, with Arland behind me. We jump over vines, duck under branches, run harder and harder until we make it to my family's "reserved" spot in less than ten minutes.

Blue and red tents grace my treasured place in the forest.

"Mom! Brit!" My heart races at a rapid pace from the run; sweat and water drip from my forehead.

"Kate?" Brit's muffled voice brings tears to my eyes.

She unzips the door and runs into my arms, nearly knocking me to the ground. "Oh my God, Kate. Are you okay? I've missed you so much, I love you," my sister says, squeezing air from my lungs.

Mom steps out, hands pressed to her mouth. She runs to smother me with her own hugs. The three of us swap *I love you*s, kisses, and tears.

Mom catches sight of Arland, then leans back and smiles.

"We don't have much time?" Mom asks, holding my head in both of her hands.

I shake my head. "No."

"Brit, gather the supplies, and let's go."

Brit runs to the tent, grabs a couple bags, and is back in an instant. Looking around, I try to find my stepdad. "Mom, where's Gary?"

"I tried to get him to come with us. Convincing these humans of our magic is not easy. He thought I had lost my mind, threatened to call the police when you and Brad didn't come home. I had to leave him behind. The spell I cast over him was so strong, he'll be positive we had a very quick divorce and you kids never want anything to do with him again," Mom says, her voice flat.

She doesn't appear as sad as I feel she should be.

"That's terrible, Mom. Gary has been so good to us. He's the only father I've ever known."

Frowning, Brit nods.

"Unfortunately, it's a price I knew I might have to pay when your father died. I had to keep you safe," Mom says, no smile, no sadness—expressionless. "We need to go."

"And Mr. Tanner? What does he think about Brad's disappearance?" I have to know the answer before I'll even consider moving back along the trail.

"Mr. Tanner thinks you and Brad are extending your time out here. He's under the impression you have finally entered into a relationship."

"But it's been weeks. How long would they expect us to stay out here?"

"To them, it's been only one week. Don't worry, dear. The spells will continue for as long as necessary. Time for them is slightly suspended right now." She nudges my shoulder.

"Huh," I say, because her explanation doesn't make sense.

"Don't worry, once Brad gets back, it will all work out. Where is he?" Mom glances around.

"*If* we can get him back. He's not here. We need antivenin, Mom. Brad has been seriously injured, and he's in a coma."

"*What?*" Brit drops the bags; tears well in her eyes.

Concern creases Mom's forehead. "If Brad has been hurt by something in Encardia, no antivenin in this world will save him. We can talk about it once we get on the other side."

We head back to the trail and race to the swimming hole, but my feet refuse to run as fast as they did before. I might not ever see Gary again. Even if I do see him, he'll think I hate him. My heart, which has broken in so many different ways, has room for one more tear . . . maybe two. This is no longer *my* home, but I guess it never was. Arland and I cannot come back here after this whole war is taken care of—there's no home to come back to.

I say goodbye to my favorite forest, my favorite swimming hole, and my favorite world. We swim through the water, then hold onto the rocks by the falls and stand in a half-circle around the portal to Encardia.

Goodbye, Gary. We may not have the closest relationship, but I love him.

Brit looks at me, another tear streaming down her face. She must be experiencing the same emotions. The last time Brit was in Encardia, she witnessed the coscarthas advancing to attack us. I hope Mom told my sister about what the people are like, how they're similar to us, and how we have to help them; otherwise, Brit wouldn't want to set foot inside this portal.

"We all go through at the same time. Hold onto our shoulders," I say, water from the falls splashing in my face. "Arland and I will stay in the front, with our weapons drawn, just in case."

"Okay," they agree at once.

Taking a deep breath, I draw my sword with my right hand. Arland holds my left and fumbles to grip his sword. Mom and Brit hang on to our shoulders.

"Ready?" I ask.

Receiving three nods, I stay vertical and step through with my sword in front of me.

We all fall on top of one another.

Chapter Nineteen

I look back toward the portal. It's closed. Getting to my feet, I dust myself off. "Did anyone get hurt?"

"I'm fine." Brit lifts the duffle bags and smiles.

Mom squeezes water from her shirt. "Me, too."

Arland grins; it's all I need to know he's fine, too. He's more than fine. We've not only shared a kiss, but he's also fulfilled his promise to me.

Thank you, God, for helping me reach my family.

I put the claymore back in my holster. Next time we go through the portal, I am going to have to find a way to pass through without getting my clothes wet. Goose bumps riddle my skin. I wring the ends of my tunic and hair, then return my attention to Arland.

"Brit, you will ride with Kate; Mrs. Wilde, with me."

Mom sucks in a sharp breath. I don't remember ever hearing her called Mrs. Wilde.

"Flanna, Cadman, you are to ride flank again," Arland says. "Kate and I are glowing so brightly, we are sure to attract the attention of daemons. We must move fast."

Brit climbs onto Mirain with me. "Why does your skin look like it's on fire?"

Warmth flashes in my cheeks from the memory of exactly *why* I'm on fire. "I'll tell you later."

I kick my heels into Mirain, and she takes off. The horses gallop as hard and as fast as they can, making the trip through the clearing in no time at all.

At the forest line, Mirain spooks and rears onto her hind legs, nearly throwing Brit. Arland, Flanna, Cadman, and Mom whisper words to the trees.

"What is it, girl?" I lean forward to get a look at her face.

She turns her head to the left.

Following her lead, I catch sight of them; hundreds of coscarthas creep between the trees. Enormous, black, wolf-like creatures travel with the daemons, eyes red and blazing. I gasp for air, bringing all of the creatures' attention upon me.

Charging through the underbrush, they come right for us.

"Arland, look to the left," I rush out my words; every fiber of my being shakes.

Arland closes his eyes, but only for a moment. His desperate look is replaced by a scowl, by his determination to live. "Hounds. We cannot go back to base while any remain alive; they will track and surround us. We will be trapped there."

"We certainly can't fight them, there are too many!" I say, waving at the army of thousands heading our way.

"They cannot"—Arland points to Brit, Mom, Flanna and Cadman—"but *we* can." Arland looks down at his glowing body, arms spread widely. The color changes from yellow to blue, and his confidence makes the flames burn even brighter.

I have never felt concern so strong in my life. If this doesn't work, everything I hold close to my heart will die—my sister, mother, Arland, and my world.

God, you have been here for me so far. Please, help me fight until Darkness leaves this land.

"Kate, you can do this," Arland reassures me.

He turns Bowen to the right. "Flanna, you and Cadman take Mrs. Wilde and Brit back, but only a few feet. We are going to focus on what approaches from the left; hopefully, nothing comes from any other side. Keep your senses keen. Abandon us if you have to."

We climb from our horses.

Arland steps around Mirain and takes me by the hand.

We stand our ground as one united force.

A flash of Arland and me standing in a patch of sunlight, happy and proud we'd killed all the daemons, enters my thoughts. I close my eyes. That was a dream. Searching my memory for details that might help us now, I remember when we turned to leave, a hound jumped at Arland from his right side. It bit his neck until he stopped breathing. The vision diminishes as abruptly as it appeared. I shudder from the memory of losing him, but take this memory as a warning; I'm sure it was sent to me for a purpose.

"We will make it through this, and we will be taking our bath together in no time," Arland says.

My soul aches at the thought of no more baths together, no more kissing, no more sleeping in his arms. I stand on my toes and place my lips on his cheek, then we draw our swords and wait for the first wave of daemons to descend upon us. They draw nearer, but I cannot be afraid.

Instincts take over. "Stop!"

Magic wakes up all around us. Carried along by the vibrant reds, blues, yellows, pinks—all the colors of magic—my voice floats though the air toward the daemons, becoming brighter and brighter until it reaches them and knocks them down.

A few coscarthas dart under bushes, trying to escape the light, but others get up and continue their forward advance—ignoring the power.

"Please, help us burn these hideous beasts, and return them to their own world," I beg of the magic.

Nothing happens.

More and more creatures get up and approach. Howls echo through the night, sucking any warmth right out of the air. Shrieks ring in my ears. The earth shakes from the daemons' stampede.

What were we thinking? How could we think we could fight? Why would anything want to hurt us like this? My heart races; my short life flashes before my eyes. "Arland, what am I supposed to do?"

He readies himself for the fight, bracing his legs apart and holding his sword in front of him. "Ask the magic to help."

In the forest, earlier, I didn't have to think about the fight. It just came to me. Here, waiting for the creatures, I don't know what to do. I don't know how to make magic respond.

"I did. Nothing happened." Fear controls me now. I can barely think, move, look at Arland, or speak. The only thing that keeps me from lying in the fetal position is the fact that I can't let him down, or Brit, my mom, Flanna, or even Cadman.

"Kate," Arland says, his skin burning brighter—the magic is obviously responding to him—"I love you."

Hearing Arland say he loves me—staring with a look of absolute adoration—and knowing this could be it, we could all die, makes me strong and determined.

We *are* going to make it through this, yet I still don't know what to do.

Arland crouches. "Think of the things you love. Think of what you need the magic to do for you."

The daemons have reached us; there's no time for me to think. I still don't know how to make magic respond, but I fight. I fight with everything in me. I stab at the coscarthas as they swipe their long claws at me. They shriek with rage when they miss. I duck, swipe, jump, run, *live*. Everything I do only aggravates them to attack harder.

Daemons advance in waves.

I kill them, one right after the other.

Arland and I separate; he fights on my right, I on his left.

Coscarthas descend on us faster than we can kill them off. We're being forced back toward the others, unable to fight them all.

"Kate, you have to use the magic." Three daemons encircle Arland, getting closer with each slash of their claws.

Mirain neighs wildly; Brit screams, a loud and bloodcurdling shriek. The two sounds combined bring my heart to a complete stop. Shaking, I turn to see what caused my sister's scream. She's not on Mirain. Brit's on the ground, trembling in fear, eyes closed.

A hound made it past Arland and me. Standing on all fours in front of her, fur raised on its haunches, the daemon sniffs her skin and snarls.

It's going to kill my sister.

"Arland!" I call, ready to run to Brit.

He stabs his sword through the chest of a coscartha. "You cannot go to her. They will kill you both. You have to find the magic."

My little sister's face is soaked with tears, bottom lip quivering. Flanna and Cadman release arrow after arrow into the daemons. My mother whispers to the trees. My love is nearly overrun by daemons.

God, my family needs you—I need you—please, help us.

Confidence blankets me, warming my skin from head to toe. I see each daemon as a target, and somehow I hear their horrible thoughts. They are eager to kill us.

I'm now aware of how each one is going to die; *I'm* going to kill them.

Energy pulses at my fingers. My body ignites in uncontrollable blue flames, different from the golden flames when I kissed Arland, more powerful, more willing to fight . . . more willing to kill.

"Stop," I yell again.

Everyone pauses—the daemons, Arland, Brit, Mom, Flanna, and Cadman—and sets their attention on me. Above our heads, a patch of Darkness breaks open, allowing the sun to shine through and illuminate the trees and underbrush. The drooping leaves and bushes spring to life, as they did between the training facility and the base, earlier. My friends, family, and enemies stare at the light in the sky.

Mom smiles and nods.

The daemons growl.

Everything buzzes with the electricity of life. Little sprite-sized beings peel themselves from trees and rise out of the ground. They come out of everything—everywhere—and fill the air all around us with bright lights. The beings are small and have little wings on their backs. All of them are different shapes; some are like the bark of trees, others like blades of grass, leaves, and they are all translucent.

They fly through the war-torn forest and bump into each other as they wake from what was certainly a very long nap. Some of them swirl around our bodies, as though trying to protect us. No one moves, other than the little beings. I get lost in their beauty, the magic of it all, and reach my finger out to touch one. A human-like face appears in the brightly colored leaf in front of me.

I hold my breath.

My finger warms as it nears her light.

She smiles, but moves away and fades back into the leaf before I reach her. Swarms of them gather in front of me, and they glance at each other, then me; they seem to be begging for direction.

I point toward the daemons. "Go, attack them . . . use fire!"

The beings transform from pieces of the forest into brilliant forms of blue fire. They dart around us, strike through our enemies, and light them in flames. The smell of burning flesh filling the air is almost impossible to inhale, but I push through.

I walk toward the hound still dazed by the magic, yet still snarling at my sister. Raising the hilt of the sword over my head, I gather all my strength, then stab the blade into his back.

He falls and lets out a loud growl as he dies.

Brit and I meet eyes.

"Get back on the horse." My voice resonates with confidence.

I rush back to Arland, then take his hand in mine. "I love you, too."

From the corner of my eye, I see him smile.

Our flames burn even brighter. I'm surer now than ever that we *are* going to be okay. I let go of Arland's hand, so we can march side-by-side into the next wave of daemons. Together, we strike and kill them with ease. The golden light swirls around us, but our bodies glow blue. The fire from our swords transfers into the daemons, allowing us to advance deeper and deeper into the army.

Every single one of these monsters will die tonight. I no longer fear them. I feel no urge to retreat, just the urge to kill the beasts that have destroyed my world, my father, Arland's mother, and so many others.

Big, black hounds lunge at us from all directions, teeth as long as my fingers protruding from their foaming jowls. The sprites take down most of the hounds in mid-air, before they can attack us. The few that get through the magic, Arland and I slaughter with our swords. More arrows fly over our heads and aid us, but they are not as efficient as Arland and I are together.

I slay the last daemon with my sword, slicing straight through its neck. I stand looking, listening for the next beast to attack, but the coscarthas have stopped shrieking from the fire, the hounds have all stopped jumping at us.

Arland and I are left standing in the middle of the forest, in a single patch of sunlight, among hundreds of burning daemon carcasses.

"We should leave now," Arland says, triggering my vision again.

I push him behind me as a hound lunges out of the tall grasses to attack us from the right. My sword impales the creature's rib cage from underneath as it tries to kill Arland. Fire erupts inside the hound, effectively taking its life.

I turn to Arland, proudly. "Now, we can go."

He cups my face in his hands. "You have now saved my life twice. I thought it was supposed to be the other way around."

"As long as we're both safe, does it matter?"

Everyone stares at us, mouths open, eyes wide.

Arland helps me onto Mirain's back, then pats her on the hindquarters. "Take her home, girl."

Brit wraps her arms around me. "You have a lot of explaining to do," she says.

I grasp her hand and squeeze. "As soon as we get somewhere safe."

Fighting something so evil, so vile, and knowing we overcame it, is exciting. No one was injured or killed, other than the creatures that needed to die.

I look over my shoulder to the scene of my first battle; the patch of daylight turns back to Darkness.

We have a lot more fighting to do.

Chapter Twenty

Arland and I steal glances at one another while we ride in silence. I'm happy my mom and Brit are here, but right now, I want nothing more than some alone time with him.

We stop in front of what appears to be more woods.

"Where are we?" Brit asks, teeth chattering.

"Nochtann." Flanna mutters the magical word, causing the stable doors to swing open.

Looking over my shoulder, I watch Brit's eyes widen.

She sucks in a breath. "Cool."

I return my gaze forward. "That's just the beginning."

She hugs me tighter.

We ride the horses into their stalls. I help Brit down, then slide from Mirain. "Thank you, Mirain. Next time, try not throwing my sister from your back."

Brit brushes Mirain with me. "Thank you."

"For what?"

My sister takes my hands in hers. "For loving me enough to save my life."

"Killing the daemon was nothing." Although it *was* something; it was scary, that's what it was.

Tears well in Brit's bloodshot eyes, threatening to spill over at any moment. "I'm not talking about right now, but thank you for that, too. I'm talking about weeks ago, when you didn't know what you were saving me from. You willingly gave up your life to save me."

"I would do it again." I wrap my arms around her.

"I love you, Kate."

"I love you, too."

Arland walks into Mirain's stall, then stands next to me.

Sniffling, I step back. "Brit, this is Arland."

She wipes her cheeks, but tears keep falling. "Hi, Arland. You better be good to my sister."

He smiles at her. "Of course, I will be good to her."

Arland puts his arm around my waist, his warmth radiating through me. "Kate, I will take care of the horses. You should spend time with your family."

I turn from my sister into Arland's embrace. He rests his hands on my lower back and clasps his fingers.

"Thank you for doing this," I say.

He squeezes me against him. "You are welcome, but I did not have much to do with it. The magic was all you."

I stare, deeply, into his emerald eyes. "You had everything to do with it."

Arland laughs, kisses my cheek, then we separate.

It's hard to walk away from him, but I do.

The onslaught of hugs, laughter, and tears my mom and Brit have for me seems never-ending. The three of us don't speak; we just keep our heads buried on each other's shoulders.

There are tons of things I need to ask my mom—things I'm upset by—but I'm just so happy she's here.

She wipes her red nose, looks at Arland in the stalls, then at me, smiles, then hugs me again . . . Mom's a bigger wreck than I've been.

Arland finishes with the horses, and our eyes meet. He joins Flanna and Cadman in an acknowledgment that my reunion will not end soon, and they begin a conversation.

Now that he's seen *why* Arland protects me, I'm sure Cadman has about a million questions. Arland doesn't protect me just because he's my Coimeádaí; he protects me for love, and for my magic.

He is more than likely instructing Cadman not to tell the others about what he witnessed this evening, which reminds me . . . .

I step back from Brit and Mom. "Arland?"

He stops talking and hurries to me. Taking my hands in his, Arland wears a look that says he'd desperately like to run away with me right now. "Is everything okay?"

"We were glowing when we passed the guards at the perimeter. Should you speak with them, too?"

"I will have Lann send them a message to speak to me as soon as they return from their posts."

Brit wraps her arm around my neck, interrupting Arland and me. "You were on fire, Kate, not glowing!"

"She wasn't on fire." Mom shakes her head. "Her essence was filled with an old magic that's been sleeping for a long time. In all my months researching what it was the Seer meant about you being Light to Darkness, I never dreamed you would actually *be* Light." She clasps her hands in front of her, her voice full of pride.

Without releasing Arland's hand, I turn to face my mom. "Arland said something similar, but I don't think I am the Light, Mom. For some reason, the Light has chosen to listen to me."

Her gaze darts between Arland and me. "Whatever it is, we'll figure it out. I'm very happy to see you have met Arland, son of my dear friend Kimball. The two of you were impressive out there. Now, where is Brad?"

My moment of happiness is gone; my shoulders slump. "He's not well, Mom. The coscarthas attacked him."

A crease forms in the center of her forehead. "Tell me what happened."

Mom's facial expressions range from anger to concern, compassion to intrigue, and finally to love while I explain the events from the time I've been here. When I finish, she remains quiet for a few moments, then snaps her fingers. "We'll have to try healing him using old magic. It's not going to be easy, if you don't know how to control it, but we will do everything we can."

In the few minutes she's been listening to me, she comes up with a plan to heal Brad's wounds and get him home. I understand why Arland said she was one of Encardia's greatest Healers. "I hope it works, Mom. You know, the first morning we were here, Brad said he didn't believe we'd traveled into a different world, and he wanted to escape back home. It's funny how he knew we had to escape here, but he didn't really believe we had gone anywhere."

"I know this is hard for you, dear. When Brad formed his attachment to you, I knew it was going to be difficult getting him to let you go, but I never imagined him actually coming here with you. If I had known now was the time, I would have been there, Kate," Mom says, her voice pleading for forgiveness.

"It's okay, Mom. What was wrong with you?" I remember how pale and weak she was the night before we left. Gary fed her crackers and water, while I held a bucket for her to throw up in.

"Nothing you need to worry yourself with. I'm fine." She's never been one to allow people fuss over her.

"Well, I'm glad you're okay, but I don't think it will be easy to convince Brad to go through the portal and leave me behind forever. I know somehow I'll have to do it." I'm trying to convince myself, more than I am them. Brad being out of my life for good will cause me a lot of pain, but won't be anything compared to what it will do to him.

Mom hugs me again. "We will talk more about this later."

"That would be nice." All the years I thought my mom was not compassionate, she was actually hiding my truth from me. I don't know why, but I'm sure she had her reasons. I'm almost afraid to find out. Every time I learn something new, my future becomes more difficult.

"How it is you've managed to rope such a hot guy already?" Brit's always been a girl who gets straight to the point.

Arland and I blush.

I dig my toe into the dirt. "Umm."

"I want details!"

This isn't exactly a conversation I want to have in front of my mom . . . or Arland. I give Brit a pointed look, bringing her questioning to a halt.

She squeezes my hand. "Later?" Brit whispers.

"Maybe . . . if you're lucky." I hug her once more, then take Arland's hand again.

Joining Cadman and Flanna, we lead our group down into the base.

Cadman's gaze bores into me.

I look back at his eyes full of hope. At the bottom of the steps, he smiles as he separates from the rest of us.

I pray he does not speak of what he saw to anyone.

Lann walks out of the communications room. "That was extraordinarily fast."

Arland glances down at me with pride. "It was an extraordinary trip."

Butterflies. He's giving me butterflies.

"What did you discover about the daemons from the woods earlier?" All pride disappears from Arland's face.

"Ogilvie and Saidear searched for an hour, but discovered nothing to track them by," Lann says.

"This is bad news."

"The spell has been recast over the perimeter."

Arland stiffens. "When? We just killed at least a thousand daemons *inside* the perimeter."

"Dunn, Tristan, Saidear, and Ogilvie are still out now. It took a lot more men than I expected, but they should return soon. We will continue searching for the three that got away."

"Where did the spell fail?" Arland asks.

"Near the river."

He rubs his chin. "And that was the only located failure?"

"Yes."

"I am aware I instructed you to bring the soldiers in, but I have changed my mind. After dinner, send everyone available out for watch duty. Cadman should remain inside to relieve you."

"Yes, sir." Lann tips his head in my mom and Brit's direction. Dark locks of hair fall in front of his eyes. "I see you made it through the portal."

"Yes."

He eyes Mom and Brit, while Arland explains how we got through the portal and how we battled the daemons. When he finishes, Lann bounds back into the communications room.

"Report back to me as soon as the soldiers are in place," Arland calls, voice riddled with concern.

"I will, sir."

Mom stares after him. "Did a Concealment spell break?"

Arland nods. "The first time in twenty years. A large population of daemons has formed between us and the Gorm Mountains—"

"*How* large?" she asks.

"Larger than what we battled tonight."

Mom shakes her head, but doesn't respond. I cannot imagine what all this must be like for her. She hasn't been here since Dad died. She never saw Encardia in Darkness.

Arland leads us down the hall, but I stop at the door before we enter the kitchen and look up at him.

"Am I still glowing?"

"No. Do not worry. I will not allow Perth to discover who you are."

"Perth Dufaigh?" Mom asks, with a hint of caution.

"Yes, Mrs. Wilde, Perth Dufaigh is here. Were you and Mr. Wilde aware of the trade?" Arland asks.

She gasps. "We were not officially made aware of the trade before we left. We knew it would happen, but why is he here?" Her voice is smooth, composed.

"Do you know how it turns out?" Arland asks the question that means more to our future than anything else in the world.

A sympathetic look crosses Mom's face.

"Not now, Arland." She obviously knows why he wants to know. There are a lot of things my mom knows that we want to hear, that we *need* to hear.

"His father put him here as a reminder of what he took from Arland," I tell her.

Mom grits her teeth. "That sounds like Dufaigh."

Pushing through the kitchen door, we find Enid serving dinner to the children.

The other night, over meal preparations, I got her story from Flanna. Enid and her family lived about a day's hike from here, through the forest, in a little stone cottage built into the side of a hill. Her husband fished the dying river; their life was quiet, simple. It had been their intention to avoid the war, and they had been doing just that for twenty years, but the daemons eventually found them.

No one knows how she managed to escape. She couldn't speak about the tragedy, other than how her family died. The children were murdered first, while Enid and her husband were forced to watch. They pleaded with the daemons, but the beasts used their poisoned claws to poke the children, over and over again. The deadly liquid delivered a slow and painful death to the two eight-year-olds. Upon their final breath, the coscarthas inhaled something from the children's mouths, then moved on to Enid's husband.

After watching their children tortured to death, Enid and her husband lost their will to live, making them less fun for the coscarthas to torture.

Her husband was murdered instantly.

Enid has been here for two months. I feel horrible for her. As much as I've tried to be kind to Enid, she's still too scared to speak to me.

Everyone looks up as our group enters the dining area.

Anna waves.

"Hi, Anna." Passing through the room, I smile at her.

"Flanna, please collect beds from the soldier's quarters and bring them to mine and Kate's room," Arland says.

My sister's gaze locks onto him. I almost hear Brit saying, "And what have you two been doing in *your* room?"

When we enter *our* room, she smiles mischievously at me.

Pretending like I don't notice, I grab Mom's arm and tug her toward the door.

"What are you doing, Kate?"

"Shouldn't we go see Brad?"

Tilting her head to the side, Mom squints her blue eyes. I know the look she's giving me; even through the candlelight, I see she feels sorry for me.

"I will get to him, soon." She pats my hand and leans in near my ear. "There are things we need to discuss, and I am worried about your sister."

I look from Mom to Brit.

My sister hugs herself, rubbing her arms.

I nod.

Flanna carries two rolled-up beds into the room. "Where do you want these?"

"One should go along the wall, and the other between the dresser and bed," Mom says.

We set up the room and decide to rotate who sleeps where.

"Arland, have you made plans to get Kate to Wickward to meet your father?" Mom wraps a sheet around one of the mattresses.

"We were planning to leave in two days."

She glances at my sister, struggling to attach a sheet to her bed. "As much as I'd like to see Kimball, I feel we should wait another week before we leave. It will give us time to work on Brad, and it will allow Brit time to acclimate to this new life, the way Kate has."

I agree with Mom. Brit clearly needs time to adjust to the lack of light, to fighting, to an anything-but-normal life.

Arland rubs his chin. "I do not like the idea of staying here, while so many daemons gather just outside our perimeter. We have already had one breach; I cannot allow that to happen again."

Mom crosses the room and places her hand over Arland's forearm. "You are a good Leader, but look at my daughter . . . ."

Brit lies on her mattress, arms wrapped around her shins.

We all turn our heads to her.

"W-what?" She sits up, but keeps herself in a ball.

"I will need to contact my father and make some additional arrangements," Arland says, bringing our attention back to him. "But, for Kate's safety, you must not refer to yourself by either your first or last name. Is there something else we can call you?"

"Morgandy Domhnaill," Mom says at once, removing her hand from his arm.

"Does it have any family meaning?"

"It's a name a Seer gave me to use."

Yes, my mom knows a lot. I'm curious to hear about myself, about my future, about her life here, and about so many things she has never shared. *Morgandy Domhnaill.* I wonder what it means, or if it means anything at all.

After our short discussion, we enter the dining room for dinner, then take seats at the table in the middle. Flanna serves the food Enid prepared. We eat, but everyone is curious about the new arrivals. On my second bite of chicken, Saidear and Tristan walk up, eyeing Brit and Mom the way they did me when I first arrived.

"Saidear, Tristan, this is my sister, Brit, and my mom, Morgandy."

"Nice to meet you, ma'am. I am glad you made it to safety." Saidear offers his hand.

Mom takes it, and he kisses her fingers, just above the knuckles.

"Nice to meet you, too." She smiles up at him.

"Kate, your sister is identical to you. You are both beautiful." There may be a little hope in Tristan's voice. He looks from Brit to me. A relationship between them will never happen; he's fifteen, she's nineteen, and way too wild for him.

I grin. "Thank you, Tristan."

The two men walk toward the kitchen and are met by Lann. All the soldiers in the room look at him. He whispers something to Saidear and Tristan, then motions for them to follow.

Chairs creak. Bowls clack onto the tables. The soldiers vacate the room, trailing behind Lann.

"Are they going to watch the perimeter?"

Arland nods. "Yes."

I lean next to Arland's ear. "Why isn't Perth going?"

"We do not trust him to fight."

Rubbing my hands together, I stare at the spot where Saidear and Tristan stood. He's just a kid. *Please take care of them, God.*

Arland places his hand over mine. "You are worried for Tristan?"

"I'm worried for all of them . . . ."

Marcus and Anna—who stayed in the dining room after the other children went to bed—run up to our table.

"Do your mother and sister handle swords as well as you do?" Marcus asks, chest heaving, smile stretched wide across his face.

Setting my concern aside, I lean forward and take his hands in mine. "They have not had the same good instructor, like I have, so we'll see how well they do."

"Marcus, you know Kate is the best sword fighter around. No one could ever be as good as her," my little cheerleader says.

"I don't know about that." I pat Anna's head.

"Marcus, Anna, I think you two should get to bed," Arland says.

"Yes, sir. See you at training tomorrow." Anna waves goodbye, grabs her brother, and they disappear.

Perth makes his way over. When he steps in front of us, Mom and Arland both stiffen.

The tension is so thick, I could make a wall with it.

"I am glad you made it. The way Kate moped around without you, it was as though she had lost all hope. How did you arrive here?" my *future husband* asks.

I shudder.

"It was a difficult trip. A lot of lives were lost along the way, but we persevered and have finally reunited with our Kate." Mom's tone is lined with formality.

She regards Perth with the same indifference the others do. I'm not sure how she recognizes him—he didn't introduce himself—but from her pursed lips and balled fists, I'd say Mom knows who he is. I'm going to need to learn how everyone differentiates between the Ground Dwellers and our own kind. He looks like a regular guy to me—albeit creepy.

"It is nice to meet you, Mrs. . . . . ?"

Mom's face is cold, as she narrows her eyes. "Mrs. Domhnaill."

"*Domhnaill?*" He shakes his head. "You are from The Meadows?"

"Yes, and we need rest, not questioning." Mom turns away from him. "So, if you will excuse us?"

Perth nods as he returns to his seat in the corner of the dining room. His cold stare pierces through me.

Chills run up my arms. "I have to head up to the stables. We haven't had a chance to feed the chickens or milk the cows today," I say, bouncing my legs. I need to get away from my *betrothed*.

"Can you excuse Kate for tonight?" Mom asks Arland. "I'd like to speak to you both."

Arland places a hand over my knee. "Of course, she may be excused."

I realize I should talk to my mom, but I made a promise to a friend. "If I don't help, Flanna will be stuck with more than her fair share of responsibility. It's already late. I'm not going to walk away from that."

"Thank you, Kate." Flanna trills from the kitchen.

Mom relents. "Go ahead. I will check in on Brad while you're working. But when you finish, I really need to speak to you both . . . privately."

"Oh. Should I take you to Brad first? Is there something you can do for him now?" I push my chair back and get up, ready to run to my best friend's side. My visits with him have been more and more difficult. Watching Brad stagnate in the same condition for weeks—barely breathing, not improving—is miserable. My mom offers him a chance to come out of this, and I want so much for Brad to heal.

Mom stands, then rubs her thumb along my cheekbone. "I'm going to check on him, dear. Tonight is not the night to work on his illness. The healing will require a lot of time and energy. Go ahead and take care of the animals."

"Okay." Hanging my head, I walk away, thinking of my friend and his smile, his laughter—how upset he's going to be when he finds out I'm with Arland. I glance over my shoulder. "And I promise we'll talk when I finish."

Flanna grabs the back of my shirt as I pass through the kitchen. "We have enough goat milk."

"Got it," I say, continuing toward the corridor.

I have my sister, my mother, and my Arland. I have friends, a purpose. Forcing a smile, I climb the stairs. This may not be what I had planned for my life, but I'm certainly surrounded by a lot more love than I ever have been. The only thing lacking is helping Brad and getting him home, but the way my mom spoke, that may not be as difficult as we thought.

Once in the stables, I feed the chickens, give them water, and collect their eggs. I hum Flanna's tune and dance around while I move on to the cows.

Milk squirts into the wooden pail, filling it halfway. Smells of hard work—of home—set me at ease. Having Mom and Brit here takes away some of the emptiness, some of the concern.

Straw rustles behind me.

Looking over my shoulder, I see Arland approach, smiling. He wraps his arms around my waist, then puts his face next to mine. Warmth radiates from him, comforting me even more.

Tingles rush down my arms and legs. "H-hi."

"Are you going to stop milking the cow, or are you going to make me wait?" he asks, enticing me to get up with his seductive voice.

I keep milking the cow, but my concentration wanes; milk sprays the ground a few times. "I'm going to make you wait."

"I will check the horses." Arland holds onto me for a moment longer, then unclasps his hands and leaves me with the cows.

He mutters something to Bowen about helping me get through stable duties, and I laugh.

Milk sloshes in the pail as I carry it to the shelf outside the cow's stall. I set the pail down, then walk toward the goats. Flanna said we still have milk remaining from yesterday, so I don't have to do anything other than check their food and water.

Wearing a grin that says his mind is in places it's never gone before, Arland blocks my entrance to their stall. "I have already taken care of them."

My heart races as he takes slow, exciting steps toward me and closes the space between us. He removes the feedbag from my hands, places it on the ground, then pulls me against him.

I rest my head on his chest and listen to him breathe. "Thank you, again."

"You are an incredible woman."

I lift my head and stare into his eyes. "You're just saying that because I saved your life."

"I say that because you have no idea how strong you are." Arland pulls away from me, takes my hand, and leads me to the corner between the goats and horses, where the straw is stored. "I have a feeling we will not be allowed much alone time, now that your mother and sister are here."

"We all have to share a room, but you and I can still find alone time."

Swarms of butterflies take over the free space in my stomach. Being with Arland has been important to both of us; I cannot imagine losing that. I suddenly want more of him, but what if I never get more? What if all there is for us is a cruel war and then death, or a forced marriage to someone who scares me? Thoughts I've never had while awake creep into my mind

"We are alone now," I say, almost too quietly for even me to hear.

His lips graze my neck. "We are."

I let my hands roam up his chest, down his back, and to his waist. Tugging at his hips, I pull him closer. Breathing is almost impossible. I gasp for air. "There is no reason for anyone else to come up here tonight."

"No, there is not." He whispers in my ear, then kisses it.

Chills course over my skin.

"I do have to talk to my mom, soon, though," I say, from the logical part of my brain. It's running through reasons why we shouldn't be up here, doing this, right now.

"So, we do not have much time." He crushes his lips onto mine.

In a hungry need for more, I wrap my arms around his neck and lean into him.

"Not nearly enough." I barely get out the words between kisses. All logic escapes me, replaced by desire, excitement, *love*.

"We will have to hurry then."

We fall back into the fresh straw.

Arland presses his body against mine.

Drawing my leg up over his waist, I throw my head back as he kisses a line down my neck. He runs his hands down my shirt, finds and loosens my belt, and then works his way up under my clothes. He caresses my bare skin with the tips of his fingers. Tingles run down my stomach; my breathing becomes rapid. He grabs my thigh, securing my leg around him. Trailing my fingers down his chest, I find and tear at the button on his pants.

Arland stops kissing me and smiles, so big, so warm, I cannot possibly wait any longer for this. I pull my shirt over my head, then pull his off.

Arland's eyes widen, then he kisses my chest softly, roaming down to my stomach.

Fire rages in me. I look down at our bodies pressed against each other; we're both glowing in warm, golden flames, and not the blue fire that engulfed us during the fight.

Arland sits back on his haunches, teases his finger down the middle of my chest, but stops at my waist.

I bite my lower lip and squirm from his tickling touch.

"Is this okay?" he asks, arching his eyebrow as he hooks his finger under my pants.

I nod.

Smiling, he leans down, creating explosions of heat everywhere our bare skin touches. He nibbles my earlobe and fumbles with the button on my pants—

"A-hem!"

"Not now, Flanna." Arland yells, voice raised and harsh.

"I am *so* sorry to interrupt, but Mrs. Wilde is growing impatient waiting for Kate. I figured you two were *very busy*, so I offered to come collect Kate for her while you finish the remaining duties," Flanna says, her voice heavily soaked in sarcasm.

The muscles in Arland's jaw contort; he wipes his hand over his face, erasing the angry expression.

Warmth fills my cheeks. Grabbing my shirt, I drape it in front of me. "Please, tell her we're finished, and I'll be there shortly."

"Make sure you pick the straw out of your hair first, Kate." Flanna turns on her toes and bounces out of the room.

Arland pulls straw from my tangled locks. "What is it you were saying about alone time?"

"That we are going to have to make a point of sneaking off as much as possible, now that my family is here." I slip my shirt over my head.

Arland does the same, and I tighten my belt, then kiss him one last time before we head downstairs.

The dining area is empty. Walking into our room, Arland and I find Mom and Brit sitting on the bed, waiting to talk to us.

He closes the door and follows behind me.

The way Mom looks at us, it's as if she knows we were making out. I hope the chagrin doesn't show on my face. Arland and I had so many opportunities to love, but now that we're ready, we have roommates.

This isn't fair.

"Kate, I have so much to tell you about yourself, and this place. I'm sure Arland has spoken a great deal about our history and your place in this war, as much as he could without knowing your entire prophecy." She looks at Arland; he stiffens, then she re-directs her attention to me. "You see, Kate, *I* cannot even tell you all of your prophecy. If you know too much, it could hinder you from making the correct choices. There are some things I can share with you, and I will certainly always be here for you along the way, but in no way will I be able to give the full prophecy, until this war has ended."

"My father has shared my entire prophecy with me. Knowledge is power. He wanted me to have as much power as possible in this fight." Arland's tone is incredulous.

"I highly doubt that, Arland Maher. Your father might have convinced you he gave your entire prophecy to you, but the Kimball I know would never have done such a thing. If you knew everything about yourself, it would not have taken you so long to figure out you were the key," she says.

Arland whispers *Solas,* then transfers his flame to another candle by the bed.

Brit watches him, eyes wide.

"Go on." He takes a seat on the bed and leans against the wooden headboard. It's clear Mom has his interest.

I sit in front of him, then cross my legs.

"I don't even need to ask; I know the two of you are in love. I was aware of your relationship, prior to Kate's birth. Your love was part of the reason her father and I made the deal with Kimball for you two to marry."

Oh, yeah, she definitely knows we were making out. My cheeks are so hot I need a fan.

"Wait, what? You didn't tell me anything about marriage, Mom," Brit says, jumping up from her cot along the wall.

"I'll tell you about it later, Brit." I don't want to think about how I'm not allowed to be with Arland, and I don't really want to tell Brit about it later, either, but I will. She deserves to know as much as I do—and more.

"No, Kate, I will fill in your sister. You have too many other things to focus on."

"But—"

"The dreams you've had have all been premonitions of your future. It doesn't mean they'll all come true, but portions of them might."

Abandoning my concerns for filling in Brit, I grip Arland's hand tighter.

My sister looks between us; she knows how much losing him would hurt me.

She's heard all the details, from me, about my dreams.

"Are you telling me Arland is going to die? He died in almost every one of my dreams." I know they can come true; I saw the vision of the hound in the forest only minutes before the daemon tried to attack Arland. What am I going to do? How will I protect him? I haven't had a chance to love him enough, yet.

He rubs my shoulders, and I lean into him for support.

"Everyone dies, Kate, but when it will happen, *your* prophecy didn't say. What I do know is that your pure, unbridled love is what fuels your power. It's necessary for you to be together." She pauses and smiles at the two of us. "Now, we've discussed it, and Brit and I are going to move in with Flanna and Lann and leave you two alone."

"What? Mom, you don't have to do that!" What is it she and Brit think Arland and I have been doing? Actually, I know exactly what it is, because we were so close to doing it in the stables. Mom wants me to *be* with Arland. Having her push me into a relationship doesn't seem right, but he and I *are* both adults—and I have no doubts about my love for him.

"I've seen how strong the two of you are together. You remind me of your father and me." She looks well past me; her normal pink hue pales, leaving her as white as a snow-capped mountain.

I've never heard her speak of my dad before. Sadness pangs in my gut. I don't know anything about him . . . I don't know anything about *her*.

"Your sister and I are not going to do anything that might come between you."

I guess Arland and I won't have to worry about our alone time. My cheeks warm from the memory of us in the straw; at least we have a bed, now.

"Before I tell you any more about your future, we need to discuss what to do about Brad. His condition is not good, Kate, but there is still hope."

Hope. Thank God—or the gods—for it. "Arland said he's never known anyone to live through an attack like that."

"It's true. Brad should not be alive, but he is, and that's a good sign. Kate, for years I prayed you would see you didn't love him. I knew the day would come when you had to say goodbye, and I knew it was going to be hard, if you hadn't figured that out yet."

"But I do love him, Mom."

Brit glares at me.

"He's my best friend, and I do love him, for all the memories we've shared through the years," I correct myself.

The nasty looks don't stop.

"*What?*"

Brit scoots herself to the middle of the bed, then crosses her legs, mimicking me. "I'm glad you've found someone else. Brad was too possessive of you. Do you remember that guy you had a crush on in the ninth grade?"

"Mark Evans?" I ask, once again remembering my biology lab partner.

"Yeah. His sister Lucy and I became good friends, over the last year. She asked me if I knew what Brad did to her brother. I had no idea what she was talking about, so I said no. Lucy said Brad approached Mark after school one day and asked if he liked you. Mark said yes, and told Brad he already asked you to the winter social. Well, supposedly, Brad punched him."

I cannot help but laugh. "So, you mean to tell me Brad fought off every guy who was ever interested in me?"

"Why would she lie to me? If you think about it, it all makes sense. Remember when Mark showed up at school with the black eye? He told you he was going to the dance with someone else. When you asked him what happened, he ignored you. Wasn't that the last time you ever talked to Mark?"

"Oh, my God. Why would Brad do that to me? Why didn't you tell me sooner?"

She rolls her eyes. "I've barely had an opportunity to talk to you without Brad around. Seriously, I think he's obsessed."

Anger, betrayal, frustration, sadness—all of these feelings surge through me. I ball my fists, take deep breaths. Arland rests his hands on my shoulders again, calming me. He's reminding me that, in the long run, it doesn't matter how Brad sabotaged my relationships. None of them would have meant anything. But, this news makes me question everything Brad and I ever did together.

"I suspected this was the case, when you first spoke of your relationship with him. He will not be easily convinced to return home, if he has been waiting around for you for years," Arland says, still holding on to me.

One more rip tears my already shredded heart. "So, what are we going to do?"

"We are going to try to heal him. If it works, I want you to tell him the truth," Mom says.

I breathe out sharply. "So he can punch Arland like he did Mark Evans?"

"No, so he knows there is no point in waiting around for you any longer." Mom's wisdom shines through.

"If everything goes according to plan, I can punch *him*. In your honor, of course." Arland teases, lightening the mood.

Everyone but me laughs at his comment. The only friend I've ever known—besides my sister—the one I've shared everything with my entire life, has been lying to me forever. When he took me to the winter social, I asked Brad to dance me around, to make Mark jealous. How stupid I must've looked. All the tears I shed over him while confiding in Brad, and he betrayed me.

"We can talk more, later," Mom says, appraising me. "In the morning, we should work on Brad. Brit will need to train if we're going to leave in a week. I'll come wake you up early." Her voice is strong.

I've never seen her like this; Mom is a natural Leader here. I like this side of her, more than the one she portrayed in our former world. She was always strong, mostly when it came to her health, but she was never a Leader.

Once they're in the hall, I gather the courage to speak again. "Good night. I'm glad you're here."

"Good night," they say together, but I catch a wink from Brit before the door closes.

Arland turns to me with a devilish smile. "Where were we?"

"I think you were about to hold me in your arms until I fell asleep."

Arland wraps his arms around me. "I am sorry Brad hurt you."

"Me, too," I say, blinded by tears.

Arland wipes them from my eyes and kisses my cheek. He hands me my nightgown, but I set it aside.

Taking off my dirty shirt and pants, I crawl under the blankets, then snuggle close to him when he joins me. My skin tingles from the touch of his mostly bare skin against mine. He caresses my arms, my stomach, my thighs.

He places his lips on mine and whispers. "The pain will go away."

I close my eyes. "I know."

Chapter Twenty-One

I awaken to a light tap on the door, reminding me of Brit's midnight knocking. I try to slink out of Arland's arms unnoticed, but he stirs and pulls me back into him.

"Are you leaving?" he asks, sounding sad, but his smile indicates otherwise.

I place my hand on his cheek. "Never. Go back to sleep. I think Brit's at the door."

Arland sucks in a deep breath, then releases my arm. He watches as I slip the white nightgown over my head.

Crossing the room, I open our door a crack. Brit's red, swollen face is the first thing I see.

"May I come in?"

Moving aside, I allow her to step through. "What's wrong? Why have you been crying?"

"We've lived our lives in the dark, Kate."

Arland climbs out of bed, and I turn my sister around while he dresses.

"I am going to check in with Lann. I will be in the communications room if you need me."

I nod.

He kisses me on the forehead, then flees, and I don't blame him. Brit and I have so much catching up to do. She also has a whole new reality to swallow.

"We never knew the truth about Dad, Mom, or even ourselves. I just graduated high school and planned on going to college with you.

Everything I thought I knew has changed. It's a lot to process." Brit sits on the edge of the bed.

I push a stray lock of hair from her tear-streaked face. "Once you accept we belong here, it will all get easier."

She throws herself back on the pile of blankets and looks up at me with a wry smile. "That's easy for you to say, with tall, dark, and handsome gushing over you."

Lying next to her, I prop myself up on my elbow.

"You're right. He's definitely made this transition easier for me. When I first got here, I was prepared to kill anyone who came near me—sort of." I remember the knife, and how I dropped it, and couldn't reach it fast enough. No, I wouldn't have killed anyone . . . I would've just made myself look stupid. "Then, I ran into Arland. From the moment I realized I wasn't dreaming, I found myself as in love with him in real life as I've been in my dreams. The first couple nights, I was scared and confused. On one hand, I had Brad, who'd professed his love for me, dying in bed. On the other hand, I had Arland, who *I've* known and loved forever, but he had no idea what I felt for him."

"So, he's the one from your dreams?" she asks, staring up at the roots poking through the ceiling.

"Sounds cheesy, huh?"

"You know what? I always felt there was some truth to your dreams. I knew when you were having them; I could almost feel your pain every time he died."

"Brit, I'm so scared one of those dreams is going to come true. One almost did tonight, but I reacted first—before the hound could kill him."

She looks straight at me. "You did a pretty good job of protecting him tonight. You'll have to remember what happened in every dream . . . . We should make a list."

"Maybe you're right. Will you work on one with me tomorrow?"

Brit's eyes widen. "Yes! Now, tell me. You've never so much as kissed a guy, and you and Arland are sleeping together. And don't even try to compare this to Brad. Sleeping with Arland is different, way different. How did it happen? I want you to spill all the details of your little love affair!" Brit sounds more like my happy sister now.

We sit up and face each other, then hold hands.

"I *have* kissed someone before. I kissed Brad. Well, he kissed me. After you made it back through the portal, when we thought we were going to die. Brad said he was sorry for holding back on me all this time."

"We've tried to tell you how much he loves you," Brit says, shaking her head. "What did you say to him when he told you?"

"I never said anything to him. There wasn't any time. Brit, I love Brad, but it's not the same way he loves me, and it's not the same way I love Arland. In a strange way, I feel like Arland and I have known each other forever. I love him for so many reasons, like his compassion for his people, his patience, his strength—"

She puts up her hands. "Okay, okay, I've got it. I know you're happy, Kate. He is *definitely* a good choice."

"He keeps the dreams away."

Brit arches her eyebrows. "What do you mean?"

"The first night he slept with me, it was because I had *the* horrible dream about him dying."

Her face softens. "The cave?"

"Yes. Arland said if he was close to me, maybe it wouldn't seem as real, but I don't have them at all now."

"That's weird, Kate. What if you need these dreams?"

"Trust me, I don't need the dreams."

"Didn't one help you protect him tonight?"

"I've got them memorized; I don't need to have them set on repeat every night."

"What else have you two been up to?"

I want to yell, "the dreams aren't necessary," at her, but I don't. I allow the conversation shift.

"Nothing. We kissed for the first time today." I leave out the activities in the stables; I'd never hear the end of her questions, if I mention anything about that.

"So, you've been sleeping in bed with Arland for three weeks, started kissing him today, and you haven't fooled around yet?"

I shake my head.

She giggles. "I should go, so you two can have more *alone* time."

"Sit down," I say, grabbing her hand as she pretends to leave. "We've been taking baths together, too." Now I'm trying to get a rise out of her.

She bows with her hands in front of her. "Oh, my God! You're my hero! And you still have your *virtue*?"

I roll my eyes. "I'll be sure to inform you when I don't."

Brit always talks a big game, but she still has her *virtue*, too. She said there wasn't a guy in the world who deserved her. Maybe that's because she was always in the wrong world.

"Oh, you won't have to tell me, I'll know."

Heat rushes into my cheeks. "You will?"

"I have a feeling everyone will know." She laughs.

"*Brit!*"

God, how I've missed her.

She looks away, glancing around the dark room like she wants to say something, but doesn't want to be the one to bring it up.

I know her too well to believe she was crying only about landing here, and life not being as it seemed. To her, this is probably like an exciting vacation. "There's something else bothering you, isn't there?"

Her smile fades, and she takes my hands in hers again. "I'm jealous of you."

"*Jealous?* Why?"

"I don't have a prophecy. We didn't live here when Mom was pregnant with me. I don't know what my future holds. It's scary that everyone seems to know their purpose but me. *And,* I started dating Taylor Evans a few months ago. I'm alone here." Her voice comes out in a whimper.

The root of her problems all comes down to a guy.

"You were dating Mark's brother and never said anything to me?"

She nods, but I don't give her a hard time for not sharing any of her life with me. Video chatting is not the same as sharing things in person, and I had been home from college for only a day.

"You aren't alone. This is your home. Your family is here, and I'm sure you will find someone as nice as Taylor to date . . . eventually." I'm trying to make her feel better, but I'm not sure if Brit will have that here. I don't know what her prophecy is. I don't even know if I'll live, or if Arland will live.

I know nothing.

She hugs me. "Thanks. You're right. I just wish I knew what I'm supposed to do here."

Arland opens the door and pokes in his head.

Brit takes it as her cue to leave. Looking between Arland and me, she smiles.

"I'll talk to you later," Brit says, then leaves.

Arland and I undress down to our underclothes, lie in bed, then he pulls the blankets over us.

"She is scared," he says.

I press my head onto his chest. "She's afraid because she doesn't have a prophecy."

"Not everyone receives a prophecy. They are reserved for Leaders and their families. She is not that different from most of my soldiers here." Arland pulls me closer.

But, Brit is a Leader; she should know. "Can a Seer give someone a prophecy after they're born?"

"If you find a good Seer, they can give you a prophecy anytime."

I wonder if I can find a Seer who will tell me about Arland, about us, about Perth, or about my sister, without holding back like my mom has.

Someone pounds on the door, rattling the wood on its hinges. An hour has passed—maybe. I don't reach out for the sun. I'm too tired to care about the time. Opening my eyes, I find Arland already dressing. I'm captivated by his half-naked body.

Turning around, he catches me staring, and smiles.

I motion with my finger, and he obeys.

Arland crawls on top of me, holding himself up by his arms. "Can I help you?"

"My mom did say she wouldn't interfere, right?" I bite my lip.

"That she did. However, I believe it would be a little obvious if we did not come out of this room for another hour . . . or two." He tempts me with a kiss on my jaw.

Pushing myself up, I kiss his neck below his ear. "Mmm, but she wouldn't mind?"

"*I* would not mind," Arland whispers, gripping my bare skin in his hands.

Another loud knock rattles the door.

Arland falls over and groans.

I already hold a grudge against whoever is knocking on our door, but I get up and get dressed.

Arland hops from the bed then stands in front of me, blocking my exit. "Today is going to be difficult, if Brad wakes up."

I look at my feet. Guilt, over how much my relationship with Arland is going to hurt Brad, has been mounting for days. "I know."

Arland lifts my chin with his finger. "You can do this. You just have to remain strong."

He places his soft lips on mine, and, for a moment, stress disappears.

Arland takes my hand in his, and we leave the room.

Mom stands outside the door with her hands on her hips.

"Sorry," I say, staring at the floor.

"Kate, I'm not upset. We need to start on Brad." A quick check of her face reveals she isn't lying. She's smiling. "Arland, can you collect Flanna and Cadman to help us?"

Arland kisses my hand. "I will return shortly."

Mom drags me by the arm toward Brad's room. After hearing of his betrayal, I have a hard time entering, a hard time not to be angry with him right now, a hard time wanting to heal him.

"Why are you so shaky?"

I take a deep breath. "I'm nervous."

"Are you worried about how Brad is going to react when he finds you're in love with Arland?"

This is the question I've been trying to avoid.

"That's one thing I'm worried about," I say. Honestly, his reaction is the biggest concern I have. What if he never wants to talk to me again? What if he throws away our friendship, because we weren't friends in the first place? If he beat up other guys who showed an interest in me, how could we be?

Mom puts her hands on my shoulders. "You have nothing to feel guilty about, dear. You never loved Brad that way. He will have to deal with that on his own. That's how life works."

"In the forest, we were getting closer than we ever had before, Mom. I was beginning to think I might have those kinds of feelings for him. He poured his heart out to me, and I jumped right in with someone else as soon as he got attacked. I would be stupid to think he wouldn't be upset by that." If I was in his place, I would hate me when I woke up; although, after years of betrayal, he more than deserves not having my friendship.

"Do you love Arland?"

I have zero doubt in my mind. "I do."

"Then you have to let your guilt over Brad go, and you have to commit to getting him home safely."

We move the chairs around Brad's bed.

Arland returns with Flanna and Cadman, but he's brought Kegan, and not my sister.

"Where's Brit?" I ask Arland, while eyeing Kegan.

"You can trust Kegan," Arland says.

"Are you sure?"

"Yes," Mom says.

Kegan gives her an appreciative smile and walks to the other side of Brad's bed, then takes his pulse.

"Where's Brit?" I ask Arland, again.

"Lann is training her. He was quite happy to do so, too."

Flanna turns up her nose as she crosses her arms. "Saidear could have trained her just as easily."

He scowls. "Saidear is in the communications room, contacting the Watchers, so they may come in for rest."

She stares at him, but doesn't speak another word.

I don't know what has her so upset. Maybe Flanna thinks Leaders shouldn't be in relationships, but that can't be true; she practically begged me to be with Arland.

"Okay, everyone, take a seat around the bed." Mom motions for me to sit in the chair closest to Brad's head. "Arland, sit as close to Kate as possible. I want everyone to hold hands, understood?"

Mom explains that when she saw Arland and me fight together last night, the magic was much more powerful when we were touching than when I acted alone. She feels our connection will give Brad a better chance of pulling through.

Arland tells her of my reaction to the coscarthas in the forest, and how he had to kiss me to get the portal to open again.

"As I said before, you two *together* are the key." She turns her eyes toward me. "Now do what comes naturally."

Taking a few deep breaths, I close my eyes and grab hold of Brad's right hand. He's warm, but not too hot; whatever medicines Kegan and Shay have given him seem to keep the fever down.

Mom sits across from me, holding Brad's left hand, Cadman next to her, then Flanna, Kegan, Arland, and me.

As we sit here together, I ask for you to heal my oldest friend Brad, please. We need to get him home to safety. I send out my prayer to the magic enchanting this land, hoping it works.

I open my eyes.

Everyone glances up, down, then at each other . . . waiting for something to happen, but nothing comes.

"You guys should ask the magic to wake up and heal him, too. *Nicely.*" I give Flanna a pointed look.

"Be nice—I can do that." She stares at her cousin and shifts in her seat.

The others close their eyes, and I hope they're sending up silent prayers.

Energy flows among us, warming my skin and rumbling in my core, but Brad still lies, almost lifeless, on the bed. There's no fire burning on my skin, or on Arland's.

He squeezes my hand as he leans into me. "Think about how much better you will feel when Brad is home."

I nod and return to concentrating on the fire, but all I think about is how much Brad hurt me, how many times he lied to me. Instead of feeling better, my chest tightens. Tears streak my face. I open my eyes and stare at him. My heart is heavy.

Mom watches me snivel like a baby. "Will you all, please, wait outside for a moment?"

Arland releases my hand and kisses my forehead.

"Except for you, Arland," she says.

Cadman and Kegan follow Flanna from the room. She glances at me before closing the door, giving me a reassuring smile.

"I know you're upset with Brad, but Kate, you must learn to control your emotions. If you can control your emotions, you can control the magic," Mom says.

I sigh. "I'm trying."

But, I don't know how to control my emotions. My best friend lied to me forever, but his actions don't genuinely matter because I have Arland . . . and love.

"You need to try harder." Mom straightens her tunic, then clasps her hands behind her back. "I'll be outside. Come get us when you're ready."

She closes the door.

I'm trapped, watching the boy who used to be my friend while he breathes.

Arland observes me staring at Brad. "Would you like for me to leave, as well?"

I lay my head in Arland's lap, and he plays with my tangled hair. "No."

My grief over Brad must hurt. "I'm sorry if I'm being selfish."

"Kate." Arland laughs. "You have not once acted selfishly. You trusted him. He took advantage of that trust, and you are hurt."

I stare up into his understanding eyes and thank the gods for giving him to me. I don't want to hurt Arland, don't want to make it appear as though I'm confused over who I love. I don't ever want to lose what we share.

"I *have* to do this."

Arland leans down and kisses my temple. "You *can* do this."

From some unknown place, a tiny bit of courage makes its way into my soul. I stand, ready to take this on. "Will you tell them they can come back in?"

"Are you sure?"

"Yes."

He opens the door and motions for everyone to rejoin us.

I point at the chairs around the bed. "Sit around him. Just like before."

When everyone takes their places, I think, not about Brad, not about the horrible things he's done, but about love. I think about my family, Arland, my desire to be alone with him—without distractions—and my desire for this war to be over, and for us all to be free.

Please, God.

On a gust of air, the sweet smell of honeysuckle drifts into the room, bringing the brilliant colors of magic. Thousands of sprites overtake the space above Brad's bed. Their tiny faces observe his mangled body.

Flanna and Cadman stare wide-eyed at the millions of little beings. They haven't experienced old magic the way Arland and I have. It protected them before, but now, with the beings filling the room and moving in the air all around us, the soldiers are touched by magic.

Blue flames cover everyone's bodies.

A few times, Kegan leans forward and tries to free his hands, as if he wants to reach out to touch the little beings—like I tried to in the forest—but Mom shakes her head, and he must think the better of it. I don't know how she stays focused; the sprites are intriguing.

"Will you heal him, please?" My question brings everyone's attention to me.

Sprites fly around each other, whispering things impossible for our ears to hear. Confusion fills their faces.

I lock eyes with my mom. I'm worried this might not work, worried Brad really might die if magic cannot help him, worried he will die and I'll still be mad at him, but her eyes remain hopeful.

The beings stop communicating with each other. At least an hour has passed since they entered the room. A swarm of blue sprites, shaped like sheets of flowing silk, covers every inch of Brad's skin and heals him before our eyes. The blisters covering his body, and the remaining fever, fade away, but he's still not moving.

When Mom first spoke of her plan, I didn't think it would work. But I thought if it did, the process wouldn't be this slow. The magic's lethargic reaction stops, and, as fast as they showed up, the sprites disappear into the earth.

Our group breaks our linked hands, and the fire on us diminishes.

My shoulders slump. "They didn't seem to know what to do."

"I don't believe they did. They have been asleep since well before Darkness entered the land. Magic hasn't had the opportunity to heal any wounds of this nature," Mom says.

"His fever and blisters are gone, though, ma'am. If we give him the antidote to the sleep he is under, do you believe he will be okay?" Kegan heads toward the dresser along the back wall.

Mom lifts one of Brad's eyelids, then takes his pulse. "It is possible that will work, but if he is not completely healed, it could cause him more trauma. We should take a break. We'll let the magic rest for a while. I need to think some things over."

We all leave the room. Everyone looks somewhat deflated, me more than anyone else. It's my friend who lies in that bed—someone who was my friend.

He may not have *ever* been my friend.

Chapter Twenty-Two

I am going to retrieve your sister from the training facility." Arland leaves me with Flanna in the kitchen.

"Okay," I say.

I refuse to meet anyone's eyes, refuse to talk, refuse to stop thinking about all the years of betrayals. Mom *and* Brad kept everything from me. At least Mom has some half-explained reasoning, but Brad? What explanation could he offer for beating up a guy I was genuinely interested in? What possessed him to hide his true feeling from me?

Flanna hands me some tomatoes and asks me to chop them for stew.

I grab a knife from the counter and set to work.

"What is wrong with you this time?" she asks, pouring a bucket of water into the pot over the fire.

"I think it's me."

"*What* do you think is you?"

"I'm so torn over Brad. I want him to wake up, and for us to be friends. At the same time, I'm mad at him, and want him to go home so I never see him again. I wonder if I'm the reason magic isn't responding well." I'm not really sure that's the reason, but I'm trying to make sense of it all.

Steam rises into the air.

Flanna takes a deep breath. "I see. Get over it, Kate. I talked to your mother and sister last night. Brad has not been good to you. He is not from here. He has to go home. Besides, you have everything you need."

I slice off the tomato stem. "Before we arrived here, almost every moment in my life had Brad in it. So, every time I think of my past, he'll be there."

Flanna gathers the chopped vegetables, then places them in a bowl. "Try to make amends with him before you convince him to leave."

If I talk things through with Brad, maybe I won't feel so guilty about sending him away. He'll have to understand we aren't from the same world. Flanna always knows what to say to make me feel better. "Hey, what was your prophecy?"

Flanna dumps the tomatoes in the pot over the fire. "It is about time you asked me that. The only part of interest to you is that I become Confidant to Light."

"Well, I didn't need a prophecy to tell me you were my friend. What about the part you don't think I'll be interested in?"

"I am still trying to figure it out." She's obviously not willing to divulge any more information.

Seems to be a common thing. Everyone's prophecies must be horrible. Arland's father never gave Arland his entire prophecy. Mom won't give me mine, and now Flanna won't share.

We have lunch ready to serve as the first waves of children enter into the dining area with Arland, Brit, and Lann. My sister runs down the stairs and over to where I'm standing in the kitchen, excitement written all over her face.

She's breathless, but smiling ear-to-ear. "I hit the bull's-eye five times in a row!"

"That's awesome. I couldn't even get the arrow to the target."

"I know." She looks over her shoulder at Arland. "He told me."

I scowl.

Crossing his arms, he shrugs and smiles.

As punishment, I send him away with bowls of stew to take out to the children.

He sets the food in front of Kent and Muriel, who recently came to one of our private training sessions. They're a couple years older than Marcus and Anna, and are fantastic sword fighters. Arland and I train Kent and Muriel a lot more often than we had expected. He said they might be ready to go out on scouting trips soon. I'm not as fond of the idea as he is, but it is the world we live in . . . as everyone always reminds me.

When the children see Arland, their faces light up. He swipes at the air a few times, like he's fighting something, and then falls over backward, gripping his heart. They laugh, and I find myself laughing, too.

Kent leans his head around Arland and waves.

I wave back.

"Will I see you again in training tomorrow?" Lann asks Brit, bringing my attention to the people standing in front of me.

Brit rocks on her toes, then smiles again. "Yep, first thing in the morning."

Lann bows. "Hello, Kate."

"Hello, Lann," I say, mimicking his formal tone.

He's the only person here who treats me like I'm some sort of queen, but I'm glad Brit found something to make her happy. I couldn't handle her being jealous of everything I do.

Once Lann is about ten paces away, she gushes over him. He's so cute, he's a great teacher, he's never seen such a natural shot, blah, blah. I would love to tell her to cool it, but what kind of hypocrite would that make me? Instead, I nod and agree at all the right times. Maybe something will happen between them, maybe it won't, but all I know is, I feel uncomfortable around Lann.

We finish lunch as Mom comes from Brad's room to gather our group, including Brit this time. Flanna brought Mom a bowl of stew earlier, but I don't think she ate much. Lost in thought, she didn't even look up when Flanna opened the door.

We leave the kitchen in the hands of Enid and go to try to save Brad, again.

Arland takes my hand as we walk down the hall. "I do not think Brad is my only competition."

My heart races. "Who else?"

The corner of his mouth twists into a wry smile. "I do believe Kent might have a crush on you."

"Oh! Well, then, you definitely have some competition. He *is* extremely handsome."

"I guess I will have to watch my back." Arland puts his arm around my shoulders and pulls me into him. "Are you still nervous?"

"Yes."

We enter the room and take our places around the bed, in almost the same order as before—Brit now stands next to Mom—then set to work again. Taking a few deep breaths, I close my eyes, calm myself, squeeze Arland's hand, and squeeze Brad's. I try to control my emotions, the way Mom said I should, try to control the magic without having to pray. I search inside myself, search for the strength, for the knowledge of how to control the power.

I think of love.

When I think of love, the magic comes to me.

Please, help me forgive Brad for the things he's done to me.

The fire in my core begins slowly, then, as if someone opened a door to a burning building—feeding the oxygen it needed to explode—the magic moves into Arland, Kegan, Cadman, Flanna, Brit, and finally Mom. All at once, they speak their requests for Brad to be healed.

I open my eyes as a flood of pink sprites enters Brad's body; they swirl around us and fill all the space in the room, then flutter toward him. Five, ten, fifteen minutes pass, before anyone dares to speak. A few sprites remain hovering over Brad and work until the rest of his blistered skin is renewed.

In the presence of the pink sprites, I'm happy, healthy, and warm. Tingles run along my arms. My stomach is full and satisfied, my thoughts excited. Tapping my toe, I hum Flanna's song and lean against Arland's shoulder.

Sprites make their way back into the earthen walls, leaving the rest of us with smiles on our faces.

"I have changed my mind, sir," Cadman says.

"About what?" Arland asks.

"I no longer wish to stop at Willow Falls. I would like to journey with you and Kate to your father's base. In fact, wherever the two of you go, I would like to serve."

Everyone bursts into laughter.

The invigorating power of the healing sprites has made Cadman want to travel with us to Wickward? I don't blame him. I feel like running a marathon. I think the sprites may have healed our spirits and tired bodies, as well as Brad's.

"What's so funny?" His voice breaks into our laughter, high-pitched and shaking.

His question only sends us deeper into our laughter, but we should be shocked Brad is awake and talking. Not even my mom can control herself. It's like we've all been drinking.

My side aches, and I gasp for breath. I know I must compose myself. Stifling the laughter, I force myself to speak. "We'll have to be careful the next time we summon healers. That was very . . . intoxicating," I say, drawing Brad's attention to me.

He sits up, lunges from bed, and lands flat on his face.

"Let me help you up," Arland says.

Our laughing stops. The redness in our cheeks fades and everyone takes deep breaths.

"No. No. I've got it." Brad hasn't moved his legs in weeks. The muscles are probably deteriorated from the lack of use. He scans the room and tries to stand again, but is still too weak.

Arland and Cadman each take one of Brad's arms and set him back on the bed.

"You need to take it easy for the next few days or so," Kegan says.

"Kate, what's going on? Where are we? Who are all of these people? Why do I feel so confused?" Squeezing his eyes closed, Brad presses his hand to his temples.

Kegan reaches into a drawer and pulls out a syringe. Surely, he doesn't think drugging Brad right now is going to help with anything. The Healer reminds me of a doctor in an old folk's home; any time the patient gets riled up, along comes a nurse ready to knock them out again.

"No, Kegan. What he needs right now is food, a bath, and information—not more drugs," I say.

Kegan looks to Arland for approval.

Arland puts up his hands. "You should listen to her or Leader Wilde."

I freeze. My mom's name is supposed to be secret. Arland just revealed who she is, and I'm sure Kegan now knows who I am, too. "Arland?"

"It is okay. Kegan and your mother are old friends."

"Kate?" Brad asks, gripping my arm with a sweaty hand.

"Brad, you have been in a coma for the last"—I look at Mom and Arland; I might as well start with the easy truths—"three weeks. We discovered how to heal you today, but it's going to take some time for your legs to get used to moving again. Cadman and Kegan will take you to the washroom to clean up. I'm sure the water will help your legs feel better. The rest of us will get some food ready." I have a lot more confidence than I did earlier.

"Please, don't leave me, Kate," he begs, squeezing my arm harder.

I cannot begin to imagine what it must feel like to wake up from a coma and discover you've been sleeping for weeks. So much has happened since he went under; some of it I don't know how to approach.

Arland and I meet eyes; he nods.

"I'll stay with you. Come on."

"Would you like me to carry him to the washroom?" Arland asks.

"No, I can handle this." I mean more than just taking Brad to wash up. I can handle being honest with my friend. He deserves the truth.

"I know you can," Arland says, and I know he understands.

Brad looks at us, but I don't give him an opportunity to say anything. Cadman and I lean our shoulders under Brad and prop his arms across our backs.

After a few failed attempts to move his feet, he gives in and allows us to carry him. But I'm too short to lift him high enough to keep his legs from dragging behind him.

The washroom feels like it's millions of miles away, with half of Brad's body weight on me. I nearly drop him when we reach the rocks surrounding the tub. I undress him down to his boxers, then move out of the way. Cadman carries Brad the remaining distance. Once Brad's situated, Cadman excuses himself to go find clean clothes and a towel.

I sit on the last stone step and hand Brad the bar of soap. "How are you feeling?"

He turns the bar over in his hands. "Confused."

"What's the last thing you remember?"

Minutes go by before he speaks again. His brain must really be mush if he's having this hard a time thinking of anything.

He looks at me, eyes lighting up. "Kissing you."

Our kiss has replaced every other bad memory in his head. My spirits—which were so lifted a short time ago—slink down and out of me. "Do you remember anything else? Like where we are, or why we kissed?"

"No, but I do remember how good you made me feel." Brad puts his wet hand on my face.

Water drips from his arm onto the stones.

I pull away.

"What's wrong?" he asks.

My apprehension is not going to be anything, compared to the heartache Brad will have when he finds out we kissed only because we thought we were going to die, *and* that I'm with someone else. So I lie. "Nothing, I'm fine."

Cadman enters with some fresh clothes; I could kiss *him* for this interruption. "Arland would like to speak to you. He is waiting outside the door."

"I'll be back in just a sec." Keeping myself from running down the steps of the enclosure and out of the room is the most difficult thing I've had to do all day. I don't want Brad to think I'm fleeing.

When I'm sure the door is closed, I throw myself into Arland's arms. "This is bad."

"Would you like me to stop hugging you?"

I glare. "I'm serious. The only thing Brad remembers is kissing me, and I might mention he seems very pleased by that. He doesn't remember why we kissed, or what happened next. How are we going to explain all of this to him without breaking his heart, or having him assume we're crazy?"

"What if we do not have to?"

"Do you suggest we take him back to the portal, throw him through, and hope he survives?" I throw up my hands, revealing how agitated I am by that thought.

"Not exactly." He laughs. "I was thinking we could cast a strong memory spell over him, and *then* send him back through the portal."

"I don't think what my mom did to Gary was fair. As much as I'm upset with Brad, I cannot allow that to happen to him."

Arland pulls away from me and tucks a strand of hair behind my ear. "He will not willingly leave you, Kate."

"Sure he will. He wanted to leave when we first got here." I know Arland is right, but I don't want to admit it.

"He wanted to leave with *you*. Try the truth. Maybe he will surprise us all and be very accepting of it."

"Well, when you put it that way, casting a spell and sending him home sounds like the perfect plan. The truth is going to hurt him." I rest my head on his chest.

"The truth usually does hurt—and we should wait until he is dressed before talking to him."

"*We?*"

"Yes. You should not have to go through this alone."

"Thank you." I stand on my toes and kiss him, then walk away.

Brad watches me as I come back into the bathroom, and somehow I cannot help but feel guilty. He knows something is bothering me, like I would recognize something bothering him.

"Are you ready to get out, sir?" Cadman asks.

Brad looks so pathetic stuck in the enclosure, unable to move on his own.

"I guess so," he says, clearly unsure of anything right now.

Cadman carries Brad down the steps, and we work together to get him dressed. As I suspected, his legs function much better after being submerged in the warm water. He's still wobbly, but being able to walk on his own is a big positive.

"Do you need our support still?" I ask.

"I think I can walk, but I wouldn't mind leaning on you." This is more like the Brad in the forest before we arrived here.

My stomach ties itself in knots.

"I will help you, sir," Cadman says, rescuing me . . . again.

Brad waves him off, but Cadman won't allow it; he has his shoulder under Brad in an instant, helping him walk out the door.

Other than our small group of trusted friends and family, no one is in the dining area when we arrive. I go into the kitchen and scoop some stew into a bowl.

"Where are all of the soldiers?" I ask Flanna.

"Arland ordered the soldiers not on watch to their quarters."

I take the bowl and place it on the table in front of Brad, then sit beside him. Arland sits next to me, along with Brit and Mom. Flanna and the others huddle around the table next to us.

"So, are you going to tell me what's going on?" Brad asks, in between bites of his stew.

I point to his meal. "Eat first."

"Can you at least tell me where we are?"

I shoot Brad a look that makes him stop asking questions—although his eyes ask a million more—but I'm not divulging anything until he eats.

My legs bounce up and down.

Arland places his hand over my left knee, but it only makes the shaking worse—I don't want Brad to see Arland's hand. I shoot Arland a look, too, and he recoils.

"Kate, I'm okay, there's no need to be so anxious." Brad's picking up on my anxiety, but for all the wrong reasons.

"I know you're okay."

He drops his spoon in his stew. "Please, tell me what's going on."

"Finish eating first."

He pushes away his bowl. "I'm done."

"Brad, it's been three weeks since you've eaten; *eat*," I say.

He returns to unwillingly spooning his stew into his mouth.

It's hard not to keep glancing at Arland. Every so often, he gives me a loving look, bringing me back to reality. Every time I look at Brad, I find he's glowering at Arland. If Brit hadn't told me about Mark, I wonder if I would've realized Brad's jealousy.

He finishes eating, then stares at me. "Well?"

I'm not ready for this yet; I need to stall. I lock eyes with Flanna.

"Kate, can you help me clean up?"

I nod, then rush from the room.

We make a quick decision to leave the dishes for later and stick to only clearing the tables.

Brad can't be a bad guy. I've known him too long to believe that. But why would he do that to Mark? Passing from the kitchen into the dining room, I avoid Brad's eyes while I gather more plates.

I stack the dishes on the counter. "Flanna, I want to flee, or stall, or hide in a corner somewhere. I can't even formulate a coherent thought right now, not to mention how badly I need to calm my nerves."

"It will all work out, Kate. Try to calm down."

Turning around, I find myself face to face with Arland.

"Follow me?" I ask.

He nods.

I go back into the dining area then collect more dishes. "I'll be right back," I tell everyone.

I drop off the bowls, then run through the corridor, past the communications room to the stairs. Sitting on the bottom step, I rest my head between my knees.

Why am I so afraid?

The sound of approaching footsteps gets my attention; Arland walks toward me. I try to smile, but fear I'm going to throw up. I have to put my head between my knees again.

He kneels in front of me, puts one hand on my thigh, then lifts my chin with the other.

His eyes are full of uncertainty.

"I am not positive the truth is the best option for Brad."

"I think you're right. Did you see the looks he was giving you?"

Arland cups his hand over my cheek. "Everyone noticed. Are you still opposed to wiping his memory?"

"It doesn't seem fair to wipe out all of his memories. His whole life would be a blur. We spent almost every moment together."

The summer after ninth grade, Brad and I *literally* spent every day together. We often referred to it as the summer of "Brate"—a conglomerate of our names, like Hollywood gives its couples. How will he remember that summer—or every one after—if his memory is tainted? He won't.

"Would it not be fair to Brad or to *you?*"

I stare at Arland, full of incredulity. Opening my mouth to protest, I realize he's right; *I* am not being fair to my former best friend. I have stumbled into a world where I've found I belong, and have fallen in love with someone, and I'm not willing to free Brad. I should give him the opportunity to go to *his* home and find someone who will love him the way he love me.

"Okay, what do we have to do?" I sigh.

"We have to answer his questions as vaguely as possible and convince him to travel to the clearing with us. Your mother and I will take care of everything else, once we get there."

Arland pulls me to my feet.

I lean into him and close my eyes as more memories of me and Brad on a tire swing flash, memories I'll never be able to talk about again.

Arland rubs my back, soothing away my worries with his touch. "You are making the correct choice."

"I hope so."

He tucks hair behind my ear. "Are you ready?"

I look up at his emerald eyes, and desire burns in me—desire to have more of him, more closeness, less stress, desire to be finished with my Brad situation. My heart races.

Arland smiles as he leans into me and pushes me up against the wall. Our lips meet. His warmth, his passion, his soft, soft lips, ignite yellow flames all over our bodies. Arland wraps his arms around me. I drape mine around his neck and get lost in him.

"What the hell is going on?" Brad screams, standing in the doorway and staring at Arland, face red and contorted.

Chapter Twenty-Three

Untangling our yellow, burning bodies from each other, Arland and I face Brad.

Heat fills my cheeks. I cannot meet his eyes. I want to run and hide . . . no, I want to avoid this confrontation completely.

Mom and Brit appear behind him, mouthing apologies. Cadman and Kegan arrive two seconds later, followed by Flanna, but they are all too late.

Brad storms down the hall, fists balled at his sides.

Arland pushes me behind him and takes a firm stance, bracing for a fight. The two stand face-to-face, staring each other down, both with clenched jaws. No one speaks, moves, or even appears to breathe.

I'm not even sure I'm breathing.

The two carry on some sort of unspoken battle with their eyes.

I glance toward the doorway. Everyone stands still, wide-eyed, mouths hanging open, and they appear to be waiting . . . waiting to see what's going to take place.

"How could you?" Brad asks, keeping his gaze focused on Arland.

Without a doubt, I know Brad is talking to me, but I cannot find the words to respond, cannot find the courage to speak to the guy who's always there when I need him. His question, I expected, but this fight, I did not.

"When you calm down, she will answer you." Arland's words ooze with confidence, revealing again why he is a Leader.

A dark look, full of contempt, passes over Brad's face; he reaches back, preparing to swing.

For a moment, everything and everyone disappear. The only things I see are Brad's fist, his anger, and his broken heart. I cannot allow this to happen. I have to stop him before this situation gets any uglier. I push myself in front of Arland, hoping to jolt Brad out of his fury.

My former best friend's fist slams into my left eye.

Cupping my face with my hand, I fall to the floor, too nauseated to stand. My ears ring. The room spins. A searing pain rips through my head.

Arland's fire changes from yellow to blue.

"Bhrú!" He yells, sending a flame from his body, which knocks Brad to the ground.

Cadman and Kegan run down the hall and grab Brad by the shirt collar.

"Let me go," he says, flailing and scratching at their arms.

"Bring him to the dining room." Cadman grabs Brad's forearm, making indentions on his skin.

Brad kicks his legs and screams at the top of his lungs while they drag him from my, and Arland's, presence.

The blood pumping through my head drowns out whatever Brad's saying.

Arland scoops me up.

"Can you see?" he asks, walking toward the kitchen while I rub my sore face.

I cannot answer, cannot think; my vision *is* blurry.

"Why the fuck won't you let me go?" Brad's curses reverberate down the hall. "Where am I? Why won't you let me see Kate?"

He's so blind with rage, I wonder if he even realizes he hit me and not Arland.

"Oh daor." Flanna sighs when we enter the kitchen. "That is going to leave a huge bruise."

"I am going to kill him," Arland says, setting me down on the counter.

Before he can go anywhere, I wrap my arms and legs around him. There's no sense in fighting. Yes, Brad is acting like a complete idiot, but we don't need to beat each other senseless over it.

"Why did you try to protect me? You do understand that Brad would not have hurt me, do you not?"

Arland's expression is hard, eyes angry; his reaction makes me cower like a small child.

"I wasn't trying to protect you as much I was trying to defuse the situation, but in hindsight, I guess it was pretty stupid." I'm ridiculous for thinking I could come between them. What I did equated to sticking my hand into a dogfight; I was bitten. I don't want Brad to be like this. If Arland had hit Brad, or vice versa, I would have been furious. It's probably better I received the blow, and no one else.

Arland rubs his fingers gently across my sore eye. "I am sorry. I am not upset with you; you have done nothing wrong. I am the one who keeps failing to protect *you*."

"Arland, do not touch it!" Flanna yells, moving between us, then she slaps a raw piece of chicken over my eye.

What I wouldn't give for a twenty-first century ice pack, right now.

Arland leans against the sink. Crossing his arms, he stares into the dining room. "We should tell Brad the truth after all."

Now he wants to hurt Brad, physically *and* emotionally.

I slide off the counter. "Okay."

After being punched, I don't care: we can wipe Brad's memory, or tell him the truth.

Arland wraps his supporting arm around me, and we leave the kitchen together.

Brad narrows his eyes, staring hard at Arland.

I look at him; his expression is stone cold, revealing no emotion at all. Arland is good at that.

Brad glances at the piece of chicken over my eye, and, instead of appearing ashamed, he returns his scowl to Arland.

We sit down at the table across from where Cadman and Kegan restrain Brad. I'm not sure how to act or what to do, so I clasp my hands together on the table and wait for someone else to start.

"Ma'am, will you allow me to sedate him?" Kegan asks.

"No." Mom and I abolish the idea together.

"Kate," Brad says, his tone curt.

I jump.

"Guilt does make you jumpy, doesn't it?" His words are snake-like.

My skin crawls.

"She has nothing to feel guilty about, boy. You are lucky you are still capable of speaking to her. Now, if you would calm down, she will explain everything to you." Cadman comes to my defense . . . again.

"Like hell she doesn't. I've been in a coma for three weeks, and she's been out screwing around with him!" Brad snaps, pointing at Arland, and then calms as quickly as a deranged mental patient. "Kate, can we talk alone?"

"Not in this lifetime. In case you do not remember, *You. Just. Hit. Her.*" Flanna shouts at him.

"It's okay. I don't mind talking to him alone." I take in everyone's shocked faces. My willingness to go anywhere with Brad surprises even me.

The muscles in Arland's face are so tight, I imagine his teeth cracking under the pressure.

"He won't hurt me," I whisper.

"She's right. I won't hurt *her*." Brad sounds nothing like the boy I grew up with.

Brit slams her hand on the table. "Shut up, Brad."

Arland appraises my wounded eye and rubs his thumb on my cheek. "You do not have to do this. You owe him nothing, now."

"You're wrong. I do owe him an explanation."

His face hardens. "We will *all* be waiting outside the door, in case you need us." Arland's soft-spoken words do not match the disapproval in his eyes.

Telling him it won't be necessary to stand outside the door would be worthless. I'm sure he would do it anyway. He may not be happy about this, but I have to talk to Brad. I have to at least try to make amends with him, like Flanna said, although she probably thinks I'm crazy for talking to him, too.

I hand her the meat. "Okay. Let's go back to your room, Brad."

Flanna growls and squeezes the chicken. She's definitely as appalled as everyone else is, but I ignore her and stand to leave with Brad. They don't know him the way I do, or did, or hope I do. He hurt me, but he's in pain, too.

Drawing in a steadying breath, I walk in silence, with Brad next to me, to what's been his room for the last few weeks.

Everyone else trails right behind us.

We enter the room, and Brad closes the door. The click makes my heart skip a few beats.

"In the bathroom, you asked if I remember why we kissed. Why *did* we kiss?"

I barely make it to one of the chairs by the bed, but thankfully, he's not yelling.

I pat the seat next to me. "Come sit by me?"

Brad walks over, lightly touches my throbbing flesh—I'm sure it's already bruised—and sits down.

He's been my best friend for years. Looking at him, I see that friend, and the memories we share. I want to hug him, want things to be the way they were—or almost the way they were. I want our friendship to be simple, the way it always was. But I guess it was always a lie, and I don't want that. I'm so confused.

"I'm so sorry. I never intended to hurt you. Seeing that . . . that guy with his hands all over you . . . ."

Avoiding what will surely cause an argument between us, I let go of his comment about *that guy*. "Are you sure there isn't anything else you remember?"

"I'm positive. The only thing I remember is kissing you." Brad pushes a hair from my face, looking at me like there's somehow still hope for an *us*.

I scoot my chair away from him. "Do you remember anything before you kissed me?"

He doesn't seem to get the point and moves closer. "There are some obscure memories, but none of them makes any sense. Why is this so important?"

"I'm hoping to re-build your memory. We found a cave. You, Brit, and me. The plan was to explore it, then head back to camp. Does this ring a bell?" I try maintaining a monotone voice, to keep him calm.

He stares at the candle flickering on the dresser; the light dances in his blue eyes. "We were camping. You and Brit wanted to show me your favorite swimming hole."

"Good. Then what happened?"

"I don't remember."

"Think harder."

Brad presses his fingers to his temples and closes his eyes. He has to search his memories and remember everything on his own. I fear if I tell him what happened, he won't believe me.

"That's when you found the cave under the water. We went to explore it. Only it wasn't a cave."

"Right. We fell on the ground when we swam through. Then what?"

"You were screaming." He opens his eyes. "I remember now; the creatures, the people rescuing us, the fever, it's all there."

Brad gets off the chair and paces back and forth between the door and me. He shakes his head and mutters inaudible words, fists balled.

I don't understand his increased agitation; I've never seen him this way.

"Brad, this world is my world. I was born here, and am back here now to help end a war, but you have to go home. Tonight, we'll ride you out to the clearing, so you can go back to your dad. Do you think you can handle that?" I ask, hoping to bring him out of his agitated state.

Brad keeps pacing and muttering. He stops and looks at me; an expression of limitless anger spreads across his face. "I *meant* it, Kate."

"You meant what?" My hands tremble. I take a deep breath. This is Brad. He won't hurt me. I shouldn't be afraid of him.

"What I said to you before the coma, that I want to marry you. I've known since the first time we met. And yet, you still don't care? Have you slept with him?" He's so close to my face; his breath warms my cheeks.

"Brad, that's none—"

"So, you have, then! I poured my heart out to you on my deathbed, and you've been fucking another guy! I thought you were better than that. I thought you had feelings for me, too. Why did you kiss me back? Why didn't you just let me die?"

Tears stream down my face. I don't dare tell Brad that Arland and I have absolutely not slept together. Brad's anger flows so freely, I'm afraid he might hurt me, on purpose this time.

He returns to pacing.

Sitting in shock, I remain silent, trying to work up enough courage to bolt from the room. I press my feet to the floor, but he blocks my escape and leans face-to-face with me.

Brad narrows his eyes. "We would've been really great together. We could've had kids, opened our own vet clinic, or operated our own farm. You would've made me the happiest man alive. I've had a ring picked out for a long time. Without your parents, I realized this trip was perfect for us to be alone. I'd planned on telling you everything, but now you've ruined *everything*! I can't believe I wanted to marry you!"

God, please, help me.

This is not the Brad I've known since we were little, not the Brad who plays with my hair when I'm stressed, or helps me with my homework. That Brad never so much as raised his voice to me. He's accusing me of ruining his life. We've kissed once; why on Earth would he have picked out a ring for me?

Mom was right. I should've told Brad how I felt, years ago, but after coming on the trip, I kind of thought there might be a future... until I met Arland. Besides that, I found out about Mark, and now, I've seen the way Brad treated Arland. Brad *is* too possessive, obsessed, even. Everything he's ever done has probably been a lie and a way to get closer to me, or to keep others from me.

He spreads out his arms, palms facing up. "Are you going to say anything?"

"I—"

There's a knock at the door.

"Kate? Your mother would like to speak to you," Flanna says.

"Leave us alone," Brad yells over his shoulder, then scowls at me. "Don't you think you owe me some kind of response?"

I close my eyes; the magic burns inside. Without looking, I know my skin is ablaze with the brilliant blue color. A renewed courage takes hold of me. Opening my eyes, I look at Brad's angry face. He doesn't step back, doesn't seem to see the fire engulfing my skin.

There's no choice. He has to go home now.

"I love you, Brad, but it's never been the same way you love me. This could've all been avoided if you had been honest with me much earlier in our lives. Please, will you ride to the clearing with us, so we can take you home?" I try hard to keep my voice void of emotion.

Brad crosses his arms. "No! I'm going to wait here until your little boyfriend drops you on your ass, and I'm going to laugh at you when he does."

He spits in my face.

"*Arland!*" I yell, knowing it's wrong, but I want Brad to hurt. He's a mean liar and deserves to be punched after his tirade.

Arland bursts through the door. "Kate, leave now!"

I run from the room and throw myself into my mother's loving arms. She brings me away from the hall, leading me toward the kitchen.

"So you're Kate's baby-sitter now? I hope you enjoyed screwing the only woman I've ever loved." Brad yells before Mom and I are out of earshot.

The door slams before I hear Arland's response.

My heart aches worse than it ever has. Tears blind me. I'm cold, but sweating.

Mom rubs my back and pulls hair out of my face as a wave of vomiting takes over. "Flanna, get something under her."

Flanna rushes a wooden bucket under my mouth, and I puke for what seems like way too long, considering how little I've eaten today.

My stomach twists and burns. With each heave, my chest constricts and my muscles weaken.

I sit on the floor, then lean against the wall.

"What happened?" Mom asks.

I tell her everything: how Brad accused me of having sex with Arland, how Brad made it seem like I was cheating on him, how he wanted to marry me, how he had a ring picked out, how he spit in my face.

She wraps her arms around me, squeezing my numb soul. "Kate, I'm so sorry. I never expected Brad to react that way. He's been hiding this very dark side of himself well."

"What do you think they're going to do to him?" I expected Arland to hit him and be out of there already, but it's been at least fifteen minutes, and I haven't heard the door open even once.

"Kegan and Arland are going to wipe his memory."

"*What?*"

"We discussed it while you were talking with Brad. If he had willingly come with us to the clearing, we would've left his memory intact, but his dark obsession with you is too powerful. I don't know if it's possible, but I fear he might try to come back through the portal."

I pull out of Mom's arms. "I didn't even get to say goodbye!"

"Why would you even want to? He spit in your face and basically told you he hopes Arland leaves you broken and miserable." Brit hops up onto the counter.

"That will never happen," Arland says, walking into the kitchen without a smile. He stares at me. His face is emotionless, but his eyes tell exactly how much he's bothered by the situation.

"Kate, will you walk with me for a moment?"

I nod.

Arland reaches out for me.

Linking my shaky arm through his, I walk with him toward Brad's room.

Arland pauses outside the door. "I did not hit him. It took a lot of restraint not to do so. We have cleaned his memory of everything that has happened since he caught us outside the communications room. Would you like to say goodbye to him now, or would you like us to finish?"

Confused by the question, I look at Arland. After everything that's happened, *do* I want to say goodbye? A moment ago, I was upset about not having the chance to say goodbye, but now that it's here, I don't want it.

"Finish it."

Arland re-enters the room.

Cadman has his hand on Brad's shoulder; the two stand by the bed.

He catches sight of me before Arland closes the door. "Kate! Let me go! I have to see her."

Before I change my mind and burst through the door, I wrap my arms around myself and run back to the kitchen. How did it come to this? How did I lose the boy I put stars on my bedroom ceiling with, when we were little? How did he turn into this monster? How come I never saw this?

"What did Arland want?" Flanna asks.

Tears stream down my face. "He gave me an opportunity to say goodbye. I didn't do it."

Flanna leads Mom, Brit, and me up to the stables, then puts us to work. I have a feeling she's doing it only for me, to help clear my head, but Mom and Brit don't complain. They take care of the cows and goats, while I spend time with Mirain.

She welcomes me in her stall, giving me little nudges with her nose. Resting my head against her chest, I listen to her breathe for a while, before I finish brushing her.

No one talks in the stables; we only work. Shovels hit the earth, and straw rustles as it's spread about. Except for an occasional sigh, it's quiet in here with Mirain. My spirit has not lifted at all, but being with her helps.

I grab some oats from a bag and offer them to her. "Who sent you to me, girl?"

Mirain eats the oats from my hand. When her mouth touches my palm, a vision flashes. A beautiful, bright-golden-skinned man with long, silver hair and a matching beard, dressed in a white robe, revealing a chest full of rippled muscles, stabs a sword into the ground, then turns to walk off. Beside him, a golden mare stands. The vision fades, but I want to see more of it. The man was elegant, warm.

Instead of giving me the same man, a second vision replaces him. Arland, Mom, Brit, Flanna, Cadman, Perth, and I all stand with our backs against a damp rock wall. Light blazes out of all of us, revealing an army of hundreds of thousands of approaching daemons.

There's nowhere to run.

The daemons are led by a man covered in blood from head to toe, wearing no clothes at all. He carries his sword, and an evil smile mars his face. His eyes are hollow and black. On the ground around our feet, and as far as can be seen in the dark, lie the dead. Daemons hover over the bodies—possibly eating them, I'm not sure. I'm so disturbed, I avert my eyes.

My knees fail me.

I fall, trembling.

This is the end.

"Brad, please don't do this!" I scream to the naked man before me.

Chapter Twenty-Four

"Tell me again. What happened?" Arland's voice thickens with concern.

"She was with the horses, while we were on the other side of the stables," Mom says. "After an hour, she started screaming. We weren't sure what happened. We found her on the floor, convulsing."

"Her eyes rolled back in her head. We could not get her to look at us or talk to us." Flanna sniffles.

Has she been crying?

"How long has she been like this?" Kegan asks.

I imagine he's ready to jab a needle into my arm, put me under the way he and Shay did to Brad. The thought of Brad sends a stabbing pain through my chest. The vision of his naked body, attacking us, killing innocent people . . . .

"She's been under nearly three hours," Mom whispers.

Three hours?

"Maybe she has a concussion from Brad punching her?" Brit chimes in.

Oh, Brit, always the drama queen; although, she makes a valid point. I haven't ever passed out this long from a vision.

"And she was with Mirain?" Arland must be coming to the same conclusion I already have, that Mirain shows me things.

"Yes," Mom, Brit, and Flanna all announce together, with a slight edge. It's clear they have told Arland this before.

"I believe she had another vision." Arland brings my hand to his mouth and gently kisses my fingers.

"Kate, if you can hear me, please, wake up."

I've been awake long enough to know how concerned they are for me; it's not fair to eavesdrop while they worry. Opening my eyes, I smile, but quickly stop. The left side of my face stings. I touch the warm, tender skin. Swelling reaches halfway down my face, over my nose, and up to my temple. The skin has to be discolored, as well.

Relief is on the faces of everyone around me, except Arland. He clenches his jaw, narrows his eyes, and his hands hold the edge of the bed, as though he wants to tear the mattress apart. He looks like he wants to run from the room, scream obscenities, and hug me, all at the same time.

"How do you feel?" Mom asks.

I'm not sure I want to look away from Arland, but I do.

Blood thrums in my ears. "L-like my eye is on fire, a little confused as to why everyone is standing around me like I'm in a hospital d-dying, and somewhat worried about some things going on in my life, but otherwise I'm fine. Thanks f-for asking." My sarcastic response does little to cover the uneasiness I'm feeling.

Mom rests her gaze on me, and everyone laughs nervously. But when I sit up, and they see I *am* fine, the joke catches on and the laughs become more honest.

Arland watches me. He hasn't spoken, hasn't touched me since he kissed my hand.

I cannot breathe. Why is he so angry? What did I do?

"Why did you pass out, Kate?" Brit asks the question that is surely on the tip of everyone's tongue, the question I don't want to answer in front of Kegan.

"I don't know. Exhaustion, maybe."

Arland looks at me cross-eyed. He knows I'm lying. I'm pretty sure everyone in the room does, too, but I don't want to tell them about my visions. Finding out what they mean is more important than causing a panic over Brad. And after the day we've had, causing a panic doesn't seem like the best idea.

Whatever is bothering Arland, he snaps out of it. His grip on the mattress relaxes; his back straightens.

"Kegan, go check in with Lann. Let him know Kate is okay, then begin inventory on our medical supplies. Send Saidear to the training facility. Have him gather all the remaining weapons, and a few targets for practice, and bring them into the sleeping quarters. Due to the daemon activity, we will not be traveling between the two buildings for the remainder of our stay. Flanna, get Brad something to eat. We will leave for the clearing at 3:00 a.m.," Arland says.

The instant the door closes, Arland sits in the chair next to the bed. His face softens. "What did you see?"

Meeting his eyes, I put my hand on his cheek. "Tell me why you're so upset, first."

He's pale and clammy; his expression shifts between angry and happy to see me.

Mom squeezes Arland's shoulder. "Kate, Arland wiped Brad's memory. When you take someone's memories from them, you get glimpses into their minds, their life, their thoughts. You see things the way they did. Anything Brad ever did with you or thought about you, Arland has seen and felt through Brad's eyes. You can imagine how hard that must have been for him."

Oh my God, *hard*? That must have been horrible. What did he see that's angered him so much? Why does he look like he wants to kill Brad? If he saw and felt what Brad was feeling, does that mean Arland is mad at *me*?

I have to know. "What did you see?"

Mom shakes her head. "I don't think it would be a good idea for Arland to tell you."

A tear hangs from Brit's chin. "Mom, I think it would be *great* for Kate to hear."

"Arland? Please?" I beg.

He sits on the bed next to me and takes my hands in his. Keeping his eyes down, Arland rubs his thumb lightly over my knuckles. "Kate, I saw a young boy who loved you very much, but as that boy grew, he became obsessed with you, when that love was not reciprocated. I saw him leading a life full of lies, so he could be close to you. He betrayed you more than once, and he enjoyed when you were hurt, so he could be closer to you. I saw a boy who was sad, who felt like a shadow in your world."

I never meant to hurt Brad, and I never expected him to hurt me. "W-what else?"

"When he saw us together, Kate, he had murderous thoughts—"

"That's enough." Mom gives Arland a stern look.

I feel like someone has taken a sledgehammer and slammed it into my chest. I'm capable of taking only short breaths. I see Arland, Mom, and Brit through the tears, but I cannot hear anything they're saying. My hands are cold. I'm sure Arland saw a lot more than he's telling me. Brad and I were friends for a long time, and he was always there, but for some reason, Mom doesn't want Arland to go on.

How could that sweet little boy from the playground turn out to be such a monster? Why did none of us recognized how bad he was? He saved his mother's life once; if he was such a bad person, why would he have done that?

Blinking the tears from my eyes, I see concern in Arland's.

No. I refuse to wallow, refuse to let Brad get the best of me, refuse to be upset over this. I'm mad. I think, for the first time in my life, I might actually hate someone.

Taking deep breaths, I focus on those in front of me, those who love me for who I am and what I want—or rather, for what I'm going to become. Wiping the tears from my face, I grip Arland's hand. "In the stables, I was feeding Mirain. I asked her who sent her to me. She showed me a vision of a man with a golden mare. He was beautiful. Before the vision faded away, he stabbed a sword into the ground and left it there."

Anger flows through me, making my skin burn. I throw the wool blankets from my legs.

Mom sits on the foot of the bed. "Is that when you fainted?"

She doesn't show it, but she must be shocked I'm not reacting worse to the news about Brad.

I'm not going to let him affect me any longer.

I take another deep breath. "No. There was another, horrible vision—"

"Hold up. Did you just say Mirain showed you the vision?" Brit asks, voice raised.

"It is not the first time Kate has experienced visions while in proximity to Mirain," Arland says, reminding me of the first vision she showed me, the one of Brad killing him.

I fight an urge to flee the room and punch Brad in *his* eye.

"Mirain was a gift from Griandor." Arland rubs his thumb over my knuckles. I think he's trying to calm me, not himself. My fury must be visible on my face, in my words, in the sweaty grip I have on him.

"I believe you are right, Arland. Griandor seems to have a lot of involvement with Kate." Mom turns to face me.

"Kate, what was the other vision?"

"Brad led the army for Darkness. Everyone had been murdered except for the four of us, Cadman, Flanna, and Perth. Brad had us cornered. I begged him to stop, but he didn't. That's when I fainted." I leave out the details of Brad being naked, with hollowed eye sockets, and covered in blood. Those details will remain locked away; they are too painful.

Arland stands so fast his chair falls back. "Can you ride?"

"I thought you'd never ask," I say.

"What are we going to do?" Brit asks, legs bouncing.

"We are not going to wait until three. Kate and I are going to get Brad out of here, now. This is not the first vision she has had of him trying to kill us. I fear the longer he is here, the more danger we are in." Arland lifts me to my feet.

I sway from standing too quickly. He pulls me into him, then wraps his arms around me. Leaning my head against Arland's chest, I listen to each of his calming breaths.

The anger begins to subside.

"I am going to get Cadman. Brit, you stay here and help Flanna. Can you two handle bringing Brad up?" Mom asks Arland.

"That sounds like the best deal for me." Brit bolts from the room.

"We will meet you in the stables with Brad," Arland says.

Mom leaves.

He stands me straight up and looks at me with questioning eyes.

I try to give him my best *I'm okay* look. It must work; he takes me by the hand and leads me from our room.

Flanna is talking to Brad in the dining area. He pauses in his conversation and looks from my hand in Arland's hands, to my eye, to Arland. I get the sinking suspicion Brad remembers me, the fight, everything. But, I think if he did, he would be trying to murder Arland right now, not sitting in his seat, looking timid and confused.

"Are you ready to return to your home?" Arland asks Brad.

The politeness infuriates me. Containing my disappointment in Brad, my resentment from his years of continuous betrayal, is impossible.

My hand shakes; Arland squeezes it. I'm almost positive the squeeze means *control your emotions*.

Brad meets my eyes. He quickly narrows his gaze and sets it on Arland. "Yes, I'd like that."

Hearing Brad speak makes my heart ache for the guy I thought I knew, for the friend I've always thought was the best, for a comforting hug from the arms I've felt around me a million times.

My muscles tense. No. I will not allow him to upset me.

Arland squeezes my hand again, sensing my emotions so well. I wonder if he knows what I'm thinking, or if my thoughts are that obvious.

"Then you must come with us, now."

Brit peeks around the wall from the kitchen; she raises her eyebrows, giving me her best *get over it* look.

I shrug.

Flanna stands and grabs Arland's forearm. "I thought we were leaving at three."

"Plan's changed." I answer for him.

She nods, then darts off toward her room.

Brad follows Arland and me through the corridor. I run up the stairs leading to the stables, with them behind me. I don't want to look at Brad, or think about him, ever again. I want to get this over with. Reaching the top, I push through the door then run to the horses' stalls.

Arland has Brad wait by the straw bay while he helps me gather the horses. I lead two of the stallions and one mare out to join Mirain and Bowen, as Mom walks in with Cadman.

"Sir, we should take four horses, so we do not have an extra on the ride back," Cadman says.

Arland nods. "Brad, would you mind riding with Cadman?"

I lead one of the stallions back to his stall.

"He can ride with me," I call over my shoulder, then close the gate.

Arland scowls at me.

If Brad ever gets his memory back, I want him to know how much I wanted him gone. I want him to suffer. Acting on revenge is nasty, but right now, it makes me feel somewhat better.

Mom watches Arland. "Kate, I don't think that's the best idea."

Brad looks between us. His blue eyes are big, round. Rubbing his hands together, he looks confused, scared

Arland glares as though he wants to hurt Brad the way he's hurt me, then Arland glares at me. I'm sure he wants to yell at me for offering a spot on my horse to Brad.

Handing the reins to Mom, I walk next to Arland and stare up into his angry eyes. "It's okay. I'm not doing this for him; I'm doing it for me."

His shoulders slump, and his anger fades. Arland puts his arms around my waist. "Kate, he does not deserve your kindness," he says, just as quietly.

"I'm not doing it to be kind."

Arland takes me by the arm to lead me inside Bowen's stall.

Before we step behind the wall, I look over my shoulder.

Brad eyes us curiously.

Mom begins a conversation with him, but Cadman stays close to her.

Everyone seems to be afraid of Brad.

"He will ride with me or Cadman, but not with you."

"Why did you bring me in here to say that?"

Arland's face is hard, nothing like the emotionless mask he normally puts on. "Kate, before, when I told you Brad was thinking murderous thoughts, he was not planning to hurt me. It was you he wanted to kill."

He balls my shirt in his fists.

My heart has already missed beats because of Brad, multiple times, actually. This news should hurt, should scare me, should make me hate him more, but it doesn't; this new information only makes me anxious to leave, ready to say goodbye forever.

Arland relaxes his hands. "Are you okay?"

"I'm fine. I just want to get this over with."

His forehead creases. "Do you still want him to ride with you?"

"Yes. I want him to hurt, if he ever remembers."

He tucks my hair behind my ears. "I do not think it is wise for you to be spiteful, Kate. It is not your nature."

"Arland—"

"Stay close to me. I do not trust him," Arland says before I can finish saying I've never been spiteful in my life, so this one time, I think everyone could excuse me.

"Thank you. I'm so sorry you had to see all of his horrible thoughts."

Arland hugs me, then brushes his lips against mine. His gesture is not nearly what I need from him—not nearly what I want.

We walk out to join the others, then mount our horses. Mom and Cadman mount theirs.

Brad looks between us all. "Who am I riding with?"

"Me," I say.

He quickly looks up to Arland.

He straightens on Bowen. "It is okay. Kate is the best rider and is the strongest of all of us."

Brad considers my offered hand. He takes it; I pull him onto Mirain with me. Keeping his palms on his thighs, he maintains a distance between us. Arland, Mom, and Cadman all stare, but if Brad tries to hurt me, Arland is close . . . and magic is on my side.

"You do realize you're going to fall off if you don't hold on to me, right?"

Brad circles his arms around my waist but doesn't hold on tight. He's trembling as if by touching me, he'll spontaneously combust.

The familiar closeness of his touch, of his warmth, everything about this reminds me of a time I took Brad riding bareback on the farm. He was never fond of riding without a saddle, not like I am. He kept his arms tightly around me; he was so scared, he didn't dare release them. He kept saying, "Saddles aren't that bad once you get used to them."

The doors swing open.

Arland gives me a pointed look. "Stay close."

Our group speeds through the dark woods like lightning through the sky on a stormy night. We bolt through the forest in a straight line, making sharp turns along the path, moving so fast that if we were glowing, there would surely be a trail of light behind us.

Mom and Cadman ride my flanks, Arland rides in front, forming a triangle of protection around me.

He stays two paces ahead, continuously looking over his shoulder at me and Brad. I'm positive Arland wants to make sure the one person I've entrusted almost everything to for my entire life, including my first kiss, doesn't kill me. The memory of that first kiss—when I thought my best friend was going to die, when I thought I was going to die—pierces my heart.

Life has changed so quickly, since my world turned upside down.

We pass the trees so fast they appear like brown blurs against the Darkness; it's like riding in a car. As a child, I used to stare straight ahead while at the same time watching the trees zip past out of the corners of my eyes.

Now, the trees zipping by don't have the same nostalgic feeling. Instead, riding with Brad is thrilling and frightening all at once. I'm happy he'll no longer be around to hurt me, to confuse me, to lie to me, but I'm scared to death he'll suddenly remember everything and try to kill me while we ride.

I pray our plan to get him home will work.

We reach the Watchers at the perimeter and bring the horses to a halt. None of the soldiers approach or ask questions, and Arland doesn't give them any orders.

Ogilvie and Dunn are on watch tonight. They stand at attention as we wait near the spot where, not that long ago, Arland and I fought a forest full of daemons, together. Where we discovered that our love for each other makes us stronger.

He turns to look at me, and smiles.

Returning his smile, my heart melts in my chest; a flash of our *alone* time in the straw speeds through my head. I wish Flanna hadn't interrupted us. I wish it was Arland's arms wrapped around my waist right now, not Brad's.

"Something about him bothers me," he whispers, bringing me from my thoughts with a jolt.

"I don't like the way he looks at you. Did he do that to your eye?"

We're at the edge of the forest, waiting for Arland to give the command to proceed. I know who Brad is speaking of, but I ask anyway. "Who?"

"Arland."

Brad thinks Arland hurt me? This, coming from the guy who beat up any guy who ever showed an interest in me, who thought about murdering me when he saw me in someone else's arms? I laugh, then stare at Arland. He has his eyes closed, listening for danger, whispering magic to the wind. "He's a good man. *He* would never hurt me."

Brad doesn't respond. He turns toward Arland. Because of the shift in body weight, Mirain strays to the left a bit.

I wonder what Brad's thinking? Does he believe I'm a girl with an abusive boyfriend?

"It seems clear. Ride fast." Arland speaks low but sternly.

We leave the cover of the surrounding forest and enter the endless sea of Darkness. Sending requests out to the magic, I try to wake it ahead of our arrival. Having the portal open and ready seems better than having everyone wait for me to do it in front of Brad; plus, he'd never understand.

We approach the spot that holds so many strange memories for me. I wonder if the area will spark any stray ones in Brad.

His blank expression doesn't change when we bring the horses to a stop in front of the portal, so I imagine the memory spell they've cast over him has worked the way it's supposed to.

We slide from the horses.

Brad stands next to me, eyebrows raised as he looks around. He probably thinks this is some kind of joke.

I point toward the glistening edges of the portal. "This might sound strange, Brad, but you just have to step through that."

He shrugs. "I don't see anything."

Brad couldn't see the portal above the water when we were on the other side, either. Ready to lead him to it, I take his hand in mine.

Before I can move forward, Arland reaches out and catches my other hand.

"You do not need to see it. Walk in the direction Kate showed you," he says, keeping a firm hold on me. "This is where we stop."

Arland thinks Brad is lying.

"I'm sorry, but I feel strange walking into something I cannot see." Darkness flashes in his eyes, reminding me of the Brad from my earlier vision.

I shudder. Gripping Arland's hand even tighter, I shake free from Brad's hold, then step back.

Responding to fear as it spreads through us, Arland and I ignite in flames.

Brad stands with his hands clasped behind his back, unfazed by our burning bodies. I don't doubt Brad cannot see the portal, but I know he has never been honest with me.

Something deep inside tells me he's not being honest right now, either.

"Do you want to go home?" My fire glows brighter, stronger.

The sweet, blue eyes of my best friend return. "Yes, but I want you to come with me."

Maybe the spell didn't work, after all? "I-I'm sorry?"

Brad brings his face within inches of mine.

Arland tugs me away.

"I know you. I don't know how, and I don't know why you act as though we've just met, but something tells me I know you very well. Why would you want to stay here—wherever the hell we are—when you can come and be free?"

Arland backs us away further. Pushing me behind him, he maintains a protective stance.

Brad watches us closely, envy on his face.

Every time I innocently fell asleep next to him, it meant something different to both of us. All those years in the dark with him—he makes me feel dirty, betrayed, and most of all, furious. Now, even after his memory has been wiped clean, he somehow still holds onto a fascination for me. I'm going to scream at him, tell him just to get the hell out of here....

"Brad, it is time for you to go home. Kate will not be coming with you," Arland yells.

Mom and Cadman stare at the flames dancing over Arland and me.

I catch Mom's eyes.

She's whispering things, probably trying to protect us with her own magic.

Brad takes five steps in the direction of the portal, stops, then turns back to us. "I remember you now. I helped you off the playground after you scraped your knee."

Arland braces himself and pushes me back further behind him.

Cadman takes up Arland's left side, Mom his right.

This is my mess. If Arland expects a fight, I'm fighting with him. I step from behind him and stand on his left, next to Cadman.

I don't think anyone was prepared for Brad to get his memory back so soon.

Watching as he shakes his head, we don't speak.

His memories must be flooding in. Brad grits his teeth, pinches his nose between his finger and thumb, and closes his eyes. "It's not just that day I remember. There are other things too, like sleeping in your bed before we went on the hike that led us here."

He lifts his head and runs to me.

"Brad, you—"

"Why are you sending me away? After everything we've been through together, why?" He looks at Arland.

"For him?" Brad cups my cheeks. "I love you! It's always been about you, Kate. You have to see that!"

I hold onto Arland so hard, I'm worried I might break the bones in his hand. My feet lose feeling. I feel like I'm floating and have no control of myself or my emotions, but I have to speak. I cannot stand here, with Brad in front of me, and not say anything.

Trying to regain some control, I take a deep breath. It's no use. I'm mad. "You lied to me for years. You fought off guys who showed an interest in me. You punched *me* when you saw Arland and me kissing. You may not ever understand why I'm staying here, but this—" I release Arland's hand, and spread my arms out wide. Almost impossibly, the blue flames become even brighter, making me feel confident. "This is my home."

Brad's expression instantly darkens. Instead of begging me to rethink my decision, he lunges. His baby blue eyes turn black, and his face contorts with rage.

Arland jumps in front of me and pushes me back.

Cadman and Mom grab my hands and pull me away, near the horses.

A wave of blue flames extends from Arland, knocking Brad to the ground. "Go through the portal, now, or we will force you through."

He scrambles to his feet. "No!"

Arland marches toward Brad—about to make good on his threat—when my ears fill with sounds of huge wings flapping in the wind. Thousands of squeaking noises fill the air, sending chills up my spine. I can't put my finger on what the shrill noises remind me of, but they come repeatedly, and from all directions. I cannot see anything over us. I know this can't be good.

My hair lifts. Goose bumps prick up my arms.

Cadman stares at the sky. "Sir, we must leave, *now*."

Arland doesn't look away from Brad. "Get on the horses. Go without me."

Mom pushes me toward Mirain.

I turn to run to Arland, but Mom wraps her arms around me and holds me tightly.

"No! I'm not leaving you." I scream, kicking and squirming.

"You must go, Kate," Arland yells.

I break free of Mom's grip but run into Cadman.

"We'll fight. Whatever it is, we'll fight. I'm not leaving you!"

He carries me to Mirain.

I try to pry his fingers from my arms, but it's no use. "I have to stay and help Arland."

Cadman is stronger than I am, and it seems Mirain is working with him. She kneels down, giving him the edge he needs to force me onto her back.

"Ma'am, we cannot fight the bats."

The squeaking sounds reminded me of bats flooding the navy-blue evening sky, on their way out of their home, looking for food. But something tells me these are no normal bats, and they won't be searching for bugs to eat. "Arland never mentioned *bats*!"

Cadman glances toward the sky. "There was no need to; we thought them to be extinct."

More familiar shrieks come from behind us.

Mirain rears and spins in circles.

I cannot see any monsters, but I know they're here. I growl. "I'm not leaving Arland."

"Kate, you have to," Mom says. "He will be okay."

I narrow my eyes. "How can you say that? If we can't fight the bats, how is Arland supposed to survive?"

I can't believe she thinks leaving him is the best idea. She must know he cannot handle an attack like this by himself. Can *we* survive this attack?

Constantly being at war is not the life I would choose for myself. I want so much more, more time discovering who I am, more time learning about animals, more time with my family, more time loving Arland . . . especially Arland.

Control your emotions, Kate. Fight this. Save Arland. If you don't, he will die. Brit's voice penetrates my thoughts, but she's not here; she can't be talking to me.

I look around for her, then shake my head at how weird that would be.

"Did you say something?" I ask Mom.

"We need to go. He will be fine, Kate," Mom says. She's afraid. Her horse stomps, shakes its tail, and spins around, taking cues from Mom's nerves.

"No, I refuse to leave."

Closing my eyes, I take deep breaths and work to calm my emotions . . . to control my emotions. I have to do this. I cannot wait. I will not leave. I will not allow Arland to be hurt. I think of love. I think of my heart. I think of our future.

Power bubbles in my core, then spreads out over every inch of my body. The flames on me become almost too blinding for me to open my eyes. "Light the air; reveal the monsters to us. Protect us, please," I ask of the magic.

Sprites burst out of the ground and flood the air, leaving holes in the earth. A patch in the Darkness opens over our heads, revealing six-winged creatures flying in circles. There are at least one hundred coscarthas steadily walking toward the portal, not even attempting to sneak.

Looking up and out at the army of daemons, I fight against the fear trying to regain control of me. I push it down and away from myself.

Brad turns his face toward the sky and looks at the daemons Cadman called bats.

Their wings are the same shape, but their bodies are anything but that of a bat. All black, and at least six feet in length, they have the heads of men; their eyes are tiny slits of orange madness; with human-like arms and legs, and hands with claws—the same sharp, deadly claws as the coscarthas. The winged creatures swoop down at us, like a normal bat would for a bug above the water, but never do more than graze us with their strangely soft wings.

A smile stretches across Brad's face. It makes no sense he would have this kind of reaction. Maybe he thinks he's dreaming. Maybe he thinks he'll wake up and have the opportunity to tell me he loves me all over again.

"Brad, you have to go through the portal or they'll kill us all," I yell, trying to pull him out of his daze.

Arland looks back at me, then at the path we rode to get here. Does he really want me to leave without him?

I shake my head.

He smiles, as if to say, "Even with all this around us, I see only you, I worry for you, I love only you." At least, that's how I feel. I no longer have any fear of these creatures, only fear that I will lose love.

I've distracted him. Brad jumps onto Arland, knocking them both to the ground. They exchange repeated blows. One stands. The other pushes him over. Brad jumps up, swings, and falters as he connects with nothing but air. Arland throws a punch, landing his fist against Brad's nose. Red dust rises around them. Their clothes are covered in dirt and blood. It's so primitive, yet hard not to watch as important pieces of my two worlds collide.

Mom tugs on my arm. "Kate, if you want to stay, you have to do something."

Death comes at us from all directions. The coscarthas run toward us, the bats swoop closer. One of the bats kicks me in the back of my head. I don't understand why they haven't killed us, but I have to do something before they do.

"*Stop!*"

My voice floats along, carried by the magic. But none of the daemons responds. Everything continues to go on as though the magic isn't here, as though there were no Light surrounding us, as though my power means nothing.

I've always thought Brad had the build to be a good fighter, but never this good. Arland is a great warrior. He has trained for this his entire life. I've seen him fight off daemons. I don't think Brad should be that hard for Arland to take down.

Ignoring the daemons around us, I focus on Brad, on the way he fights, on the way he seems to be able to move inhumanly fast, before Arland can land a punch. Brad seems to hit Arland more powerfully than any human's fists should.

Two bats swoop down, kicking Arland as they did me. Like they're trying to help Brad.

If Darkness can taint a Draíochta's soul through dreams, I imagine it can taint a human soul, too. Brad was sleeping for weeks, giving plenty of opportunities for Darkness to slip into his mind.

"Help Arland," I beg of the magic.

Blue flames shoot from my chest, changing into a warm, golden color the closer they get to Arland. They swirl around his body, brighter, stronger than ever before.

He jumps to his feet.

Brad cannot touch Arland, but continues to try to hit him, to kick him, to knock him over, but Brad's efforts are worthless.

Arland has magical protection . . . *my* magical protection.

The coscarthas stop their advance.

The bats swoop away from us.

The daemons seem to be waiting for something.

"Please, take Brad home, heal his angry soul, and allow him to find happiness. Close the portal behind him, too," I ask, adding the last part with hope that no one or nothing can ever get through the portal again.

Nothing happens.

"Go home, Brad, or the only woman you ever loved will be killed." Arland repeats the line Brad said out of anger, before his memories were temporarily erased.

He catches my gaze. "I already told her I was going to stay here and watch her suffer."

The sweet smile on the face of the boy I've always thought was my friend doesn't fit the anger, the rage, I know he's feeling inside. I don't recognize this new person standing in front of me at all.

"Sir, we have to leave him," Cadman says.

Arland looks at me.

I nod.

I don't want to watch Arland and Brad fight anymore. I've done my part. I've tried to get him home. He's his own responsibility now, even though leaving Brad ensures my visions will come true. Maybe that's a future we cannot escape. Maybe what I saw was a warning. One we could do nothing about.

Arland leaves Brad staring up at the sky, and jumps on Bowen.

"You should have left me," Arland says, taking his place next to me.

"I will never leave you."

He grabs my hand.

Relief floods my soul.

Blood flows from his nose. Dirt covers his body. Yet, I see him smiling at me. I breathe for what feels like the first time since we got here.

We're all protected and joined as one force.

Concentrating on the power in my core, I will the magic to move from me into Mom and Cadman.

Everyone ignites in flames. Mom, Cadman, and Arland whisper incantations at the daemons.

I don't recognize their words, but I understand their meaning: they're trying to make the daemons go away without more fighting.

Two words come to mind. I don't know what they mean or what they'll do, but I shout them anyway. "Logh dó!"

A smile lights Mom's face.

Arland laughs so hard he nearly falls from Bowen.

Cadman watches Brad.

A tornado of sprites explodes from around Brad's feet, illuminating the dry earth and the side of the mountain where the rippling portal is located. They swirl around Brad, picking him up and hurtling him toward home.

A bat drops from the sky, like a hawk for its prey, and grabs Brad from the sprites' control. The daemon carries Brad, screaming and writhing to get away, and takes him fifteen feet in the air. Another bat joins the one carrying Brad, flapping enormous black wings and blocking our view of him.

I can't leave Brad now. It's impossible for me to move. I know he's been bad to me, but I cannot allow them take him.

"Protect him," I cry out to the magic.

Sprites fly up to Brad, but more bats swoop in. Forming a circle around him, the flying daemons prevent the magic from entering.

Sprites try to get through, but their Light fades once inside the circle. They fall to the ground, dead.

"Why isn't it working?"

My question receives no response. Everyone stares at the sky, watching, whispering, begging that this doesn't end badly.

"I'm sorry, Kate. I never meant to hurt you." Brad screams as another bat approaches, with claws stuck out like knives.

They spin him around in the air to face us.

They want *me* to see this?

Panic spreads through me like poison.

Fear makes everything in front of me swirl.

Terror brings my heart to a skidding halt.

Tears spill over my eyes. My emotions have spiraled out of control.

"Stop them," I scream at the magic, pointing toward the bats.

Sprites swarm around the daemons, but they're far too powerful for even the most ancient of magic to stop.

Brad watches, eyes wide with fear and full of tears, as the bat jabs a claw through his chest. Blood flows and spills to the dry earth, immediately soaking into the ground, leaving the dirt stained red.

His head sags. His body falls slack.

"No," I cry.

The bats fly off with Brad in their grasp, bobbing in the air as they go.

I'm too shocked, too scared, too upset to send any more magic after them. My memories of Brad—good and bad—loop through my mind as I watch the bats fly off with his body, out of the light, away from the portal, away from us, away from his home.

Away from me.

Dead.

I remember sleeping in his arms in the tent the morning before we came here. The smile in his eyes when he saw me watching him while we swam. His fingers running through my hair when he tried to calm me. Him howling *I love you* when he was drinking. Him holding my hand at concerts, putting stars on my ceiling in my bedroom. I remember him punching me, yelling at me, wanting to kill me . . . .

Arland squeezes my hand I forgot he was holding. "We have to go, Kate."

"I was mad, Arland, but I didn't want him to die. Why? Why did they kill only Brad?"

He looks around. "We have to go."

The shrieking of the coscarthas breaks into my brain, over the memories, over the pain. Taking another deep breath, I realize I have to save Arland, my mom, and Cadman. I cannot allow them to be killed, too.

"Kill the daemons." I command the magic with as much strength and control as I can muster.

Sprites fly into the clearing where the coscarthas are trying to hide from the Light. The magic wastes no time, stabbing through the mangled creatures and creating a path for us to pass through.

"Can you ride?" Arland's voice is muffled.

Do I need to answer his question? I close my eyes.

Brad was murdered.

Worse yet, I'm afraid he wanted to die.

The way he smiled at the bats, but then he said he was sorry. Why did he apologize?

Arland shakes my shoulder. "Kate! Can you ride?" he asks, louder.

I blink tears from my eyes. "Yes."

"Stay close," he says, kicking his heels into Bowen's belly.

Following behind him, I turn and watch the war between the coscarthas and the sprites go on as we race back to base.

Chapter Twenty-Five

No one speaks.

I don't look up from Mirain's brilliant, white mane. Shedding any more tears seems pointless. I don't blame myself for Brad's death. I'm furious for wanting to get back at him, terrified by how happy he looked to see the bats, and by the panic in his eyes before the daemon drove its claw through his chest . . . and I'm confused by his apology.

My breath catches.

Brad is dead.

"Give me your hand."

All that blood . . . .

"Kate?"

His smile . . . .

"Can you hear me?"

All our memories.

"Kate!"

I glance to my right.

Arland shakes my thigh. "Give me your hand, and I will help you down."

Looking around, I find we're in the stables. I don't remember passing through the doors. Don't remember the ride back. My brain is flooded with images of death.

Taking his hand, I slide from Mirain's back. Knees buckling beneath me, I falter.

Wrapping his arms around mine, Arland keeps me upright. We're still radiating the bright light. It makes my eyes ache. Makes the tears more blinding.

I cannot go downstairs right now, not where Perth can see me, not where *anyone* can see me. My body weighs a thousand pounds.

Mom and Cadman join us in Mirain's stall, then hug me, holding me up with their support.

My spirit is reduced to nothing.

Stepping back, their foreheads crease with concern.

"Everything is going to be okay." Arland murmurs in my ear.

"I hope so." I bury my head in his chest. "You were right. I shouldn't have been spiteful."

He smoothes my hair with his palm. "Kate, do not blame yourself for this."

"I don't. I have a feeling those daemons were waiting for us. Maybe instead of rushing to get Brad home, we should have protected him after I had the vision."

Unwilling to look anyone in the eyes, I keep my head against Arland. His shirt muffles my voice.

Mom squeezes my shoulder. "Kate, we will figure out what your visions mean. We will review every single one of your dreams. We will be more careful."

"Brit wanted to do the same thing, but it's too late for B-Brad." I gasp. Too soon to speak his name....

"We will work on it when you're ready. Cadman, can you clear the way for Kate and Arland to enter the base without being seen?"

The Light has faded from Mom and Cadman.

"Yes, ma'am," he says. "I will return when it is safe."

She watches him leave, then turns to me. "Kate, Brad was never part of your prophecy. If the daemons were waiting for us, then I suspect the leader of Darkness has been given information about you. I think Brad is going to be used against you, as you saw in your vision, but we know he will not be Brad. Do you understand?"

"Control my emotions, right?" I sigh. Controlling my emotions may be more difficult than it sounds. I had a slight grasp on them at the clearing, but I was able to protect only Arland. I couldn't save Brad.

She nods.

Backing away from me, Arland turns to my mom.

"Are you suggesting one of our own has given information to our enemies?" he asks, his eyebrows arched, his voice raised.

The absence of his support makes me breathless, tired, and weak. I'd like to go to sleep in his arms and not think about the rest of the world for a while.

"I'm not positive, Arland. How else would you explain what happened tonight?"

I look for a place to sit. If they're going to talk about who betrayed us, it's going to take awhile. I'm going to seat myself before I fall.

Leaving them, I drop down onto one of the straw bales in the storage bay. Putting my head between my knees, I listen to their conversation while trying to breathe, trying to control.

They discuss what happened to Brad, skipping over the horrible details, but leaving in enough to make me feel sick.

The bat stabs its claw through his heart, over and over again, in my mind. A wave of nausea hits the pit of my stomach. Salty fluids fill my mouth. I spit on the straw beneath my feet, then take deep breaths.

His murder was so awful, so tragic . . . .

How are we going to explain his loss to Mr. Tanner? He's already grieving over losing his wife, now his only son. Mom said her spells would work on him for however long we needed, but does that include death?

Closing my eyes, the face of the boy from the playground flashes before me. His baby blues were so big, so honest, so concerned when he picked me up from the asphalt. I was crying, and he was the only one who offered to help me. Blood ran down my knee, staining my white socks. Little black stones stuck to my tender skin.

"You're Kate, right?" he asked me.

We'd gone to the same school since kindergarten, but I'd never paid attention to him before.

"Y-yeah," I said through sobs, wondering how he knew my name.

"My name is Brad."

"T-thank you, B-Brad," I said when we reached the sterile, gray nurse's office.

He sat me in a plastic chair, and stood next to me with his hands clasped in front of him, shifting from foot to foot. Brad lingered as though waiting for me to say something, but I continued to cry. He took the blue seat next to mine and told me stories, while blowing cool air on my knee, like my mom would've if she'd been there. Brad told bad one-line jokes, making me laugh.

A stray tear falls from my chin, then drips onto the dirt. I don't know how much time has passed since I've been sitting here. So far, I've been able to keep myself from throwing up, from losing control, from allowing myself to feel guilt, but I don't know how long I can keep it up.

"I will speak with every one of my men right now." Arland's voice draws me from my misery.

His comment makes my brain snap back into the present, out of its weakness. Arland is going to walk into the base, glowing, and question everyone about me? Does he want Perth to find out? Does Arland want the guilty person to run away before we get the information we need?

He doesn't need to speak to every one of his men. It takes me about three seconds to run down the list of those who know about me.

"Arland, wait." I stand. My legs tremble. The room spins.

Closing my eyes, I wait for the dizziness to pass. When I'm sure I'm not going to be sick, I join Mom and Arland. "Flanna, Lann, Kegan, Cadman, Mom, Brit, possibly Gavin, and Dunn—they're the only ones who know about me. I can account for their whereabouts, with the exception of Gavin, Dunn, and Lann."

"I spoke to Gavin and Dunn after they saw us return from the clearing; neither noticed anything out of the ordinary." Arland pauses. "I do not believe it was Lann, or anyone close to us. I would have sensed something."

Mom meets my eyes, holding my gaze . . . she doesn't blink. "Arland, we should take some time to think before we speak with anyone about our suspicions. Kate has had a very difficult day. I think it would be wise for you both to rest."

So many years, I thought Mom didn't care about my feelings, didn't worry about things that got me down. There wasn't much for me to complain to her about, other than my visions, but those were the most haunting parts of my life. Now, she's here, she's supportive, caring. I want to hug her for suggesting Arland and I need to relax, but I don't.

"You are right. We should rest."

My skin is cold. I'm exhausted, hungry, empty—so many different emotions I'm failing to control.

He looks down at me. "I am sorry. I was upset at the suggestion someone had turned against us . . . against you, Kate. I stopped thinking about what you needed."

I lean into his side. "It's okay."

Arland puts his arm across my back, soothing me with his warmth.

"Kate, the magic you have been conjuring is powerful, and it can drain you . . . as it did your father. You must rest after using so much of it."

"H-how much do you know, Mom? Is anyone else I love going to die? Is it even possible for me to fight against Darkness? How long do I have to rest? How long will this pain remain in my chest? Why does it hurt so much?"

"Your path is clear." Cadman's voice sends a shock through me.

I didn't even hear him come up the stairs.

"Thank you, Cadman." Mom calls over her shoulder, then returns her gaze to me. "The pain will go away, Kate. These things take time. And tonight is not the night to discuss your prophecy."

Arland's stomach growls. "We should eat."

"Okay." Although I'm hungry, the thought of eating brings on another wave of nausea.

Flanna and Brit serve us stew in the dining room.

Mom goes over the details of everything that happened with the others, while keeping them away from Arland and me.

Brit catches my eyes a few times as she walks around, performing various mundane tasks I normally do. I need to talk to Brit about her voice in my head, and about Brad. Even though she wasn't his biggest fan, she must be hurting. But I can't. I can't think about him, or about what happened. I'm too tired, too sick of feeling depressed to grieve over him.

Arland rests his hand on my leg, calming, but not stopping, my shaking fits. His fingers are stiff, tense. I'm sure worrying about who betrayed us is driving him crazy, but he needs rest as much as I do. While I've been the one conjuring the magic, he's been using it quite well when it envelops him. He appears lost in his thoughts; his eyes are focused on something across the room.

Pushing away my bowl, I think about my dad, while Arland dabs his spoon at his food.

My dad was able to conjure old magic, maybe not the same way I do, but he was capable. What other things do I share with him? What other things made him special that I should know about? I wish I knew him, wish I could talk to him now. What would he say, watching his little girl fight daemons he saw only a few times? Would he be proud of me, or would he think I needed to be doing more, be more fearless?

Arland rubs his hand along my leg; it bounces wildly. The more I think, the more tired I become. His warm, soothing touch creates goose bumps all over my skin.

Lifting my head from my hands, I look at his face.

He gives me the same longing gaze he had in the stables yesterday, or the day before—I've lost track of time.

I smile at him, heart thudding rapidly. I don't know how it's possible for me to feel this way, after everything that's happened, but Arland somehow drowns out all the bad and makes me happy.

"If you do not mind, Mrs. Wilde, I would like to steal Kate for the remainder of the evening." Arland regards my mom with formality.

She and Cadman came to sit with us after Flanna and Brit went up to the stables.

"You take all the time you need to rest. We can save our discussion for tomorrow." Mom gives me a warm smile, then returns to her quiet conversation with Cadman.

Arland leads me out to the courtyard I almost forgot existed. We haven't come here since the first day we met. Nothing has changed, although the chestnut tree appears to be leaning a little more, and the plants growing along the walls are dried up, and with the help of a little wind, will blow away any day.

"Do you remember what I told you about this place?" Arland asks.

"It's protected by magic," I say, void of my normal tone of voice, shocking myself with how monotone it is.

He laughs. "Well, yes, it is protected by magic. But do you remember why we come out here, Kate?"

"To draw, after bad battles."

Arland wants me to draw out the scenes of what happened tonight?

I'm not going to do it.

I refuse.

"No!"

He holds my gaze, eyes pleading with me.

"Kate, you loved Brad. I know you are hurting in so many different ways, and I know he caused a lot of that pain. But what you felt for him was innocent, pure." Arland rubs my shoulders. "You need to deal with this."

I shake my head. I'm not ready to face reality. I'm not ready to accept Brad's gone. I don't want to think about death. Panic bubbles in my core. I want to flee. I don't want Brad to go up on these walls. "No! Let's go back inside, please? I'm tired."

"Kate," Arland says, lifting my chin, "it will help."

"Fine!" I grab a small twig from near my feet, draw a stick figure of Brad, then jab the twig through his chest. I glower at Arland.

"Are you happy now?"

He takes me in his arms, and I bury my face in his tunic.

"I am sorry. I should not have pressured you."

I try to push the thoughts of Brad being stabbed out of my mind. "I'm sorry, too."

Arland and I leave the courtyard, hand in hand. He leads us to our room, but we only stay long enough for him to grab clothes and towels. "Will you take a bath with me?" he whispers.

We haven't bathed in days. After all the puking, the fighting, the raw meat on my bruised face, I'm disgusting. My hair is painfully tangled, my clothes are dirty, and my skin is dry. "Yes."

Arland lights candles in the dark washroom.

I stand in the middle, so exhausted that collapsing right where I stand seems like a good option.

He kneels to untie my boots. Arland holds my legs steady as he slides the boots from my feet, then unbuttons my pants. "I am sorry."

I stare blankly at him. "Let's not talk about it."

He takes my face in his palms. "Kate, you cannot ignore the pain."

Closing my eyes, I avoid looking into his, avoid a talk I'm not ready to have, a reality I'm not sure belongs to me. "I know I have to deal with it, but not right now."

Arland pulls my pants from my legs. His warm lips graze my knees, my thighs, and my hips as he stands back up. Lifting my shirt over my head, he trails his mouth over my bare shoulders and neck, then removes his clothes.

Arland's touch, his kisses, weaken me and make me stronger, all at the same time. I realize how empty I've felt since Brad punched me, how much I need Arland's love, his tenderness, his tiny little affections meaning more than an *I want you*. They mean *I love you*.

Lifting me, he returns his mouth to mine, and I give in to his kiss, to his lips, to his love.

When Arland sets me down again, I'm a little more awake, a little more alive, and a little less empty.

On normal nights, we bathe with our undergarments on, to save a little of our modesty, but tonight I don't care about modesty. Now, more than ever, I understand this could be our last night alone, our last opportunity to love each other. Brad's life was so easily taken from him. There might not be a tomorrow, or a week from now, for Arland and me. I have to love him every chance I get.

I reach around my back to unhook my bra, but he stops me.

"Not tonight," Arland says, fastening the hooks.

A tear betrays me. I don't want to be rejected. I want to be loved, to make this emptiness go away. "There might not be another night."

He pushes my tangled locks away from my eyes. "Kate, there will be other nights, plenty of other nights. Someone you spent your childhood with was murdered in front of you. I know how I felt when I lost my mother. I know what an enormous amount of pain you must feel, and I know you are trying to mask that pain."

"I do hurt, but I love you. I won't regret this. Please?" I try to seduce him with my eyes, but I'm sure I failed the super-model-sexy-look class years ago.

"You have no idea how difficult this is. Please, do not beg me."

"*Please?*" I break his hold on me, kiss his chest, and rub my hands down the front of his sculpted abs.

Arland takes my shoulders and holds me at arm's length. "Please, do not mix our love with the death of your friend."

I open my mouth to protest, then snap it shut. Arland is right, but I do want him. I want to love him. But he deserves something special. A night dedicated to him, to us. Not a night full of sadness.

"I'm sorry," I say, looking at my feet and biting my lip. I should not have been so forward with him. Ever. My constant pressuring is unfair, but then again, this world needs us to be together.

"Do not be sorry for loving me." He returns his lips to my neck, to my shoulders, then takes my hands in his.

"You are such an incredibly strong woman."

I don't respond. What can I say to that? Should I say he's incredible, too? Instead of saying anything, I press myself against the bare skin on his chest, desiring more, but not pushing.

Arland lifts me, carries me up the stairs to the stone enclosure, then sets me in the water. It's perfect, as always. He steps in after, pulls me close, then trails his fingers along my skin.

Resting my head on his chest, I listen to his heart. At first, it's a normal beat, but then it speeds up, returns to normal, then speeds up again.

He lets out a few deep breaths, but his heart doesn't seem to calm.

"What's wrong?" I ask, moving to sit in front of him. I touch the side of his face, trying to read his eyes, trying to understand what's upsetting him.

Arland is sad, tired. The youthful look that appeared on his face on the other side of the portal has been replaced with the same rugged, worn look he always carries here.

He wipes his thumb across my black eye, without causing any pain. "I was afraid I was going to fail you at the clearing. Between Brad, the bats, and the coscarthas, I fear I am not doing enough for you. We could have all been killed tonight, if the daemons tried. Yet *you* saved *us* again. I do not deserve your protection, and you deserve better than what I am giving you."

A lump forms in the back of my throat. How could he think he doesn't deserve my protection? Does he think I would be better off without him? Does he think it's possible someone else could protect me better? Even after seeing how strong we are together—when we're connected?

My jaw falls slack.

"Are *you* okay?" Arland asks, appraising my changed expression.

"No. I'm scared," I say, thinking of all the different ways Darkness might use Brad against us, thinking of the horrible images of him approaching us, covered in blood, naked, and eager to kill.

"We will get through this." Arland has said this to me so many times already. "What are your fears about?"

"I'm scared for many reasons: for me, for you, for us, my sister, my mom. But mostly I'm scared you're going to tell me I should find another Coimeádaí."

Arland chuckles. "Why would I want you to be with another? I did swear to stay with you until I die, did I not?"

"You did swear, as my Coimeádaí."

He sits up and takes my face in both of his hands. His emerald eyes burn into mine. "Kate, I will stay with you as long as you want. However you want me."

I move closer and kiss the side of his face, teasing him. "What do *you* want us to be?"

"Mmm. First, I am interested in hearing what you want," Arland says, sliding me on top of him.

"That's not fair!"

He smiles wryly, then kisses my neck, making it impossible for me to breath, impossible for me to think, and lifting my spirit, all at once. "I think it is fair."

"I wish we could be somewhere away from this war, doing what we want to do, when we want to do it. I don't want to worry about daemons, saving the world, or being given away for someone *else* to marry . . . ." The smile stretching across Arland's face stops me . . . and my heart.

"That all sounds very good." His voice is deep, raspy with seduction.

"And you?"

"I will tell you later." He's still smiling.

I splash water at his face. "Tell me now."

Arland shakes his head, sprinkling me with stray beads of water from the ends of his hair.

"Please," I say.

Our mostly naked bodies press against each other. The muscles in his forearms tense, and he pulls me closer. His heart pounds against my chest.

Fire burns on us, even in the water.

"Soon."

His lips graze my jaw while his hands roam down my back, down my legs. My skin tingles with pleasure from his touch. My body cries out to be closer to him. He moves his hands up to my face and pulls me into his lips.

We ignore a knock on the door.

Another, louder knock . . . .

Arland growls.

"Give you two guesses who that is," I say, breathless.

"I need only one to know it is Flanna."

Arland climbs from the enclosure.

I watch him take every step—watch, while biting my lower lip.

He wraps a towel around himself, then opens the door.

Flanna pops her head in, waves at me, then drops a couple fresh towels on the counter. "Thought you might need these soon. You should both get some sleep."

With a wink, she's gone.

Arland picks up the towels, then uses one to dry his hair.

I leave the comfort of the warm water in the stone enclosure where we have shared so many intimate moments.

Arland watches *me*—eyes wide and full of yearning—as I descend the stairs to get dressed. He holds open a towel and wraps me in it, squeezing me.

"You are the most beautiful creature in *any* world. Please, allow me to love you forever."

Standing on my toes, I kiss his nose. "Permission granted."

He gives a little eye-roll, then helps slip my nightgown over my head.

I slide off my wet things from under the dry gown.

We bring a couple of candles from the bathroom and set them on the table next to our bed. I lift the blankets, but Arland grabs me around the waist and pulls me into him before I crawl under the wool covers.

"I owe you an answer," he says.

I swallow hard. "You do."

"The worlds we grew up in are very different, Kate. What we are doing right now, what we have been doing in the washroom and in the stables, it is not accepted unless it happens between a fear céile and bean chéile."

"What does that mean?"

Our eyes lock.

"It means I want you to be mine, and me to be yours. I want what happens between us to be allowed, accepted. I wish for you to be buried with my people after living a long, happy life together."

"Y-you m-mean you want your original future back?" I ask, not wanting to say the words Bound, marriage, wife, husband, or anything like that.

"We would make good Leaders, a good family."

"We would." I've thought, many times, of how good Arland is with his people, with children, with me. The idea of marriage has never scared me; the idea of marrying Arland actually excites me. It seems fast for people who've known each other for such a short time to want to commit themselves, but this is a different world; we might not live long enough to wait, might not have continual opportunities.

Flanna said that by the age of fifteen, people here usually begin families. By Encardia's standards, we're considered old.

"Katriona, I want to be with you forever. I want to have a million moments like this one, but I do not want you to be killed for loving me."

"Who would kill me?" This might be all I get of Arland, ever. The thought sends a tear racing down my cheek.

Arland wipes my face with his thumb.

With my swollen eye, I can barely see as it is, but crying makes it impossible to see anything but blurs.

"As it stands, the Ground Dwellers will likely kill me when they discover who you are, and that I have been sleeping in the same room as you, but they might also take *your* life if we have made love. It means too much. I should never have allowed us to get this far, Kate."

"Because of Perth? Because I'm supposed to be Bound to him?"

He nods.

"We'll hide. And even if we're caught, Arland, if I die having loved you, then that's the best death I can wish for. If I have to live a life never having loved you, then I will feel as though I haven't lived."

"I have failed in every attempt to protect you; I will not fail you in this way, too." Arland grips at my waist, pulls me closer to him, making me feel as though he wants to do exactly as he says he won't.

I am not going to be told who, how, or when I can love. I will not have Arland living a life that could end in his death—both of our deaths—for loving me.

Reaching down, I grab the bottom of my nightgown then slip it over my head, revealing my naked skin to Arland. Sitting on the bed, I ease myself onto my back, never taking my eyes from his. I'm not doing this to mask the pain of Brad, I'm not doing this to defy the Leaders of this world; I'm doing this for love.

Looking at my naked form, Arland gasps as his eyes widen.

I wait for him to lie next to me, but he just stands there, with confusion written on his face . . . pain . . . desire.

"Do you know how weak you are making me feel right now?" His tone is uncontrolled, constricted, yet excited.

"I'm not trying to make you feel weak," I say, trying to maintain a level of dignity. I didn't think it would take him this much deliberation. "I need to make you understand I love you, and no matter what this world *wants* me to do, I'm going to do what *I* want to do."

Arland mutters inaudible words, stands in place, then looks up and down the length of my body. Sitting on the bed next to me, he puts his hand on my face, leans in and kisses me.

But I want more.

Wrapping my arms around his waist, I desperately pull him closer to me.

He straddles my legs, brushes his lips on my neck, down the center of my chest and stomach.

My skin tingles with excitement.

Arland trails his hands down my legs, tickling me with his fingertips as he works his way up my stomach and shoulders. Holding himself up by his arms, he dips his head and returns his mouth to mine.

I tug at his shirt, trying to lift it over his head.

He pulls it back down, then stops kissing me. "I cannot do this."

"*What?* Why?" How could he tease me this way? How could he build up my broken spirit, and then leave me hanging? I slide out from under him, sit up on the bed, then pull the blankets over myself.

Arland passes me my nightgown. "I did not say I do not want to do this."

Ignoring the garment in his hand, I allow tears to stream down my face again. "What is it then?"

He slips the gown over my head. "I already told you. I cannot allow you to die for me."

"Arland—"

He kisses my forehead. "I love you, Kate. We will find a way to get around this, but not tonight."

"I love you." I whisper, allowing him to stroke my face as I lie next to him and cry.

I cry for Brad, for Arland. I grieve over all the losses I've endured. He was right not to make love to me, but I cry about that, too. Arland holds me closely, calming the shaking fits, the fears, the nerves, while I sob for hours. When the tears dry, when my head throbs, when I no longer remember why I'm upset, I close my eyes and allow Arland's soothing touch to lull me to sleep.

Chapter Twenty-Six

*H*ome, sweet home. Bright yellow rays beam down onto the rolling green pastures of our farm. Standing on the bottom rail of the split-wood fence, I making clicking sounds, calling to my new brown and white horse.

She trots up to me, ears pricked forward.

Gary hangs over the fence and laughs. "She already loves you."

Arland is in the barn, shoveling out old manure, and spreading fresh straw.

Inhaling a deep, renewing breath, I set to train the little horse. It's a long day of good, hard work, but it's all worth it to be home again.

When the day is ending, and the fireball in the sky peeks over the top of the Blue Ridge Mountains, we call it quits and head to our house. The wooden boards creak as Arland, Gary, and I step onto the porch where Mom, Brit, and Perth are already eating dinner. Everyone smiles and laughs.

Brad and Mr. Tanner ride up the circular driveway in their truck; the familiar sputtering of the diesel engine is like sweet music to my ears.

Everything is normal. Better than normal.

I take Arland's hand in mine, and we go to the rock-lined driveway to meet them.

Brad jumps down from the truck, gravel crunching under his feet, and he fixes his narrowed eyes on me.

"What's wrong?" I ask.

His eye color changes from blue to black. "You aren't dead."

A shiver runs through me. I open my swollen, burning eyes. I haven't dreamed in weeks. Rubbing the bed next to me, I feel for Arland.

He's not here.

"Solas." I squeeze my hand into a fist, then open it. A small, blue flame dances on my palm. I smile. I've finally mastered the trick Arland tried to teach me. Grabbing the candle from next to the bed, I transfer the flame to the wick.

A dark figure passes in front of the dresser.

I bring the sheets to my chin. "Who's there?"

Brad emerges from the shadows and stands next to my bed.

Am I still dreaming? "B-Brad?"

"Hi, Kate," he says, locking his ice-cold fingers around my arm.

What's happening? This isn't Brad, and I'm not sure this is a dream.

I look around the little room, but it's so dark. I cannot see anything past the wooden posters of the bed. For all I know, Arland could be lying dead on the floor. My heart races out of control. Taking short breaths, I focus on building the courage to speak.

Brad squints his eyes. He watches me . . . waiting. A wicked smile twists his face.

Seconds tick by, turning into minutes.

Who is this? Why isn't he saying anything?

Arland. Why isn't he with me?

"Where is Arland?" I ask, sounding stronger than I feel.

"Tell me why you betrayed me, then I'll tell you what I did with him," Brad's ghost—or whatever this is—demands, cool and calm.

"I didn't betray you. Now where is he?"

Illuminate my room, right now, please.

White sprites appear in the room, as though I flicked a light switch, revealing that I'm alone with Brad.

I take a deep breath. Relief floods me. Arland isn't here, but where could he be?

"There was a lot of noise coming from the hall. Arland went to check it out. You may see him again someday, . . . you may not. My servants could not find you, though. Such stupid creatures. The rest of the pathetic Draíochta were easy for them to capture." He waves a hand, like we're having a casual conversation.

"C-capture?" I hope I heard him wrong.

"Oh no, you heard me correctly."

I stare at the strange orange eyes where Brad's used to be. He can hear my thoughts?

The imposter nods. "You are all so easily fooled by my servants' tricks. I have had two living amongst you for weeks, watching and waiting for the perfect moment to strike. I do plan on killing whoever it was that protected you before you could be captured," he says, one arm across his chest, the other stroking his chin.

Mom was right. Oh God, where is everyone?

"W-who are you?"

Brad's baby blues shine through the sadistic façade of the being before me. For a moment, I see pain, a struggle within those eyes. "You do not recognize me? We have known each other our entire lives."

"You're D-Darkness, not Brad." My breath forms white clouds in front of me. "Get out!"

He shakes his head. "Darkness. What a ridiculous name they have given to a god."

He huffs a short, agitated laugh.

His proximity to my face is unnerving. Hoping not to provoke Darkness any further, I push myself back, but he jumps on the bed and forces his lips onto my mouth.

He's kissing me.

Punching his chest, I scream, kick, and scratch. "Get off me!"

He cringes, then licks my face with a rough, snake-like tongue. Resting his chest on mine, he nearly suffocates me with his weight.

"*Help*! Take him out of here." I beg the magic—or anyone who can hear me.

No one responds.

Darkness' face sours. He lifts off me, then stands next to the bed. "Your magic cannot help you in your dreams, girl. I wanted to see what it was about you that pleased the human boy so much, but you are as deplorable as the rest of the Draíochta."

His form twists from Brad into something so scary, I have the urge to bring the blanket over my head. Shaking, I look away, instead.

"You should get a good look at the face of your enemy."

Working up courage, I face Darkness again. His body shifts among different conglomerations of his daemons, never resting on one form for longer than a second. He has claws as long as the coscarthas', surely filled with the same poison. His eyes are orange and beady like those of the bats, then they transform to black, hollowed sockets, then to blood red orbs. Wings of a hawk sprawl from his back, then those of a bat. The head of a hound sits on his neck one moment, then one of a man. His chest is human, and his legs are of a bristly ox. The scaly tail swishing behind him terrifies me more than anything else.

He watches as I absorb what his horrifying transformations mean: how little I still know of what dangers are in Encardia. How little anyone knows of the dangers in Encardia.

"As you can see, there are quite a few of my servants you have not yet met. Do not fear, child. When they find you, they are only permitted to torture you. Killing you will be my pleasure, alone." Darkness licks his blackened lips.

"What's the point? What do you gain from killing me and all these innocent people?" I slap my hand over my mouth.

"I am five thousand years old; entertainment is difficult to find."

He destroys life because he's *bored?*

"I would not expect you to understand, mortal." Darkness clenches his jaw, muscles rippling all over his body.

"You do not deserve the powers my brother and sister have so foolishly given you. However, your powers will aid *me* greatly in this war, after I kill you."

The reckless god's bones crack and bend in impossible directions.

I cringe, then look away.

Snarls echo around the room. A foul odor, ten times worse than sewage, fills the air. My cheek warms, then cools, over and over again.

He's panting on me.

I tense and hold my breath, lungs burning from the lack of air. One, two, three, four . . . Darkness growls . . . two, no, five, six . . . hot liquid drips onto my hand.

"Foolish indeed. You cannot even control your fear. I will rather enjoy sucking the Light from your soul—"

I open my eyes to see why he's stopped talking.

Darkness has transformed into a hound, black fur raised on its neck. It stares at a golden light—more brilliant than anything that has shone on my body—flooding into the room and swirling around us.

Pleasant, warm, smelling of sweet honeysuckle, the Light lifts my hair and caresses my skin with its comfort.

Darkness growls, a low, guttural noise. The hound dissolves, shifting into a normal-looking but naked man, with shoulder length, curly, jet-black hair, and snow-white skin. He's breathtaking. Like the man in the vision Mirain showed me, but not as pure. There's something evil, something sinister about Darkness' beauty.

He touches my cheek with his finger, burning my skin.

I recoil.

"I will see you again, soon," he says, dissipating into thin air.

The golden light takes on the form of a god, Griandor. I recognize him from my vision.

Air returns to my lungs, but I'm trembling like a dry leaf in the wind, and hanging onto my sanity like the leaf would cling to the branch. Trying to avoid falling off. Trying to prevent being blown into the vast openness of the world.

A blanket of Light drapes over me, calming the shaking. "Peace, child. I am not here to harm you, and Dughbal cannot hurt you."

A lump forms in my throat. I swallow it. "A-am I-I dreaming?"

"Not exactly. Neither Dughbal nor I have been in your room this morning. We are merely apparitions." Griandor's words sound like the joyous songs of angels. He smiles, eyes radiating kindness.

"Dughbal said I was dreaming, but I felt him on me. He kissed me. His weight smothered me." I cringe at the memory of Dughbal's rough tongue flicking against my cheek.

The muscles in Griandor's jaw jut out. "Unfortunately, my brother is dishonest, and very powerful. I assure you, he cannot do anything more than what you experienced tonight. Otherwise, I fear he would have already taken your life."

I know Griandor said Dughbal was not in my room, but I cannot help but try to rub the feeling of his ice-cold body off me.

"Katriona, the gifts my sister and I have bestowed upon you are undeniably very powerful. Most Draíochta, and even the Daonna from your former home, may be swayed and even killed in their dreams, but you, and the Draíochta near you, will be safe as long as you all remain on the path of Light."

"But Dughbal said he had servants here. People have been hurt. Brad died. Am I not on the path of Light?" I ask, shaking my head.

"You are on the correct Path, child."

"I'm s-sorry. If you are a god, why do you not end this war yourself?" I hope not to sound petulant, but having humans fight a war between gods . . . ?

Griandor's smile falls. Yellow flames burn in his distant eyes.

Balling the bed sheet in my sweaty hands, I wait while he formulates his response.

"During a battle, many centuries ago, we fought brutally against each other. One of our worlds, Elysia, was obliterated from the path of destruction forged between the gods. It was our most prized world. The inhabitants were beautiful, peaceful, loving. There were endless treasures to be found there. After we decimated Elysia, we vowed never to directly battle each other again."

"Why did you fight?"

"Balance."

"*Balance?*"

Griandor nods. "There are eight primary gods. Before destroying Elysia, there were eight worlds, and then Heaven. A constant shift of control must be made in order to maintain balance in any world. My brother wanted permanent control over Elysia. He began spending more time with the mortals of that world, hoping they would pray to him. But Dughbal was not kind, and therefore the people prayed against him. He refused to leave. Fear multiplied in Elysian hearts. My sister and I tried to convince him to return home . . . . That is when the war began."

"So, if he vowed never to battle again, why are we here?"

"After Elysia died, we lived in peace, but over time Dughbal grew restless. Desiring conflict, he began causing trouble in the heavens. Our father punished him, sending Dughbal to dwell with man in all forms for three centuries."

"Your father sent him here? If your brother wanted conflict, why send him somewhere people are easily destroyed?"

Pursing his lips, Griandor scowls. "His punishment was intended to make him grow fond of life, not want to destroy it. My father knew not the depths of evil in his son."

"I-I'm s-sorry." I look away. I cannot bear the shame his scowl makes me feel.

Placing his finger under my chin, he turns my face toward him. "You are intelligent, Katriona. You should never be ashamed to ask questions."

His touch is comforting, similar to how Arland soothes me, but a million times more powerful.

"In the underworld of Daigre, Dughbal whispered to the corpses of beings from old worlds. He promised the souls power, magic, and most importantly, new life, if they would agree to fight for him. Dughbal expected his actions to bring us out of our vow of peace and fight against him. When we did not, he punished this world, for it is closest in beauty to Elysia. Since the magic of the gods was no longer being used here, it was easy for Dughbal to take over."

"Old magic is magic of the gods?"

"Yes, child. The Draíochtas' intentions to protect themselves from the Daonna were honorable, but in doing so, they separated themselves from the ways of old magic. Over time, most lost faith that old magic ever existed. Many lost faith that *we* ever existed. There were a few who continued to practice, like your father's family, but not enough to protect the world from my brother." Griandor pauses, shaking his head.

"I don't understand. How would practicing magic keep us safe from a god?"

"How many daemons have you fought since you have been here?"

"Too many."

Griandor laughs. "I agree, you have fought more than a fair share. Had you ever fought *anything* before coming here?"

"No."

"Can you imagine how easy it would be to fight the daemons if everyone possessed the same power as you?"

"So why not give everyone the power to do the same as me?"

"Katriona, these people made practicing old magic a crime. Most of them forgot it ever existed. We needed someone who would not be afraid of the punishment the leaders of this world would inflict upon them."

I lean forward. "That's why my parents had to leave with me? Why not more? Why didn't you send thousands of us away?"

He sighs. "Our powers cannot be split, and we felt putting them into one Draíochta would be better than two."

"But if there are seven good gods, you could have made at least five others like me."

"My father cannot give his powers away; it would be foolish. And my other siblings feared that, if they did as my sister and I have done, Dughbal would kill them first."

"What have you and your sister done?"

"We gave you our magic, our strength. Years before the battle began, Gramhara and I were given a prophecy of what was to come.

We searched long and hard for a soul deserving enough of our powers of Light and Love. When your mother and father conceived you, we knew you were the right soul. You have a pure heart, courage, fire."

I wonder whether they picked the right soul or not. I have not been courageous. My heart has been broken repeatedly. I guess I might have fire, but only in a literal sense . . . and that's not even mine.

Griandor purses his lips again. "Do not doubt yourself, Katriona. Have you questioned your place in this world since you arrived?"

Before I answer, I think back over all the time I've been here. "I don't know."

"We have been watching you. Even yesterday, while sending your friend away, you told him this was your world. Could you not feel the power flowing through you at that moment? The moment when you realized this is where you want to be?" His voice rises.

Is he growing impatient?

"I-I c-could feel the flames grow stronger, blinding, but I have no control. I couldn't save Brad."

"You try too hard. You over-think what you need to do. When you first discovered your powers, did you think? No. You reacted to the situation as it presented itself. Since then, you have begged for help, questioned the power, tried to silence your emotions. You should control your emotions—as your mother has instructed you—but do not subdue them. It is the fire, the love, the rage, the *passion* inside you that will end this war. And you did save your friend. You asked for his forgiveness before he was killed."

"I did?" I don't remember asking for that.

"Logh dó,"—Griandor says—"means forgive him. And we did forgive him, not that he had much to be forgiven for."

I might rip the ball of sheets in my hands to shreds. "*What?* He hit me. He hurt me for many years. All the memories Arland took from him were awful."

"Your Brad did not do those things. Dughbal tried to taint your friend years before the two of you ever entered Encardia. My brother heard your prophecy. He traveled to Earth, hoping to find you, but your mother's protections over you were powerful. Dughbal found Brad in the forest, but was unable to turn him. The boy's mind is strong. However, the poison of the coscarthas was stronger."

"So, when he was lost in the forest when he was ten, really Dughbal had captured him?" Another lump forms in my throat.

Griandor nods.

Tremors take control of my hands. Brad was so frightened. I thought he'd never go in the woods again. "Why didn't he remember anything?"

"Your mother erased the memory of the encounter."

She lied? Why didn't she tell me the truth? I understand why she didn't tell me before I came here, but why not now? "Did my mom know Brad was going to be a part of this war?"

Griandor arches his eyebrows. "Your mother knows much. She is a fool to keep it from you, but I understand why she has. Her desire for you to stay on the path of Light is her way of protecting you. Find a way to forgive her; she has lost everything, much as you have."

I nod, but Griandor's plea for forgiveness does not make me any happier. Mom may have her reasons, but she needs to keep me in the loop. I don't want to be surprised. I want to know if someone else I love is going to die, so I can spend as much time with that person as possible.

"What about Mark Evans?" I ask, remembering I still have a reason to be mad at Brad.

Griandor places his hand on my shoulder. "That was a misunderstanding, Katriona. Mark Evans had intentions for you Brad was not fond of . . . neither was I."

My heart sinks to my feet. I shouldn't have doubted Brad, or thought he was a monster. I shouldn't have brought him here. Tears fill my eyes. I cover my face with the sheet.

"None of this is your fault. Brad was not right for you. I believe you are aware of that, but you can still help him. When the war is over, I will see to it that his life is returned to him, that he is sent home, and that his heart is mended from the loss of you in it."

I stifle my tears and look up at the kind god. "How do I end the war?"

Griandor smiles. "What Dughbal does not know is our father stripped his immortality from him when he was cast down from the heavens. Dughbal may have great power, and continue to steal great power from innocent lives, but he can be killed. You must seek him out, fight him, burn him as you do his daemons," he says, eyes flashing with golden flames.

"You need to stop him soon. Daemons draw the magic out of their victims and become stronger with each new life they steal, making Dughbal more powerful. We fear he may venture into the remaining seven worlds and decimate life there, the way he has here. The gods and goddesses are at an impasse with Dughbal. If we fight, our battle might destroy worlds, and the life they carry. If we do not fight, our lack of interference could do the same."

Overwhelmed. That's how I feel. "How am I supposed to get to him? I couldn't even kill his bats."

"You need to establish your own army. It will not be easy for you to convince Maher, Dufaigh, and Murchadha to follow you—"

"Who is Murchadha?"

"He is another Leader of Encardia. The three have grown fearful of Dughbal and are afraid of any more blood being shed. You must do *whatever* it takes to convince them."

Putting my head between my knees, I swallow hard. "I have to work with the Ground Dwellers?"

Griandor places his hand on my head. "You must find a way to unite *everyone*."

"And the others? Dughbal said he captured them," I say, not wanting to think of the Ground Dwellers or of a marriage to Perth. Instead, I worry about the children, my family, and my heart.

"It will be your first test to find them and save them. There will be many more tests along the way."

"How—?"

"Going forward, you must trust in yourself and those around you. Most importantly, you must trust in those you love. You will need no other guide. You could fail, Katriona, but we hope you do not." Griandor removes his hand from my head and clasps his fingers in front of him, eyes staring beyond me again.

"My sister predicts you will revolutionize this world. She predicts you will surprise many . . . even yourself. Be strong, child. We will be watching, and will send messages when we can. However, the closer you are to Arland Maher, the harder it will be for us to communicate. He protects you in more ways than one."

Griandor grins, then fades from a man back into the swirling golden light.

"Wait!"

He pauses, not returning to his human form, but floating in the air around me.

"Who betrayed us? Dughbal said there were two of his servants living amongst us."

"Katriona," Griandor says, his melodic voice vibrating on my skin, "you must discover this on your own. Trust yourself."

Before he disappears, his light touches my face, taking the pain out of my eye. My skin is still swollen, but the ache is gone.

I'm alone.

I don't have to leave this room to know Arland is gone, Brit is gone, Mom is gone, *everyone* is gone. Pulling clothes from the drawers that have been maintained for me by dedicated soldiers of Arland's . . . of mine, I get dressed.

Sliding my claymore through its holster, I walk out of the bedroom, probably for the last time ever. I turn to close the door, but cannot see it. It's as if no room exists on the other side, just as the stables didn't appear until Arland whispered *Nochtann*.

I'm not sure what everything Griandor told me means, but I *will* go forward. I *will* find the soldiers, my family, and my heart.

I *will* seek out Dughbal and destroy him for hurting those I love.

My name is Katriona Wilde, and I have fire.

Flip the page for a taste of...

Chapter One

Everything of importance in my new world has disappeared. The people I hold dear to my heart have been betrayed by two of our own who have been working for Darkness. The children, my sister, my mom, my friends, and *my Arland*—they were taken while I was asleep. But for whatever reason, someone protected me before I could be captured.

A few weeks ago, I didn't know Flanna, Lann, Tristan, or anyone else from Encardia aside from Arland—and him I knew only through dreams—but now that I do, I know I have to save them.

Saving things seems to be what my life is all about, at least according to the sun god, Griandor. He may have told me who I am and what I'm capable of, but knowledge doesn't do much to fill the hole in my chest.

I have to fight a fallen god, kill his army of daemons, and hide my identity from the Ground Dwellers. The only people of this world who'd like to see me fail.

And I've already failed everyone in so many ways, but I will find them, and I will do what I must to rid this world of Darkness.

"Hello, *Katriona*," a man calls, low and guttural, from behind me.

My body ignites in flames, fueled by fear and old magic. I draw my sword and turn from the empty space where my bedroom used to be, bracing for my first fight—of many fights to come—and I see Perth.

"Do you intend to kill me with that . . . *wife?*"

He regards me with the same ice-cold gaze he did the first time I met him in the training room. The blue flames reflecting in his pale, green eyes don't help much.

"I will kill you, if you take another step forward," I say with as much confidence as possible. I will not be forced into a marriage with Perth to repay the Ground Dwellers for building the bases. I will end this war between the gods, and I will free myself of this world's desires for my future . . . somehow.

"What if I take two?" he asks, moving forward *three* steps, leaving about enough distance for me to easily strike through him with my claymore.

"*Don't. Test. Me!*"

Perth takes one more step. A wicked smile stretches across his ivory face, and I push the tip of my sword into a spot above his heart.

"How foolish do you and Arland think I am?"

Arland. Anger fills me at the mere mention of his name.

"Why? Why did you betray all these people? Was it just to prove a point?" My voice comes out in a growl.

"*Me* betray these people? I did no such thing," Perth says, shaking his head.

Inching forward, I push the sword harder against his chest. "If you didn't betray everyone, why are you still here?"

"If you would stop trying to kill your future husband, I would be happy to tell you," he says, taking a step back when I pierce his skin with the tip of the claymore. Blood soaks through his white linen tunic and forms a red stain down to his belt.

I'm not playing games. Stepping toward him, I dig the blade back into his chest over the bleeding wound. "Why shouldn't I kill you? Right here, right now?"

Perth puts up his hands in surrender. "Because we are not so different, you and I."

"Go on. I'm listening," I say, *without* backing off.

"I had trouble sleeping and was walking in the forest. That is why I was not taken with everyone else. The children were screaming. I ran here to see what was going on, but there were too many daemons for me to try to do anything. When I entered the base to check if anyone was left, I found you."

I point to the closest table with my sword. "Sit."

Perth takes a chair at the table in the center of the room.

I seat myself opposite of him. "Why are we not so different?"

I have not sheathed my sword. I don't trust Perth as far as I can throw him . . . and since I'm short and don't weigh more than one-hundred and twenty pounds, I'm guessing I can't throw him very far.

Our eyes lock.

"We are both just pawns in a power play. I did not ask to be used against your family any more than you asked to be Bound to me," he says without any edge of humor to his tone.

I'm speechless. I think I *might* believe him. When people lie, they don't do it looking you straight in the face.

"How did you know who I am?"

"I visited a Seer on my own, three years ago. She told me my hatred of the Light Lovers would come crashing down the day I met *the* Light. I laughed at her. The thought of *not* hating the Light Lovers was absurd." The normal Perth has just returned. He leans back in his chair, fingers clasped behind his head, and a smart smile plays on his face.

I glare. If he's trying to help his case by telling me this . . . it's not working.

"Just hear me out, please." He rights himself in the chair. The smile vanishes.

I nod.

"For all my mocking, the Seer did not stop giving me the prophecy. She said I would recognize the Light immediately because she would not look at me as a monster, at least not the first time we met. The Seer also told me the Light was not my rightful future, and if I tried to obtain that future, I would live a life without love. She said the Light belongs to Arland Maher and him to the Light."

Closing my eyes, I think of Arland's smile, of his warmth. We were made for one another, to come together and fight a war, and yet we're apart. Separated by God only knows how much distance. I have to get to him.

"I love my father, Katriona," Perth says, drawing my eyes open. "I would not want to do anything to displease him, but when I met you—a Light Lover—and you did not look at me as a monster, my heart felt something it never had before."

"And what's that?"

"Hope. Hope that our two kinds could live in a world without turmoil."

"So, why did you try to kill me that day in the training room?" I hope his head still hurts where I hit him with my sword.

He laughs. "I was not attempting to take your life. I was angry. The Seer was right, and I knew I was going to have to fight against my father."

I want to take Perth for his word, but if he desires our two kinds to be united, why has he kept this from Arland? "Why haven't you said anything before now?"

"Do you believe Arland—or anyone—would have trusted me? He has told you about my kind. How did his mood change when he spoke of me?"

"Point taken."

The first time I asked about Perth, Arland ignored my question. He had to take me out to his favorite thinking spot by the river—as close to The Meadows as he could get . . . as close to his mother.

Resting the sword on the table, I release my grip on the hilt. I don't think Perth is making up this story. The sun god, Griandor, told me to trust in those around me, and since Perth is the only one left at base . . . I should start with him.

"Why are you telling *me*?" I ask.

"There are three reasons. You are the only other Draíochtan here, and you are going to need me if you want to survive. And Morgandy Domhnaill." The corners of his mouth twist up into a wry smile.

"Morgandy Domhnaill? My mom's fake name?"

"Yes. My Aunt Shylay used to tell me stories about Morgandy Domhnaill. She was a fabled, ancient goddess who lived by the sea. She treated the mortals with love and took care to ensure they always had food and a place to sleep. She was a goddess of kindness, and everyone trusted her."

"What does this have to do with my mom?"

"I believed her stories to be just that, but my Aunt told me if I ever met someone who called herself by the goddess' name, I should trust her and those she loves. When your mother spoke her name, I was taken aback. I never expected to hear the name 'Morgandy Domhnaill' again in all my life. I should have confessed then, but the way your mother regarded me—the way they all do—made me second guess what my Aunt instructed me to do."

Something tells me my mom knew Perth wasn't all rotten. I bet she even had a reason to treat him the way she did that night. My mom knows so much. I need to get back to her. There are so many things we need to discuss. No matter what impact she thinks it may have on my future, I want to know . . . everything.

"Why do our two kinds fight for power?" If I am supposed to unite everyone and form an army, I should be aware of exactly what divided us.

Perth raises his eyebrow. "Arland has not informed you of this? What *have* you two been up to?"

"You are not in a good position to ask questions you have no business knowing the answers to," I say, putting my hand back on the sword.

He watches my fingers thrum against the metal. "You enjoy killing things?"

I stand. "*Perth.*"

"Fine, fine." He waves. "Long ago, we were all considered equals, but Foghlad, the Leader of my kind at the time, wanted more."

Sitting back down, I release my death grip on my sword.

"Thank you." Perth tips his head in the direction of my clasped hands. "He used our magic against the Light Lovers, twisting the thoughts in their heads, turning them into spies, killers, whatever he needed them to do at the time."

"But how? Flanna mentioned your powers are used for dark things, but Arland said our powers cannot be used to fight."

"I wish I knew. Our magical powers are not supposed to be used to fight, but somehow he manipulated the magic to work against nature."

"And your people just supported him?" I ask, leaning forward.

Perth snorts. "Foghlad spoke eloquently to his followers, and over time—and I imagine with the help of magic—all of my kind believed in his mission to conquer the Meadows and take control of Encardia."

I narrow my eyes. "Why? What was he going to do with the control if he got it?"

"He was an evil man. Plain and simple. I am not positive what his final plans were, but Foghlad taught all of my people how to use our beautiful magic in dark ways. The battles have gone on for so long, not many of my kind understand how peaceful life could be if we would stop trying to conquer the world."

I lean back in my seat; the twisted roots of the chair poke into my shoulders. "Have you ever told anyone this?"

Perth shakes his head. "Unfortunately, if my father or anyone knew how I felt, I am sure they would kill me."

I feel as though uniting all of the Draíochta to fight might be more difficult than Griandor led me to believe—not that he gave me much information in the first place. "How long have the Ground Dwellers been fighting for power?"

"The first battle began one hundred and twenty-three years ago."

One hundred and twenty-three years? Uniting them after that much time might not be difficult—it might be impossible. "So, what do we do now?"

Perth smiles crookedly. "Since you are the one glowing with ancient magic, I was hoping you would come up with a plan."

He may find this funny, but I'm *not* smiling. I narrow my eyes.

"Sorry. The blue flames *are* somewhat distracting." He wipes his hand over his face, smoothing his expression.

I draw in deep breaths. My mind reaches out to all corners of my body, grabbing the flames and folding them in. I'm taking control. Not asking, just doing—like Griandor told me. The magic works its way into my chest, and the fire disappears above my heart.

The room is now pitch-black.

"Solas." I light a candle sitting in the center of the table with a spark from my hand.

"If I had any remaining doubts about your identity, your control over old magic just made them all wash away," Perth says, with childlike eyes.

"Did you see where the others were taken?"

"I followed them to a cave three miles north of here. I am not sure if they entered, but with only a knife for protection, it was too far for me to continue on alone."

"Are the animals—?"

"Daemons have no use for our animals; they are fine."

"Good, then let's ride out to the cave and check it out. If they aren't there, we'll come back. If they are, we'll fight."

"You want to ride straight into a trap?" Perth crosses his arms over his chest, looking at me like I'm an idiot. "The daemons will expect retaliation. We need to track them, gather information, and attack when the time is right."

"Well, we can't stay here. We have to get to them soon, or the daemons will kill them!" A lump forms in my throat. I have to save the others before it's too late; if a single life is lost, it will be too much for me to handle.

"You are correct. We cannot stay here." Perth tips his head toward the hall. "It appears someone hid your room, which tells me *someone* believes whoever called for the attack knows who you are.

The daemons know you are here; they will wait for you. They might be mounting another attack as we speak. We should move to Willow Falls. There will be other soldiers who can help us. We can use the chatter box in the communications room to send word we are coming."

It's apparent Perth wants me to abandon the idea of finding the soldiers. He's never seen me fight; he has no idea what I'm capable of. Until my conversation with the sun god, *I* had no idea what I'm capable of.

"We don't need to bring any other soldiers into this. I can handle the daemons that took the others. We'll send word to Willow Falls about their capture, and we'll let the Leaders know as soon as we rescue everyone, we'll go there." I had no trouble fighting off hundreds of coscarthas and hounds in the forest, and that was before I knew much about myself.

"It will be a suicide mission."

It's also apparent Perth has no faith in me.

"Are you going to come with me, or am I going alone?"

"What kind of man would I be if I allowed a woman to go into a battle on her own?" He places his cold hand over the back of mine. "Especially one who belongs to me."

I jerk my hand free. "Thank you, but I don't belong to you."

"Try telling my father that." Clasping his fingers on *his* side of the table, Perth laughs. "And do not thank me. We are both going to die. So, do you know how to use the chatter box?"

"No."

"Neither do I. You should try to use the magic you have been blessed with," Perth says, heavy on the sarcasm.

Grabbing my sword, I point it toward the kitchen. "Lead the way."

Wilde's Army (Darkness Falls, Book Two)
is available on **Amazon.com**, **Barnes & Noble**,
***iTunes**, **Kobo**, and other retailers.*

Thank You For Reading

© 2012 Krystal Wade
http://krystalwade.blogspot.com

Curiosity Quills Press
http://curiosityquills.com

Please visit http://curiosityquills.com/reader-survey/ to share your reading experience with the author of this book!

About the Author

Krystal Wade can be found in the sluglines outside Washington D.C. every morning, Monday through Friday. With coffee in hand, iPod plugged in, and strangers – who sometimes snore, smell, or have incredibly bad gas – sitting next to her, she zones out and thinks of fantastical worlds for you and me to read.

How else can she cope with a fifty mile commute?

Good thing she has her husband and three kids to go home to. They keep her sane.

Wilde's Army, by Krystal Wade

"Hello, Katriona." Those two words spark fear in Katriona Wilde and give way to an unlikely partnership with Perth, the man she's been traded to marry for a favor. Saving her true love and protector Arland, her family, and their soldiers keeps her motivated, but the at-odds duo soon realizes trust is something that comes and goes with each breath of Encardia's rotting, stagnant air.

Now, Kate must unite her clashing people, and form an army prepared to fight in order to defeat Darkness. When so many she's grown fond of die along the journey, will she still be Katriona Wilde, the girl with fire?

Wilde's Meadow, by Krystal Wade

Happy endings are hard to find, and even though Katriona is in the middle of a war with someone who's already stolen more than she can replace, she aches for a positive future with her Draiochtans. Armed with hope, confidence in her abilities, and a strange new gift from her mother, Kate ventures into the Darkness to defeat a fallen god.

Losses add up, and new obstacles rise to stand in the way. Is the one determined to bring Encardia light strong enough to keep fighting, or will all the sacrifices to stop those who seek domination be for nothing?

Legasea, by Krystalyn Drown

When sixteen-year-old Aileen Shay sees a dead girl floating in the bay during a midnight yacht party, she never imagines Jamie Flannigan, her new boyfriend, may be involved. When another girl is attacked, Aileen learns that Jamie's family belongs more to myths and legends than they do in the real world—they are selkies.

But they aren't the only ones in her small fishing town who can keep a secret. As Aileen uncovers the truth, she learns why her own soul is bonded to the sea–and faces a painful and dangerous choice.

Death By Chocolate, by Johanna Pitcairn

Julie deals with more problems than most teenagers her age. A runaway, she quickly ends up homeless and broke. When an old Gypsy woman offers to read her future in exchange for a meal, the tarot cards reveal a great destiny, and perilous journey–and a red heart shaped box of chocolates melts reality and fantasy into one never ending nightmare where failure equals death.

In an unwelcoming world filled with danger, will her guide, Evan, truly help her when she needs him most? Demons of a long forgotten past haunt her dreams and seek revenge for something she doesn't remember. Too many questions receive too little answers. Will Julie accept the truth to survive?

The Gathering Darkness, by Lisa Collicutt

They say: "the third time's the charm" and for sixteen-year-old Brooke Day, they had better be right.

She doesn't know it yet but she's been here before—twice in fact. Though, she's never lived past the age of sixteen.

Now in her third lifetime, Brooke must stay alive until the equinox, when she will be gifted with a limited-time use of ancient power. Only then will she be able to defeat the evil that has plagued her for centuries.

Ever, by Jessa Russo

Some girls lose their hearts to love. Some girls lose their minds. Seventeen year-old Ever Van Ruysdael could lose her soul.

Ever's love life has been on hold for the past two years. She's secretly in love with her best friend Frankie, and he's completely oblivious. Of course, it doesn't help that he's dead, and waking up to his ghost every day has made moving on nearly impossible.

Frustrated, and desperate to move on, Ever finds herself falling for her hot new neighbor Toby. His relaxed confidence is irresistible, and not just Ever knows it. But falling for Toby comes with a price that throws Ever's life into a whirlwind of chaos and drama.

Please visit CuriosityQuills.com for more great books!

Fade, by A.K. Morgen

When Arionna Jacobs meets Dace Matthews, everything she thought she knew about herself and the world around them begins to fall apart. Neither of them understands what is happening to them, or why, and they're running out of time to figure it out.

An ancient Norse prophesy of destruction has been set into motion, and what destiny has in store for them is bigger than either could have ever imagined.

18 Things, by Jamie Ayres

A young girl struggles to live again after a lightning strike kills the best friend she was secretly in love with.

Her therapist suggests she write a life list of eighteen things to complete the year of her eighteenth birthday, sending her and her friends, including the new hottie in town, on an unexpected journey they'll never forget.

As she crosses each item off her list, she must risk her own heart, but if she fails, she risks losing herself and her true soul-mate forever

Lightning Source UK Ltd.
Milton Keynes UK
UKOW07f2037091114

241367UK00017B/437/P